Nora Roberts is the number one *New York Times* bestselling author of more than one hundred novels, including *Birthright, Chesapeake Blue, Three Fates, Face the Fire,* and *Midnight Bayou*. She has eighty-six *New York Times* bestsellers to her name, twenty-two of which debuted at #1. Under the pen name J. D. Robb, she is also the author of the #1 *New York Times* bestselling futuristic romantic suspense series featuring Lieutenant Eve Dallas and Roarke. With more than 200 million copies of her books in print, Nora Roberts is indisputably the most celebrated and beloved women's fiction writer today.

Visit her website at www.noraroberts.com

D0766178

Ceremony in Death

Nora Roberts

writing as

J.D. Robb

PIATKUS

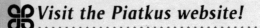

Visit the Piatkus website!

Piatkus publishes a wide range of bestselling fiction and non-fiction, including books on health, mind, body & spirit, sex, self-help, cookery, biography and the paranormal.

If you want to:

- read descriptions of our popular titles
- buy our books over the internet
- take advantage of our special offers
- enter our monthly competition
- learn more about your favourite Piatkus authors

VISIT OUR WEBSITE AT: www.piatkus.co.uk

Copyright © 1997 by Nora Roberts
Material excerpted from *Vengeance in Death* by Nora Roberts writing as
J.D. Robb copyright
© 1997 by Nora Roberts

This edition published in Great Britain in 2003 by
Piatkus Books Ltd of
5 Windmill Street, London WIT 2JA
email: info@piatkus.co.uk

Reprinted 2004, 2005

First published in the United States in 1997 by Berkley Publishing Group, a division of
Penguin Putnam Inc., New York.

The moral right of the author has been asserted

A catalogue record for this book is available from the British Library

ISBN 0 7499 3412 3

Typeset in Times by Palimpsest Book Production Limited,
Polmont, Stirlingshire

Printed and bound in Great Britain by
Mackays of Chatham Ltd, Chatham, Kent

There are more things in heaven and earth, Horatio,
Than are dreamt of in your philosophy.

SHAKESPEARE

We may not pay Satan reverence, for that would be
indiscreet, but we can at least respect his talents.

MARK TWAIN

Chapter One

Death surrounded her. She faced it daily, dreamed of it nightly. Lived with it always. She knew its sounds, its scents, even its texture. She could look it in its dark and clever eye without a flinch. Death was a tricky foe, she knew. One flinch, one blink, and it could shift, it could change. It could win.

Ten years as a cop hadn't hardened her toward it. A decade on the force hadn't made her accept it. When she looked death in the eye, it was with the cold steel of the warrior.

Eve Dallas looked at death now. And she looked at one of her own.

Frank Wojinski had been a good cop, solid. Some would have said plodding. He'd been affable, she remembered. A man who hadn't complained about the bilge disguised as food at the NYPSD Eatery, or the eye-searing paperwork the job generated. Or, Eve thought, about the fact that he'd been sixty-two and had never made it past the rank of detective sergeant.

He'd been on the pudgy side and had let his hair gray and thin naturally. It was a rare thing in 2058 for a man to bypass body sculpting and enhancements. Now, in his clear-sided view casket with its single spray of mournful lilies, he resembled a peacefully sleeping monk from an earlier time.

He'd been born in an earlier time, Eve mused, coming into the world at the end of one millennium and living his life in the next. He'd been through the Urban Wars, but hadn't talked of them as so many of the older cops did. Frank hadn't been one for war stories, she recalled. He was more likely to pass around the latest snapshot or hologram of his children and grandchildren.

He liked to tell bad jokes, talk sports, and had a weakness for soydogs with spiced pickle relish.

A family man, she thought, one who left behind great grief. Indeed, she could think of no one who had known Frank Wojinski who hadn't loved him.

He had died with half his life still ahead of him, died alone, when the heart everyone had thought so huge and so strong had just stopped.

'Goddamn it.'

Eve turned, laid a hand on the arm of the man who stepped up beside her. 'I'm sorry, Feeney.'

He shook his head, his droopy camel's eyes filled with misery. With one hand he raked through his wiry red hair. 'On the job would have been easier. I could handle line of duty. But to just stop. To just check out in his easy chair watching arena ball on the screen. It's not right, Dallas. A man's not supposed to stop living at his age.'

'I know.' Not knowing what else to do, Eve draped an arm over his shoulder and steered him away.

'He trained me. Looked after me when I was a rookie. Never let me down.' Pain radiated through him and glinted dully in his eyes, wavered in his voice. 'Frank never let anyone down in his life.'

'I know,' she said again, because there was nothing else that could be said. She was accustomed to Feeney being tough and strong. The delicacy of his grief worried her.

She led him through the mourners. The viewing room was packed with cops as well as family. And where there were cops and death, there was coffee. Or what passed for it at such places. She poured a cup, handed it to him.

2

'I can't get around it. I can't get a hold of it.' He let out a long, uneven breath. He was a sturdy, compact man who wore his grief as openly as he wore his rumpled coat. 'I haven't talked to Sally yet. My wife's with her. I just can't do it.'

'It's all right. I haven't talked to her, either.' Since she had nothing to do with her hands, Eve poured a cup for herself that she didn't intend to drink. 'Everybody's shook up by this. I didn't know he had a heart problem.'

'Nobody did,' Feeney said quietly. 'Nobody knew.'

She kept a hand on his shoulder as she scanned the over-crowded, overwarm room. When a fellow officer went down in the line of duty, cops could be angry, they could be focused, fix their target. But when death snuck in and crooked a capricious finger, there was no one to blame. And no one to punish.

It was helplessness she felt in the room and that she felt in herself. You couldn't raise your weapon to fate, or your fist.

The funeral director, spiffy in his traditional black suit and as waxy-faced as one of his own clients, worked the room with patting hands and sober eyes. Eve thought she'd rather have a corpse sit up and grin at her than listen to his platitudes.

'Why don't we go talk to the family together?'

It was hard for him, but Feeney nodded, set the untouched coffee aside. 'He liked you, Dallas. "That kid's got balls of steel and a mind to match," he used to tell me. He always said if he was ever jammed, you'd be the one he'd want guarding his back.'

It surprised and pleased her, and it simultaneously added to her sorrow. 'I didn't realize he thought of me that way.'

Feeney looked at her. She had an interesting face, not one he'd have called a heart-stopper, but it usually made a man look twice with its angles and sharp bones, the shallow dent in the chin. She had cop's eyes, intense and measuring, and he often forgot they were a dark golden brown. Her hair was the same shade, cut short and badly in need of some shaping. She was tall and lean and tough-bodied.

3

He remembered it had been less than a month since he had come across her, battered and bloodied. But her weapon had been firm in her hand.

'He thought of you that way. So do I.' While she blinked at him, Feeney squared his hunched shoulders. 'Let's talk to Sally and the kids.'

They slipped through the crowd jammed together in a room oppressed with dark simulated wood, heavy red draperies, and the funereal smell of too many flowers crammed into too small a space.

Eve wondered why viewings of the dead were always accompanied by flowers and draping sheets of red. What ancient ceremony did it spring from, and why did the human race continue to cling to it?

She was certain that when her time came, she wouldn't choose to be laid out for study by her loved ones and associates in an overheated room where the pervasive scent of flowers was reminiscent of rot.

Then she saw Sally, supported by her children and her children's children, and realized such rites were for the living. The dead were beyond caring.

'Ryan.' Sally held out her hands – small, almost fairy-like hands – and lifted her cheek to Feeney's. She held there a moment, her eyes closed, her face pale and quiet.

She was a slim, soft-spoken woman who Eve had always thought of as delicate. Yet a cop's spouse who had survived the stress of the job for more than forty years had to have steel. Against her plain black dress she wore her husband's twenty-five-year NYPSD ring on a chain.

Another rite, Eve thought. *Another symbol*.

'I'm so glad you're here,' Sally murmured.

'I'll miss him. We'll all miss him.' Feeney patted her back awkwardly before drawing away. Grief was in his throat, choking him. Swallowing it only lodged it cold and heavy in his gut. 'You know if there's anything . . .'

'I know.' Her lips curved slightly, and she gave his hand a quick and comforting squeeze before turning to Eve. 'I appreciate you coming, Dallas.'

'He was a good man. A solid cop.'

'Yes, he was.' Recognizing it as high tribute, Sally managed a smile. 'He was proud to serve and protect. Commander Whitney and his wife are here, and Chief Tibble. And so many others.' Her gaze drifted blindly around the room. 'So many. He mattered, Frank mattered.'

'Of course he did, Sally.' Feeney shifted from foot to foot. 'You, ah, know about the Survivor's Fund.'

She smiled again, patted his hand. 'We're fine there. Don't worry. Dallas, I don't think you really know my family. Lieutenant Dallas, my daughter Brenda.'

Short, with rounded curves, Eve noted as they clasped hands. *Dark hair and eyes, a bit heavy in the chin. Took after her father.*

'My son Curtis.'

Slim, small boned, soft hands, eyes that were dry but dazed with grief.

'My grandchildren.'

There were five of them, the youngest a boy of about eight with a pug nose dashed with freckles. He eyed Eve consideringly. 'How come you've got your zapper on?'

Flustered, Eve tugged her jacket over her side arm. 'I came straight from Cop Central. I didn't have time to go home and change.'

'Pete.' Curtis shot Eve an apologetic wince. 'Don't bother the lieutenant.'

'If people concentrated more on their personal and spiritual powers, weapons would be unnecessary. I'm Alice.'

A slim blonde in black stepped forward. She'd have been a stunner in any case, Eve mused, but having sprung from such basic stock, she was dazzling. Her eyes were a soft, dreamy blue, her mouth full and lush and unpainted. She wore her hair

5

loose so that it rained straight and glossy over the shoulders of her flowing black dress. A thin silver chain fell to her waist. At the end of it was a black stone ringed in silver.

'Alice, you're such a zip head.'

She flicked a cool glance over her shoulder toward a boy of about sixteen. But her hands kept fluttering back to the black stone, like elegant birds guarding a nest.

'My brother Jamie,' she said in a silky voice. 'He still thinks name-calling deserves a reaction. My grandfather spoke of you, Lieutenant Dallas.'

'I'm flattered.'

'Your husband isn't with you tonight?'

Eve arched a brow. *Not just grief*, she deduced, *but nerves*. It was easy enough to recognize. Signals as well, but they weren't clear. *The girl was after something*, she mused. *But what?*

'No, he's not.' She shifted her gaze back to Sally. 'He sends his sympathies, Mrs Wojinski. He's off planet.'

'It must take a great deal of concentration and energy,' Alice interrupted, 'to maintain a relationship with a man like Roarke while pursuing a demanding, difficult, even dangerous career. My grandfather used to say that once you had a grip on an investigation, you never let go. Would you say that's accurate, Lieutenant?'

'If you let go, you lose. I don't like to lose.' She held Alice's odd gaze for a moment, then on impulse crouched down and whispered to Pete. 'When I was a rookie, I saw your grandfather zap a guy at ten yards. He was the best.' She was rewarded with a quick grin before she straightened. 'He won't be forgotten, Mrs Wojinski,' she said, offering her hand. 'And he mattered very much to all of us.'

She started to step back, but Alice laid a hand on her arm, leaned close. The hand, Eve noted, trembled slightly. 'It was interesting meeting you, Lieutenant. Thank you for coming.'

Eve inclined her head and slipped back into the crowd.

6

Casually, she reached a hand into the pocket of her jacket and fingered the thin slip of paper Alice had pushed inside.

It took her another thirty minutes to get away. She waited until she was outside and in her vehicle before she took the note out and read it.

Meet me tomorrow, midnight. Aquarian Club.
TELL NO ONE. Your life is now at risk.

In lieu of a signature, there was a symbol, a dark line running in an expanding circle to form a sort of maze. Nearly as intrigued as she was annoyed, Eve stuffed the note back in her pocket and started home.

Because she was a cop, she saw the figure draped in black, hardly more than a shadow in the shadows. And because she was a cop, she knew he was watching her.

Whenever Roarke was away, Eve preferred to pretend the house was empty. Both she and Summerset, who served as Roarke's chief of staff, did their best to ignore the other's presence. The house was huge, a labyrinth of rooms, which made it a simple matter to avoid one another.

She stepped into the wide foyer, tossed her scarred leather jacket over the carved newel post because she knew it would make Summerset grind his teeth. He detested having anything mar the elegance of the house. Particularly her.

She took the stairs, but rather than go to the master bedroom, she veered off to her office suite.

If Roarke had to spend another night off planet as expected, she preferred to spend hers in her relaxation chair rather than their bed.

She often dreamed badly when she dreamed alone.

Between the late paperwork and the viewing, she hadn't had time for a meal. Eve ordered up a sandwich – real Virginia ham on rye – and coffee that jumped with genuine caffeine.

When the AutoChef delivered, she inhaled the scents slowly, greedily. She took the first bite with her eyes closed to better enjoy the miracle.

There were definite advantages to being married to a man who could afford real meat instead of its by-products and simulations.

To satisfy her curiosity, she went to her desk and engaged her computer. She swallowed ham, chased it with coffee. 'All available data on subject Alice, surname unknown. Mother Brenda, née Wojinski, maternal grandparents Frank and Sally Wojinski.'

Working ...

Eve drummed her fingers, took out the note and reread it while she polished off the quick meal.

Subject Alice Lingstrom. DOB June 10, 2040. First child and only daughter of Jan Lingstrom and Brenda Wojinski, divorced, Residence, 486 West Eighth Street, Apartment 4B, New York City. Sibling, James Lingstrom, DOB March 22, 2042. Education, high school graduate, valedictorian. Two semesters of college: Harvard. Major, anthropology. Minor, mythology. Third semester deferred. Currently employed as clerk, Spirit Quest, 228 West Tenth Street, New York City. Marital status, single.

Eve ran her tongue around her teeth. 'Criminal record?'

No criminal record.

'Sounds fairly normal,' Eve murmured. 'Data on Spirit Quest.'

Spirit Quest. Wiccan shop and consultation center, owned by Isis Paige and Charles Forte. Three years in Tenth Street location.

Annual gross income one hundred twenty-five thousand dollars. Licensed priestess, herbalist, and registered hypnotherapist on site.

'Wicca?' Eve leaned back with a snort. 'Witch stuff? Jesus. What kind of scam is this?'

Wicca, recognized as both a religion and a craft, is an ancient, nature-based faith which—

'Stop.' Eve blew out a breath. She wasn't looking for a definition of witchcraft, but an explanation as to why a steady-as-a-rock cop ended up with a granddaughter who believed in casting spells and magic crystals.

And why that granddaughter wanted a secret meeting.

The best way to find out, she decided, was to show up at the Aquarian Club in a bit over twenty-four hours. She left the note on the desk. It would be easy to dismiss it, she thought, if it hadn't been written by a relative of a man she'd respected.

And if she hadn't seen that figure in the shadows. A figure she was sure hadn't wanted to be seen.

She walked to the adjoining bath and began to strip. It was too bad she couldn't take Mavis with her for the meet. Eve had a feeling the Aquarian Club would be right up her friend's alley. Eve kicked her jeans aside, leaned over to stretch out the kinks of a long day. And wondered what she would do with the long night ahead.

She had nothing hot to work on. Her last homicide had been so open and shut that she and her aide had put it to bed in under eight hours. Maybe she'd spend a couple hours glazing out watching some screen. Or she could pick a weapon out of Roarke's gun room and go down and run a hologram program to burn off excess energy until she could sleep.

She'd never tried one of his auto-assault rifles. It might be interesting to experience how a cop took out an enemy during the early days of the Urban Wars.

She stepped into the shower. 'Full jets, on pulse,' she ordered. 'Ninety-eight degrees.'

She wished she had a murder to sink her teeth into. Something that would focus her mind and drain her system. And damn it, that was pathetic. She was lonely, she realized. Desperate for a distraction, and he'd only been gone three days.

They both had their own lives, didn't they? They'd lived them before they met and continued to live them after. The demands of both their businesses absorbed much time and attention. Their relationship worked – and that continued to surprise her – because they were both independent people.

Christ, she missed him outrageously. Disgusted with herself, she ducked her head under the spray and let it pound on her brain.

When hands slipped around her waist, then slid up to cup her breasts, she barely jolted. But her heart leaped. She knew his touch, the feel of those long, slim fingers, the texture of those wide palms. She tipped her head back, inviting a mouth to the curve of her shoulder.

'Mmm. Summerset. You wild man.'

Teeth nipped into flesh and made her chuckle. Thumbs brushed over her soapy nipples and made her moan.

'I'm not going to fire him.' Roarke trailed a hand down the center of her body.

'It was worth a shot. You're back . . .' His fingers dipped expertly inside her, slick and slippery, so that she arched, moaned, and came simultaneously. 'Early,' she finished on an explosive breath. 'God.'

'I'd say I was just on time.' He spun her around, and while she was shuddering and blinking water out of her eyes, he covered her mouth in a long, ravenous kiss.

He'd thought about her on the interminable flight home. Thought about this, just this: touching and tasting and hearing

10

that quick catch in her breath as he did. And here she was, naked and wet and already quivering for him.

He braced her in the corner, gripped her hips, and slowly lifted her off her feet. 'Miss me?'

Her heart was thundering. He was inches away from driving into her, filling her, destroying her. 'Not really.'

'Well, in that case . . .' He kissed her lightly on the chin. 'I'll just let you finish your shower in peace.'

In a flash, she wrapped her legs around his waist, took a firm hold of his wet mane of hair. 'Try it, pal, and you're a dead man.'

'In the interest of self-preservation then.' To torture them both, he slipped into her slowly, watched her eyes go opaque. He closed his mouth over hers again so that her shallow breaths shuddered through him.

The ride was slow and slippery, and more tender than either had expected. Climax came on a long, quiet sigh. Her lips curved against his. 'Welcome home.'

She could see him now, those stunning blue eyes, the face that was both saint and sinner, the mouth of a doomed poet. His hair was streaming with water, black and sleek, just touching broad shoulders roped with subtle and surprisingly tough muscle.

Looking at him after these brief, periodic absences always made something unexpected lurch through her. She doubted she would ever get used to the fact that he not only wanted her but loved her.

She was smiling still as she combed her fingers through his thick, black hair. 'Everything okay with the Olympus Resort?'

'Adjustments, some delays. Nothing that can't be dealt with.' The elaborate space station resort and pleasure center would open on schedule, because he wouldn't accept any less.

He ordered the jets off, then took a towel to wrap around

her when she would have used the drying tube. 'I began to understand why you stay in here while I'm away. I couldn't sleep in the Presidential Suite.' He took another towel, rubbed it over her hair. 'It was too lonely without you.'

She leaned against him a moment, just to feel the familiar lines of his body against hers. 'We're getting so damn sappy.'

'I don't mind. We Irish are very sentimental.'

It made her smirk as he turned to get robes. He might have had the music of Ireland in his voice, but she seriously doubted if any of his business friends or foes would consider Roarke a sentimental man.

'No fresh bruises,' he observed, helping her into her robe before she could do it for herself. 'I take that to mean you've had a quiet few days.'

'Mostly. We had a john get a bit overenthusiastic with a licensed companion. Choked her to death during sex.' She belted the robe, scratched fingers through her hair to scatter more water. 'He got spooked and ran.' She moved her shoulders as she stepped into the office. 'But he lawyered up and turned himself in a few hours later. PA took it down to manslaughter. I let Peabody handle the interview and booking.'

'Hmm.' Roarke went to a recessed cabinet for wine, poured them both a glass. 'It's been quiet then.'

'Yeah. I had that viewing tonight.'

His brow furrowed, then cleared. 'Ah, yes, you told me. I'm sorry I couldn't make it home in time to go with you.'

'Feeney's taking it really hard. It would be easier if Frank had gone down in the line of duty.'

This time Roarke's brow quirked. 'You'd prefer that your associate had been killed rather than, say, go gently into that good night?'

'I'd just understand it better, that's all.' She frowned into her wine. She didn't think it wise to tell Roarke she'd prefer

12

a fast and violent death herself. 'There is something odd, though. I met Frank's family. The oldest granddaughter's on the weird side.'

'How?'

'The way she talked, and the data I accessed on her after I got home.'

Intrigued, he lifted his wine to sip. 'You ran a make on her?'

'Just a quick check. Because she passed me this.' Eve walked to the desk, picked up the note.

Roarke scanned it, considered. 'Earth labyrinth.'

'What?'

'The symbol here. It's Celtic.'

Shaking her head, Eve eased closer to look again. 'You know the strangest things.'

'Not so strange. I spring from the Celts, after all. The ancient labyrinth symbol is magical and sacred.'

'Well, it fits. She's into witchcraft or something. Got herself the start of a top-flight education. Harvard. But she drops out to work in some West Village shop that sells crystals and magic herbs.'

Roarke traced the symbol with a fingertip. He'd seen it before, and others like it. During his childhood, the cults in Dublin had run the range between vicious gangs and pious pacifists. All, of course, had used religion as the excuse to kill. Or be killed.

'You have no idea why she wants to meet you?'

'None. I'd say she figures she read my aura or something. Mavis ran a mystic grift before I busted her for pinching wallets. She told me people will pay most anything if you tell them what they want to hear. More, if you tell them what they don't want to hear.'

'Which is why cons and legitimate businesses are very much the same.' He smiled at her. 'I take it you're going, anyway.'

13

'Sure, I'll follow through.'

Naturally she would. Roarke glanced at the note again, then set it aside. 'I'm going with you.'

'She wants—'

'It's a pity what she wants.' He sipped his wine, a man accustomed to getting precisely what he wanted. One way or another. 'I'll stay out of your way, but I'm going. The Aquarian Club is basically harmless, but there are always unsavory elements that leak through.'

'Unsavory elements are my life,' she said soberly, then cocked her head. 'You don't, like, own the Aquarian, do you?'

'No.' He smiled. 'Would you like to?'

She laughed and took his hand. 'Come on. Let's drink this in bed.'

Relaxed by sex and wine, she fell peacefully asleep, draped around Roarke. That's why she was baffled to find herself suddenly and fully awake only two hours later. It hadn't been one of her nightmares. There was no terror, no pain, no cold, clammy sweat.

Yet she had snapped awake, and her heart wasn't quite steady. She lay still, staring up through the wide sky window over the bed, listening to Roarke's quiet, steady breathing beside her.

She shifted, glanced down at the foot of the bed, and nearly yelped when eyes glowed out of the dark. Then she registered the weight over her ankles. *Galahad*, she thought and rolled her eyes. The cat had come in and jumped onto the bed. That's what had awakened her, she told herself. That's all it was.

She settled again, turned onto her side, and felt Roarke's arm slide around her in sleep. On a sigh, she closed her eyes, snuggled companionably against him.

Just the cat, she thought sleepily.

But she would have sworn she'd heard chanting.

14

Chapter Two

By the time Eve was elbow deep in paperwork the next morning, the odd wakefulness in the night was forgotten. New York seemed to be content to bask in the balmy days of early autumn and behave itself. It seemed like a good time to take a few hours and organize her office.

Or rather to delegate Peabody to organize it.

'How can your files be this skewed?' Peabody demanded. Her earnest, square face expressed deep remorse and disappointment.

'I know where everything is,' Eve told her. 'I want you to put everything where I'll still know where it is, but where it also makes sense for it to be. Too tough an assignment, Officer?'

'I can handle it.' Peabody rolled her eyes behind Eve's back. 'Sir.'

'Fine. And don't roll your eyes at me. If things are a bit skewed, as you put it, it's because I've had a busy year. As we're in the last quarter of this one and I'm training you, it falls to me to dump this on you.' Eve turned and smiled thinly. 'With the hope, Peabody, that you will one day have an underling to dump shit assignments on.'

'Your faith in me is touching, Dallas. Chokes me up.' She hissed at the computer. 'Or maybe it's the fact that you've got yellow sheets in here from five years ago that's choking me. These should have been downloaded to the main and cleared out of your unit after twenty-four months.'

'So download and clear now.' Eve's smile widened as the machine hacked, then droned out a warning of system failure. 'And good luck.'

'Technology can be our friend. And like any friendship, it requires regular maintenance and understanding.'

'I understand it fine.' Eve stepped over, pounded her fist twice on the drive. The unit hiccupped back into running mode. 'See?'

'You have a real smooth touch, Lieutenant. That's why the guys in Maintenance shoot air darts at your picture.'

'Still? Christ, they hold a grudge.' With a shrug, Eve sat on the corner of the desk. 'What do you know about witchcraft?'

'If you want to cast a spell on your machine here, Dallas, it's a little out of my field.' Teeth clenched, she juggled and compressed files.

'You're a Free-Ager.'

'Lapsed. Come on, come on, you can do it,' she muttered at the computer. 'Besides,' she added. 'Free-Agers aren't Wiccans. They're both earth religions, and both are based on natural orders, but . . . son of a bitch, where'd it go?'

'What? Where did what go?'

'Nothing.' Shoulders hunched, Peabody guarded the monitor. 'Nothing. Don't worry, I'm on it. You probably didn't need those files, anyway.'

'Is that a joke, Peabody?'

'You bet. Ha ha.' A line of sweat dribbled down her back as she attacked the keys. 'There. There it is. No problem, no problem at all. And off it goes into the main. Neat and tidy.' She let out an enormous sigh. 'Could I maybe have some coffee? Just to keep alert.'

Eve shifted her gaze to the screen, saw nothing that looked ominous. Saying nothing, she rose and ordered coffee from the AutoChef.

'Why do you want to know about Wicca? You thinking

of converting?' At Eve's bland look, Peabody tried a smile. 'Another joke.'

'You're full of them today. Just curious.'

'Well, there's some overlap on basic tenets between Wiccans and Free-Agers. A search for balance and harmony, the celebration of the seasons that goes back to ancient times, the strict code of nonviolence.'

'Nonviolence?' Eve narrowed her eyes. 'What about curses, casting spells, and sacrifices? Naked virgins on the altar and black roosters getting their heads chopped off?'

'Fiction depicts witches that way. You know, 'Double, double, toil and trouble.' Shakespeare. *Macbeth*.'

Eve snorted. '"I'll get you, my pretty, and your little dog, too"' The Wicked Witch of the West. Classic vid channel.

'Good one,' Peabody admitted. 'But both examples feed into the most basic of misconceptions. Witches aren't ugly, evil crones mixing up cauldrons of goop or hunting down young girls and their friendly, talking scarecrows. Wiccans like to be naked, but they don't hurt anything or anyone. Strictly white magic.'

'As opposed to?'

'Black magic.'

Eve studied her aide. 'You don't believe in that stuff? Magic and spells?'

'Nope.' Revived with coffee, Peabody turned back to the computer. 'I know some of the basics because I have a cousin who shifted to Wicca. He's into it big time. Joined a coven in Cincinnati.'

'You've got a cousin in a coven in Cincinnati.' Laughing, Eve set her own coffee aside. 'Peabody, you never cease to amaze me.'

'One day I'll tell you about my granny and her five lovers.'

'Five lovers isn't abnormal for a woman's lifetime.'

'Not in her lifetime; last month. All at the same time.'

Peabody glanced up, deadpan. 'She's ninety-eight. I hope to take after her.'

Eve swallowed her next chuckle as her tele-link beeped. 'Dallas.' She watched Commander Whitney's face swim on-screen. 'Yes, Commander.'

'I'd like to speak with you, Lieutenant, in my office. As soon as possible.'

'Yes, sir. Five minutes.' Eve disengaged, shot a hopeful glance at Peabody. 'Maybe we've got something going. Keep working on those files. I'll contact you if we're heading out.'

She started out, stuck her head back in. 'Don't eat my candy bar.'

'Damn,' Peabody said under her breath. 'She never misses.'

Whitney had spent most of his life behind a badge and a large part of his professional life in command. He made it his business to know his cops, to judge their strengths and weaknesses. And he knew how to utilize both.

He was a big man with workingman hands and dark, keen eyes that some considered cold. His temperament, on the surface, was almost terrifyingly even. And like most smooth surfaces, it coated something dangerous brewing beneath.

Eve respected him, occasionally liked him, and always admired him.

He was at his desk when she stepped into his office, lines of concentration puckering his brow as he read over some hard copy. He didn't glance up, merely gestured toward a chair. She sat, watched an air tram rumble by his window, baffled as always by the number of passengers with binoks and spy glasses.

What did they expect to see behind the windows where cops worked? she wondered. *Suspects being tortured, weapons discharged, victims bleeding and weeping? And why would the fantasy of such misery entertain them?*

'I saw you at the viewing last night.'

Eve shifted her thoughts and attention to her commander. 'I imagine most every cop in Central made an appearance.'

'Frank was well-liked.'

'Yes, he was.'

'You never worked with him?'

'He gave me some pointers when I was a rookie, helped out on legwork a couple of times, but no, I never worked with him directly.'

Whitney nodded, kept his eyes on hers. 'He was partnered with Feeney, before your time. You were partnered with Feeney after Frank shifted from the streets to a desk,'

She began to get an uncomfortable feeling in the gut. *Something here*, she thought. *Something's off.* 'Yes, sir. This has hit Feeney pretty hard.'

'I'm aware of that, Dallas. Which is why Captain Feeney isn't here this morning.' Whitney propped his elbows on his desk, linked his fingers, folded his fingers over. 'We have a possible situation, Lieutenant. A delicate situation.'

'Regarding DS Wojinski?'

'The information I'm going to relay to you is confidential. Your aide can be apprised per your discretion, but no one else on the force. No one in the media. I am asking you, ordering you,' he corrected, 'to essentially work alone, on this matter.'

The discomfort in her stomach spread into little licks of fear as she thought of Feeney. 'Understood.'

'There is some question regarding the circumstances of DS Wojinski's death.'

'Question, Commander?'

'You'll require some background data.' He laid his folded hands on the edge of the desk. 'It has come to my attention that DS Wojinski was either pursuing an investigation of his own off the clock or involved with illegals.'

'Drugs? Frank? Nobody was cleaner than Frank.'

Whitney didn't so much as blink. 'On September twenty-second of this year DS Wojinski was spotted by an undercover

19

illegals detective allegedly conducting business in a suspected chemical distribution center. The Athame is a private club, religious in theme, which offers its members group and individual ritual services and is licensed for private sexual functions. The Illegals Division has had it under investigation for nearly two years. Frank was seen making a buy.'

When Eve said nothing, Whitney drew a long breath. 'This situation was subsequently reported to me. I questioned Frank, and he was not forthcoming.' Whitney hesitated, then followed through. 'Frankly, Dallas, the fact that he would neither confirm nor deny, refused to explain or discuss, seemed very out of character. And it worried me. I ordered him to submit to a physical, including a drug scan, advised him to take a week's leave. He agreed to both. The scan was, at that point, clear. Due to his record and my personal knowledge and opinion of him, I did not mark the incident in his file, but sealed it.'

He rose then, turned to his window. 'Perhaps that was a mistake. It's possible if I had pursued the matter at that point, he would still be alive, and we wouldn't be having this discussion.'

'You trusted your judgment and your man.'

Whitney turned back. His eyes were dark; they were intense but not cold, Eve thought. They felt. 'Yes, I did. And now I have more data. The standard autopsy on DS Wojinski detected traces of digitalis and Zeus.'

'Zeus.' Now Eve rose. 'Frank was not a user, Commander. Putting aside who and what he was, a chemical as powerful as Zeus shows. You see it in the eyes, in the personality shift. If he'd been using Zeus, every cop in his division would have known it. The drug scan would have picked it up. There has to be a mistake.'

She dug her hands into her pockets, willed herself not to pace. 'Yeah, there are cops who use, and there are cops who figure their badges shield them from the law. But not Frank. No way was he dirty.'

'But the traces were there, Lieutenant. As well as traces of other chemicals, identified as designer clones. The combination of those chemicals resulted in cardiac arrest and death.'

'You suspect he OD'd, or self-terminated?' She shook her head. 'That's wrong.'

'I repeat, the traces were there.'

'Then there had to be a reason. Digitalis?' She frowned. 'That's heart medicine, isn't it? You said he'd had a physical a couple of weeks ago. Why didn't it show he had heart trouble?'

Whitney's gaze remained level. 'Frank's closest friend on the force is the top E-detective in the city.'

'Feeney?' Eve took two strides forward before she could stop herself. 'You think Feeney covered for him, doctored his records? Damn it, Commander.'

'It's a possibility I can't ignore,' Whitney said evenly. 'Nor can you. Friendship can and does shadow judgment. I am trusting that your friendship with Feeney will not, in this case, shadow yours.'

He walked to the desk again, his position of authority. 'These allegations and suspicions must be investigated and resolved.'

The hot licks in her stomach had grown and were burning like acid. 'You want me to investigate fellow officers. One of which is dead, leaving a grieving family behind. The other of which was my trainer and is my friend.' She put her hands on the desk. 'Is your friend.'

He'd expected the anger, accepted it. Just as he expected she would do the job. He wouldn't accept less. 'Would you prefer I gave this to someone who didn't care?' His brow lifted on the question. 'I want this done quietly, with each piece of evidence and all investigative records sealed for my eyes only. It may be necessary for you to speak with DS Wojinski's family at some point. I trust you will do so discreetly and tactfully. There is no need to add to their grief.'

'And if I turn something up that smears a lifetime of public service?'

'That will be for me to deal with.'

She straightened. 'It's a hell of a thing you're asking me to do.'

'Ordering you to do,' Whitney corrected. 'That should make it easier, Lieutenant. On you.' He handed her two sealed discs. 'View these on your home unit. Any and all transmissions on this matter are to be sent from your home unit to my home unit. Nothing is to go through Cop Central until I tell you differently. Dismissed.'

She turned on her heel, walked to the door. There she paused but didn't look back. 'I won't roll over on Feeney. Damned if I will.'

Whitney watched her stride out, then closed his eyes. She would do what needed to be done, he knew. He only hoped it wasn't more than she could live with.

Her temper was bubbling by the time she got back to her own office. Peabody sat in front of the monitor, smirking.

'Just about got it knocked. Your unit's a real whiner, Dallas, but I've been slapping it into shape.'

'Disengage,' Eve snapped and grabbed up her jacket and bag. 'Get your gear, Peabody.'

'We've got a case?' Revving up, Peabody jumped out of the chair and hustled after Eve. 'What kind of case? Where are we going?' She broke into a trot to keep up. 'Dallas? Lieutenant?'

Eve slapped the control on the elevator, and the single furious look she shot at Peabody was enough to stifle any further questions. Eve stepped into the elevator, shuffled into position with several noisy cops, and stood in stony silence.

'Hey, Dallas, how's the newlywed? Why don't you get your rich husband to buy the Eatery and stock some real food.'

She flicked a steely glare over her shoulder, stared into a face of a grinning cop. 'Bite me, Carter.'

'Hey, I gave that a shot three years ago, and you nearly broke all my teeth. Holding out for a civilian,' he said when laughter erupted.

'Holding out for somebody who isn't the major asshole of Robbery,' someone else put in.

'Better than being the minor one, Forenski. Hey, Peabody,' Carter continued. 'Want me to bite you?'

'Is your dental plan up to date?'

'I'll check on that and get back to you.' With a wink, Carter and several others piled out.

'Carter puts the moves on anything female,' Peabody said conversationally, worried that Eve continued to stare straight ahead. 'Too bad he's an asshole.' No response. 'Ah, Forenski's kind of cute,' Peabody continued. 'He doesn't have a steady personal partner, does he?'

'I don't poke into the private lives of fellow officers,' Eve snapped back, and strode out onto the garage level.

'You don't mind poking into mine,' Peabody said under her breath. She waited while Eve uncoded her car locks, then climbed into the passenger seat. 'Am I to log in destination, sir, or is it a surprise?' Then she blinked when Eve simply laid her head against the wheel. 'Hey, are you all right? What's going on, Dallas?'

'Log in home office.' Eve drew a breath, straightened. 'I'll fill you in on the way. All information you're given and all records on the ensuing investigation are to be coded and sealed.' Eve maneuvered out of the garage and onto the street. 'All said information and records are confidential. You are to report only to me or the commander.'

'Yes, sir.' Peabody swallowed the obstruction that had lodged in her throat. 'It's internal, isn't it? It's one of us.'

'Yeah. Goddamn it. It's one of us.'

*

Her home unit didn't have the eccentricities of her official computer. Roarke had seen to that. The data scrolled smoothly on-screen.

'Detective Marion Burns. She's been undercover at The Athame for eight months, working as a bartender.' Eve pursed her lips. 'Burns. I don't know her.'

'I do, slightly.' Peabody scooted her chair a bit closer to Eve's. 'I met her when I was . . . you know, during the Casto thing. She struck me as a solid, eyes-on-the-job sort. If memory serves, she's third generation cop. Her mother's still on the job. Captain, I think, in Bunko. Her grandfather went out line of duty during the Urban Wars. I don't know why she'd have fingered DS Wojinski.'

'Maybe she reported what she saw, or maybe it's something else. We'll have to find out. Her report to Whitney's pretty cut and dried. At one hundred thirty hours, September 22, 2058, she observed DS Wojinski seated at a private booth with known chemical dealer Selina Cross. Wojinski exchanged credits for a small package, which appeared to contain an illegal substance. The conversation and exchange lasted fifteen minutes, at which time Cross moved to another booth. Wojinski remained in the club another ten minutes, then left. Detective Burns tailed the subject for two blocks at which time he engaged a public transport.'

'So she never saw him use.'

'No. And she never saw him return to the club that night or on any subsequent night during her watch. Burns goes top of our list for questioning.'

'Yes, sir. Dallas, since Wojinski and Feeney were tight, wouldn't it follow that Wojinski would have confided in him? Or failing that, that Feeney would have noticed . . . something.'

'I don't know.' Eve rubbed her eyes. 'The Athame. What the hell's an athame?'

'I don't know.' Peabody pulled out her palm PC and

requested the data. 'Athame, ceremonial knife, a ritual tool normally fashioned of steel. Traditionally the athame is not used for cutting, but for casting or banishing circles in earth religions.'

Peabody glanced up at Eve. 'Witchcraft,' she continued. 'That's quite a coincidence.'

'I don't think so.' She took the note from Alice out of her desk drawer, passed it to Peabody. 'Frank's granddaughter slipped this to me at the viewing. Turns out she works at some shop called Spirit Quest. Do you know it?'

'I know what it is.' Troubled now, Peabody set the note down. 'Wiccans are peaceful, Dallas. And they use herbs, not chemicals. No true Wiccan's going to buy, sell, or use Zeus.'

'How about digitalis?' Eve cocked her head. 'That's kind of an herb, isn't it?'

'It's distilled from foxglove. It's been used medicinally for centuries.'

'It's what, like a stimulant?'

'I don't know that much about healing, but yeah, I'd think.'

'So's Zeus. I wonder what kind of effect you'd get combining the two. Bad mix, wrong dosage, whatever, I wouldn't be surprised if you'd get heart failure.'

'You think Wojinski self-terminated?'

'The commander suspects it, and I've got questions,' Eve said impatiently. 'I don't have answers. But I'm going to get them.' She picked up the note. 'We'll start tonight, with Alice. I want you there at eleven, in civilian clothes. Try to look like a Free-Ager, Peabody, not a cop.'

Peabody winced. 'I've got this dress my mother made for my last birthday. But I'll get really pissed off if you laugh.'

'I'll try to control myself. For now, let's see what we can dig up on this Selina Cross and The Athame Club.'

Five minutes later, Eve was smiling grimly at her machine. 'Interesting. Our Selina's been around. Spent some time in a cage. Just look at this yellow sheet, Peabody. Soliciting sex without a license, '43, '44. Assault charge also in '44, subsequently dropped. Ran into Bunko in '47, running a medium scam. What the hell do people want to talk to the dead for, anyway? Suspected of animal mutilations, '49. Not enough evidence for arrest. Manufacturing and distribution of illegals. That's what tagged her and put her away from '50 to '51. All small-time shit, though. But here in '55, she was brought in and questioned in connection with the ritual slaying of a minor. Her alibi held.'

'Illegals has had her under observation since she was sprung in '51,' Peabody added.

'But they haven't brought her in.'

'Like you said, she's small-time. They must be looking for a bigger fish.'

'That would be my take. We'll see what Marion has to say. Look here, it says Selina Cross owns The Athame Club, free and clear.' Eve pursed her lips. 'Now, where would a small-time dealer get the credit power to buy and run a club? She's a front. I wonder if Illegals knows for who. Let's take a look at her. Computer, display image of subject, Cross, Selina.'

'Whew.' Peabody gave a little shudder as the image floated on-screen. 'Spooky.'

'Not a face you'd forget,' Eve murmured.

It was sharp and narrow, the lips full and vibrant red, the eyes black as onyx. There was beauty there, in the balance of features, the white, smooth skin, but it was cold. And as Peabody had observed, spooky. Her hair was as dark as her eyes, parted perfectly in the center, and it hung straight. There was a small tattoo over her left eyebrow.

'What's that symbol?' Eve wondered. 'Zoom and enhance segment twenty to twenty-two, thirty percent.'

'A pentagram.' Peabody's voice quivered, causing Eve to glance over curiously. 'Inverted. She's not Wiccan, Dallas.' Peabody cleared her throat. 'She's a Satanist.'

*

Eve didn't believe in such things – the white or the black of it. But she was prepared to believe others did. And more inclined to believe that some used that misguided faith to exploit.

'Be careful what you discount, Eve.'

Distracted, she glanced over. Roarke had insisted on driving. She couldn't complain as any one of his vehicles beat the hell out of hers.

'What do you mean?'

'I mean, when certain beliefs and traditions survive for centuries, there's a reason for it.'

'Sure there is, human beings are, and always have been, gullible. And there are, and always have been, individuals who know how to exploit that gullibility. I'm going to find out if someone exploited Frank's.'

She had told Roarke everything, and had justified it professionally by telling herself since she couldn't tap Feeney for his computer expertise, she could, and would, tap Roarke for his.

'You're a good cop and a sensible woman. Often, you're too good a cop and too sensible a woman.' He stopped for traffic, turned to her. 'I'm asking you to be particularly careful when delving into an area such as this.'

His face was in shadows, and his voice much too serious. 'You mean witches and devil worshipers? Come on, Roarke, we're into the second millennium here. Satanists, for Christ's sake!' She pushed her hair back from her face. 'What the hell do they think they'd do with him if he existed and they managed to get his attention?'

'That's the problem, isn't it?' Roarke said quietly and turned west toward the Aquarian Club.

'Devils exist.' Eve frowned as he slid his vehicle up to a second-level spot on the street. 'And they're flesh and blood, they walk on two legs. You and I have seen plenty of them.'

She got out, took the ramp down to street level. It was

27

breezy, and the freshening wind had cleared the smells and smoke away. Overhead, the sky was a thick black, unrelieved by moon or stars. Crisscrossing beams from sluggish air traffic flickered, chased by the muffled grumble of engines.

Here on the street was an arty, up-market part of town where even the glida grill on the corner was spotless, and its menu ran to fresh hybrid fruit rather than smoked soy-dogs. Most of the street vendors had closed up for the night, but during the day, they would unfold their carts and discretely hawk offerings of handmade jewelry, hooked rugs and tapestries, herbal baths, and teas.

Panhandlers in this area would likely be polite, their licenses clearly displayed. And they would probably spend their daily earnings on a meal rather than a chemical high.

The crime rate was low, the rents murderous, and the median age of its residents and merchants carelessly young.

She would have hated to live there.

'We're early,' she murmured, scanning the street as a matter of habit. Then her mouth curved into a smirk. 'Look at that, will you? The Psychic Deli. I guess you go in, order the veggie hash, and they claim they knew you were going to do that. Pasta salad and palm readings. They're open.' On impulse, she turned to Roarke. She wanted something that would turn her sour mood. 'You game?'

'You want your palm read?'

'What the hell.' She grabbed his hand. 'It'll put me in the groove for investigating Satanic chemi-dealers. Maybe they'll cut us a deal and do yours for half price.'

'No.'

'You never know unless you ask.'

'I'm not having mine read.'

'Coward,' she muttered and tugged him through the door.

'I prefer the word *careful*.'

She had to admit, it smelled wonderful. There was none of the usual overlay of onion and heavy sauces. Instead, there was a light fragrance of spice and flowers that meshed perfectly with the airy music.

Small white tables and chairs were arranged at a nice distance from the display counter where bowls and plates of colorful food were presented behind sparkling glass. Two customers sat together over bowls of clear soup. Both of them sported flowing white robes, jeweled sandals, and shaved heads.

Behind the counter was a man with silver rings on every finger. He wore a wide-sleeved shirt in quiet blue. His blonde hair was neatly braided and twined with silver cord. He smiled in welcome.

'Blessed be. Do you wish food for the body or for the soul?'

'I thought you were supposed to know.' Eve grinned at him. 'How about a reading?'

'Palm, Tarot, runes, or aura?'

'Palm.' Enjoying herself, Eve stuck her hand out.

'Cassandra is our palmist. If you'd take a comfortable seat, she'll be happy to help you. Sister,' he added as she started to turn, 'your auras are very strong, vibrant: You are well-matched.' With this, he picked up a wooden stick with a rounded edge and ran it gently over the rim of a white frosted bowl.

Even as the vibration sang, a woman stepped through the beaded curtain separating a back room. She wore a silver tunic with a silver bracelet coiled above her elbow. Eve noted that she was very young, barely twenty, and like the man, her hair was blonde and coiled into a braid.

'Welcome.' Her voice held a hint of Ireland. 'Please be comfortable. Would you both like a reading?'

'No, just me.' Eve took a seat at a far table. 'What's it run?'

'The reading is free. We request a donation, only.' She sat gracefully, smiled at Roarke. 'Your generosity will be appreciated. Madam, the hand you were born with.'

'I came with both of them.'

'The left, please.' She cupped her fingers under Eve's offered hand, barely touching at first. 'Strength and courage. Your fate was not set. A trauma, a break in the lifeline. Very young. You were only a child. Such pain, such sadness.' She lifted her gaze, clear gray. 'You were, and are, without blame.'

She tightened her grip when Eve instinctively drew back. 'It's not necessary to remember all, until you're ready. Sorrow and self-doubt, passions blocked. A solitary woman who chose to focus on one goal. A great need for justice. Disciplined, self-motivated . . . troubled. Your heart was broken, more than broken. Mauled. So you guarded what was left. It's a capable hand. One to trust.'

She took Eve's right hand firmly, but barely looked at it. Those clear gray eyes stayed on Eve's face. 'You carry much of what was inside you. It will not be quiet, it will not rest. But you've found your place. Authority suits you, as does the responsibility that marches with it. You're stubborn, often single-focused, but your heart is greatly healed. You love.'

She flicked a glance at Roarke again, and her mouth softened when she looked back at Eve. 'It surprises you, the depth of this. It unnerves you, and you are not easily unnerved.' Her thumb skimmed over the top of Eve's palm. 'Your heart runs deep. It is . . . choosy. It is careful, but when it's given, it's complete. You carry identification. A badge.' She smiled slowly. 'Yes, you made the right choice. Perhaps the only one you could have made. You've killed. More than once. There was no alternative for you, yet this weighs heavy on your mind and heart. In this, you find it difficult to separate the intellect from the emotion. You'll kill again.'

The gray eyes went glassy, and the light grip tightened. 'It's dark. The forces are dark here. Evil. Lives already lost, and others yet to lose. Pain and fear. Body and soul. You must protect yourself and those you love.'

She turned to Roarke, snagging his hand and speaking rapidly in Gaelic. Her face had gone very white, and her breath hitched.

'That's enough.' Shaken, Eve snatched her hand back. 'Hell of a show.' Irritated that her palm tingled, she rubbed it hard against the knee of her slacks. 'You've got a good eye, Cassandra, is it? And an impressive spiel.' She dug into her pocket, took out fifty in credits and laid them on the table.

'Wait.' Cassandra opened a small, embroidered pouch at her waist, plucked out a smooth stone in pale green. 'A gift. A token.' She pushed it into Eve's hand. 'Carry it with you.'

'Why?'

'Why not? Please come again. Blessed be.'

Eve caught one last glance at her pale face before Cassandra hurried into the back room with a musical jingle of beads.

'Well, so much for "You're taking a long ocean voyage,"' Eve muttered as she headed for the door. 'What did she say to you?'

'Her dialect was a bit thick. I'd say she's from the west counties.' He stepped outside, oddly relieved to draw in the night air. 'The gist was that if I loved you as much as she believed, I would stay close. That you're in danger of losing your life, perhaps your soul, and you need me to survive it.'

'What a crock.' She glanced down at the stone in her hand.

'Keep it.' Roarke closed her fingers over it. 'Couldn't hurt.'

With a shrug, Eve pushed it into her pocket. 'I think I'm going to steer clear of psychics.'

'An excellent idea,' Roarke said with feeling as he walked with her across the street and into the Aquarian Club.

Chapter Three

It was quite a place, Eve mused, and certainly quieter than any club she'd been in before. Both conversation and music were muted, and both had an elegant little lilt. Tables were packed together as was the norm, but they were arranged to provide circular traffic patterns that reminded Eve of the symbol at the base of Alice's note.

Ringing the walls were mirrors fashioned into the shapes of stars and moons. Each held a burning candle, a white pillar, that reflected light and flame. Between each mirror were plaques of symbols and figures she didn't recognize. The small dance floor was circular as well, as was the bar where patrons sat on stools that depicted signs of the zodiac. It took her a moment to place the woman seated on the twin-faces of Gemini.

'Jesus, that's Peabody.'

Roarke shifted his gaze, focused on the woman in a long, sweeping dress in swirling hues of blue and green. Three long strands of beads sparkled to her waist, and earrings of varicolored metals jingled beneath the fringes of her straight, cropped hair.

'Well, well,' he said and smiled slowly, 'our sturdy Peabody makes quite a picture.'

'She sure . . . blends,' Eve decided. 'I have to meet with Alice alone. Why don't you go over and talk to Peabody?'

'A pleasure. Lieutenant . . .' He took a long look at her

worn jeans, battered leather jacket, and unadorned ears. 'You don't blend.'

'Is that a dig?'

'No.' He flicked a finger over the dent in her chin. 'An observation.' He strolled over, slid onto the stool beside Peabody. 'Now, let's see, what would be the standard line? What's a nice witch like you doing in a place like this?'

Peabody slid him a sidelong look, grimaced. 'I feel like an idiot in this getup.'

'You look lovely.'

She snorted. 'Not exactly my style.'

'You know the fascinating thing about women, Peabody?' He reached out, tapped a finger against her dangling earrings to send them dancing. 'You have so many styles. What are you drinking?'

Ridiculously flattered, she struggled not to flush. 'A Saggitarius. That's my sign. The drink's supposed to be metabolically and spiritually designed for my personality.' She sipped from the clear chalice. 'Actually, it's not bad. What's your, you know, birth sign?'

'I have no idea. I believe I was born the first week of October.'

Believe; Peabody mused. *How odd not to know.* 'Well, that would make you Libran.'

'Well then, let's be metabolically and spiritually correct.' He turned to order drinks, watched Eve sitting at a table. 'What sign would you attribute to your lieutenant?'

'She's a tough one to pin down.'

'Indeed she is,' Roarke murmured.

From her table on the outer circle, Eve watched everything. There was no band or holographic image of one. Instead, the music seem to come from nowhere and everywhere. Windy flutes and plucked strings, a soothing female voice that sang with impossible sweetness in a language Eve didn't recognize.

She saw couples in earnest conversations, others laughing quietly. No one flicked an eyelash when a woman in a sheer white sheath rose to dance alone. Eve ordered water and was amused when it was served in a goblet of simulated silver.

She tuned in to the conversation at the table behind her and was further amused to hear the group's sober discussion on their experiences with astral projection.

At a table in the next ring, two women talked about their former lives as temple dancers in Atlantis. She wondered why former lives were always more exotic than the one being lived. The only shot a person had, in her opinion.

Harmless weirdos, Eve thought, but caught herself rubbing her still tingling palm on her jeans.

She saw Alice the minute the girl walked in. *Agitated*, Eve thought. *Nervous hands, tensed shoulders, jittery eyes*. She waited until Alice scanned the room, spotted her, then she inclined her head in acknowledgment. With a last backward glance at the door, Alice hurried over.

'You came. I was afraid you wouldn't.' Quickly, she dipped into her pocket and drew out a smooth black stone on a silver chain. 'Put this on. Please,' she insisted when Eve only studied it. 'It's obsidian. It's been consecrated. It'll block evil.'

'I'm all for that.' Eve slipped the chain around her neck. 'Better?'

'This is the safest place I know. The cleanest.' Still darting glances around the room, Alice sat. 'I used to come here all the time.' She gripped the amulet she wore in both hands as a server glided to the table. 'A Golden Sun, please.' She took a deep breath as she looked back at Eve. 'I need courage. I've tried to meditate all day, but I'm blocked. I'm afraid.'

'What are you afraid of, Alice?'

'That those who killed my grandfather will kill me next.'

'Who killed your grandfather?'

'Evil killed him. Killing is what evil does best. You won't believe what I tell you. You're too grounded in what can be seen only with the eyes.' She accepted the drink from the server, closed her eyes a moment as if in prayer, then slowly lifted the cup to her lips. 'But you won't ignore it, either. You're too much a cop. I don't want to die,' Alice said and set her cup down.

That, Eve thought, was the first sensible statement she'd heard. The fear was genuine enough, she decided, and unmasked tonight. At the viewing, Alice had been careful to slick on a layer of composure and calm.

For her family, Eve realized.

'Who are you afraid of, and why?'

'I have to explain. All of it. I have to purge before I can atone. My grandfather respected you, so I come to you in his memory. I wasn't born a witch.'

'Weren't you?' Eve said dryly.

'Some are, and some, like me, are simply drawn to the craft. I became interested in Wicca through my studies, and the more I learned, the more I felt a need to belong. I was drawn to the rituals, the search for balance, the joy, and the positive ethics. I didn't share my interest with my family. They wouldn't have understood.'

She dipped her head and her hair flowed down like a curtain. 'I enjoyed the secrecy of that and was still young enough to find the experience of going skyclad at an outdoor celebration slightly wicked. My family . . .' She lifted her head again. 'They're conservative, and a part of me simply wanted to do something daring.'

'A small rebellion?'

'Yes, that's true. If I had left it at that,' Alice murmured, 'if I had truly accepted my initiation into the craft, and what it meant, everything would be different now. I was weak, and my intellect too ambitious.' She picked up her drink again, wet her dry throat. 'I wanted to know. To compare and analyze, rather like a thesis, the contrasts of white and black magic. How could I fully appreciate the one without fully understanding its antithesis? That was my rationale.'

'Sounds logical.'

'False logic,' Alice insisted. 'I was deluding myself. The ego and the intellect were so arrogant. I would study the black arts on a purely scholarly level. I'd talk to those who had chosen the other path and discover what had turned them away from the light. It would be exciting.' She smiled tremulously. 'I thought it would be exciting, and for a short time, it was.'

A child, Eve thought, *in the body of a stunning woman. Bright and curious, but a child, nonetheless.* It was pitifully easy to tug information from the young. 'Is that how you met Selina Cross?'

Paling, Alice made a quick forking gesture with her forefinger and pinky. 'How do you know of her?'

'I did some research. I didn't walk in here blind, Alice. As a cop's granddaughter, you shouldn't have expected me to.'

'Be afraid of her.' Alice compressed her lips. 'Be afraid of her.'

'She's a second-rate grifter and chemi-dealer.'

'No, she's much more.' Alice gripped her amulet again. 'Believe that, Lieutenant. I've seen. I know. She'll want you. You'll challenge her.'

'Do you believe she had something to do with Frank's death?'

'I know she did.' Tears swam into her eyes, deepening the soft blue. One huge and lovely drop spilled over and slid down her white cheek. 'Because of me.'

Eve leaned closer to comfort, and to block the tearful face from any onlookers. 'Tell me about it, about her.'

'I met her nearly a year ago. On the sabbat of Samhain. All Hallow's Eve. More research, I told myself. I didn't realize how deeply I'd already been drawn in, how utterly seduced I was by the power, the pure selfish greed of the other side. I hadn't performed any of the rituals, not then.

I was still observing. Then I met her, and the one they call Alban.'

'Alban?'

'He, serves her.' Alice lifted a hand, laid her fingers against her mouth. 'That night still isn't clear in my mind. I realize now they cast a spell over me. I let them lead me into the circle, strip off my robes. I heard the bells ring, and the chant to the dark prince. I watched the sacrifice of the goat. And I shared in the blood.'

Her head drooped again as shame whirled inside her. 'I shared in it, drank of it, and enjoyed. I was the altar that night. I was tied to the stone. I don't know how or by whom, but I wasn't afraid. I was aroused.'

Her voice dropped to a whisper. The music changed, slid from strings to drums and bells, cheerfully sexual. Alice never lifted her gaze.

'Each member of the coven touched me, rubbed oils and blood over me. The chanting was inside me, and the fire was so hot. Then Selina laid over me. She . . . did things. I'd never had any sexual experience. Then while she slid up my body, Alban straddled me. She watched me. His hands were on her breasts and he was inside me. And she watched my face. I wanted to close my eyes, but I couldn't. I couldn't. I couldn't stop looking into her eyes. It was like she was the one – the one inside me.'

Her tears plopped on the table now. Even though Eve had shifted to sheild her from most of the room, and Alice's voice was barely more than a whisper, several heads were turning curiously.

'You were drugged, Alice. And exploited. You have nothing to be ashamed of.'

Her eyes lifted briefly and threatened to break Eve's heart. 'Then why am I so ashamed? I was a virgin, and there was pain, but even that was arousing. Unbearably. And the pleasure that came with it was huge, monstrous. They used me, and I begged

37

to be used again. And was, by the entire coven. By sunrise I was lost, enslaved. I woke in bed, between them. Alban and Selina. I'd already become their apprentice. And their toy.'

Tears were running down her cheeks as she drank again. 'Sexually, there was nothing I would not allow them, or one of their choosing, to do to me. I embraced the dark. And I became careless in my arrogance. Someone told my grandfather. He would never give me a name, but I know it was a Wiccan. He confronted me, and I laughed at him. I warned him to stay out of my affairs. I thought he had.'

Saying nothing, Eve slid her water across the table. Gratefully, Alice picked it up, drained it. 'A few months ago, I discovered Selina and Alban were performing private rituals. I'd come down from college a day early. I went to their house, and I heard the ceremonial chant. I opened the door of the ritual room. They were there, together, performing a sacrifice.' Her hands shook. 'Not a goat this time, but a child. A young boy.'

Eve's hand closed tight over Alice's wrist. 'You saw them murder a child?'

'Murder is too tame a word for what they did.' The tears dried up in horror. 'Don't ask me to tell you. Don't ask me that.'

She would have to, Eve knew, but it could wait. 'Tell me what you can.'

'I saw . . . Selina, the ritual knife. The blood, the screams. I swear you could see the screams like black smears on the air. It was too late to stop it.'

She looked at Eve again, those swimming eyes begging to be believed in this one thing. 'I was too late to do anything for the boy, even if I'd had the power or the courage to try.'

'You were alone, shocked,' Eve said carefully. 'The woman was armed, the boy was dead. You couldn't have helped him.'

For one long moment, Alice stared at her, then covered her

face with her hands. 'I try to believe that. Try so hard. Living with it is destroying me. I ran away. I just ran.'

'You can't change it.' Eve kept her hand on Alice's wrist, but her grip gentled. She had once seen a child mutilated, had been too late. Seconds too late. She hadn't run, she had killed. But the child was just as dead, either way. 'You can't go back and change it. You have to live with what is.'

'I know. Isis tells me that.' Alice took a shuddering breath, lowered her hands. 'They were engrossed in their work and never saw me. Or I pray they never saw me. I didn't go to my grandfather or the police. I was terrified, sick. I don't know how much time went by, but I went to Isis, the high priestess who had initiated me into Wicca. She took me in; even after all I'd done, she took me in.'

'You didn't tell Frank what you'd seen?'

Alice winced at the bite in Eve's voice. 'Not then. I spent time in reflection and purification. Isis performed several cleansing rites and auric healings. Isis and I felt it best that I stay in seclusion for a while, concentrate on finding the light, and atonement.'

Eve's eyes were hot and hard as she leaned closer. 'Alice, you saw a child murdered and told no one but your neighborhood witch?'

'I know how it sounds.' Her lip quivered before she caught it between her teeth and steadied it. 'The child's physical being was beyond help. I could do nothing for him but pray for the safe passage of his soul to the next plane. I was afraid to tell Grandpa. Afraid of what he might do and what Selina would do to him. When I did go to him last month, I told him everything. Now he's dead, and I know she's responsible.'

'How do you know?'

'I saw her.'

'Wait.' Eyes narrowed, Eve held up a hand. 'You saw her kill him?'

'No, I saw her outside my window. I looked out the night

he died, and she was standing below, looking up. Looking up at me. The call came from my mother to tell me Grandpa was dead. And Selina smiled. She smiled and she beckoned to me.' Alice buried her face in her hands again. 'She sent her forces against him. Used her power to stop his heart. Because of me. Now the raven comes every night to my window and watches me with her eyes.'

Christ, Eve thought, where were they going with this? 'A bird?'

Alice laid her trembling hands on the table. 'She's a shape-shifter. She takes what form she wills. I've protected myself as best I can, but my faith may not be strong enough. They're pulling at me, calling to me.'

'Alice.' While sympathy remained, Eve found her patience waning. 'Selina Cross might have had a part in your grandfather's death. If we find that he didn't die of natural causes, it wasn't some spell; it was calculated, simple murder. If so, there'll be evidence, and a trial, and she'll be dealt with.'

'You can't find smoke.' Alice shook her head. 'You won't find evidence in a curse.'

Enough was enough. 'At this point, you're a witness to a crime. Potentially the only witness, and if you're afraid, I can arrange a safe house for you.' Her voice was flat and brisk, all cop. 'I need you to give me a description of the child so that I can check missing persons. With your formal statement, I can get a warrant to search the room where you allegedly witnessed the murder. I need you to give me details, straight details. Times, places, names. I can help you.'

'You don't understand,' Alice said, shaking her head slowly. 'You don't believe me.'

'I believe you're an intelligent and curious woman who got in over her head with some very nasty people. And I believe you're confused and upset. I have someone you can talk to who can help you sort things out.'

'Someone?' Alice's eyes went cold and her voice hard. 'A

40

psychiatrist? You think I'm imagining things, making them up.' Her body trembled as she surged to her feet. 'It's not my mind that's in danger, it's my life. My life, Lieutenant Dallas, and my soul. If you find yourself in battle with Selina, you'll believe. And may the goddess help you.'

She whirled and ran out, leaving Eve cursing.

'That seemed remarkably unsuccessful,' Roarke commented as he came up behind her.

'The girl's whacked out, but she's terrified.' Eve heaved a long breath and rose. 'Let's get the hell out of here.' She signaled Peabody, then headed for the door.

Outside, a thin fog crept along the ground, stealthily, like twining gray snakes. Rain, thin and chilly, was just beginning to slick the street.

'There she is,' Eve murmured when she caught sight of Alice rushing around the corner. 'Headed south. Peabody, tail her, make sure she gets home safe.'

'Got her,' Peabody headed off at a half trot.

'That kid's a mess, Roarke. They've fucked with her in every way possible.' Disgusted, she dug her hands into her pockets. 'I probably could've handled it better, but I don't see how it would help to encourage her delusions. Spells and curses and shape shifters. Jesus.'

'Darling Eve.' He kissed her brow. 'My own practical cop.'

'The way she tells it, she was practically the bride of Satan.' Grumbling, Eve started for the car, turned on her heel, and paced back. 'I'll tell you how it went, Roarke. She wanted to play, wanted to dabble in the occult, and she ran into real bad news. She's a naive, pretty girl, and it doesn't take a crystal ball to see it. So she went to one of their meetings, or whatever the hell you call them, and they drugged her. Then they gang-raped her. Bastards. She's drugged and in shock and vulnerable to suggestions, and it's easy for a couple of professional cons to convince her she's part of their cult. Pull a couple of magic

41

tricks out of their hat and fascinate her. Use sex to keep her in line.'

'She got to you,' Roarke murmured and touched her hair, brushing away the wet.

'Maybe she did. Damn it, did you look at her? She's well-named. Looks like that kid in the fairy story. Probably believes in talking rabbits, too.' Then she sighed, struggled to put her emotions back into place. 'But we're not in a fairy story here. She claims she walked in on a ritual murder. A little boy, she said. I've got to get her in to Mira. A shrink will be able to sort out the fact from fiction. But I believe that murder was fact, and if they killed one child, they've killed more. People like them prey on the helpless.'

'I know.' He reached out to rub the tenstion in her shoulders. 'Close to home?'

'No. It's not like what happened to me. Or you.' But there were enough echoes to unnerve her. 'We're still here, aren't we?' She laid a hand on his but frowned into the shadows. 'Why didn't Frank make a log of what she'd told him? Why the hell did he go solo on this?'

'Maybe he did make a log. A private one.'

She blinked, stared at him. 'God, how could I be so slow!' She clapped her hands on either side of his face and kissed him hard. 'You're brilliant.'

'Yes, I know.' He jerked her back as a figure darted out of the shadows and over the ramp. 'Black cat,' he said, simultaneously uneasy and amused at himself. 'Bad luck.'

'Yeah, right.' She started up the ramp, cocked her head as the cat sat at the side of Roarke's car, watching her out of bright and glittering green eyes. 'You don't look hungry, ace. Too sleek and glossy for an alley cat. Too perfect,' she realized. 'Must be a droid.' Still, she crouched, reached out to stroke. The cat hissed, arched, and swiped. Eve would have found her palm laid open if she hadn't been quick enough to dodge. 'Well, that's friendly.'

'You should know better than to offer your hand to strange animals – or droids.' But he stepped in front of Eve to uncode the car and kept his eyes on the gleaming green of the cat's. When Eve was in the car, he spoke softly. The cat's fur bristled, its tail switched, then it leaped nimbly from the ramp to the street, and it was swallowed by the fog.

Roarke couldn't have said why he'd given the order to go in Gaelic. It had simply come out that way. He was still pondering it when he slid in beside Eve.

'Listen, Roarke, I can't tap Feeney for any E-work on this. At least not until the commander loosens up. I may have to go to the family for access to Frank's personal records, but if I do that, I'll have to tell them something.'

'And you'd rather not.'

'Not yet, in any case. So how do you feel about using your . . . skills to access Frank's personal unit and logs?'

His mood lifted as he started the car, guiding it down to street level. 'That depends, Lieutenant. Do I get a badge?'

Her lips twitched into a smirk. 'No. But you get to have sex with a cop.'

'Do I get to pick the cop?' He only smiled when she punched his arm. 'I'd pick you. Probably. And I suppose you want me to begin my unofficial consultation tonight.'

'That's the idea.'

'All right, but I want sex first.' He tucked his tongue in his cheek as she chuckled. 'How long do you think Peabody's going to be busy? Just joking,' he said quickly, but shifted into autodrive just in case Eve got violent. 'She did look quite appealing tonight though.'

Laughing, he caught her fist in his hand, then snuck the other one up to her breast. 'Listen, pal, you're in deep enough without trying that. Engaging in any sexual act in a moving vehicle is in violation of inner city codes.'

'Arrest me,' he suggested and nipped her bottom lip.

'I might. When I'm done with you.' She wiggled free and

shoved him back. 'And just for that smart-ass remark about my aide, no sex until after the consult.'

He disengaged auto, then slid her a slow, smiling glance. 'Wanna bet?'

She met that arrogant glance narrow-eyed. 'Fifty credits, even odds.'

'Done.' And he whistled his way through the iron gates that led home.

Chapter Four

'Pay up.'

Eve rolled over, rubbed her bare butt, and wondered if she'd have rug burns. Still vibrating from the last orgasm, she closed her eyes again. 'Huh?'

'Fifty credits.' He leaned over, gently kissed the tip of her breast. 'You lost, Lieutenant.'

Her eyes blinked open and stared into his gorgeous and very satisfied face. They were sprawled on the rug of his private room, and their clothes, as best she could recall, were scattered everywhere. Starting at the stairway where he'd trapped her against the wall and had started to . . . win the bet.

'I'm naked,' she pointed out. 'I don't generally keep credits up my—'

'I'm happy to take your IOU.' He rose, all graceful, gleaming muscles, and took a memo card from his console. 'Here you are.' Handed it to her.

She stared down at it, knowing dignity was as lost as the fifty credits. 'You're really enjoying this.'

'Oh, more than you can possibly imagine.'

Scowling at him, she engaged the memo. 'I owe you, Roarke, fifty credits, Dallas, Lieutenant Eve.' She shoved the memo at him. 'Satisfied.'

'In every possible way.' He thought, sentimentally, that he would tuck the memo away with the little gray suit button he'd kept from their very first meeting. 'I love you, Dallas, Lieutenant Eve, in every possible way.'

She couldn't help it. She went soft all over. It was the way he said it, the way he looked at her that had rapid pulses beating under melting skin. 'Oh, no, you don't. That kind of thing's how you took me for fifty.' She scrambled up before he could distract her again. 'Where the hell are my pants?'

'I haven't the faintest idea.' He walked to a section of the wall, touched a mechanism. When the panel slid open, he drew out a robe. It was silk and thin and made her eyes narrow again.

He was always buying her things like that, and they always seemed to find their way to various parts of the house. Conveniently.

'That's not working attire.'

'We can do this naked, but you'd certainly lose another fifty.' When she snatched the robe out of his hand, he turned and took out another for himself. 'This could take some time. We'll want coffee.'

As she went to the AutoChef to get coffee, Roarke moved behind the console. The equipment here was first flight, and unregistered. CompuGuard couldn't track it nor block him from hacking into any system. Still, even with those advantages, finding a personal log that may or may not have existed was like separating individual grains of sand from a bucketful.

'Engage,' he ordered. 'More likely his home unit, wouldn't you think?'

'Anything on his unit at Cop Central would have been transferred, and official units record all logging. If he wanted to keep something to himself, he'd have used a private system.'

'Do you have his home address? Never mind,' he said before Eve could speak. 'I'll get it. Data, Wojinski, Frank . . . what was his rank?'

'Detective Sergeant, attached to Records.'

'Data on screen one, please.'

As it began to scroll, Roarke reached for the coffee Eve held out to him, then waved his fingers when his 'link beeped. 'Get that, would you?'

It was the careless order of a man used to giving them. Automatically, she bristled, then just as quickly bumped aside the annoyance. She supposed the situation called for her to act as assistant.

'Roarke's residence. Peabody?'

'You didn't answer your communicator.'

'No, I . . .' God knew where it was, she thought. 'What's up?'

'It's bad. Dallas, it's bad.' Though her voice was steady, her face was dead white, and her eyes too dark. 'Alice is dead. I couldn't stop it. I couldn't get to her. She just—'

'Where are you?'

'On Tenth Street, between Broad and Seventh. I called the MTS, but there was nothing—'

'Are you in jeopardy?'

'No, no. I just couldn't stop her. I just watched while—'

'Secure the scene, Officer. Relay to Dispatch. I'm on my way. Call backup as required, and stand. Understood?'

'Yes, sir. Yes.'

'Dallas out. Oh, Christ,' she murmured when she disengaged.

'I'll take you.' He was already up, his hand on her shoulder.

'No, this is my job.' And she prayed it wasn't her doing. 'I'd appreciate it if you'd stay here and get whatever data you can.'

'All right. Eve.' He took both of her shoulders now, firmly, before she could turn away. 'Look at me. This was not your fault.'

She did look at him, and there was grief in her eyes. 'I hope to God it wasn't.'

*

There wasn't a crowd. Eve could be grateful for that. It was after two in the morning, and only a few gawkers huddled together behind the barricade. She saw a Rapid Cab tipped drunkenly on the curb and a man sitting beside it, his head in his hands, as an MT spoke with him.

On the rain-slicked street, lit dimly by the glow of a security light with fog billowing like clouds, was Alice. Her body sprawled there, faceup, her arms and legs flung out as if in wild welcome. Blood, her own, had soaked through the filmy material of her dress and turned it to dark, doomed red.

Peabody stood by her, assisting a uniform in the erecting of a privacy screen.

'Officer Peabody.' Eve said it softly, waited for Peabody to turn, straighten her shoulders, and cross to her. 'Your report?'

'I followed the subject to her residence, as per your orders, Lieutenant. I watched her enter the building, and subsequently observed the light go on in the second window from the east, third floor. On my own initiative, I decided to keep watch for a period of fifteen minutes, to insure the subject remained inside. She did not.'

Peabody trailed off, and her gaze shifted to the body. Eve sidestepped, blocked the view. 'Look at me when you report, Officer.'

'Yes, sir.' Peabody snapped back. 'Subject exited building approximately ten minutes later. She appeared agitated, continually looked over her shoulder as she walked west at a rapid pace. She appeared to be crying. I maintained the standard distance. That's why I couldn't stop her.' Peabody had to suck in air. 'I maintained the standard distance.'

'Stop it.' Eve snapped it out, gave Peabody a quick shake. 'Complete your report.'

Peabody's eyes went flat and cold as they met Eve's. 'Yes, sir. The subject stopped suddenly, took several steps in retreat. She spoke. I was too far away to discern what she said, but it was my impression that she was speaking to someone.'

She played it back through her mind, every step, leaning on her training like a crutch. 'I closed the distance somewhat, in the event the subject was in jeopardy. I observed no one on the street other than the subject herself. The fog may have been a factor, but there was no one on the sidewalk or the street that I could see.'

'She stood there, talking to no one?' Eve asked.

'That's how it appeared, Lieutenant. She became increasingly agitated. She begged to be left alone. Her words were, "Haven't you done enough, haven't you taken enough? Why won't you leave me in peace."'

Peabody stared back at the sidewalk, saw it all again. Heard it as well. That hitch of desperation and despair in Alice's voice. 'I thought I heard a response, but can't be definite. The subject was speaking too loudly and too rapidly for me to make a clear statement on that. I decided to move closer, to make myself known.'

A muscle in her jaw jumped as she continued to stare over Eve's shoulder. 'At this time, a Rapid Cab, traveling east, approached. The subject turned and ran into the street, directly into the path of the oncoming vehicle. The driver attempted to stop and evade, but was unable to do so and struck the subject head-on.'

She paused just long enough to take another breath. 'Road conditions were fair to poor, and played a minor factor. Even with optimum conditions, it would be my opinion the driver would have been unable to avoid the collision.'

'Understood. Continue.'

'I reached the body within seconds, and though I observed that she was already dead, I called for the medical technicians, then attempted to contact you via your communicator. When this was unsuccessful, I utilized the portalink in my bag and reached you at home to report the situation. Following your

49

orders, I relayed to Dispatch and requested a uniform, then secured the scene.'

It was hell to be too late, Eve knew, and no amount of sympathy could ease that bitter guilt. So she offered none. 'Very well, Officer. That's the driver?'

Peabody continued to stare straight ahead, and her voice was hollow. 'Yes, Lieutenant.'

'Arrange for his vehicle to be taken in for analysis, then consult with the MTs and find out if he's in shape to give a statement.'

'Yes, sir.' Peabody clutched her hand into a fist at her side. She kept her voice low, but it vibrated with emotion. 'You had a drink with her barely an hour ago. And it doesn't mean a damn to you.'

Eve took the hit and waited until Peabody turned away before she walked back to Alice. 'Yes, it does,' she murmured. 'And that's the problem.'

Opening her field kit, she crouched down to do her job.

It wasn't homicide. Technically, Eve should have turned the matter over to Traffic after Peabody's report and the ensuing statement from the weeping cabbie. But she watched Alice's body being loaded into the morgue wagon and knew she had no intention of doing so.

She took a last look at the scene. The rain had nearly stopped and wouldn't wash away the blood. The few gawkers who had gathered were already breaking up and moving along, tearing the last thin curtains of fog as they shuffled home.

Across at the curb, a city tow unit was already hitching up the damaged cab for transferral to the police compound.

Accidents, some would say, happened all too often. And so, Eve thought, did murder. All too often.

'You've had a long night, Peabody. You're off duty.'

'I would prefer to stay on, Lieutenant, and see this through.'

'You won't help her or me unless you can see it through objectively.'

'I can do my job, sir. My feelings are my own business.'

Eve hitched up her field kit, took a long look at her aide. 'Yes, they are. Just don't let them get in my way.' She took her recorder out of her kit, held it out to Peabody. 'On record, Officer. We'll examine the subject's residence.'

'Do you intend to notify the next of kin? Sir?'

'When we're done here.'

They headed east, back to Alice's building. She hadn't gotten far, Eve thought, barely a block. What had driven her back out? And what had driven her into the path of the cab?

The building was a pretty, restored brownstone of three stories. The entrance doors sported beveled glass with an etched design of peacocks. The security camera was in full repair, and the locks coded for palm prints. Eve disarmed them with a master code and entered a small, well-scrubbed foyer with faux marble floors. The elevator had a mirrored bronze sheen and ran with silent efficiency.

Alice, she thought, had had taste and the financial resources to indulge it. There were three apartments on the third floor, and again Eve used her master to gain entrance.

'Dallas, Lieutenant Eve, and aide, Peabody, Officer D., entering residence of deceased for standard examination. Lights,' she ordered, then frowned when the room remained dark.

Peabody reached around the door, flicked a switch. 'She must have preferred manual to voice-activated.'

The room was cluttered and colorful. Pretty scarves and throws were draped over chairs, tables. Tapestries depicting attractive naked people and mythological animals romped over the walls. Candles were everywhere, on tables, on shelves, on the floor, as were bowls of colored stones, of herbs, of dried flower petals. Chunks and wands of crystal, sparkling clean, crowded every flat surface.

A mood screen was engaged and showed a wide field of meadow grass and wildflowers blowing gently in the breeze. Its audio played the song of birds and zephyrs.

'She liked pretty things,' Eve observed. 'And lots of them.' Moving over, she glanced at the controls of the mood screen and nodded as they corroborated her thought. 'She flipped this on as soon as she walked in. Wanted to mellow out, I'd say.'

Leaving Peabody to follow, she walked into the adjoining room. The bedroom was small, cozy, and again cluttered. The spread on the narrow bed was embroidered with stars and moons. A glass mobile, dancing with fairies, hung above it and even now clinked musically in the breeze through the open window.

'This would have been the window, the light you saw come on.'

'Yes, sir.'

'So she flipped on the screen, then came straight into the bedroom. Probably wanted to change, get out of the damp dress. But she didn't.' Eve stepped on to a small area rug with the face of a smiling sun. 'It's cluttered, but tidy in its way. No sign of disturbance or struggle.'

'Struggle?'

'You said she was agitated, crying when she came back out. The country meadow program didn't mellow her, or didn't have enough time to.'

'She didn't bother to shut it down again.'

'No,' Eve agreed. 'She didn't. There's the possibility someone was here when she got home. Someone who upset or frightened her. We'll check the security logs.' She opened what she assumed was a closet, and let out a hum. 'Well, look at this. She'd turned it into a room of some kind. Not a lot of clutter here. Get this on record.'

Peabody stepped up, scanned the recorder over a small, white-walled room. The floor was wood with a white pentagram

52

painted on it. A ring of white candles were arranged in careful symmetry around the edge. A small table held a clear crystal ball, a bowl, a mirror, and a dark-handled knife with a short, blunted blade.

Eve sniffed the air, but caught no hint of smoke or candle wax. 'What do you figure she did in here?'

'I'd say it was kind of ritual room, for meditation, or casting spells.'

'Jesus.' With a shake of her head, Eve stepped back. 'We'll leave that for now and check out her 'link. If no one was here to scare her back out, maybe she got a call that did. She came into the bedroom first,' Eve murmured, wandering back to the small bedside 'link. 'Maybe she intended to go in there and play witch after she'd changed and calmed down. She wasn't carrying anything when she went back out. She didn't come in here to get something and go out again. She was upset, she came home.'

Eve engaged the 'link, requested a replay of the last call transmitted or received. And the room filled with low, rhythmic chanting.

'What the hell is that?'

'I don't know.' Uneasy, Peabody stepped closer.

'Replay,' Eve demanded.

Hear the names. Hear the names and fear them. Loki, Beelzebub, Baphomet. I am annihilation. I am revenge. In nomine Dei nostri Santanas Luciferi excelsi. Vengeance for you who strayed from the law. Hear the names and fear.

'Stop.' Eve gave a quick, involuntary shudder. 'Beelzebub, that's devil shit, isn't it? The bastards were playing with her, tormenting her. And she was already on the edge. No wonder she ran out of here. Where were you, you son of a bitch, where were you? Location of last transmission. Display.' Her mouth thinned as she read the data. 'Tenth and Seventh, right down the goddamn street. Probably a public 'link. Fuckers. She was heading right for them.'

'There wasn't anyone there.' But Peabody was watching Eve's face now, and the fury that fired in her eyes. 'Even with the fog, the rain, I would have seen someone if they'd been laying for her. There wasn't anything there but a cat.'

Eve's heart took a bad jump. 'A what?'

'Just a cat. I caught a glimpse of a cat, but there was no one on the street.'

'A cat.' Eve walked to the window. Suddenly, she felt the need for a good gulp of air. There, on the sill, she saw the long, black feather. 'And a bird,' she murmured. She took out tweezers, held the feather up to the light. 'We've still got the occasional crow in New York. A crow's the same thing as a raven, isn't it?'

'More or less. I think.'

'Bag it,' Eve ordered. 'I want it analyzed.' She rubbed her fingers over her eyes as if to push away fatigue. 'Next of kin would be Brenda Wojinski, mother. Run that for an address.'

'Yes, sir.' Peabody took out her PPC, then simply held it while shame washed over her. 'Lieutenant, I'd like to apologize for my earlier comment and my behavior.'

Eve took the disc from the 'link, sealed it herself. 'I don't recall any comment, Peabody, or any unsatisfactory behavior.' She gave Peabody a level look. 'While the recorder is still engaged, do another scan of the apartment.'

Understanding, Peabody inclined her head. 'I'm aware the recorder is still engaged, Lieutenant. I want this on the record. I was insubordinate and out of line both professionally and personally.'

Damn stiff-necked idiot, Eve thougth and bit back an oath. 'There was no insubordination in my opinion or in my recollection, Officer.'

'Dallas.' Peabody loosed a sigh. 'I damn well was. I was shaky and having a hard time dealing with the situation. It's one thing to see a body after it's done, and another to see a woman get tossed ten feet in the air and land on the pavement. She was under my watch.'

'I was rough on you.'

'Yes, sir, you were. And you needed to be. I thought that because you were able to maintain, you were able to do your job, it meant you didn't care. I was wrong, and I'm sorry.'

'Acknowledged. Now, put this on record, Peabody. You followed orders, you followed procedure. You were not at fault for what happened tonight. You could not have prevented it. Now, put it aside so we can find out why she's dead.'

Eve thought that a cop's daughter knew when another cop knocked on the door at five in the morning, it was with news of the worst kind. She saw, the minute Brenda recognized her, that she was right.

'Oh God. Oh God. Mama?'

'No, it's not your mother, Ms Wojinski.' There was only one way, Eve knew, and that was fast. 'It's Alice. May we come in?'

'Alice?' She blinked glazed eyes, propped a hand on the door for balance. 'Alice?'

'I think we should go inside.' As gently as possible, Eve took her arm, stepped through the door. 'Let's go in and sit down.'

'Alice?' she said again. Grief cracked the glaze over her eyes. Tears poured through. 'Oh no, not my Alice. Not my baby.'

Brenda swayed, would have slid to the floor, but Eve tightened her grip and headed quickly for the nearest seat. 'I'm sorry. I'm so sorry for your loss, Ms Wojinski. There was an accident early this morning, and Alice was killed.'

'An accident? No, you've made a mistake. It was someone else. It wasn't Alice.' She clutched at Eve, flooded eyes pleading. 'You can't be sure it was my Alice.'

'It was. I'm sorry.'

She collapsed then, burying her face in her hands, pressing her hands to her knees so her body was balled in a defensive shield.

'I could make her some tea,' Peabody murmured.

'Yeah, go.' It was the part of the job that made Eve feel the most helpless, the most inadequate. There was no solution for fresh grief. 'Is there someone I can call for you? Do you want me to contact your mother? Your brother?'

'Mama. Oh God, Alice. How will we bear it?'

There was no answer for that, Eve thought. Yet they would. Life demanded it. 'I can give you a soother, or contact your doctor, if you'd prefer.'

'Mom?'

As Brenda continued to rock, Eve looked over. The boy stood in the doorway, blinking sleepy, confused eyes. His hair was tousled from sleep and he wore grubby sweatpants with holes at the knees.

Alice's brother, Eve remembered. She'd forgotten.

Then he focused on Eve, his eyes suddenly alert, and much too adult. 'What's wrong?' he demanded. 'What's happened?'

What the hell was his name? Eve struggled to remember, then decided it didn't matter at the moment. She rose. He was a tall boy, she realized, with sleep creases in his cheeks and a body already braced to take the worst. 'There's been an accident. I'm sorry but—'

'It's Alice.' His chin quivered, but his eyes stayed steady on hers. 'She's dead.'

'Yes, I'm sorry.'

He continued to stare at her as Peabody came in with a cup of tea, set it awkwardly on the table. 'What kind of accident?'

'She was hit by a car early this morning.'

'Hit and run?'

'No.' Eve watched him carefully, considering. 'She stepped

56

into the path of a cab. The driver was unable to stop. We're in the process of analyzing his vehicle and the scene, but there was a witness who corroborates the driver's statement. I don't believe he was at fault. He didn't attempt to flee the scene, and his driving record is clean.'

The boy simply nodded, dry-eyed, while his mother's weeping filled the room. 'I'll take care of her. It'd be best if you left us alone now.'

'All right. If you have any questions, you can reach me at Cop Central. I'm Lieutenant Dallas.'

'I know who you are. Leave us alone now,' he repeated and went to sit by his mother.

'The kid knows something,' Eve stated as they stepped outside.

'That would be my take. Maybe Alice felt more comfortable talking to him than other members of the family. They were pretty close in age. Brothers and sisters squabble, but they confide in each other.'

'I wouldn't know.' She started her car, pined for coffee. 'Where the hell do you live, Peabody?'

'Why?'

'I'll drop you at home. You can catch some sleep, report to Central at eleven.'

'Is that what you're going to do, catch some sleep?'

'Yeah.' That was probably a lie, but it served her purposes. 'Which way?'

'I live on Houston.'

Eve winced only a little. 'Well, if it's going to be inconvenient, it might as well be way inconvenient.' She headed south. 'Houston? Peabody, you bohemian.'

'It was my cousin's place. When she decided to move to Colorado and weave rugs, I took it over. Rent control.'

'A likely story. You probably spend all your free time hanging at poetry bars and performance art clubs.'

'Actually, I prefer the mating lounges. Better food.'

'You'd probably get more sex if you didn't think about it so much.'

'No, I tried that, too.' She yawned, abruptly and hugely. 'Sorry.'

'You're entitled. When you report in, check on the status of the autopsy. I want to be sure there's nothing weird in the tox report. And make sure to change out of that silly dress.'

Peabody shifted on her seat. 'It's not that silly. A couple guys at the Aquarian seemed to like it. So did Roarke.'

'Yeah, he mentioned it.'

Jaw dropped, Peabody swiveled her head. 'He did? Really?'

Foolishness, Eve thought, *helped soothe*. 'He said something about you looking appealing. So I hit him. Just in case.'

'Appealing. Jesus.' Peabody patted her heart. 'I'm going to have to dig through some of the other stuff my mother's made for me. Appealing.' She sighed. 'Roarke doesn't have any brothers, cousins, uncles, does he?'

'As far as I know, Peabody, he's one of a kind.'

She found him dozing. Not in bed, but on the sofa in the sitting area of the master suite. The moment she stepped into the room, his eyes opened.

'You've had a long, rough one, Lieutenant.' He reached out a hand. 'Come here.'

'I'm going to grab a shower, some coffee. I've got some calls to make.'

He'd tagged onto the police scanner and knew exactly what she'd been dealing with. 'Come here,' he repeated, and closed his hand over hers when she reluctantly obliged. 'Are the calls going to make any difference if you make them an hour from now?'

'No, but—'

So he tugged until she tumbled onto the sofa with him. Because her struggle was only halfhearted, he managed to

58

snuggle her down beside him quickly. And wrapping an arm around her, he kissed her hair. 'Sleep a little,' he said quietly. 'There's no need to exhaust yourself.'

'She was so young, Roarke.'

'I know. Close it off, just for a little while.'

'The data? Frank's log. Did you find anything?'

'We'll talk about it after you sleep.'

'An hour. Just an hour.' Linking her fingers with his, she let herself go under.

Chapter Five

Sleep helped. So did the hot shower and the food Roarke ordered up. Eve shoveled eggs into her mouth as she studied the data he'd unearthed on-screen.

'More like a diary than an investigative log,' she decided. 'Lots of personal comments, and obviously he was worried about Alice. *"I'm not sure how deeply they've influenced her mind, or hurt her heart."* He was thinking like a grandfather, not like a cop. You got this off his home unit?'

'Yes. He had it coded and passkeyed. I suspect he didn't want his wife stumbling across it.'

'If he had it coded, how did you access?'

Roarke took a cigarette from a carved box, studied it. 'You don't really want me to explain that, do you? Lieutenant?'

'No.' Eve forked up more eggs. 'Guess not. Still, his personal thoughts and worries aren't going to be a lot of help. I need to know what he found out, and how far his private investigation went before he died.'

'There's more.' Roarke scrolled over dates. 'There, he talks about tailing Selina Cross, and lists some of her . . . associates.'

'But there's nothing there. He suspects she's dealing illegals. He believes she's holding unacceptable ceremonies in her club and perhaps her home. He observes suspicious characters coming and going, but he bases it all on emotion. No facts. Frank had been off the streets too long.' Eve set her plate aside and rose. 'If he didn't want to involve cops, why the hell didn't he at least hire a PI to handle the legwork? What's this?'

Frowning, she stepped closer to the screen.

I think she made me. Can't be sure, but it's almost as though she's leading me along now. I'm going to have to make a move soon. Alice is terrified, begging me to stay away from Cross, and from her. The poor kid spends too much time with that Isis character. Isis may be a harmless weirdo, but she can't be a good influence on Alice. I've told Sally I'm working late. Tonight, I'm going in. Cross spends Thursday nights at the club. The apartment should be empty. If I can get inside and find anything, anything at all to prove Alice saw a child murdered, I can report to Whitney anonymously. She's going to pay for what she and her filthy lover did to my little girl. One way or the other, she's going to pay.

'Christ, nighttime breaking and entering, illegal search and seizure.' Frustrated, Eve dragged both hands through her hair. 'What the hell was he thinking? He had to know that anything he found would get tossed out in court. He'd never nail them this way.'

'I have a feeling he wasn't worried about court, Eve. He wanted justice.'

'And now he's dead, isn't he? And so's Alice. Where's the rest?'

Roarke scrolled to the last entry.

Security's too tight on the building, couldn't get through it. I've been off the streets too damn long. I may have to tag someone to help me on this after all. I'm going to see that witch pays if it's the last thing I do.

'That's all on this – that entry was logged on the night before he died. There may be more, under a different code.'

So, he hadn't made her pay, Eve thought. *And he hadn't had time to get help. Not enough time*, she thought again with twin surges of relief and sorrow. The entries went a long way toward clearing both Frank and Feeney.

'But you don't think so. You don't think there's anything else.'

'No, I don't. There's the timing, of course. And he wasn't that clever with electronics,' Roarke explained. 'It was child's play to find this. Still, we'll look. It'll take some time to break through if there's anything there. And it'll have to be later. I have several meetings this morning.'

She turned to him. Odd, she realized, she'd forgotten for a moment he wasn't working with her. His business and the direction of it was in a much different sphere from hers. 'So many billions, so little time.'

'How true. But I should be able to fiddle a bit more this evening.'

She knew he hadn't so much as glanced at the stock reports or taken the morning calls that never failed to come in daily. 'I'm taking up a lot of your time.'

'You are, indeed.' He came around the console, leaned back against it. 'And the payment will be your time, Lieutenant. A day or two away when we can both manage it.' Then his smile faded. He took her hand, ran his thumb over the carving on her wedding ring. 'Eve, I don't like to interfere with your work, but I'll ask you to be particularly careful in this matter.'

'A good cop's always careful.'

'No,' Roarke said, looking into her eyes, 'she's not. She's courageous, she's smart, she's driven, but she's not always careful.'

'Don't worry, I've dealt with worse than Selina Cross.' She kissed him lightly. 'I've got to go in, check on some reports. I'll try to let you know if I'm going to be late.'

'Do that,' he murmured, and watched her go.

She was wrong, he mused. He doubted very much if she'd

ever dealt with worse than Selina Cross. And he had no intention of letting her deal with it alone. Moving to the 'link, Roarke called his assistant and arranged to have all his off-planet and out-of-town trips for the next month canceled.

He intended to stay very close to home. And his wife.

'No drugs,' Eve stated as she looked over the toxicology report on Alice. 'No alcohol. She wasn't under the influence. But you heard her talking to someone who wasn't there, and she runs out into the path of an oncoming cab. She's worked herself up into a state of terror, then was triggered by the chanting on the phone. They knew how to get to her, how to manipulate her.'

'It's not illegal to chant over a 'link.'

'No.' Eve considered. 'But is it illegal to threaten to harm over a public transmitter.'

'That's reaching,' Peabody returned. 'And it's only a misdemeanor.'

'It's a start. If we manage to tie the transmission to Selina Cross, we can hassle her. In any case, I think it's time we met. How about a little trip to Hell, Peabody?'

'I've been dying to go.'

'Who isn't?' But before she could rise, Feeney burst into her office. His eyes were shadowed, his face unshaven.

'Why are you primary on Alice's case? A traffic accident. Why the hell is a homicide lieutenant handling a traffic fatality?'

'Feeney—'

'She was my goddaughter. You didn't even call me. I heard it on the goddamn news.'

'I'm sorry. I didn't know. Sit down, Feeney.'

He jerked away when she touched his arm. 'I don't need to sit down. I want answers, Dallas. I want some fucking answers.'

'Peabody,' Eve murmured, and waited until her aide had

gone out and closed the door. 'I am sorry, Feeney, I didn't know you were her godfather. I spoke to her mother and her brother, and simply assumed they would let the rest of the family know.'

'Brenda's under sedation,' Feeney tossed out. 'What the hell do you expect? She lost her father and her daughter within days of each other. Jamie's only sixteen. By the time he called a doctor and saw to his mother, got a hold of Sally, I'd already heard it on-screen. Jesus, Jesus, she was just a kid.'

He turned away, pulled at his hair. 'I used to give her piggyback rides, sneak her candy.'

This was what it was like to lose someone you loved, she thought. And was grateful she loved so few. 'Please sit down, Feeney. You shouldn't have come in today.'

'I said I don't need to sit down.' His voice leveled as he turned back to study her. 'I want an answer, Dallas. Why are you on Alice's accident?'

She couldn't afford to hesitate, couldn't afford not to lie. 'Peabody was a witness,' she began, grateful she could give him that much. 'She was on a free evening, and she'd been to a club. She saw the accident. It shook her, Feeney, and she called me. It was knee-jerk, I guess. I couldn't be sure what had happened, so I told her to relay to Dispatch, to secure the scene, and I responded. Since I had, and I had all the data, I notified next of kin. I figured it would be easier on the family if I handled it.' She moved her shoulders, bitterly ashamed at using old friends. 'I thought it was the least I could do, for Frank.'

He never took his eyes off her face. 'Is that all of it?'

'What else is there? Listen, I just got the tox report. She wasn't using, Feeney. She wasn't drunk. Maybe she was still upset about Frank, or something else. I don't know. Could be she didn't even see the damn cab. It was a lousy night, fog, rain.'

'The bastard was speeding, wasn't he?'

'No.' She couldn't give him anyone to blame, couldn't offer even that prickly comfort. 'He was within the limit. His record's clean, and so was the on-site drug and alcohol. Feeney, she bolted out in front of him, and there was nothing he could do. I want you to understand that. I talked with the driver myself, and I investigated the scene. It wasn't his fault. It wasn't anyone's.'

It had to be someone's, he thought. He couldn't lose two people back to back for no reason. 'I want to talk to Peabody.'

'Give her a little time, will you?' Layers of guilt added onto the burden she already carried. 'It really wrecked her. I'd really like to keep her focused on something else until she settles with it.'

He drew a deep breath, shuddered it out. Beneath his tearing grief was gratitude that someone he trusted would care for his godchild. 'You'll close it then, personally? And give me all the data?'

'I'll close it, Feeney. I promise you.'

He nodded, rubbed his hands over his face. 'Okay. I'm sorry I jumped you.'

'It's all right. It doesn't matter.' She hesitated, then put her hand on his arm, squeezed lightly. 'Go home, Feeney. You don't want to be here today.'

'I guess I will.' He put a hand on the door. 'She was a sweetheart, Dallas,' he said quietly. 'My God, I don't want to go to another funeral.'

When he left, Eve sank into her chair. Misery and guilt and anger twisted around her throat like barbs. She rose again, grabbed her bag. She was, she told herself, in the perfect mood to meet Selina Cross.

'How do you want to play it?' Peabody asked as they pulled up in front of an elegant old building downtown.

'Straight. I want her to know Alice talked to me, and that I

65

suspect her of harassment, dealing, and conspiracy to murder. If she's got any brains, she'll know I don't have anything solid. But I'll give her something to think about.'

Eve stepped out of the car, ran her gaze over the building with its carved glass windows and grinning gargoyles. 'She lives here, she's not hurting financially. We're going to have to find out just where she gets her money. I want everything on record, Peabody, and keep your eyes open. I want your impressions.'

'I'll give you one right now.' Peabody clamped her recorder onto her uniform jacket, but kept her eyes on the topmost window of the building, a wide, round glass intricately carved. 'That's another inverted pentagram. Satanic symbol. And those gargoyles don't look friendly.' She smiled wanly. 'You ask me, they look hungry.'

'Impressions, Peabody. Try to keep the fantasies down to a minimum.' Eve approached the security screen.

'Please state your name and your business.'

'Lieutenant Eve Dallas and aide, NYPSD.' She held up her badge to be scanned. 'To see Selina Cross.'

'Are you expected?'

'Oh, I don't think she'll be surprised.'

'One moment.'

While she waited, Eve studied the street. There was plenty of pedestrian and vehicular traffic, she noted. But most of those who walked used the other side of the street, and many of those eyed her and the building warily.

Oddly, there wasn't a single glida grill or street hawker in sight.

'You are cleared to enter, Lieutenant. Please proceed to elevator one. It is already programmed.'

'Fine.' Eve looked up, caught the shadow of movement behind the topmost glass. 'Look official, Peabody,' she murmured as they approached the heavily grilled front doors. 'We're under observation.'

The grills slid back, locks snicked open. The light on a recessed security panel blinked from red to green. 'A lot of hardware for an apartment building,' Peabody commented, and ignoring the fluttering in her stomach, stepped in behind Eve.

Like a viewing parlor, the lobby area was heavily into red. A two-headed serpent slithered over the bloodred carpet, the gold threads of its eyes glinted as it watched a black-robed figure slice a curved knife over the throat of a white goat.

'Lovely art.' Eve lifted a brow as Peabody carefully picked her way around the snake. 'Wool doesn't bite.'

'You can't be too careful.' She glanced back as they stepped to the elevator. 'I really hate snakes. My brother used to catch them out in the woods and chase me with them. Always had a phobia.'

The ride up was smooth and fast, but it gave Eve enough time to detect yet another security camera in the small, black-mirrored car.

The doors opened into a spacious foyer with floors of black marble. Twin red velvet settees flanked an archway and boasted carved arms of snarling wolves. A floral arrangement speared out of a pot shaped like a boar's head.

'Wolfbane,' Peabody said quietly, 'belladonna, foxglove, skullcap, peyote.' She shrugged at Eve's considering look. 'My mother's an amateur botanist. I can tell you that's not your usual flower arrangement.'

'But the usual is so tedious, isn't it?'

They got their first face-to-face look at Selina Cross exactly as she wanted to be seen. Flanked by the archway in a snug black dress that brushed the floor, her feet bare with the toenails painted a violent red, she posed. And smiled.

Her skin was vampire white, the slash of red over her full lips glossy as fresh blood. Her eyes glittered green and feline in a narrow, undoubtedly witchlike face that wasn't beautiful, but was eerily compelling. Her hair fell, black against black, from that rigid center part, to her waist.

The hand she gestured with held rings on every finger and her thumb. A silver chain was attached to each and twisted into an intricate mesh over the back of her hand.

'Lieutenant Dallas and Officer Peabody, isn't it? What interesting visitors on such a dull day. Will you come in . . . to my parlor?'

'Are you alone, Ms Cross? It would simplify this if we could speak with Mr Alban as well.'

'Oh, what a shame.' She turned, silks whispering, and slipped through the arch. 'Alban's busy this morning. Sit down.' She gestured again, encompassing a generous room crowded with furniture. Every seat boasted the heads or claws or beaks of some predator. 'Can I offer you something?'

'We'll skip the refreshments.' Considering it apt, Eve chose a chair with the arms of a hound.

'Not even coffee? That is your drink, isn't it?' Then she shrugged, slicked a fingertip over the pentagram above her eyebrow. 'But suit yourself.' With that same studied skill, she lowered to a curved settee that stood on cloven feet and draped her long arms over the back. 'Now, what can I do for you?'

'Alice Lingstrom was killed early this morning.'

'Yes, I know.' She continued to smile pleasantly, as though discussing the nice run of weather. 'I could tell you I witnessed the . . . accident through my scrying mirror, but I doubt you'd believe that. Of course, I'm not one to disdain technology and often watch the news and other forms of entertainment on-screen. The information's been public for hours.'

'You knew her.'

'Of course; she was a pupil of mine for a time. A dissatisfactory one as it turned out. Alice complained to you about my tutelage.' It wasn't formed as a question, but she waited, as if for an answer.

'If you mean she reported to me that she was drugged, sexually abused, and was a witness to an atrocity, then yes, she complained.'

'Drugs, sex, and atrocities.' Selina let out a low, purring laugh. 'What an imagination our little Alice had. A shame she couldn't use it to broaden her vision. How is your imagination, Lieutenant Dallas?' She flicked the hand gloved with mesh. In the small marble fireplace, flames burst to life.

Peabody jolted, didn't manage to muffle a yelp, but neither woman acknowledged her. They continued to stare, unblinking at each other.

'Or may I call you Eve?'

'No. You can call me Lieutenant Dallas. It's a little warm for a fire, don't you think? And a bit early in the day for parlor tricks.'

'I like it warm. You have excellent nerves, Lieutenant.'

'I also have low tolerance for grifters and dealers and child killers.'

'Am I all of that?' Selina tapped her sharp red nails on the back of the settee, her only outward sign of annoyance in Eve's lack of response. 'Prove it.'

'I will. Where were you last night between the hours of one and three A.M.?'

'I was here, in my ritual room, with Alban and a young initiate we call Lobar. We were engaged in a private sexual ceremony from midnight until nearly dawn. Lobar is young and . . . enthusiastic.'

'I'll want to talk to them both.'

'You can contact Lobar any evening between eight and eleven at our club. As for Alban, I don't keep his schedule, but he is generally here or at the club most nights. Unless you believe in magic, Lieutenant, you're wasting your time. I could hardly have been here, fucking two very entertaining men, and out luring poor Alice to her death.'

'Is that what you consider yourself, a magician?' Eve glanced toward the still burning fire with a mild sneer. 'That's nothing more than trickery and distraction of the eye. You can be licensed to juggle on the streets for two thousand credits a year.'

Selina's muscles quivered as she sat forward. Her eyes were burning now, as the fire did. 'I am a high priestess of the dark lord. Our numbers are legion, and I have powers that would make you weep.'

'I don't cry easily, Ms Cross.' *Ah, a temper*, Eve thought with satisfaction. *And easily ruffled pride*. 'You're not dealing with an impressionable eighteen-year-old girl now, or her frightened grandfather. Which one of your legion called Alice last night and played a tape of chanting threats?'

'I have no idea what you're talking about. And you're beginning to bore me.'

'The black feather on the windowsill was a nice touch. Or simulated feather, I should say, but she wouldn't have known that. Are you into droid pets, Ms Cross?'

Idly, Selina lifted a hand, skimmed it through then down her hair. 'I don't care for . . . pets at all.'

'No? No cats and ravens?'

'How predictable that would be.'

'Alice believed you were a shape-shifter,' Eve said and watched as Selina smiled. 'Care to give us a demonstration of that little talent?'

Selina's nails began to tap again. Eve's tone was as insulting as a backhanded slap. 'I'm not here to entertain you. Or to be mocked by your small mind.'

'Is that what you call it? Were you entertaining Alice with cats and birds and threatening chants over her 'link? How could she feel safe in her own home? Was she such a threat to you?'

'She was nothing to me but an unfortunate failure.'

'You were seen selling illegals to Frank Wojinski.'

The abrupt switch had Selina blinking. When her lips curved now, the smile didn't reach her eyes. 'If that were true, we wouldn't be having this discussion here in my home, but in

Interview. I'm an herbalist, again licensed, and I often sell or trade perfectly legal substances.'

'Do you grow your herbs here?'

'As a matter of fact, I do, and distill my potions and medications.'

'I'd like to see them. Why don't you show me your work area?'

'You'll need a warrant for that, and we both know you haven't cause for one.'

'You're right. I guess that's why Frank didn't bother with a warrant.' Eve rose slowly, spoke softly. 'You knew he was onto you, but did you suspect he might get in here, inside? You didn't see that in your magic ball, did you?' Eve said when Selina's breath shortened and thickened. 'What would you think if I told you he was in your house, and he documented what he saw, and what he found.'

'You have nothing. Nothing.' Selina sprang to her feet. 'He was an aging man with slow wits and bad reflexes. I made him for a cop the first time he tried to tail me. He was never in my home. He told you nothing when he was alive, and he can't tell you anything now.'

'No? Don't you believe in talking to the dead, Ms Cross? I make my living at it.'

'And do you think I don't recognize smoke and mirrors, Lieutenant?' Her spectacular breasts strained against the material of her dress as she struggled to even her breathing. 'Alice was a foolish girl who believed she could flirt with dark forces, then run back to her pathetic white magic and tidy little family. She paid the price for her ignorance and her cowardice. But not at my hand. I have nothing more to say to you.'

'That'll do for now. Peabody?' She started toward the archway. 'Your fire's going out, Ms Cross,' she said mildly. 'Pretty soon you're going to have nothing but a mess of ashes.'

Selina stood where she was, shaking with rage. When the

71

door closed and security engaged, she balled her hands into fists and screamed with temper.

A panel on the wall slid open. The man who stepped out was tall and golden. His chest gleamed and rippled with muscle. The tattoo over his heart was of a horned goat. He wore only an open black robe carelessly belted at the waist with silver cord.

'Alban.' Selina ran to him, threw her arms around him.

'There, my love.' His voice was deep, soothing. On the hand that stroked her hair was a large silver ring carved with an inverted pentagram. 'You mustn't unbalance your chakras.'

'Fuck my chakras.' She was weeping now, wildly, pounding on him like a child in a blind tantrum. 'I hate her. I hate her. She has to be punished.'

With a sigh, he let her go to storm the room, cursing, smashing crockery. He knew the temper would pass more quickly if he stood back and let it purge.

'I want her dead, Alban. Dead. I want her to suffer agonies, to scream for mercy, to bleed and writhe and bleed. She insulted me. She challenged me. She all but laughed in my face.'

'She doesn't believe, Selina. She has no vision.'

Exhausted as always after a fit of temper, she collapsed on the settee. 'Cops. I've hated them all my life.'

'I know.' He picked up a tall, slim bottle, poured her some thick, cloudy liquid. 'We'll have to be careful with her. She's very high-profile.' He passed her a chalice. 'But we'll think of something, won't we?'

'Of course we will.' She smiled again, sipped slowly at the brew. 'Something very special. The master would want something . . . inventive in her case.' Now she laughed, full-throated, head thrown back. The police had been the bane of her existence – until she'd discovered a higher power. 'We'll make a believer out of her, won't we, Alban?'

'She'll believe.'

She drank deeply now, felt the lovely haze coat her tangled emotions. And let the chalice drop. 'Come here, and take me.' Eyes glittering, she slid down. 'Force me.'

And when he covered her body with his, she turned her head, bared her teeth, and dug them into his shoulder to draw blood.

'Hurt me,' she demanded.

'With pleasure.' he replied.

And when they lay apart, their violent passion sated, he lay quiet beside her. She would revive now, he knew. She would cool and she would calm, and she would think.

'We should preform a ceremony tonight. Call together the entire coven for a Black Mass. We need power, Alban. She isn't weak, and she wants to destroy us.'

'She won't.' With affection now, he stroked her cheek. 'She can't. After all, she's only a cop with no past and a limited future. But you're right, of course, we'll call the coven. We'll perform the rite. And, I think, we'll provide Lieutenant Dallas with a distraction – or two. She won't have the time or inclination to worry overmuch about little Alice for long.'

Fresh arousal rippled through her, a dark wave that flooded into her eyes. 'Who dies?'

'My love.' He lifted her, speared her, sighed when her muscles clamped viciously around him. 'You have only to choose.'

'You really pissed her off.' Peabody struggled to ignore the light sweat of fear that dried on her skin as Eve drove away from the building.

'That was the idea. Now that I know control isn't her strong point, I'll be sure to piss her off again. She's all ego,' Eve decided. 'Imagine, thinking we'd fall for a second-rate trick like the fire.'

'Yeah.' Peabody managed a sickly smile. 'Imagine.'

Eve tucked her tongue in her cheek and decided against

ragging on her aide. 'Since we're into witches, let's swing by and check out this Isis at Spirit Quest.' She slid her eyes right. Well, maybe she'd rag just a little. 'You can probably buy a talisman or some herbs,' she said solemnly. 'You know, to ward off evil.'

Peabody shifted in her seat. Feeling foolish wasn't nearly as bad as worrying about being cursed. 'Don't think I won't.'

'After we deal with Isis, we can grab a pizza sub – with plenty of garlic.'

'Garlic's for vampires.'

'Oh. We can have Roarke get us a couple of his antique guns. With silver bullets.'

'Werewolves, Dallas.' Amused at both of them now, Peabody rolled her eyes. 'A lot of good you're going to do if we have to defend ourselves against witchcraft.'

'What does it to witches, then?'

'I don't know,' Peabody admitted. 'But I'm damn sure going to find out.'

Chapter Six

Shopping wasn't something Eve considered one of the small pleasures in life. She wasn't a browser, a window shopper, or a electronic catalogue surfer. She avoided, whenever possible, the shops and boutiques in, above, and below Manhattan. She shuddered at the very thought of a trip to one of the sky malls.

She imagined her outward resistance to the consumption of merchandise was the primary reason Isis pegged her as a cop the minute she stepped into Spirit Quest.

As stores went, Eve considered it tolerable. She wasn't interested in the crystals and cards, the statues and candles, even though they were attractively displayed. The background music was soft, more of a murmur than a tune, and the light was allowed to play over the edges of raw crystals and polished stones in pretty rainbows.

The place smelled, she thought, not offensively of forest.

If witches were what she was dealing with, Eve decided, Isis and Selina couldn't have been more dramatically opposed in appearance. Selina had been pale and slim and feline. Isis was an exotic amazon of a female with gypsy curls of flaming red, round black eyes, and cheekbones that could have carved wood. Her skin was the soft gold of a mixed-race heritage, her features bold and broad. Eve measured her at just over six feet and a well-packed and curvy one-seventy.

She wore a loose, flowing robe of blinding white with a belt studded with rough stones. Her right arm was wound with gold coils from elbow to shoulder, and her large hands winked and flashed with as many as a dozen rings.

'Welcome.' The voice suited her, oddly accented and throaty. Her lips curved, but it was a smile of grieving rather than pleasure. 'Alice's cop.'

Eve lifted a brow as she took out her shield. She figured she looked like a cop. And, since Roarke, her face had been in the media relentlessly. 'Dallas. You'd be Isis, then?'

'I would. You'll wish to talk. Excuse me.' She walked to the door. Graceful, Eve observed, the way an athlete is graceful. She turned an old-fashioned hand-lettered sign to Closed, pulled the shade over the glass of the door, and flicked a thumb latch.

When she turned back, her eyes were intense, her mouth grim. 'You bring dark shadows into my light. She clings – such a stench.' At Eve's narrowed look, she inclined her head. 'Selina. One moment.'

She went to a wide shelf and began to light candles and cones of incense. 'To purify and shield, to protect and defend. You have shadows of your own, Dallas.' She smiled briefly at Peabody. 'And not just your aide.'

'I'm here to talk about Alice.'

'Yes, I know. And you're impatient with what you see as my foolish window dressing. I don't mind. Every religion should be open to questions and change. Will you sit?'

She gestured to a corner where two chairs flanked a round table etched with symbols. Again, she smiled at Peabody. 'I can get another chair from the back for you.'

'No problem. I'll stand.' She couldn't help it; her gaze traveled the room, lingering now and then wistfully on some pretty bauble.

'Please feel free to browse.'

'We're not here to shop.' Eve took a seat, shot Peabody a withering glance. 'When did you last see or speak with Alice?'

'On the night she died.'

'At what time?'

'I believe it was about two A.M. She was already dead,' Isis added, folding her large, beautiful hands.

'You saw her after she was dead.'

'Her spirit came to me. You find this foolish; I understand. But I can only tell you what is, and was. I was asleep, and I awoke. She was there, beside the bed. I knew we'd lost her. She feels she's failed. Herself, her family, me. Her spirit is restless and full of grief.'

'Her body's dead, Isis. That's my concern.'

'Yes.' Isis picked up a smooth, rose-colored stone from the table, worried it in her hand. 'Even for me, with my beliefs, it's difficult to accept her death. So young, so bright.' The huge, dark eyes swam. 'I loved her very much, as you would a younger sister. But it wasn't meant for me to save her in this life. Her spirit will return, be reborn. I know we'll meet again.'

'Fine. Let's concentrate on this life. And this death.'

Isis blinked back the tears and managed a quick, genuine smile. 'How tedious you must find all of this. You have such a logical mind. I want to help you, Dallas, for Alice. For myself, perhaps for yourself as well. I recognize you.'

'I gathered that.'

'No, from another time. Another place. Another plane.' She spread her hands. 'I last saw Alice alive on the day of her grandfather's memorial service. She blamed herself, was determined to make an atonement. She'd strayed for a time, been misled, but she had a strong and bright heart. Her family was dear to her. And she was afraid, desperately afraid of what Selina would do to her – body and soul.'

'You know Selina Cross?'

'Yes. We've met.'

'In this life?' Eve asked dryly, and made Isis smile again.

'In this life, and others. She's no threat to me, but she is dangerous. She seduces the weak, the confused, and those who prefer her way.'

'Her claims to be a witch—'

'She is no witch.' Isis drew her shoulders back, lifted her head. 'We who embrace the craft do so in the light and live by an unbreakable code. *And it harm none.* She used what pitiful power she has to call on the dark, to exploit its violence, its ugliness. We know what evil is, Dallas. We've both seen it. Whatever form it takes doesn't change its basic nature.'

'We can agree on that. Why would she harm Alice?'

'Because she could. Because she would enjoy it. There's no question that she's responsible for this death. You won't find it easy to prove it. You won't give up.' Isis kept her eyes on Eve's, looking long, looking deep. 'Selina will be surprised and infuriated by your tenacity, your strength. Death offends you, and the death of the young cuts small slices from your heart. You remember too well, but not all. You weren't born Eve Dallas, but you've become her, and she you. When you stand by the dead, stand for the dead, nothing moves you aside. His death was necessary for your life.'

'Stop,' Eve ordered.

'Why should it haunt you?' Isis's breathing was slow and thick, her eyes dark and clear. 'The choice was made correctly. Innocence was lost, but strength took its place. For some, it must be so. You'll need all before this cycle passes. A wolf, a boar, and a silver blade. Fire, smoke, and death. Trust the wolf, slay the boar, and live.'

Abruptly, she blinked. Her eyes clouded as she lifted a hand to press fingers to her temple. 'I'm sorry. I didn't intend—' She let out a quiet moan, squeezed her eyes shut. 'Headache. Vicious. Excuse me one minute.' She got shakily to her feet and hurried into the back.

'Jesus. Dallas, this is getting way too weird. Do you know what she was talking about?'

'His death was necessary for your life.' Her father, Eve thought, fighting off a shudder. A cold room, a dark night, and blood on the knife clutched in a desperate child's hand.

'No, it's just jibberish.' Her palms were damp, infuriating her. 'These people figure they have to pull out some magic tricks to keep us interested.'

'I studied at the Kijinsky Institute in Prague,' Isis said as she stepped back into the room. 'And was studied.' She set a small cup aside, managed a smile as the headache eased. 'My psychic abilities are documented – for those who need documentation. But I apologize, Dallas. I didn't intend to drift in that manner. It's very rare for it to happen without my consciously controlling it.'

She came back to sit as she spoke, spread the skirts of her robe gracefully. 'It would be sheer hell to be privy to thoughts and memories without some power to control and block. I don't like to pry into personal thoughts. And it hurts,' she added, gently rubbing her temple again. 'I want to help you do what Alice wanted, so she can rest. I want, for personal and selfish reasons, to see Selina pay the proper price for what she's responsible for. I'll do whatever I can, whatever you'll allow me to do, to help you.'

Trust didn't come easily for Eve, and she would check very thoroughly into Isis's background. But for now, she'd use her. 'Tell me what you know about Selina Cross.'

'I know she's a woman without conscience or morals. I would think your term would be *sociopath*, but I find that too simple and too clean for what she is. I prefer the more direct term of *evil*. She's a clever woman with a skill for reading weaknesses. As for her power, what she can read or see or do, I can't say.'

'What about Alban?'

'About him I know next to nothing. She keeps him close. I assume he's her lover and she finds him useful or she would have – dispatched him by now.'

'This club of hers?'

Isis smiled thinly. 'I don't frequent such . . . establishments.'

'But you know of it?'

'One hears rumors, gossip.' She lifted her broad shoulders.

'Dark ceremonies, Black Masses, the drinking of blood, human sacrifice. Rape, murder, infanticide, the calling up of demons.' Then she sighed. 'But then, you might hear such talk about Wiccans from those who have no understanding of the craft and who see black draped crones and eye of newt when they think of witches.'

'Alice claimed to have seen a child murdered.'

'Yes, and I believe she did. She couldn't have invented such a thing. She was in shock and ill when she came to me.' Isis pressed her lips together, shuddered out a breath. 'I did what I could for her.'

'Such as encouraging her to report the incident to the police?'

'That was for her to decide.' Isis lifted her chin again, met the iced anger in Eve's eyes. 'I was more concerned with her emotional and spiritual survival. The child was already lost; I had hoped to save Alice from the same fate.' Her eyes dropped now, and dampened. 'And I regret, bitterly, that I didn't act differently. And that, in the end, I failed her. Perhaps it was pride.' She looked at Eve again. 'You'd understand the power and the deception of personal pride. I thought I could handle it, that I was wise enough, strong enough. I was wrong. So, Dallas, to atone, I'll do anything you ask, avail you of all knowledge and any power the goddess grants me.'

'Information will do.' Eve angled her head. 'Selina treated us to a little demonstration of what she'd call power. It impressed Peabody.'

'It caught me off guard,' Peabody muttered, studying Isis warily. She didn't think she was up for another demonstration. To Peabody's surprise, and Eve's, Isis threw back her magnificent head and laughed. It was like hearing silver buoys clang in pearly fog.

'Should I call up the wind?' With one hand pressed to her breast, she chuckled. 'Summon the dead, strike the cold fire? Really, Dallas, you believe in none of that, so it would be a waste of my time and energy. But perhaps you'd be interested

80

in observing one of our gatherings. We have one at the end of next week. I can arrange it.'

'I'll think about it.'

'You smirk,' Isis said lightly, 'yet the pledge you wear on your finger carries the ancient symbol of protection.'

'What?'

'Your wedding ring, Dallas.' With that quiet smile, Isis lifted Eve's left hand. 'It's carved with an old Celtic design for protection.'

Baffled, Eve studied the pretty etching in the slim gold ring. 'It's just a design.'

'It's a very specific and powerful one, to give the wearer protection from harm.' Amused, she raised her brows. 'I see you didn't know. Is it so surprising, really? Your husband has the blood of the Celts, and you lead a very precarious life. Roarke loves you very much, and you wear the symbol of it.'

'I prefer facts to superstitions,' Eve said and rose.

'As you should,' Isis agreed. 'But you will be welcome at the next gathering, should you choose to attend. Roarke will also be welcome.' She smiled at Peabody. 'And your aide. Will you accept a gift?'

'It's against the rules.'

'And rules are to be respected.' Rising, Isis moved behind a display counter, took out a small, clear bowl with a wide lip. 'Then perhaps you will buy this. I have, after all, lost potential business by closing to speak to you. Twenty dollars.'

'Fair enough.' Eve dug into her pocket for credits. 'What is it?'

'We'll call it a worry bowl. In this you place all your pain, your sorrow, your worries. Set it aside and sleep without shadows.'

'Such a deal.' Eve set the credits on the counter and waited for Isis to wrap the bowl in protective paper.

Eve got home early, a rarity. She thought she could dive into work in the quiet of her home office. She could get past

Summerset easily enough, she mused as she pulled up at the end of the drive. The butler would simply sniff and ignore her. She'd have a couple of hours clear to run data on Isis and to contact Dr Mira's office and make an appointment with the psychiatrist. It would, Eve decided, be interesting to get Mira's take on personalities such as Selina Cross and Isis.

Eve got no farther than the front door when her plans disintegrated.

Music pounded, blasting out of the front parlor like compact nuclear explosions. Staggering against the waves, Eve slapped her hands over her ears and shouted.

She didn't have to be told it was Mavis. No one else in her sphere would play clashing, discordant notes at that decibel. When she reached the doorway, the volume was still revved high. Her shouted demands reached neither the remote nor the single occupant of the room.

Alone, decked out in a micro robe of searing magenta that echoed the spiral curls shooting out of her head, Mavis Freestone lounged on the couch, doing the impossible. She slept like a baby.

'Jesus Christ.' Since vocal commands were useless, Eve risked her eardrums and dropped her hands to fumble with the recessed control unit. 'Off, off, off!' She shouted stabbing buttons. The noise shut down in midblast and made her moan.

Mavis's eyes popped open. 'Hey, how's it going?'

'What?' Eve shook her head to try to dispel the high-pitched ringing. 'What?'

'That was a new group I picked up this morning. Mayhem. Pretty decent.'

'What?'

With a chuckle, Mavis unfolded her neat little body and bounced to a cabinet. 'Looks like you could use a drink, Dallas. I must have zoned. Up pretty late the last few nights. Wanted to talk to you – about stuff.'

'Your mouth is moving,' Eve observed. 'Are you talking to me?'

'It wasn't that loud. Have a drink. Summerset said it would be all right if I hung for awhile. Didn't know when you'd check in.'

For reasons that eluded Eve, the stiff-necked butler appeared to have a major crush on Mavis. 'He's probably in his cage, composing odes to your legs.'

'Hey, it's nothing sexual. He just likes me. So.' Mavis clunked her glass against Eve's. 'Roarke's not around, right?'

'With that music blasting?' Eve snorted, sipped. 'Figure it out.'

'Well, that's good, because I wanted to roll it out with you.' But she sat, twisted the glass in her hands, and said nothing.

'What's the problem? You and Leonardo have a fight or something?'

'No, no. You can't really fight with Leonardo. He's too sweet. He's in Milan for a few days. Some fashion deal.'

'Why didn't you go with him?' Eve sat, rested her booted feet on the priceless coffee table, crossed her ankles.

'I've got the gig at the Down and Dirty. I wouldn't let Crack down after he bailed me.'

'Hmm.' Eve rolled her shoulders and began to relax. Mavis's career as a performer – it was difficult to use the term *singer* when defining Mavis's talents – was moving along. There had been some serious roadblocks, but they'd been overcome. 'I didn't figure you'd work there much longer. Not with a recording contract.'

'Yeah, well, that's the thing. The contract. You know, after finding out Jess was using me – and you and Roarke – for his mind games, I didn't figure the demo I'd cut with him would go anywhere.'

'It was good, Mavis; flashy, unique. That's why it got picked up.'

'Is it?' She rose again, a tiny woman with wild hair. 'I found

83

out today that Roarke owns the recording company that offered the contract.' Gulping her drink, she paced away. 'I know we go back a ways, Dallas, a long ways, and I appreciate you putting Roarke up to it, but I don't feel right about it. I wanted to thank you.' She turned then, her silver eyes tragic and bleak. 'And tell you that I'm going to turn it down.'

Eve pursed her lips. 'Mavis, I don't know what the hell you're talking about. Are you telling me that Roarke, the guy who lives here, is producing your disc?'

'It's his company. Eclectic. It produces everything from classical to brain drain. It's *the* company. Totally mag, which was why I was so wired up about the deal.'

Eclectic, Eve mused. *The company*. It sounded just like him. 'I don't know anything about it. I didn't ask him to do anything, Mavis.'

She blinked, lowered slowly to the arm of a chair. 'You didn't? Solid?'

'I didn't ask,' Eve repeated, 'and he didn't tell me.' Which was also just like him. 'I'd have to say that if his company is offering you a contract, it's because Roarke, or whoever he's put in charge of that stuff, figures you're worth it.'

Mavis took slow breaths. She'd worked herself up to the selfless sacrifice, unwilling to take advantage of friendship. Now she teetered. 'Maybe he arranged it, like a favor.'

Eve cocked a brow. 'Roarke's business is business. I'd say he figures you're going to make him richer. And if he did do it as a favor, which I doubt, then you'll just have to prove to him that you're worth it. Won't you, Mavis?'

'Yeah.' She let out a long breath. 'I'm going to kick ass, you wait and see.' Her smile beamed out. 'Maybe you could come by the D and D tonight. I've got some new material, and Roarke could get another close-up of his latest investment.'

'Have to pass tonight. I've got work. I've got to check out The Athame.'

Mavis grimaced. 'What the hell are you going there for? Nasty place.'

'You know it?'

'Only by rep, and the rep's down below bad news.'

'Someone I've got to talk to there, connected with a case I'm working on.' She considered. There was no one she knew more likely to have a line on the unusual. 'Know any witches, Mavis?'

'Yeah, sort of. A couple of servers down at the Blue Squirrel were into it. Brushed a few way back when I was on the grift.'

'You believe in that stuff? Chanting and spells and palm reading?'

Mavis cocked her head and looked thoughtful. 'It's major bullshit.'

'You never fail to surprise me,' Eve decided. 'I figured you'd be into it.'

'I ran a con once. Spirit guide. I was Ariel, reincarnation of a fairy queen. You'd be amazed how many straights paid up for me to contact their dead relatives or tell them their future.'

To demonstrate, she let her head fall back. Her eyes fluttered, her mouth went slack. Slowly, her arms lifted, palms turned up. 'I feel a presence, strong, seeking, sorrowful.' Her voice had deepened, attained a faint accent. 'There are dark forces working against you. They hide from you, wait to do harm. Beware.'

She dropped her arms and grinned. 'So, you tell the mark you need to have trust in order to offer protection from the dark forces. All they have to do is put say, a thousand cash – cash is all that works – in an envelope. Seal it. You make sure you tell them to seal it with this special wax you're going to sell them. Then you're going to do this cool chant over it, and bury the envelope in a secret place under the dark of the moon. After the moon's cycled, you'll dig up the envelope and give it back. The dark forces will have been vanquished.'

'That's it? People just hand over the money?'

'Well, you string it out a little longer, do some research so you can hit them with names and events and shit. But basically, yeah. People want to believe.'

'Why?'

'Because life can really suck.'

Yes, Eve thought when she was alone agian, she supposed it could. Hers certainly had for long stretches of time. Now she was living in a mansion with a man who, for some reason, loved her. She didn't always understand her life or the man who now shared it, but she was adjusting. So well, in fact, that she decided not to go bury herself in work, but to go outside, into the golden autumn evening and take an hour for herself.

She was used to streets and sidewalks, crowded skyglides, jammed people movers. The sheer space Roarke could command always astonished her. His grounds were like a well-tended park, quiet and lush, with the foliage of rich man's trees in the dazzling flame of fall. The scents were of spicy flowers, the faintly smoky fragrance of October in the country.

Overhead, the sky was nearly empty of traffic, and even that was a dignified hum. No rumbling airbuses or lumbering tourist blimps over Roarke's land.

And the world she knew, and that knew her, was beyond the gates and over the walls, in the seamy dark.

Here she could forget that for a short time. Forget New York existed with its death and its anger – and its perpetually appealing arrogance. She needed the quiet and the air. As she walked over thick, green grass, she worried the ring with its odd symbols on her finger.

On the north side of the house was an arbor of thin, somehow fluid iron. The vines twisting and tumbling over it were smothered with flowers wildly red. She had married him there, in an old, traditional ceremony where vows were exchanged and promises made. A ceremony, she thought now. A rite that included music, flowers, witnesses, words that were repeated time after time, place after place, century through century.

And so, she thought, other ceremonies were preserved and repeated and believed to hold power. Back to Cain and Abel, she mused. One had planted crops, the other tended a flock. And both had offered sacrifice. One had been accepted, the other dismissed. Thus, she imagined, some would say good and evil were born. Because each needed the balance and challenge of the other.

So it continued. Science and logic disproved, but the rites continued, incense and chanting, offerings and the drinking of wine that symbolized blood.

And the sacrifice of the innocent.

Annoyed with herself, she rubbed her hands over her face. Philosophizing was foolish and useless. Murder had been done by human force. And it was human force that would dispense justice. That was, after all, the ultimate balance of good and evil.

She sat on the ground under the arbor of bloodred blossoms and drew in the burning scent of evening.

'This isn't usual for you.' Roarke came up quietly behind her – so quietly, her heart gave a quick trip before he settled on the grass beside her. 'Communing with nature?'

'Maybe I spent too much time inside today.' She had to smile when he handed her one of the red flowers. She twirled it in her fingers, watched it spin before she looked over at him.

He was relaxed, his dark hair skimming his shoulders, as he leaned back on his elbows, legs stretched out, feet crossed at the ankles. She imagined his pricey and beautiful suit would pick up grass stains that would horrify Summerset. He smelled male, and expensive. Lust curled comfortably in her stomach.

'Successful day?' she asked.

'We'll have bread on the table another day or two.'

She flicked her fingers at the ends of his hair. 'It's not the money, is it? It's the making it.'

'Oh, it's the money.' His eyes laughed at her. 'And the

making it.' In a quick move she told herself she should have seen coming, he reached up, cupped the back of her neck, and overbalanced her onto him and into a hot kiss.

'Hold on.'

She didn't squirm quickly enough and ended up under him.

'I am.'

His mouth fastened greedily on her throat and sent little licks of heat straight down her body to her toes.

'I want to talk to you.'

'Okay, you talk while I get you out of these clothes. Still wearing your weapon,' he observed as he hit the release for the harness. 'Thinking of zapping some wildlife?'

'That's against city ordinance. Roarke.' She caught his wrist as his hand closed sneakily over her breast. 'I want to talk to you.'

'I want to make love with you. Let's see who wins.'

It should have infuriated her, the fact that he already had her shirt open and her breasts aching. Then his mouth closed over that sensitive flesh and had her eyes all but crossing in pleasure. Still, it wouldn't do to let him win too easily.

She let her body go limp, moaned, and combed her fingers through his hair, ran them over his shoulders. 'Your jacket,' she murmured and tugged at it. When he shifted to shrug free, she had him.

It was a basic tenet of hand-to-hand. Never lower your guard. She scissored, shoved, and pinned him with a knee to the crotch and an elbow to the throat.

'You're tricky.' He calculated he could dislodge the elbow, but the knee . . . There were some things a man didn't care to risk. He kept his eyes on hers and slowly, carefully skimmed his fingertips up her bare torso, circled her breast. 'I admire that in a woman.'

'You're easy.' His thumb brushed lightly over her nipple, quickening her breath. 'I admire that in a man.'

'Well, you've got me now.' He unsnapped her waistband, teased her stomach muscles to quiver. 'Be kind.'

She grinned, levered her elbow away to brace her hands on either side of his head. 'I don't think so.' Lowering her head, she caught his mouth with hers.

She heard his breath suck in, felt his arms come around her, fingers digging in. His groan thundered through her pulse.

'Your knee,' he managed.

'Hmm?' Lust was full-blown now and raging. She shifted lips and teeth to his throat.

'Your knee, darling.' She moved to attack his ear and nearly unmanned him. 'It's very effective.'

'Oh, sorry.' Snorting, she lowered her knee, lowered her body, and let him roll her over. 'Forgot.'

'A likely story. You may have caused permanent damage.'

'Aw.' With a wicked grin, she tugged open his trousers. 'I bet we can make it all better.'

His eyes went dark when she stroked him, stayed open and on hers when their lips met again. This kiss, surprisingly tender, twined that terrifyingly strong emotion with the easy lust.

The lower edges of the sky were as wildly red as the blossoms arching over them. The shadows were long and soft. She could hear birdsong and the whisper of air through the dying leaves. The touch of his hands on her was like a miracle, chasing away all the ugliness and pain of the world she walked in.

She didn't even know she needed to be soothed, he thought as he stroked, and he soothed, so that arousal was slow and warm and liquid. Perhaps neither had he, until they held like this, touched like this. The romance of the air, the light, the gradual surrender of a strong woman was gloriously seductive.

He eased into her, watching her face as the first orgasm rolled through her, feeling her body clench, shudder, go pliant as his fueled it and filled it.

She kept her eyes open, as fascinated by the intensity of

his stare as the silvery ripples of sensation that pumped through her. She matched his pace, silky and smooth even as her breath tore. And when she saw those dark Celtic eyes cloud, go opaque, she framed his face with her hands, pulled his mouth to hers to savor his long, long groan of release.

When his body was ranged weightily over hers; his face buried in her hair, she wrapped her arms companionably around him. 'I let you seduce me.'

'Uh-huh.'

'I didn't want to hurt your feelings.'

'Thank you. You tolerated it all so stoically, too.'

'It's the training. Cops have to be stoic.'

He reached out, ran a hand over the grass, and plucked up her shield. 'Your badge, Lieutenant.'

She snickered, slapped him on the ass. 'Get off me. You weigh a ton.'

'Keep sweet-talking me, and God knows what could happen.' Lazily, he rolled aside, noted that the sky had gone from cloudy blue to pearl gray. 'I'm starving. You distracted me and now it's well past dinnertime.'

'It's going to be a little more past.' She sat up and began to tug on her clothes. 'You had your sex, pal. Now it's my turn. We have to talk.'

'We could talk over dinner.' He sighed when she sent him a steely stare. 'Or we could talk here. Problem?' he asked and skimmed his thumb over the dent in her chin.

'Let's just say I have some questions.'

'I might have the answers. What are they?'

'To begin with—' She broke off, blew out a breath. He was sitting there, mostly naked, looking very much like a sleek, well-satisfied cat. 'Put some clothes on, will you? You're going to distract *me*.' She tossed his shirt at him when he only grinned. 'Mavis was waiting for me when I got home.'

'Oh.' He shook out his shirt, noted its deplorable condition, but slipped it on. 'Why didn't she stay?'

'She's got a gig at the Down and Dirty. Roarke, why didn't you tell me you own Eclectic?'

'It's not a secret.' He hitched into his slacks, then handed her her weapon harness. 'I own a number of things.'

'You know what I'm talking about.' She would be patient here, Eve told herself, because it was a delicate area for everyone. 'Eclectic's offered Mavis a contract.'

'Yes, I know.'

'I know you know,' she snapped, slapping away his hand as he attempted to smooth down her hair. 'Damn it, Roarke, you could have told me. I'd have been prepared when she asked me about it.'

'Asked you what? It's a standard contract. She'll certainly want an agent or representative to look it over, but—'

'Did you do it for me?' she interrupted, and her eyes were focused on his face.

'Did I do what for you?'

Now her teeth went on edge. 'Offer Mavis the recording contract.'

He folded his hands, cocked his head. 'You're not planning on giving up law enforcement to be a theatrical agent, are you?'

'No, of course not. I—'

'Well then, it has nothing to do with you.'

'You're not going to sit there and tell me you like Mavis's music.'

'Music is a term I'm not sure applies to Mavis's talents.'

'There.' She jabbed a finger into his chest.

'That talent, however, is – I believe – commercial. Eclectic's purpose is to produce and distribute commercial recording artists.'

She sat back, tapped her finger on her knee. 'So it's a business thing. Straight business.'

'Naturally. I take business very seriously.'

'You could be snowing me,' she said after a moment. 'You're good enough.'

'Yes, I am.' Pleased that he was one of the very few who could snow her, he smiled at her. 'Either way, the deal's done. Is that all?'

'No.' She hissed out a breath, then leaned forward and kissed him. 'Thanks, either way.'

'You're welcome.'

'Next, I have to hit The Athame tonight, check a guy out.' She saw the flicker in his eyes, the tensing of his jaw. 'I'd like you to go with me.' She had to bite her tongue to keep from snickering when he narrowed those eyes at her.

'Just like that? It's police business, but you're not going to make an issue out of it?'

'No, first because I think you might be helpful, and second because it saves time. We'd argue about it, and you'd just go, anyway. This way, I ask you to come and you go, understanding I'm in charge.'

'Clever of you.' He took her hand and drew her to her feet. 'Agreed. But after dinner. I missed lunch.'

'One more thing. Why did you have a Celtic symbol of protection carved into my wedding ring?'

He felt the jolt of surprise, covered it smoothly. 'Excuse me?'

'No, you weren't quick enough that time.' It pleased her that she'd spotted that minute and masterfully covered awareness. 'You know exactly what I'm talking about. One of our friendly neighborhood witches tagged it today.'

'I see.' *Caught*, he realized, and he stalled by lifting her hand to examine the ring. 'It's an appealing design.'

'Don't bullshit me, Roarke. I'm a professional.' She stepped in until their eyes were level again. 'You buy into it, don't you? You actually buy all this hocus-pocus.'

'It's not a matter of that.' He fumbled and knew it when she furrowed her brow.

92

'You're embarrassed.' Her brow cleared in surprise and amusement. 'You're never embarrassed. By anything. This is weird. And kind of sweet.'

'I'm not embarrassed.' *Mortified*, he decided, *but not embarrassed*. 'I'm simply . . . not entirely comfortable explaining myself. I love you,' he said and stilled her muffled chuckle. 'You risk your life, a life that's essential to me, just by being who you are. This . . .' He brushed his thumb over her wedding band. 'Is a small and very personal shield.'

'That's lovely, Roarke. Really. But you don't really believe all that magic nonsense.'

His gaze lifted, and as twilight turned to night, his eyes glinted in the dark. Like a wolf's, she thought.

And it was a wolf, she remembered, she was to trust.

'Your world is relatively small, Eve. You couldn't call it sheltered, but it's limited. You haven't seen a giant's dance, or felt the power of the ancient stones. You haven't run your hand over the Ogham carving in the trunk of a tree petrified by time or heard the sounds that whisper through the mist that coats sacred ground.'

Baffled, she shook her head. 'It's, what, an Irish thing?'

'If you like, though it's certainly not limited to a single race or culture. You are grounded.' He ran his hands up her arms to her shoulders. 'Almost brutal in your focus and your honesty. And I've lived, let's say, a flexible life. I need you, and I'll use whatever comes to hand to keep you safe.' He lifted the ring to his lips. 'Let's just call it covering the bases.'

'Okay.' This was a new aspect of him it would take time to explore. 'But you don't have, like, a secret room where you dance around naked and chant?'

He tucked his tongue in his cheek. 'I did, but I turned it into a den. More versatile.'

'Good thinking. Okay, let's eat.'

'Thank God.' He took her hand and tugged her toward the house.

Chapter Seven

The Athame slicked a high-gloss sheen over depravity, like the baby-kissing smile on a corrupt politician. One scan convinced Eve she'd have preferred to spend an evening in a low-level dive, smelling stale liquor and staler sweat.

Dives didn't bother with disguises.

Revolving balconies of smoky glass and chrome trim ringed the main level in two tiers so that those who preferred a loftier view could circle slowly and check out the action. The central bar speared out in five points, and each was crowded with patrons perched on high stools fashioned to resemble optimistically exaggerated body parts.

A couple of women decked out in micro skirts sat spread-legged on a pair of bulging, flesh-toned cocks and laughed uproariously. A skinheaded bar surfer checked them out by prying his hand down their snug blouses.

All the walls were mirrored, and they pulsed with cloudy red lights. Some of the tables flanking the dance floor were tubed for privacy, some were smoked so that silhouettes of couples in various states of fornication wavered against the glass to entertain the crowd, and all were coated with a shiny black lacquer that made them resemble small, dark pools.

On a raised platform, the band pumped out harsh and clever rock. Eve wondered what Mavis would think of their wildly painted faces, tattooed chests, and black leather cod-pieces studded with silver spikes. She decided her friend would probably have dubbed them mag.

'Do we sit?' Roarke murmured in her ear, 'or case the joint?'

'We go up,' she decided. 'For the overview. What's that smell?'

He stepped onto the auto-stairs with her. 'Cannabis, incense. Sweat.'

She shook her head. There was something under that mix, something metallic. 'Blood. Fresh blood.'

He'd caught it as well. That broody underlayer. 'In a place like this, they put it in the air vents for mood enhancement.'

'Charming.'

They stepped off onto the second level. Here, rather than tables and chairs, there were floor pillows and thick rugs where patrons could lounge as they sipped their brew of choice. Those on the prowl leaned on the ornate chrome rail, scoping, Eve imagined, for a likely partner to lure into one of the privacy rooms.

There were a dozen such rooms on this level, all with heavy black doors bearing chrome plaques with such names as Perdition, Leviathan, and – more direct, in Eve's opinion – Hell and Damnation.

She could too easily imagine the personality type who would find such invitations seductive.

As she watched, a man whose eyes were glazed with liquor began to slurp his way up his companion's legs. His hand snuck under her crotch-skimming skirt as she giggled. Technically, she could have busted them both for engaging in a sexual act in public.

'What would be the point?' Roarke commented, reading her perfectly. His voice was mild. Anyone taking a casual glance would have seen a man faintly bored with the ambiance. But he was braced to attack or defend, whichever became necessary.

'You've got more interesting things to do than toss a horny couple from Queens in lockup.'

That wasn't really the point, Eve thought as the man tugged apart the self-stick fly on his baggy blue trousers. 'How do you know they're from Queens?'

Before he could answer, a young, attractive man with a flowing mane of blond hair and bare, gleaming shoulders, hunkered down beside the busy couple. Whatever he said had the woman giggling again then grabbing him into a sloppy kiss.

'Why don't you come, too?' she demanded in an unmistakable accent. 'We could have ourselves a manage and twas.'

Eve lifted a brow at the borough massacre of the French term, and at the easy skill with which the bouncer disengaged himself and led the staggering couple off.

'Queens,' Roarke said, smug. 'Definitely. And that was smoothly done.' He inclined his head as the couple was taken through a narrow door. 'They'd add the price of the privacy room to the tab, and no harm done.' There was a scream of female laughter as the bouncer came back out and secured the door. 'Everyone's happy.'

'Queens might not be in the morning. The cost of a privacy room in a place like this has to hurt. Then again . . .' She scanned the crowd. Ages varied from the very young – many of whom she was sure had gained entrance with forged ID – to the very mature. But from the wardrobe and jewelry, the tone of faces and bodies that slyly hinted at salon enhancements, the clientele was solidly upper middle-class.

'Money doesn't look to be a problem here. I've spotted at least five high-credit licensed companions.'

'My count was more like ten.'

She quirked a brow. 'Twelve bouncers with low-grade palm zappers.'

'On that count, we agree.' He slipped an arm around her waist and walked to the rail. Below, the dance floor was packed, bodies rubbing suggestively against bodies. Wild laughter bounced off the mirrored walls and shot upward.

The band was into their performance mode. The two female vocalists were being bound to dangling silver chains with leather straps. The music pounded, heavy on the drums. The dancers surged forward, closing in, as eager as a mob at a lynching. Audience participation was realized as a man was brought forward and accepted the invitation to strip the women out of their flimsy robes. Beneath, they were naked but for glittery stars over nipples and pubes.

The crowd began to chant and howl as he coated them with thick oil, and they writhed and screamed and begged for mercy.

'That's skirting the line,' Eve muttered.

'Performance art.' Roarke watched the man scourge the first vocalist with a velvet cat 'o nine tails. 'Still within the law.'

'A simulation of debasement encourages the real thing.' She set her teeth as a band member began to lightly slap the second vocalist as their voices soared in fervent duet. 'We're supposed to be beyond this kind of female exploitation. But we're not. We never are. What are they looking for?'

'Thrills. Of the cheaper and meaner variety.' His hand soothed the base of her back. She knew what it was to be bound, to be abused. There was nothing artful and nothing entertaining about it. 'There's no need to watch this, Eve.'

'What makes them do it?' she wondered. 'What makes a woman let herself be used that way, in simulation or in reality? Why doesn't she kick his balls into his throat?'

'She's not you.' He kissed her on the brow and firmly turned her away.

The railing was thick with people, now straining to see the show.

As they took a quick tour of the top floor, a woman in a sheer black gown glided up to them. 'Welcome to The Master's Level. Do you have a reservation?'

97

Enough was enough, Eve thought. She flipped out her badge. 'I'm not interested in what you're selling here.'

'Fine food and wine,' the hostess said after only a quick hitch at the sight of police identification. 'You'll find we're completely within code here, Lieutenant. However, if you wish to speak with the owner—'

'I've already done that. I want to see Lobar. Where do I find him?'

'He doesn't work this level.' With the subtlety and discretion that would have made the poshest maître d' proud, the hostess steered Eve back toward the stairs. 'If you will go to the main level, you will be met, and a table provided. I'll contact Lobar and send him to you.'

'Fine.' Eve studied her, saw an attractive woman in her mid-twenties. 'Why do you do this?' she asked and glanced at one of the screens where a woman screamed and struggled as she was strapped to a raised slab of marble. 'How can you do this?'

The hostess merely glanced down at Eve's badge, then smiled sweetly. 'How can you do that?' she countered and drifted away.

'I'm letting it get to me,' Eve admitted as they headed down to the main level. 'I know better.'

The band continued to play, the music a frenzy now. But the performance aspect had switched to a huge view screen that filled the wall behind the stage. It took Eve only a glance to see why. The club wasn't licensed for live sex acts, but such minor inconveniences were transcended by video.

The female vocalists were still bound, still singing their hearts out without missing a beat. But they were behind the stage now, on camera, along with the man from the audience and a second man who wore nothing but an ornate mask of a boar's head.

'Pigs,' was all Eve had to say, then looked into gleaming red eyes.

'Your table is this way.' The young man smiled, revealing

gleaming teeth with incisors sharpened to vicious fangs. He turned. His hair streamed down his naked back, black, tipped with red like flames. He opened the rounded door on a privacy tube, stepped in ahead of them.

'I'm Lobar.' He grinned again. 'I've been expecting you.'

He might have been pretty without the affectation of vampire fangs and demon eyes. As it was, Eve thought he looked like an overgrown child dressed up for Halloween. If he was of legal age, she deduced it couldn't have been by much. His chest was thin and hairless, his arms slim as a girl's. But she didn't think it was the red tint of his eyes that took away his innocence. It was the look in them.

'Sit down, Lobar.'

'Sure.' He dropped into a chair. 'I'll have a drink. You're buying,' he told Eve. 'You want my time during work hours, you gotta pay.' He punched out a selection on the electronic menu, adjusted his chair so that he could see the view screen. 'Great show tonight.'

Eve glanced over.

'The script could use work,' she said dryly. 'You got ID, Lobar?'

He peeled his lips back from his fangs, lifted his hands, palm out. 'Not on me. Unless you think I got secret pockets in my skin.'

'What's your legal name?'

His smile disappeared, and his eyes were suddenly the sulky eyes of a child. 'It's Lobar. That's who I am. I don't have to answer your questions, you know. I'm cooperating.'

'You're a real sterling citizen.' Eve waited while his drink slid out of the serving slot. Another show; she mused, as the heavy glass chalice smoked with some murky gray brew. 'Alice Lingstrom. What do you know about her?'

'Not much, except she was a dumb bitch.' He sipped the drink. 'She hung around for awhile, then went crying off. It was fine with me. The master doesn't need any weaklings.'

99

'The master.'

He sipped again, smiled. 'Satan,' he said, relishing it.

'You believe in Satan?'

'Sure.' He leaned forward, slid his hand with its long, black-painted nails toward Eve. 'And he believes in you.'

'Careful,' Roarke murmured. 'You're too young and stupid to loose a hand.'

Lobar snorted, but he slid his hand back again. 'Your watchdog?' he said to Eve. 'Your rich watchdog. We know who you are,' he added, fixing his red eyes on Roarke. 'Big fucking deal. You don't have any power here. And neither does your cop bitch.'

'I'm not his cop bitch,' Eve said mildly, shooting a warning glance at Roarke. 'I'm my own cop bitch. And as to power . . .' She leaned back. 'Well, I've got the power to take you down to Cop Central and slap you into Interview.' She smiled, letting her gaze run over the naked chest and gleaming nipple rings. 'The guys would just love to get a load of you. Cute, isn't he, Roarke?'

'In an apprentice demon sort of fashion. You must have a very . . . interesting dentist.' As it was a privacy booth, he took out a cigarette, lighted it.

'I could use one of those,' Lobar said.

'Could you?' With a shrug, Roarke slid another cigarette onto the table. When Lobar picked it up, looked at him expectantly, Roarke grinned. 'Sorry, you want a light? I assumed you'd shoot flame out of your fingertips.'

'I don't do tricks for straights.' Lobar leaned forward, sucking on the filter as Roarke flicked his lighter at the tip. 'Look, you want to know about Alice, and I can't help you. She wasn't my type. Too inhibited, and always asking questions. Sure I banged her a couple of times, but those were like community fucks, you know? Nothing personal.'

'And on the night she was killed?'

He blew out smoke, sucked more in. He hadn't had real

tobacco before, and the expensive drug made him light-headed and relaxed. 'Never saw her. I was busy. I had a private ceremony with Selina and Alban. Sexual rites. After, we fucked around most of the night.'

He took another deep drag, holding it in as he would a toke from a prime joint, then exhaling lustily through his nostrils. 'Selina likes double bangers, and when she's done, she likes to watch and get herself off. Was dawn, easy, before she'd had enough.'

'And the three of you were together the entire night. No one left, even for a few minutes.'

He moved his bony shoulders. 'That's the thing about three people. No waiting.' He lowered his gaze suggestively to her breasts. 'Want to try it?'

'You don't want to solicit a cop, Lobar. And I like men. Not skinny boys in silly costumes. Who called Alice and played the recording. The chant?'

He was sulky again, his ego pricked. If she'd come alone, he thought, he'd have shown her a few things. A bitch was a bitch as far as he was concerned, badge or no badge. 'I don't know what you're talking about. Alice was nothing. Nobody gave a shit about her.'

'Her grandfather did.'

'Heard he was dead, too.' The red eyes gleamed. 'Old fart. Desk cop, button pusher. Means nothing to me.'

'Enough to know he was a cop,' Eve put in. 'A cop who rode a desk. How'd you know that, Lobar?'

Realizing his mistake, he crushed out what was left of the cigarette in quick, vicious little jabs. 'Somebody must've mentioned it.' He exposed his fangs in a wide grin. 'Probably Alice did, while I was banging her.'

'Doesn't say much for your performance rating, does it, if she was talking about her grandfather when you were . . . banging her.'

'I heard it somewhere, all right?' He grabbed his drink,

101

gulped deeply. 'What's the big fucking deal where? He was old, anyway.'

'Did you ever see him? In here?'

'I see a lot of people in here. I don't remember any old cop.' He waved a hand. 'Place rocks like this most every night. How the hell do I know who comes in? Selina hired me to keep the occasional asshole in line, not to remember faces.'

'Selina's got quite the enterprise going here. Is she still dealing? She deal for you?'

His eyes went sly. 'I get power from my beliefs. I don't need illegals.'

'Have you ever participated in human sacrifice? Ever slice up a child for your master, Lobar?'

He polished off his drink. 'That's an outsider's hallucination. People like you like to make Satanists out to be monsters.'

'People like us,' Roarke murmured, skimming his gaze over Lobar from the fire-tipped hair to the nipple rings. 'Yes, obviously we're biased when anyone can see you're simply . . . devout.'

'Look, it's a religion, and we've got freedom of religion in this country. You want to push your God down our throats? Well, we reject him. We reject him and all his weak-kneed creeds. And we'll rule in Hell.'

He shoved back from the table and stood. 'I've got nothing more to say.'

'All right.' Eve spoke quietly, looking up into his eyes. 'But you think about this, Lobar. People are dead. Somebody's going to be next. It might just be you.'

His lips trembled, then firmed. 'It might just be you,' he shot back and slammed out of the booth.

'What an attractive young man,' Roarke commented. 'I do believe he'll be a delightful addition to Hell.'

'That may be where he's going.' After a quick glance around, Eve nudged the empty glass into her bag. 'I want to find out where he came from. I can run his prints at home.'

'Fine.' He rose, took her arm. 'But I want a shower first. This place leaves something nasty coated on the skin.'

'I can't argue with that.'

'Robert Allen Mathias,' Eve stated, reading data off her monitor. 'Turned eighteen six months ago. Born in Kansas City, Kansas, son of Jonathan and Elaine Mathias, both of whom are Baptist deacons.'

'A PK.' Roarke put in. 'Preacher's kid. Some can rebel in extreme manners. Looks like little Bobby has.'

'History of problems,' Eve continued. 'I got his juvie file here. Petty theft, break in, truancy, assault. Ran way from home four times before he hit thirteen. At fifteen, after a joy ride that landed him a grand theft auto, his parents had him termed legally incorrigible. Did a year at a state school, which ended with him being kicked to a state institution after an attempted rape on a teacher.'

'Bobby's a sweetheart,' Roarke murmured. 'I knew there was a reason I wanted to jab his little red eyes out. They kept latching onto your breasts.'

'Yeah.' Unconsciously, Eve rubbed a hand over them as if to erase something vile. 'Psych profile's pretty much what you'd expect. Sociopathic tendencies, lack of control, violent mood swings. Subject harbors deep, unresolved resentment toward parents and authority figures, particularly female. Displays both fear and resentment toward females. Intelligence rating, high, violence quotient, high. Subject displays complete lack of conscience and an abnormal interest in the occult.'

'Then what is he doing out on the street? Why isn't he in treatment?'

'Because it's the law. You have to kick him when he turns eighteen. Until you nail him as an adult, he's clear.' Eve puffed out her cheeks, blew out the air. 'He's a dangerous little bastard, but there's not much I can do about him. He corroborates Selina's statement for the night of Alice's death.'

103

'He'd have been instructed to,' Roarke pointed out.

'Still sticks – unless I can break it.' She pushed back. 'I've got his current address. I can check it out, knock on doors. See if his neighbors can give me something on him. If I can get him in on something, lay on some pressure, I think little Bobby would break.'

'Otherwise?'

'Otherwise, we keep digging.' She rubbed her eyes. 'We'll deal with him. Sooner or later, he'll revert to type – bust somebody's face, assault some woman, kick the wrong ass. Then we'll lock him in a cage.'

'Your job is miserable.'

'Most of the time,' she agreed, then looked over her shoulder. 'Are you tired?'

'Depends.' He glanced at the screen where Lobar's data scrolled. He had an image of her diving deeper, spending the quiet hours of night wading through the muck. He didn't bother to sigh. 'What do you need?'

'You.' She could feel her color rise as he lifted a curious brow. 'I know it's late, and it's been a long day. I guess I was thinking of it kind of like the shower. Something to wash away the grime.' Embarrassed, she turned back, stared hard at the screen. 'Stupid.'

It was always hard for her to ask, he mused. For anything. 'Not the most romantic proposal I've ever had.' He laid his hands on her shoulders, massaged gently. 'But far from stupid. Disengage,' he ordered and the screen went dark. He turned her chair around, drew her to her feet. 'Come to bed.'

'Roarke.' She put her arms around him, held tight. She couldn't explain how or why the images she'd seen that night had left something inside her shaky. With him, she didn't have to. 'I love you.'

Smiling a little, she lifted her head and looked into his eyes. 'It's getting easier to say. I think I'm starting to like it.'

With a short laugh, he pressed a kiss to her chin. 'Come to bed,' he repeated, 'and say it again.'

The rite was ancient, its purpose dark. Cloaked and masked, the coven gathered in the private chamber. The scent of blood was fresh and strong. The flames spearing above black candles flickered to send shadows slithering over the walls like spiders hunting prey.

Selina chose to be the altar and lay naked, a candle burning between her thighs, a bowl of sacrificial blood nestled between her generous breasts.

She smiled as she glanced toward the silver bowl overflowing with the cash and credits the membership had paid for the privilege to belong. Their wealth was now her wealth. The master had saved her from a scrabbling life on the streets and brought her here, into power and into comfort.

She had gladly traded her soul for them.

Tonight there would be more. Tonight there would be death, and the power that came from the rending of flesh, the spilling of blood. They would not remember, she thought. She had added drugs to the blood-laced wine. With the right drugs, in the right dosage, they would do and say and be what the master wanted.

Only she and Alban would know that the master had demanded sacrifice for his protection, and the demand had been happily met.

The coven circled her, their faces hooded, their bodies swaying, as the drug, the smoke, the chanting hypnotized them. At her head stood Alban, with the boar's mask and the athame.

'We worship the one,' he said in his clear and beautiful voice.

And the coven answered. 'Satan is the one.'

'What is his, is ours.'

'Ave, Satan.'

As Alban lifted the bowl, his eyes met Selina's. He took up a sword, thrust it at the four points of the compass. The princes of hell were called, the list long and exotic. Voices were a hum. Fire crackled in a blackened pot set on a marble slab.

She began to moan.

'Destroy our enemies.'

Yes, she thought. *Destroy.*

'Bring sickness and pain on those who would harm us.'

Great pain. Unbearable pain.

When Alban laid a hand on her flesh, she began to scream. 'We take what we wish, in your name. Death to the weak. Fortune to the strong.'

He stepped back, and though it was his right to take the altar first, he gestured to Lobar. 'Reward to the loyal. Take her,' he commanded. 'Give her pain as well as pleasure.'

Lobar hesitated a moment. The sacrifice should have come first. The blood sacrifice. The goat should have been brought out and slaughtered. But he looked at Selina, and his drug-clouded brain shut off. There was woman. Bitch. She watched him with cold, taunting eyes.

He would show her, he thought. He would show her he was a man. It wouldn't be like the last time when she had used and humiliated him.

This time, he would be in charge.

He cast aside his robe and stepped forward.

Chapter Eight

The steady beep of an alarm had Eve rolling over and cursing. 'It can't be time to get up. We just went to bed.'

'It's not. That's security.'

'What?' Now she sat up quickly. '*Our* security?'

Roarke was already out of bed, already pulling on slacks, and answered with a grunt. Instinctively Eve reached for her weapon first, clothes second. 'Someone's trying to break in?'

'Apparently someone has.' His voice was very calm. As the lights were still off, she could see only his silhouette in the scattered light of the moon through the sky window. And joining that silhouette was the unmistakable outline of a gun in his hand.

'Where the hell did you get that? I thought they were all locked up. Goddamn it, Roarke, that's illegal. Put it away.'

Coolly, he plugged a round in the chamber of the antique and banned-for-use Glock nine millimeter. 'No.'

'Damn it, damn it.' She snatched up her communicator, shoved it in the back pocket of her jeans out of habit. 'You can't use that thing. I'll check it out – that's my job. You call Dispatch, report a possible intruder.'

'No,' he said again and started for the door. She was on him in two steps.

'If someone's on the grounds or in the house, and if you shoot him with that, I'm going to have to arrest you.'

'Fine.'

'Roarke.' She grabbed at him as he reached for the door. 'There's procedure for something like this, and reasons for that procedure. Call it in.'

His home, he thought. Their home. His woman, and the fact that she was a cop didn't mean a damn at the moment. 'And won't you feel foolish, Lieutenant, if it's a mechanical malfunction?'

'Nothing of yours ever malfunctions,' she muttered and made him smile despite the circumstances.

'Why, thank you.' He opened the door, and there was Summerset.

'It appears someone is on the grounds.'

'Where's the breech?'

'Section fifteen, southwest quadrant.'

'Run a full video scan, employ full house security when we're out. Eve and I will check the grounds.' Absently, he ran a hand down her back. 'A good thing I live with a cop.'

She looked down at the gun in his hand. Attempting to disarm him would likely prove unsuccessful. And it would take too much time. 'We're going to talk about this,' she said between her teeth. 'I mean it.'

'Of course you do.'

They went side by side down the stairs, through the now silent house. 'They haven't gotten in,' he said as he paused by a door leading onto a wide patio. 'The alarm for a breech of the house is different. But they're over the wall.'

'Which means they could be anywhere.'

The moon was waxing toward full, but the clouds were thick and shadowed its light. Eve scanned the dark, the sheltering trees, the huge ornamental bushes. All provided excellent cover for observation. Or ambush. She heard nothing but the air teasing leaves going brittle with age.

'We'll have to separate. For Christ's sake don't use that weapon unless your life's threatened. Most B and E men aren't armed.'

And most B and E men, they both knew, didn't attempt to ply their trade on a man like Roarke. 'Be careful,' he said quietly and slipped like smoke into the shadows.

He was good, Eve assured herself. She could trust him to handle himself and the situation. Using the dim and shifting moonlight as a guide, she headed west, then began to circle.

The quiet was almost eerie. She could barely hear her own footsteps on the thick grass. Behind her, the house stood in darkness, a formidable structure of old stone and glass, guarded, she thought, by a skinny snob of a butler.

Her lips curled. She'd love to see an unsuspecting burglar come up against Summerset.

When she reached the wall, she scanned for any breech. It was eight feet high, three feet thick, and wired to deliver a discouraging electric shock to anything over twenty pounds. Security cameras and lights were set every twelve feet. She whispered out an oath when she noted the narrow beams were blinking red rather than green.

Disengaged. Son of a bitch. Weapon drawn and ready, she circled to the south.

Roarke did his own circuit in silence, using the trees. He'd bought this property eight years before, had had it remodeled and rehabbed to his specifications. He'd supervised the design and implementation of the security system personally. It was in a very real sense his first home, the place he'd chosen to settle after too many years of wandering. Beneath the icy control, as he slipped from shadow to shadow, was a bubbling, grinding fury that his home had been invaded.

The night was cool, clear, quiet as a tomb. He wondered if he was up against a very ballsy thief. It could be as simple as that. Or it could be something, someone much more dangerous. A pro hired by a business competitor. An enemy – and he hadn't fought his way to where he was without making them. Particularly since many of his interests had been on the dark side of the law.

Or the target could be Eve. She, too, had made enemies. Dangerous enemies. He glanced over his shoulder, hesitated. Then told himself not to second-guess his wife. He knew of no one better equipped to take care of herself.

But it was that hesitation, that instinctive need to protect that turned his luck. As he paused in the shadows, he caught the faint sound of movement. Roarke took a firmer grip on the gun, stepped back, stepped to the side. And waited.

The figure was moving slowly, in a crouch. As the distance between them melted away, Roarke could hear the puff of nervous breathing. Though he couldn't make out features, he judged male, perhaps five-ten, and on the lean side. He could see no weapon, and thinking of the difficulty Eve might have explaining why her husband had held off an intruder with a banned handgun, tucked the Glock into the back of his slacks.

He braced, looking forward to a little hand-to-hand, then lunged when the figure slunk by. Roarke had an arm around a throat, a fist clenched and raised in anticipation of quiet, perhaps petty revenge, when he realized it wasn't a man, but a boy.

'Hey, you son of a bitch, let go. I'll kill you.'

A very rude and very frightened boy, Roarke decided. The struggle was short and all one-sided. It took seconds only for Roarke to pin the boy against the trunk of a tree. 'How the hell did you get inside?' Roarke demanded.

The kid's breath was coming in whistles, and his face was pale as a ghost. Roarke could hear the audible click in his throat as he swallowed. 'You're Roarke.' He stopped struggling and tried to smirk. 'You've got pretty good security.'

'I like to think so.' *Not a thief*, Roarke decided, *but ballsy, certainly*. 'How did you get past it?'

'I—' He broke off, eyes going huge as they shot over Roarke's shoulder. 'Behind you!'

With a smoothness the boy would later appreciate, Roarke

pivoted, keeping his grip unbreakable. 'We have our intruder, Lieutenant.'

'So I see.' She lowered her weapon, ordered her heart to slow to normal. 'Jesus, Roarke, it's just a kid. It's—' She stopped, narrowed her eyes. 'I know this kid.'

'Then perhaps you'd introduce us.'

'It's Jamie, right? Jamie Lingstrom. Alice's brother.'

'Good eye, Lieutenant. Now, you want to tell him to stop choking me?'

'I don't think so.' She holstered her weapon, stepped up. 'What the hell are you doing, breaking into private property in the middle of the night? You're a cop's grandson, for Christ's sake. You want to end up in juvie?'

'I'm not your big problem right now, Lieutenant Dallas.' He made a valiant attempt to sound tough, but his voice wavered. 'You've got a dead body outside the wall. Really dead,' he added and began to shake.

'Did you kill someone, Jamie?' Roarke asked mildly.

'No, man. No way. He was there when I came by.' Terrified his stomach would revolt and humiliate him, Jamie swallowed hard again. 'I'll show you.'

If it was a trick, Eve considered it a fine one. She couldn't take a chance. 'All right. Let's go. And if you try to run, pal, I'll zap you.'

'Wouldn't make any sense to run, would it, when I went to all this trouble to get in? This way.' His legs were rubber, and he sincerely hoped neither of them noticed that his knees kept knocking together.

'I'd like to know how you got in,' Roarke said as they headed for the main gate. 'How you bypassed security.'

'I fool around with electronics. A hobby. You've got a really high-grade system. The best.'

'So I thought.'

'I guess I didn't disengage all the alarms.' Jamie turned his head, tried another weak smile. 'You knew I was here.'

'You got in,' Roarke repeated. 'How?'

'This.' Jamie pulled a small palm-sized unit out of his pocket. 'It's a jammer I've been working on for a couple of years. It'll read most systems,' he began, frowning when Roarke plucked it out of his hand. 'When you engage this,' he continued, leaning over to point, 'it'll scan the chips, run a cloning program. Then it's just a matter of backing out the program step by step. Takes some time, but it's pretty efficient.'

Roarke stared at the mechanism. It was no bigger than one of the E-games one of his companies manufactured. Indeed, the casing looked distressingly familiar. 'You adapted a game unit into a jammer. Yourself. One that read and cloned and breached my security.'

'Well, most of it.' Jamie's eyes clouded in annoyance. 'I must have missed something, one of the backups maybe. Your system must be ultra mag. I'd like to see it.'

'Not in this lifetime,' Roarke muttered and shoved the unit into his pocket.

When they reached the gates, he disengaged and opened them manually, sliding a narrow look at Jamie as the boy craned over his shoulder to see.

'Way impressive,' Jamie commented. 'I didn't figure I could get through this way. That's why I had to come over the wall. Needed a ladder.'

Roarke simply closed his eyes. 'A ladder,' he said to no one in particular. 'He climbed up a ladder. Lovely. And the cameras?'

'Oh, I blanked them from across the street. The unit's got a range of ten yards.'

'Lieutenant.' Roarke snagged Jamie by the collar. 'I want him punished.'

'Later. Now, where's this body you're supposed to have seen?'

The cocky smile fell away from his face. 'To the left,' he told her, paling again.

'Keep a hold of him, Roarke. Stay here.'

'I've got him,' Roarke replied, but he'd be damned if he'd stay back. He tugged Jamie through the gate, met Eve's annoyed stare blandly. 'Our home, our problem.'

She said something nasty under her breath and turned left. She didn't have to go far. It wasn't hidden, it wasn't subtle.

The body was naked and strapped to a wooden form in the shape of a star. No, she realized. A pentagram. Inverted so that the head with its dead doll eyes and gaping throat hung over the bloody sidewalk. The arms were outstretched, the legs parted in a wide vee. The center of his chest was a mass of black blood and gore, the hole hacked out of it bigger than a man's fist.

She doubted the ME would find a heart inside when he opened the body for autopsy.

She heard the choked sound behind her and turned to see Roarke shift his grip on Jamie and step over to shield the boy from the view.

'Lobar,' was all he said.

'Yeah.' She stepped closer. Whoever had taken his heart had also plunged a knife through a sheet of paper and through his groin.

DEVIL WORSHIPPER
BABY KILLER
BURN IN HELL

'Take the boy inside, will you, Roarke?' She glanced at the collapsible ladder tilted against the wall. 'And get rid of that. Pass the kid off to Summerset for now. I can't leave the scene.' She turned, her face blank and impassive. Her cop face. 'Will you bring me my field kit?'

'Yes. Come on, Jamie.'

'I know who he is.' Tears swam in Jamie's eyes and were viciously blinked away. 'He's one of the bastards who killed my sister. I hope he rots.'

Because his voice had broken at the end, Roarke slipped an arm around his shoulder. 'He will. Come inside. Let the Lieutenant do her job.' Roarke sent Eve one last look before hefting the ladder and leading Jamie back through the gates.

With her gaze still fixed on the body, Eve pulled out her communicator. 'Dispatch, Dallas, Lieutenant Eve.'

'Dispatch, acknowledged.'

'Reporting homicide, requesting assistance.' She gave the necessary data, then replaced her communicator. Turning, she stared across the wide, quiet street into the dark, shifting shadows of the great park. In the east the sky was stripping off the first layers of night, and the stars, such as they were, were blinking out.

Murder had come into her life before and would again. But someone would pay for bringing it into her home.

She turned as Roarke approached not only with her field kit but her battered leather jacket. 'It gets chilly this close to dawn,' he said and handed it to her.

'Thanks. Jamie all right?'

'He and Summerset are eyeing each other with mutual dislike and distrust.'

'I knew I liked that kid. You can go inside and referee,' she told him as she took out Seal-It and clear-coated her hands, her boots. 'I've called it in.'

'I'm staying.'

Since she'd already figured he would, she didn't argue. 'Then make yourself useful and record the scene.' She took her recorder out of the kit, passed it to him, then covered his hand with hers. 'I'm sorry.'

'You're too smart to be sorry for something that isn't your responsibility. He wasn't killed here, was he?'

'No.' Confident that Roarke could function as her aide until Peabody arrived, Eve approached the body again. 'Not nearly enough blood. He'd have gushed from the jugular. That was likely the cause of death. We'll find the other wounds are postmortem. In any case, there'd be splatters all over hell and back. We'd be wading in it. Record on?'

'Yes.'

'Victim identified as Robert Mathias, aka Lobar. White male, eighteen years of age. Preliminary visual exam indicates death was caused by a sharp-bladed instrument that severed the throat.' Shutting off everything but training, she took out a pencil light, examined the chest wound. 'Additional insults include a wound in the chest, probably inflicted by the same weapon. The victim's heart has been removed. The organ is not on scene. I need close-ups here,' she said to Roarke.

She took instruments out of her kit to calibrate. 'The throat wound is six and a quarter inches across, approximately two inches deep.' Quickly, competently, she measured and recorded the other wounds. 'A knife, black-handled with carving, was left in the body in the groin area to anchor what appears to be a computer-generated note on treated paper.'

She heard the shrill sound of sirens coming closer. 'Uniforms,' she told Roarke. 'They'll secure the scene. Not much traffic out this way at this time of night.'

'Fortunately.'

'The body has been strapped by leather strips to a wooden structure, pentagram shape. The small amount of blood and blood patterns indicate victim was killed and mutilated elsewhere and transported to scene. Perimeter security to be scanned. Possibility of breech onto private property beyond security gate and wall. Body discovered at approximately four-thirty A.M. by Lieutenant Eve Dallas and Roarke, residents.'

She turned and walked over as the first black-and-white screeched up to the curb. 'I want a privacy screen employed. Now. Block off the street in a twenty-foot perimeter. I don't want gawkers here. I don't want the fucking media. Got it?'

'Sir.' The two uniforms hustled out of the car and to the trunk. They wrestled out the privacy screen.

'I'm going to be awhile,' she told Roarke. Taking the

recorder from him, she passed it to another uniform. 'You should go inside, keep an eye on the kid.' Wearily, she watched the cruiser cops erect the screen. 'He should call his mother or something. But I don't want him to leave until I talk to him again.'

'I'll take care of it. I'll cancel my appointments for the day. I'll be available.'

'That would be best.' She started to touch him, wanted to badly, then realized her sealed hands were smeared with blood and dropped them again. 'It would help if you kept him occupied, kept his mind off of it for now. Goddamn it, Roarke, this bites.'

'A ritual killing,' he murmured, and understanding, laid a hand on her cheek. 'But which side did it?'

'I guess I'm going to be spending a lot of time interviewing witches.' She huffed out a breath, then frowned when she saw Peabody striding double-time down the street. 'Where the hell's your vehicle, Officer?'

Her uniform might have been pressed to within an inch of its life, but her face was flushed and her breathing short. 'I don't have a vehicle, Lieutenant. I use city transpo. The closest public stop is four blocks from here.' She slanted a look at Roarke as though it was his personal responsibility. 'Rich people don't use public transportation.'

'Well, requisition a damn vehicle,' Eve ordered. 'We'll be in as soon as we're done out here,' she told Roarke, then turned away. 'Body's behind the screen. Get the recorder from the uniform, I don't trust his eye, and his hands are shaking. I want measurements on the blood pool and stills of the wounds, all angles. Seal up. I don't think the sweepers are going to find much here, but I don't want anything compromised. I'll do the prelim for time of death. The ME's on the way.'

Roarke watched her march off, flip through the screen, and figured she was finished with him.

Inside the house, he found Jamie, guarded by a visibly irritated

116

Summerset. 'You will not be allowed free range of this house,' Summerset snapped out. 'You will touch nothing. If you break one piece of crockery, soil one centimeter of fabric, I will resort to violence.'

Jamie continued to pace, continued to paw the statuary in the small – and as Summerset thought of it lesser – parlor. 'Well, now I'm shaking. You really put the fear of God in me, old man.'

'Your manners continue to disintegrate,' Roarke commented as he stepped into the room. 'Someone should have taught you to show some respect for your elders.'

'Yeah, well, someone should have taught your guard dog to be polite to guests.'

'Guests don't tamper with security systems, climb over walls, and skulk around private property. You are not a guest.'

Jamie deflated. It was tough to stand up under those cool blue eyes. 'I wanted to see the Lieutenant. I didn't want anyone to know.'

'Next time, try using the 'link,' Roarke suggested. 'It's all right, Summerset, I'll deal with this.'

'As you wish.' Summerset shot Jamie one last withering look, then stalked, stiff-backed, out of the room.

'Where'd you find Count Boredom?' Jamie asked and slumped into a chair. 'The morgue?'

Roarke sat on the arm of a sofa, took out a cigarette. 'Summerset can eat runts like you for breakfast,' he said mildly and flicked on his lighter. 'I've seen him.'

'Right.' Still Jamie sent a cautious look toward the doorway. Nothing in this house was what he'd expected, so he wouldn't underestimate the butler. 'Speaking of breakfast, you got anything to eat around here? It's been like hours since I had anything.'

Roarke blew out smoke. 'You want me to feed you now?'

'Well, you know. We got to hang anyway. Might as well eat.'

Cheeky little bastard, Roarke thought, not without admiration. Only youth, he supposed, could have an appetite after seeing what was outside the wall. 'And what did you have in mind? Crêpes, an omelette, perhaps a few bowls of sugar-soaked cereal?'

'I was thinking more of pizza, maybe a burger.' He fixed on a winning smile. 'My mom's a real nutrition fanatic. We only get health shit at home.'

'It's five in the morning, and you want pizza?'

'Pizza goes down smooth anytime.'

'You may be right.' And he thought he could use something, himself, after all. 'Let's go then.'

'It's like a museum in here,' Jamie said as he followed Roarke into the hall with its luminous paintings and gleaming antiques. 'I mean, in a good way. You must be rolling in it.'

'I must be.'

'People say you just touch something and the credits fly out.'

'Do they?'

'Yeah, and you didn't make all of it exactly on the upside, you know? But being hooked up with a cop like Dallas, you'd have to be straight.'

'One would think,' Roarke murmured and swung through a door into a huge kitchen.

'Wow. Ultimate. You got people who, like, cook things – by hand and stuff?'

'It's been known to happen.' Roarke watched the boy prowl, toy with controls on the compu-range, the subzero refrigerator. 'It's not going to happen this morning.' He walked to a large AutoChef. 'What is it then, pizza or burger?'

Jamie grinned. 'Both? I could probably drink a gallon of Pepsi.'

'We'll start with a tube.' Roarke programmed the AutoChef, then went to the refrigerator himself. 'Sit down, Jamie.'

'Frigid.' But he kept his eye on Roarke as he slid onto the padded bench of a breakfast nook.

After a short debate, Roarke punched in for two tubes, slipped them out of the door slot when they slid down. 'You'll want to contact your mother,' he said. 'You can use the 'link there.'

'No.' Jamie put his hands under the table, rubbed them on his jeans. 'She's zoned. She can't handle it. Alice. She's tranqued out. We – the viewing's tonight.'

'I see.' And because he did, Roarke let it drop. He handed the drink to Jamie, then took a large bubbling pizza from the AutoChef. He set it, then the burger that followed, on the table.

'Rocking A.' With the appetite of the young, Jamie grabbed the burger and bit in. 'Man! Man, it's meat,' he said with his mouth full. 'It's meat.'

It took a master not to let his mouth twitch. 'You'd prefer soy?' Roarke asked politely. 'Veggie?'

'No way.' Jamie wiped his mouth with the back of his hand, grinned. 'Really decent. Thanks.'

Roarke got two plates and a slicer. He went to work on the pizza. 'I suppose breaking and entering stimulates the appetite.'

'I'm always hungry.' Without shame, Jamie transferred the first slice to his plate. 'Mom says it's growing pains, but I just like to eat. She's real worried about junk intake, so I've got to sneak real food in. You know how moms are.'

'No, actually, I don't. I'll take your word.' And because he'd never been quite as young as Jamie, or quite as innocent, he took a slice for himself and prepared to enjoy watching the boy devour the rest.

'Parents are okay.' Jamie shrugged, alternating between the pizza and the burger. 'I don't see my father – not in a few years.

He's got a life over in Europe, the Morningside Community outside London.'

'Structured, programmed residential,' Roarke put in. 'Very tidy.'

'Yeah, and very boring. Even the grass is programmed. He digs on it, though, him and his foxy new wife – his third already.' He jerked a shoulder, sucked on the Pepsi. 'He isn't much on the father game. It bothered Alice a lot. Me, I can take it or leave it.'

No, Roarke thought, he didn't think so. Wounds were there. Odd what deep and permanent injury a parent could cause a child. 'Your mother hasn't married again?'

'Nah. She's not into it. She was bummed pretty bad when he took off. I was six. I'm sixteen now, and she still thinks I'm a kid. I had to nag for weeks to get her to let me go for my vehicle license. She's okay really. She's just . . .' He trailed off, stared down at his plate as if he wondered how food had gotten there. 'She doesn't deserve this. She does the best she can. She doesn't deserve this. She loved Grandpa. They were really tight. And now Alice. Alice was really weird, but she . . .'

'She was your sister,' Roarke said quietly. 'You loved her.'

'It shouldn't have happened to her.' He lifted his gaze slowly, met Roarke's with a kind of terrifying fury. 'When I find them, the one who hurt her, I'm going to kill them.'

'You want to be careful what you say, Jamie.' Eve stepped in. Her eyes were shadowed, her face pale with fatigue. Though she'd been careful, there were a few smears of blood on her jeans. 'And you want to put away any thoughts of revenge and leave investigation to the cops.'

'They killed my sister.'

'It hasn't been determined that your sister was a victim of homicide.' Eve headed to the AutoChef, programmed coffee. 'And you're in enough trouble,' she added before he could speak, 'without hassling me.'

'Be smart,' Roarke said when Jamie opened his mouth again. 'Be quiet.'

Peabody stood in the humming silence. She studied the boy, felt a little tug. She had a brother his age. With this in mind, she slapped on a smile. 'Pizza for breakfast,' she said with determined cheer. 'Got more?'

'Help yourself,' Roarke invited and patted the bench beside him in invitation. 'Jamie, this is Officer Peabody.'

'My grandfather knew you.' Jamie studied her with cautious, appraising eyes.

'Did he?' Peabody picked up a slice. 'I don't think I ever met him. I knew about him, though. Everybody at Central was sorry when he died.'

'He knew about you. He told me Dallas was molding you.'

'Peabody's a cop,' Eve broke in, 'not a lump of clay.' Annoyed, she picked up the last slice of pizza, bit in. 'This is cold.'

'It's great cold.' Peabody winked at Jamie. 'Nothing better than cold pizza for breakfast.'

'Eat while you can.' Respecting her own advice, Eve took another bite. 'It's going to be a long day.' She pinned Jamie with a glance. 'Starting now. Until you have a guardian or representative present, I can't record your statement or officially question you. Do you understand?'

'I'm not an idiot. And I'm not a child. I can—'

'You can be quiet,' Eve interrupted. 'With or without representation, I can toss you into juvenile lockup for trespassing. If Roarke chooses to press charges—'

'Eve, really—'

'You be quiet, too.' She rounded on him, all frustration and fatigue. 'This isn't a game, it's murder. And the media is already outside, sniffing blood. You're not going to be able to step outside your own house without having them jump you.'

'Do you think that disturbs me?'

'It disturbs me. It damn well disturbs the hell out of me. My job doesn't come here. It doesn't come here.' She stopped herself, turned away.

This, she realized abruptly, was what ate at her insides, chewed at her control. There was blood on her home, and she had brought it there.

Steadier, she turned back. 'That's all beside the point for now. You have some explaining to do,' she said to Jamie. 'Do you want to do it here or down at Central after I contact your mother?'

He didn't speak for a moment, just watched her as if measuring. It was, she realized, the same look that had been in his eyes when she had told him his sister was dead. It was very adult, very controlled.

'I know who the dead guy is. His name is Lobar, and he's one of the bastards who killed my sister. I saw him.'

Chapter Nine

Jamie's eyes were fierce, furious. Eve kept hers on his as she laid her palms on the table and leaned forward. 'Are you telling me that you saw Lobar kill your sister?'

Jamie's mouth worked as if he was chewing the words, and the words were bitter. 'No. But I know. I know he was one of them. I saw him with her. I saw all of them.' His chin wobbled and his voice cracked, reminding her he was only sixteen. But his eyes stayed ageless. 'I got in one night. In that apartment downtown.'

'What apartment?'

'Spooky Selina and Asshole Alban.' He shrugged a shoulder, but the movement was more nervous than cocky. 'I watched one of their devil shows.' His hand wasn't quite steady as he picked up his drink and sucked down the last of the Pepsi.

'They let you observe a ceremony?'

'They didn't *let* me do anything. They didn't know I was there. You could say I let myself in.' He glanced at Roarke. 'Their security isn't nearly as jazzy as yours.'

'There's good news.'

'You've been a busy boy, Jamie,' Eve said evenly. 'Planning on cat burglary as a career?'

'No.' He didn't smile. 'I'm going to be a cop. Like you.'

Eve blew out a breath, scrubbed her hands over her face, and sat. 'Cops who make a habit of illegal entry end up on the wrong side of a cage.'

'They had my sister.'

'Were they holding her against her will?'

'They messed with her mind. That's the same thing.'

Touchy area, Eve mused. She couldn't go back and stop the kid from breaking into private property. His grandfather had been a solid cop, she remembered, and had tried to do the same. The boy had simply succeeded.

'I'm going to do you a favor because I liked your grandfather. We're going to keep this off the record. As far as the record goes, you were never there. Never inside that place. You got that?'

'Sure.' He jerked a shoulder. 'Whatever.'

'Tell me what you saw. Don't exaggerate, don't speculate.'

Jamie's lips curved a little. 'Grandpa always said that.'

'That's right. You want to be a cop, give me a report.'

'Okay. Cool. Alice was in Weird City, right? She'd been cutting classes, making noises about dropping out. Mom was really wrecked over it. She thought it was a guy, but I knew it wasn't. Not that she was talking to me. She'd stopped talking to me.'

He broke off then, his eyes dark and miserable. Then he shook his head, sighed once, and continued. 'But I knew her. Alice would get all moony over a guy, dreamy-eyed and spastic. But with this, she was different. I figured she'd started experimenting. Illegals. I know my mom had talked to my grandfather, and he'd talked to Alice, but nobody was getting anywhere. So I figured I'd check it out. I followed her a couple times. I thought it would be good practice. Surveillance. She never tagged me. None of them did. A lot of people don't see kids, or if they do, they think they're harmless idiots.'

Eve kept her eyes hard on his face. 'I don't think you're harmless, Jamie.'

His lips twisted in a smirk. He recognized that Eve's statement wasn't exactly flattering. 'So I tailed her to that club. The Athame. First time I had to wait outside. I wasn't prepped for it. She went in about ten, came out about twelve, with the ghoul patrol.'

He smirked again when Eve lifted a brow. 'Okay, subject exited premises in the company of three individuals, two male, one female. You already got their descriptions, so I'll say they were later identified by investigator as Selina Cross, Alban, and Lobar. They proceeded east, on foot, then entered multiunit housing structure owned by Selina Cross. Investigator observed light go on in top window. After weighing the options, investigator decided to enter building. Security was bypassed with minimal to average effort. Can I have another Pepsi?'

Saying nothing, Roarke took the empty tube, slipped it into the recycling slot, and fetched the boy another.

'It was really quiet inside,' Jamie continued as he broke the seal. 'Like dead. Dark. I had a minilight, but I didn't use it. I got upstairs, bypassed the palm plate and the cameras. The locks weren't that tricky. I figure they didn't think anybody'd have the nerve to come that far without an invite, you know? I got inside and the place was empty. I couldn't figure it. I'd seen them go in, I'd seen the light, but the place was empty. So I poked around. They've got some screwy stuff in there. And it smelled . . . off. Sorta like the incense and junk in a Free-Agers' shop, but different. Just off. I was in one of the bedrooms. There's this wild statue in there. This guy with a pig head and a man's body with a really monster cock at full alert.'

He stopped, flushed a little as he remembered he was talking to females as well as cops. 'Sorry.'

'I've seen cocks at full alert before,' Eve said mildly. 'Go on.'

'Okay. So I was just sort of looking at it, and this guy comes in. I thought, *Shit, I'm busted*, but he didn't see me. He got something out of a drawer, turned around, and walked out. Never even looked my way.' Jamie shook his head, sipped deeply, as he reexperienced the bowel-liquefying fear. 'I got to the doorway just as he was going through the wall. Secret panel,' he explained with a quick grin. 'I thought they were only in old videos. I gave it a couple of minutes and went in after him.'

At this, Eve simply pressed her hands to her face, digging her fingers into the knots. 'You went in after him.'

'Yeah, my luck was holding pretty good. There's this stairway, narrow. I think it was stone. I could hear music. Not really music, more like voices, sort of humming. And that off smell was stronger. The stairway turns and there's this room. About half the size of this one, with mirrored walls. Lots of candles and more horny statues. It's smoky. Something's in the smoke, because it makes me light-headed. I try to be careful not to breathe too much in.'

He stared down at the drink in his hand. This part was hard, he realized. Harder than he'd thought it would be. 'There's this raised platform, all this carving. Some sort of words, I think, but I can't make it out. Alice is lying on it. She's naked. The three of them are standing over her saying something. Singing it, I guess, but I can't understand them. They're doing things to her, to each other.'

He had to swallow again. His face was bone white with high, red blotches on the cheeks. 'They've got like sex toys and she's . . . letting them. Both of them. And she lets them, she lets them do her while that Cross bitch watches. Alice just lets them . . .'

Without realizing it, Eve reached out, took his hand, let him grip her fingers hard enough to rub bone.

'I couldn't stay there. I was sick, seeing that, and the smoke, the sounds. I had to get out.' His eyes were wet now as he looked up. 'She wouldn't have let them do that if they hadn't messed with her mind. She wasn't a slut. She wasn't.'

'I know. Did you tell anyone?'

'I couldn't.' He swiped the back of one hand over his face. 'It would've killed my mom. I wanted to hit Alice with it, hit her hard with it. I was so pissed off. But I couldn't. I was embarrassed I'd seen her like that, I guess. My sister.'

126

'It's all right.'

'I went back to the club a couple nights later and got in.'

'They let you inside?'

'I got fake ID. Places like that, they don't care if you look twelve if you got ID that says different. Security's tighter there. They've got scanners, electronic and human, every damn where. I spotted Alice with that Lobar creep. They went upstairs, all the way up to the fancy level. I couldn't get in, but I got close enough to see they'd disappeared again. So I figure there must be a room up there, too. Like the one in the apartment. I was working out a way to get in after hours, then Alice ditched them. She moved in with that Isis character for awhile, got her own place and that job. And she didn't go to the club anymore, or back to the apartment.'

He let out a sigh. 'I thought she'd straightened herself out, that it had gotten through what creeps they were. She talked to me a little.'

'Did she tell you about the people she'd been involved with?'

'Not really. She just said she'd made a mistake, a terrible one. That she was like, atoning, cleansing, that zip brain stuff of hers. I knew she was scared, but she talked to my grandfather, so I figured things would be mellow again. Did they kill him, too?'

'There's no evidence of that. I'm not going to discuss it with you,' she added when he lifted his haunted eyes to hers. 'And you're not to discuss this with anyone. You're not to go near that club or that apartment again. If you do and I find out – and I will find out – I'll slap a security bracelet on you and you won't be able to burp without a scanner picking it up.'

'It's my family.'

'Yes, it is. And if you want to be a cop, you'd better learn that if you can't be objective, you can't do the job.'

'My grandfather wouldn't have been objective,' Jamie said quietly. 'And now he's dead.'

She had no answer for that, so she rose. 'Now the problem is getting you out of here and keeping your involvement out of the media. They'll be watching the gate.'

'There's always an alternative,' Roarke commented. 'I'll arrange it.'

She had no doubt he could, and nodded. 'I've got to change, get down to Central. Peabody.' She flicked a meaningful look in Jamie's direction. 'Stand by.'

'Yes, sir.'

'She means guard dog me,' Jamie muttered as Eve and Roarke left the kitchen.

'Yeah.' But Peabody flashed a companionable smile. 'Want another Pepsi?'

'I guess.'

She got up to play with the delivery slot on the fridge, helped herself to a cup of Roarke's magnificent coffee. 'So how long have you wanted to be a cop?'

'For as long as I remember.'

'Me, too.' She settled down to talk shop.

'I'll take him out by air,' Roarke told her as he and Eve cleaned up and changed in the bedroom.

'By air?'

'I've been meaning to take the minichopper out for a spin, anyway.'

'This area isn't zoned for personal choppers.'

Wisely, he disguised a laugh with a cough. 'Say that again when you're wearing your badge.'

She muttered to herself and pulled on a clean shirt. 'Take him home, will you? I appreciate it. The kid's lucky to be alive.'

'He's resourceful, bright, focused.' Roarke smiled as he picked up the jammer, admired it. 'Now, if I'd had one of these at his age . . . ah, the possibilities.'

'You do well enough with your magic fingers.'

'True.' He tucked the jammer in his pocket. He was going to

have one of his engineers analyze and very possibly reproduce it. 'I'm afraid youth today doesn't appreciate the satisfaction of hands on. If young Jamie changes his mind about law enforcement, I think I could find a nice slot for him in my little world.'

'Don't even mention it. You'll corrupt him.'

Roarke picked up his slim gold wrist unit, fastened it on. 'You did very well with him. Firm without being cold. A nice, authoritative, yet maternal style.'

She blinked. 'Huh?'

'You're good with children.' He grinned as she paled.

'I'd wondered.'

'Get a grip. A good strong grip,' she advised and strapped on her weapon harness. 'I'm going to hit Central first, file my report, feed Whitney the data that's not going into it. Officially, Jamie's name isn't going to be linked with this. I'm sure, if necessary, the two of you can work out a plausible story for his mother.'

'Child's play,' Roarke said with tongue in cheek.

'Hmm. From my prelim, Lobar was killed at oh three thirty. That would be about an hour after we left the club. Hard to tell how long he'd been propped outside the gate, but at a guess, no more than fifteen minutes or so before Jamie happened on him. It's not likely that whoever left Lobar hanging, let's say, stuck around. But if they did, and spotted Jamie, he could be a target. I want the kid under surveillance, and until Whitney uncuffs me, I can't use a cop.'

'Would you like me to put one of my trusted employees on him?'

'No, but that's what I'm going to ask you to do.' She turned to the mirror, raked fingers through her hair in lieu of a comb. 'I'm bringing this home, too many angles of it. I'm sorry.'

He walked to her, turned her around, caught her face in his hands. 'You can't separate what you do from who you are. I don't expect or want you to. What touches you, touches me. That's what I expect and what I want.'

'The last case that touched me almost killed you.' She wrapped her hands around his wrist, squeezed. 'I need you too much. It's your own fault.'

'Exactly.' He bent down, kissed her. 'That's what I want as well. Go to work, Lieutenant.'

'I'm going.' She strode to the door, paused, glanced back. 'I don't want to hear from Traffic that my husband was hotdogging the skyways in his minichopper.'

'You won't. I bribe too well.'

It made her laugh as she headed back down to fetch Peabody and face the first media onslaught.

She'd no more than strapped into her vehicle when she heard the throaty purr of an expensive engine. Wincing only a little, she glanced east and saw the sleek little copter with its tinted one-way glass cabin and whirling silver blades rise, circle playfully – and illegally – before bulleting off.

'Wow! What a machine. Is that Roarke's? Have you been up?' Peabody craned her head to try to get a last look. 'That is one rapid mother.'

'Shut up, Peabody.'

'I've never been up in a personal.' With a wistful sigh, Peabody settled. 'Makes the units Traffic use look like dog meat.'

'You used to be intimidated when I told you to shut up.'

'Those were the good old days.' Grinning, Peabody crossed her ankles. 'You handled the kid really well, Lieutenant.'

Eve rolled her eyes. 'I know how to interview a cooperative witness, Peabody.'

'Not everybody can handle a teenager. They're brutal, and fragile. That one's seen more than anyone should.'

'I know.' So had she by that age, Eve remembered. Perhaps that's why she'd understood. 'Prepare yourself, Peabody. The sharks are circling.'

Peabody grimaced at the pack of reporters crowded outside the gate. There were minicams, recorders, and hungry looks. 'Gee, I hope they get my best side.'

'Tough when you're sitting on it.'

'Thanks. I've been working out.' Automatically, Peabody wiped off the grin and assumed a blank, professional expression. 'I don't see Nadine,' she murmured.

'She's around.' Eve hit the remote for the gates. 'Furst wouldn't miss this one.' She timed it, opening the gates seconds before the nose of the car would have brushed iron. Reporters streamed forward, engulfing the car, aiming their cameras, shouting their questions. One or two were ballsy or stupid enough to step onto private property. Eve took note, switched the volume on her outside speakers to blast.

'The investigation is ongoing,' she announced. 'There will be an official statement at noon. Any media representative who trespasses on this property will not only be prosecuted but will be blocked from all data.'

She all but slammed the gates on scrambling feet. 'Where the hell are the uniforms I left on duty?'

'Probably eaten alive by now.' Peabody stared through the reporter who plastered himself against her side of the windshield. 'This one's kind of cute, Lieutenant. Try not to damage his face.'

'His choice.' She kept driving. Someone bounced off her fender and cursed. There was a slight bump, and a very loud scream.

'That's ten points for the foot,' Peabody commented, secretly thrilled. 'See if you can swipe that one there. The woman with the yard of legs in the green suit. That'll get you five more.'

The reporter clinging to the windshield slid off as Eve juggled the wheel. 'Missed her. Well, can't win them all.'

'Peabody.' Eve shook her head, hit the accelerator, and headed downtown. 'Sometimes I worry about you.'

She wanted to see Whitney first, but wasn't surprised to find Nadine waiting in ambush at the first-level interior glide at Central.

'Busy night, Dallas.'

'That's right, and I'm still busy. There'll be a press release by noon.'

'You can give me something now.' Nadine elbowed her way onto the glide. She wasn't a big woman, but she was a sneaky one. You didn't get to be one of the top on-air reporters in the city without some quick moves. 'Just a nibble, Dallas. Something I can take to the public for my ten o'clock bumper.'

'Dead guy,' Eve said shortly, 'identification withheld until next of kin are notified.'

'So you know who he was. Got any leads on who opened his throat?'

'My professional opinion would be someone with a sharp implement,' Eve said dryly.

'Um-hmm.' Nadine's eyes narrowed. 'There's a rumor rolling around that there was a message left at the scene. And that it was a ritual killing.'

Goddamn leaks. 'I can't comment on that.'

'Wait a minute.' At the top of the glide, Nadine took Eve's arm. 'You want me to hold something, you know I'll hold it. Give me something, and let me work.'

Trusting the media was a dicey business, but she'd trusted Nadine before. To their mutual benefit. As a research tool, Eve knew Nadine was a finely honed instrument. 'If it was a ritual killing, which is not substantiated and not for broadcast, my next step would be to gather all pertinent data on established cults and their members – registered and otherwise – in the city.'

'There are all kinds of cults, Dallas.'

'Then you'd better get busy.' She shook her arm free before dropping one more crumb. 'Funny, cult must be the root word for occult. Or maybe it's just a coincidence.'

'Maybe it is.' Nadine swung to the downward glide. 'I'll let you know.'

'That was tidy,' Peabody decided.

'Let's hope it stays that way. I'm for Whitney. I want you

132

to find out the names of every uniform that was on scene this morning. I want to have a talk about internal security with every one of them.'

'Ouch.'

'Damn right,' Eve muttered and stalked to the elevator.

Whitney didn't make her wait. She noted as she took her seat in his office that he didn't appear to have slept any more than she the night before.

'Internal Affairs is beefing on the Wojinski matter. They're pushing for an official investigation.'

'You can't hold them off.'

'Not past end of shift today.'

'My report should help.' She took a disc out of her bag. 'There is absolutely no evidence that DS Wojinsky was using illegals. There's every indication that he was running his own sting on Selina Cross. His reasons were personal, Commander, but even IAD should understand them. I have Alice's statement, recorded, and fully transcribed in the report. In my opinion, she had been drugged, and her . . . naïveté exploited. She was used sexually. She became involved with the cult established by Selina Cross and Alban. And when she broke with them, she was threatened, and she was frightened. Eventually, she went to Frank.'

'Why did she break loose?'

'She claims she witnessed the ritual slaying of a child.'

'What?' His knuckles went white as he surged up from his desk. 'She witnessed a murder, reported this to Frank, and he didn't file?'

'She waited some time before telling him, Commander. There was no evidence to support her allegations. I can't substantiate them now. But I can say that Alice believed she saw the killing. And she was terrified for her life. She also felt she was responsible for the death of her grandfather. She believed, strongly, that he had been murdered because of his private investigation of Selina Cross. Her claim was that Selina Cross has expert knowledge of chemicals and essentially poisoned Frank.'

'We don't have enough to prove foul play.'

'Not yet. Alice was certain she would be next, and she died the same night she gave her statement to me. She also claimed Cross was a shape-shifter.'

'Excuse me?'

'She believed that Cross could take other forms. A raven, for one.'

'She thought Cross could become a crow and fly? Jesus, Dallas, the boys in IAD are going to love that one.'

'It doesn't have to be real for her to have believed it. She was a terrified young girl, tormented by these people. I found a black feather on her windowsill the night she died – a simulated feather, and there was a threatening message on her 'link. They were tormenting her, Commander. There's no mistake there. What Frank did, he did to try to protect his family. Maybe he went about it wrong, but he was a good cop. He died a good cop. IAD isn't going to change that.'

'We'll make sure they don't.' He locked the disc away. 'For now, this stays here.'

'Feeney—'

'Not at this time, Lieutenant.'

Damn if she'd be brushed off like a fly, she thought, and set her jaw. 'Commander, my investigation to this point discloses absolutely no connection between DS Wojinski's private investigation and Captain Feeney. I can find no evidence that Feeney tampered with any records for Frank.'

'Do you actually believe Feeney would leave evidence, Dallas?'

She kept her eyes level. 'I'd know if he was involved. He's grieving for both his friend and his goddaughter, and he doesn't know anything other than the official line on either. He doesn't know, Commander, and he has a right to.'

It was going to cost them, Whitney knew. All of them. But it couldn't be helped. 'I can't take his personal rights into consideration, Lieutenant. Believe me, IAD won't. All data here is on need-to-know only. It's a rough spot. You'll have to handle it.'

It ate a hole in her gut, but she nodded. 'I'll handle it.'

'What connection is this to the body left outside your home this morning?'

Left with no choice, she fell back on training and delivered data. 'Robert Mathias, known as Lobar, white male, eighteen years. My report on cause of death is the throat wound, but the body was also mutilated. The victim was a member of Cross's cult. I also interviewed him last night at his place of employment. A club called The Athame, owned by Selina Cross.'

'People you talk to are ending up dead very quickly, Dallas.'

'He was Cross's alibi for the night Alice was killed. Hers and Alban's. He corroborated this during questioning.' She opened her bag. 'He wasn't killed at the scene, and he was left there in a manner designed to indicate a ritual killing.' She placed one of the death stills on Whitney's desk.

'The murder weapon was likely the knife he's got stuck in his groin. It's an athame – a ritual knife. Supposedly, Wiccans dull the blade and use it only for symbolism.' She took out another shot, a close-up of the note. 'The message appears to indicate the murder was done by an enemy of the Church of Satan.'

'Church of Satan,' Whitney muttered. The death photo didn't sicken him, it tired him. He'd seen far too many. 'The ultimate oxymoron. Someone took a dislike to the practices and took him out.'

'The scene was set that way. It's possible, and I've got a couple of lines I can tug on that angle.'

He looked up from the photo. 'You're thinking Cross had a hand in this. She'd execute her own alibi.'

'She'd execute her own progeny if she had any. I think she's smart,' Eve continued. 'And I think she's crazy. I'll be consulting with Mira on that end. But I also think she'd get a real bang out of doing this, out of rubbing it in my face. She didn't need him anymore. I had his statement.'

Whitney nodded, pushed the photos back to her. 'Talk to her again. And this Alban.'

'Yes, sir.' She put the photos away. 'There's more. It's . . . delicate.'

'What?'

'I've deleted any reference to this from the official report. Slightly altered the timing. For the record, Roarke and I were awakened by the security alarm, which was tripped when the body was placed against the perimeter wall. Off the record, we didn't discover the body initially. Jamie Lingstrom did.'

'Jesus,' Whitney said after a long minute. He pressed his fingers over his eyes. 'How?'

Eve cleared her throat and gave a quick and concise report of everything that took place after the alarm. She concluded with what Jamie had told her at the breakfast table.

'I don't know how much of that you want to feed to IAD. Jamie's statement corroborates Alice's contention that Frank was trying to trap Cross.'

'I'll filter out what I can.' He continued to rub his eyes. 'First his granddaughter, now his grandson.'

'I think I shook him enough to keep him in line.'

'Dallas, teenagers are remarkably hard to shake. I've been there.'

'I do want him to have some protection, as well as surveillance. Using my own judgment, I'm arranging for this privately.'

Whitney lifted a brow. 'You mean Roarke's arranging it?'

Eve folded her hands. 'The boy will be watched.'

'We'll leave it at that.' He leaned back. 'A homemade, hand-held jammer, you said? One the kid jerry-rigged that managed to bypass the outer layers of the security on that fortress you live in?'

'So it would seem.'

'Where is it? You didn't give it back to him.'

'I'm not an idiot,' she said as if she'd been slapped on the wrist. 'Roarke has it.' And as she completed the sentence, and the thought, her training slipped enough for her to wince.

'Roarke has it.' Despite the situation, Whitney threw back his head and laughed. 'Oh that's rich. You gave the wolf the key to the henhouse.' He caught her narrow-eyed scowl and muffled the next chuckle. 'Just trying for a little levity, Lieutenant.'

'Yes, sir. Ha ha. I'll get it back.'

'No offense, Dallas, but if you're taking bets, I've got a hundred I'll put on Roarke. In any case, unofficially, the department appreciates his assistance and cooperation.'

'You'll excuse me if I don't relay that. It'll only go to his head.' Recognizing dismissal, she rose. 'Commander, Frank was clean. IAD is going to confirm that. Whether his death was of natural causes or induced is going to be more difficult to establish. I could use Captain Feeney.'

'You know you don't need Feeney on this, Dallas, not in an investigative sense. I appreciate your feelings, but this stays here until further notice. You might find yourself sitting in this chair one day,' he said and watched her brow furrow in surprise. 'Difficult decisions sit here with you. And giving unpleasant orders is every bit as frustrating as taking them. Keep me posted.'

'Yes, sir.' She walked out, knowing that she didn't want his chair, his rank, or his responsibilities.

Chapter Ten

Her first duty was to inform Lobar's next of kin. Once it was done, Eve spent a few moments pondering family. They hadn't cared. The woman's face on-screen had stayed blank, as if Eve had informed her of the death of a stranger rather than a son she had birthed and raised. She had thanked Eve politely, asked no questions, agreed that the remains be sent home when released.

They would, she'd said, give him a decent, Christian burial.

She imagined they would have done the same for a family pet.

What calcified the feelings to that extent? she wondered. *If there had been feelings to begin with. What made one mother grieve so pitifully, as Alice's mother was, and another take the news of her child's death without a single tear?*

What had her own mother felt on her birth? Had she been happy, or simply relieved to have the nine-month intruder finally evicted from her body?

She had no memory of a mother, not even some shadowy female form in her life. Only of her father, of the man who had dragged her from place to place, kept her in locked rooms. Who had raped her. And the memories of him, after so many years of denial, were much too clear.

Perhaps some people were fated to survive without family, she thought. *Or simply to survive them.*

Because her thoughts were dark, it was with mixed feelings she called Dr Mira's office for a consultation. After she'd managed to intimidate Mira's assistant into squeezing her in the next day, she grabbed her bag, beeped Peabody, and headed out.

She didn't miss Peabody's wary expression as they pulled up in front of Selina's apartment, but she ignored it. It was starting to rain, a nasty, surprisingly cold drip out of suddenly leaden skies. The wind was up, whistling down the long canyon of street and biting where it struck exposed flesh.

On the opposite sidewalk, a man rushed east, huddled under a black umbrella. He turned quickly into a shop with a grinning skull and the words The Arcane painted on the door.

'Perfect day to pay a visit to Satan's handmaid.' Peabody strained for false cheer and surreptitiously fingered a bit of Saint-John's-wort she'd stuck in her pocket. Her mother's advice for protection against black magic. The stalwart Peabody had discovered she believed in witches after all.

They went through the same routine with security, only the wait was longer and more unpleasant as the rain began to stream down in earnest. Nasty forks of lightning jabbed at the sky, their tines bright bloodred at the edges.

Eve glanced up, then back at her aide. Her smile was hard and cold. 'Yeah, perfect.'

They trailed water into the lobby, into the elevator, and into the foyer of Selina Cross's apartment.

And it was Alban who greeted them. 'Lieutenant Dallas.' He offered a beautifully sculptured hand graced with a single ring of thick brushed silver. 'I'm Alban, Selina's companion. I'm afraid she's meditating at the moment. I hesitate to disturb her.'

'Let her meditate. You'll do for now.'

'Well then, come in and sit down. Please.' His manner was sophisticated, faintly formal, and at odds with the barechested black leather unisuit he wore. 'Can I get you something? Some tea perhaps to ward off the chill. Such an interesting change in the weather.'

'Nothing.' Eve thought she'd have preferred a quick hit of Zeus to anything brewed in that place.

The gloom suited it, she decided. *The dank light, the wicked hiss of rain and wind on the windows. Then there was Alban, with his pretty poet's face and warrior god body. A perfect fallen angel.*

'I'd like your whereabouts for last night between the hours of three hundred and five hundred hours.'

'Three and five A.M.?' He blinked as if translating the military time. 'Last night – or this morning, rather. Why, here. I think we got back from the club a bit before two. We haven't been out yet today.'

'We?'

'Selina and myself. We had a coven meeting, which concluded around three. We cut it a little short as Selina wasn't feeling herself. Normally, we might entertain afterwards, or continue with a smaller, more private rite.'

'But you didn't do so last night.'

'No. As I said, Selina wasn't feeling well, so we went to bed early. Early for us,' he explained with a smile. 'We're night people.'

'Who attended the coven meeting?'

His smile shifted into a serious, almost studious expression. 'Lieutenant, religion is a private matter. And still in this day and age, one such as ours is persecuted. Our membership prefers discretion.'

'One of your membership was indiscreetly murdered last night.'

'No.' He rose, slowly, keeping his hand braced on the arm of his chair as if unsteady. 'I knew it was something horrible. She was so disturbed.' He took a deep breath as if preparing both mind and body. 'Who?'

'Lobar.' Selina said the name as she stepped through a narrow archway. She was deathly pale, her cat's eyes shadowed. She wore her black hair loose today, with a wide dip over generous breasts. 'It was Lobar,' she repeated. 'I saw it just now, in the smoke. Alban.' She pressed a hand to her head, swayed.

140

'Quite a show,' Eve murmured as Alban rushed across the room to catch her, to hold her against him. 'You saw it in the smoke.' Eve cocked her head. 'That's handy. Maybe I should take a look at the smoke myself, see who cut his throat.'

'There's nothing in the smoke for you but your own ignorance.' Leaning on Alban, Selina walked slowly to the sofa. She sat with a rustle of her robes, lifted a hand to Alban's. 'I'm all right.'

'My love.' He brought her hand to his lips. 'I'll get you a soother.'

'Yes, yes, thank you.'

She bowed her head while he went quietly out. Oh, it was hard to keep a cat grin off her face, to stop the glorious images from playing back in her brain of the rite, the sacrifice, the blood.

And only she and Alban knew of the excitement, the power of that moment when Lobar had been offered to the master.

Only she fully understood the thrill of making that sacrifice with her own hand. She shuddered once with dark pleasure, stirred by the memory. The way Lobar's eyes had met hers, the way the athame had fit cold in her hand. Then the hot fountain of blood when she'd used it.

Imagining the shock, the fury Eve must have felt when she'd found Lobar so carefully positioned at the entrance to her own sanctuary, Selina nearly snickered. She pressed her fingers to her lips a moment, as if holding back a sob.

Alban was a genius, she thought, for truly only a genius would have created such beautiful irony.

'Visions can be a blessing or a curse.' She continued in a voice strained with weariness. 'I prefer to think of them as blessings, even when they cause me sorrow. Lobar is a heavy loss.'

'Laying it thick, aren't you?'

Selina's head shot up, and her eyes glimmered with something more of hate than grief. 'Don't mock my feelings, Dallas. Do you think power such as mine means I don't have them? I feel, I experience. I bleed,' she added and, with a lightning movement, raked one of her long, lethal nails over her own palm. Blood welled dark and red.

'A demonstration wasn't necessary,' Eve said easily. 'I know you bleed. Lobar certainly did.'

'His throat. Yes, that's what I saw in the smoke.' She reached out for Alban when he came in, carrying a shallow silver bowl. 'But there was more. Something else.' She took the bowl, tipped it up to her lips. 'Mutilation. Oh, how they despise us.'

'They?'

'The weak and the white.'

She took a black swatch of cloth from the pocket of her robe, passed it to Alban. He lifted her injured hand, raised it to his lips. With quick efficiency, he bound up her wounded palm. Selina never spared him a glance.

'Those who view our master with hate,' she continued. 'And more, those who practice the magic of the foolish.'

'So, in your opinion, this was a religious murder?'

'Of course; I have no doubt.' She finished the soother, set the bowl aside. 'Do you?'

'Quite a number of them; but then, I have to investigate the old-fashioned way. I can't call up the devil and ask for a consult. Lobar was here last night.'

'Yes, until nearly three. He would have taken the mark soon.' Selina sighed, idly running her red-tipped nails up and down Alban's arm. 'One of his last acts was to join his body with mine.'

'You had sex with him last night.'

'Yes. Sex is an important part of our rituals. I chose him last night.' She shuddered again because the choice had been hers. And the deed. 'Something must have told me.'

'A bird maybe. A big black bird.' Lifting a brow, Eve studied Alban. 'So, it's no problem with you to watch while other men have sex with your . . . companion. Most men are a little territorial. They might harbor unhealthy resentments.'

142

'We don't believe in monogamy. We find it limiting and foolish. Sex is pleasure, and we don't put restrictions on our pleasures. Consensual sex in a private home or licensed club isn't against your laws, Lieutenant.' He smiled. 'I'm sure you engage in it yourself.'

'You like to watch, Alban?'

His brows lifted. 'Is that an invitation?' At Selina's quick chuckle, he shifted and took her hand. 'There, you're feeling better now.'

'Grief passes, doesn't it, Selina?'

'It must,' she agreed, nodding at Eve. 'Life is to be lived. You'll look for who did this, and perhaps you'll find them. But the punishment of our master is greater and more terrible than any you could invent.'

'Your master isn't my concern. Murder is. Since you have an interest in the deceased, maybe you'll let me take a look around.'

'Get a warrant, and you're welcome.' The tranq had clouded her eyes, but her voice was strong enough when she stood. 'You're more a fool than I originally thought if you believe I had anything to do with this. He was one of ours. He was loyal. It is against the law to harm a loyal member of the cult.'

'And he talked to me last night in a privacy booth. Did the smoke tell you what he told me, Selina?'

Her eyes shifted, darkened. 'You'll have to find other waters to fish in, Dallas. I'm tired, Alban. Show them out.' She glided a way, back through the arch.

'There's nothing we can do for you, Lieutenant. Selina needs to rest.' He glanced toward the arch, worry in his eyes. 'I need to tend her.'

'Got you trained, does she?' With light disdain coating her voice, Eve rose. 'Do you do tricks, too?'

Sadly, he shook his head. 'My devotion to Selina is personal. She has powers, and the powerful have needs. I meet hers, gratefully.' He walked back into the foyer, opened the door.

'We would like to take Lobar's body when it's possible. We have our death ceremony.'

'So does his family, and they come ahead of you.'

'What do we have on this Alban?' Eve demanded the moment they were outside in the now drenching rain.

'Next to nothing.' Peabody ducked into the car and immediately felt more at ease. She knew it was foolish to hope she never had to go back inside that building, but she hoped in any case. 'No priors, next to no background. If he was born with a name other than Alban, it doesn't pop.'

'There's more. There's always more.'

Not so, Eve thought, drumming her fingers against the wheel. She'd once investigated another suspicious character and had found little to nothing. His only name was Roarke.

'Look again,' she ordered and pulled away from the curb.

'Funny, isn't it?' she continued while Peabody plugged in her data unit. 'There's next to no traffic on this block. Turn the corner . . .' She did so and immediately hit a snarl of nasty and comforting vehicular traffic, bumping bad-temperedly through the rain. People hustled along sidewalks and glides, huddled in doorways. Two glide-cart operators on opposing corners hunched under ratty awnings and scowled at each other.

'People have instincts they're not even aware of.' Still less than comfortable, Peabody glanced back, as if expecting something not quite human might be scrabbling behind them. 'There's a bad feeling around that building.'

'It's brick and glass.'

'Yeah, but places tend to take on the personalities of the people who live in them.'

A car turned the corner ahead, blasting its horn at the sea of pedestrians who streamed across against the go light. Insults were cheerfully hurled both verbally and through equally graphic hand signals. Someone spat.

Steam poured up through the vents from the underground

system in dirty clouds. It tangled thickly with the smoke belching from a ratty and obviously under code glida grill fighting its way through the mass of wet humanity. A level up, the nearest skywalk shuddered to a halt and sent all its passengers into a riot of cursing and complaints.

Overhead, a tourist blimp blasted out a spiel of the advantages and highlights of living in an urban wonderland.

Peabody took a cleansing breath, pleased to be back in the midst of the arrogant and crowded New York she understood. 'Take Roarke's place,' she continued. 'It's grand and elegant and intimidating, but it's also sexy and mysterious.' She was too busy fiddling with the unit to notice the amused look Eve shot her. 'My parents' place? It's all open and warm and a little confused.'

'What about your place, Peabody? What's that?'

'Temporary,' Peabody said definitely. 'Dallas, your car unit isn't cooperating here. I should be able to transfer data to—' She broke off as Eve leaned over, smacked the dash above the car screen. An image popped on, wobbling drunkenly. 'That's some better,' Peabody decided and requested a run on Alban.

Alban – no known alternate name – born 3–22–2020 Omaha, Nebraska.

'Funny,' Eve interrupted, 'he didn't look corn fed.'

ID number, the computer continued with a definite hiccup in its program, 31666-LRT-99. Parents unknown. Marital status, single. No known means of support. No financial data available.

'Interesting. Sounds like he's leeching off Selina. Criminal records, all arrests.'

No criminal record.

'Education?'

Unknown.

'Our boy's wiped, or had somebody wipe records,' Eve told Peabody. 'You don't get to be nearly forty years old without generating more data than this. He's got connections somewhere.'

She needed Feeney, she thought grumpily. Feeney could tickle the computer and trick additional data. Instead, she was going to have to go to Roarke and add another layer to his involvement.

'Well, shit.' She pulled up in front of Spirit Quest, frowned at the Closed sign on the door. 'Run up for a look-see, Peabody. Maybe she's inside.'

'Got an umbrella or a rain shield?'

Eve arched a brow. 'Are you trying to be funny?'

Peabody only sighed, then pushed out of the car. She plodded and splashed through the rain, peered into windows. Shivering a little, she turned back, shook her soaking head, then groaned when Eve jerked a thumb toward the apartment over the shop. Resigned, Peabody trudged around the side, climbed a set of rickety metal stairs. Moments later, she was back, streaming water.

'No answer,' she told Eve. 'Minimal security. Unless you count the swatch of Saint-John's-wort over the entrance.'

'She has a swatch of warts? That's disgusting.'

'Not warts.' Despite her wet uniform and dripping hair, Peabody indulged in a good laugh. 'It's a plant. Saint-John's-wort.' Amused enough, she dug into her pocket for her sprig. 'Like this. It's for protection. Guards against evil.'

'You carry plants in your pocket, Officer?'

146

'I do now.' Peabody pushed it back in her pocket. 'Want some?'

'No, thanks, I prefer trusting my weapon to guard against evil.'

'I consider this my clutch piece.'

'Whatever works for you.' Eve scanned the area. 'Let's try that café place across the street. Maybe they know why she's closed in the middle of a business morning.'

'Maybe they've got decent coffee,' Peabody said and sneezed twice, hard. 'If I catch a cold, I'll kill myself. It takes me weeks to throw one of those suckers off.'

'Maybe you need a plant to cart around that wards off common germs.' Leaving it at that, Eve hopped out of the car, coded the locks, and jogged across the street into Coffee Ole.

The stab at a Mexican theme wasn't bad, she decided. Bright colors – heavy on orange – gave it a sunny appearance even on a filthy day. It might have fallen far short of Roarke's gorgeous villa on the west coast of Mexico, but it had a certain tacky charm with its plastic flowers and papier-mâché bulls. Bright mariachi music piped through the speakers.

Either the rain or the ambiance had brought in a crowd. But as Eve scanned the room, she noted that the people packed around tables weren't wolfing down plates of enchiladas. Most were huddled over single stingy cups of what smelled remotely like overboiled soy coffee.

'Baseball's closing in on the league titles, isn't it, Peabody?'

Peabody sneezed again. 'Baseball? I guess. Arena ball's my game.'

'Uh-huh. Seems to me there a pennant race going on. Pivotal game today. I imagine lots of money's going to change hands.'

Peabody's head was starting to feel stuffy – a very bad sign – but it was still clear enough for her to latch on. 'You figure this is a front, an illegal betting parlor.'

'Just a hunch. We may be able to use it.' She sidled up to the counter, tagged a harassed-looking man. Short of stature, dark of complexion, weary of eye.

'Eat in or carry out?'

'Neither,' she began, then relented as she heard Peabody sniffle. 'One coffee, for her. And a couple of answers.'

'I've got coffee.' He swiveled around to plug thick dark brew into a cup barely bigger than a thimble. 'I got no answers.'

'Maybe you should hear the questions.'

'Lady, I got a full house here. I serve coffee. I got no time for conversation.' He dumped the cup on the counter and would have backed away, but Eve snagged his wrist. 'What are the house odds on the game today?'

His eyes shifted left and right before settling on her face. But he'd spotted Peabody and her uniform. 'Don't know what you're talking about.'

'You know, if me and my pal here settle in for a few hours, your business is going into the recycler. Personally, I don't give a good damn about your business, any of your business. But I could.' Still holding his wrist, she turned her head and stared hard at two of the men seated at the counter.

It took less than ten seconds for them to decide to drink coffee elsewhere. 'How long do you think it'd take me to clear this place out?'

'What do you want? I make my contribution. I'm covered.'

She let him go. It annoyed her to find out that he had cop protection. Didn't surprise her, just annoyed. 'I'm not going to interfere unless you irritate me. Tell me about the shop across the street. Spirit Quest.'

He snorted, visibly relaxed. She wasn't after him. Feeling cooperative, he refilled Peabody's cup, then picked up a rag and wiped the counter. He ran a clean place. 'The witch? She don't come in here. Don't drink coffee, if you know what I mean.'

148

'She's closed today.'

'Yeah?' He narrowed his eyes to try to see through the window, through the rain. 'Not usually.'

'When did you see her last?'

'Shit.' He scratched the back of his neck. 'Let's see. Seems I saw her yesterday. Closing time? Yeah, yeah, she closes about six, and I was washing the front windows. You gotta keep on the windows in this city. Dirt just jumps right on them.'

'I bet. She closed about six. Then what?'

'Went off with that guy she lives with. Walking. They don't got transpo.'

'You haven't seen her today?'

'Now that you mention it, guess not. She lives up above, you know. Me, I live across town. Keep business and personal life separate, that's my motto.'

'Any of her people ever come over here?'

'Nah. Some of her customers, sure. And some of mine go over there looking for lucky charms. We bump along okay. She ain't no problem for me. Even bought the wife a birthday present over there. Pretty little bracelet, colored stones. Kinda stiff in the price, but women like that glitter shit.'

He tossed the rag aside and ignored the request for coffee from down the counter. 'Look, she in trouble? She's okay in my book. Weird maybe, but ain't no harm in her.'

'What do you know about the girl who used to work there? Young girl, about eighteen. Blonde.'

'The spooky one? Sure, I used to see her come and go. Always looking over her shoulder that one, like somebody was going to jump out and say boo.'

Someone did, Eve thought. 'Thanks. If you see Isis come back today, give me a call.' She slipped a card onto the counter along with credits for the coffee.

'No problem. Wouldn't like to see her get in trouble, though. She's okay for a whacko. Hey.' He lifted a finger as Eve started to turn. 'Speaking of whackos, I saw one a couple of nights ago when I was closing up.'

'What sort of whacko?'

'Just a guy. Well, might have been a woman. Couldn't tell 'cause they was all wrapped up in this black robe, hood and everything. Just standing there on the curb, staring across the street at her place. Just standing and staring. Gave me the creeps. I walked the other way. Twice as far to the bus stop, but I didn't like the feel of it. And you know what? I looked back, and there wasn't no one there. Nothing but a damn cat. Whacko, huh?'

'Yeah,' Eve murmured. 'Whacko.'

'I saw a cat,' Peabody began when they headed back to the car, 'on the street when Alice was killed.'

'There are lots of cats in the city.'

But Eve remembered the one on the ramp. Sleek and black and mean. 'We'll follow up with Isis later. I want to check with the ME before I feed the statement to the media.' She uncoded the car as Peabody sneezed again. 'Maybe he'll have something for that cold.'

Peabody rubbed her hand under her nose. 'I'd just as soon stop by a pharmacy, if you don't mind. I don't want Dr Death treating me until absolutely necessary.'

After she was back in her office and Peabody was off changing into a dry uniform and dosing herself with a small fortune of over-the-counters, Eve studied the autopsy report on Lobar.

She'd had the time of death right in the prelim, and the cause. Then again, she mused, it was tough to miss a mile-wide gash in the throat and a crater in the chest. And, fancy that, there had been traces of a hallucinogen, a stimulant, and a mind hazer – all of the illegals variety – in his bloodstream.

So he'd died sexually fulfilled and zoned. Some, she imagined, would say that wasn't such a bad deal. But then, most of them hadn't had a knife raked over their throats.

She lifted the sealed weapon, studied it. No prints, of course, and none expected. No blood on it but for the victim's. She studied the carved black handle, scanning the symbols and letters that meant nothing to her. It appeared to be old and rare, but she doubted that would help her pin ownership. The blade was under legal limit, required no registration.

Still, she would check antique shops, knife shops, and, she supposed, witch shops. That would only take weeks, she thought in disgust, and was unlikely to lead anywhere.

Since she had twenty minutes before she had to face the media, she turned to her machine and got started. She'd no more than plugged in the description of the weapon when Feeney walked in, shut her door.

'Heard you had a rude awakening this morning.'

'Yeah.' Her stomach clutched, not in memory of what had come into her home, but at knowing she would have to weigh every word with him. 'Not the kind of package I like to receive.'

'You need help on it?' He smiled wanly. 'I'm looking for busywork.'

'I've got it covered for now, but I'll let you know.'

He paced to her narrow window, back to her door. He looked exhausted, she thought. So tired. So sad.

'What's the story? Did you know the guy?'

'Not really.' Oh, Christ, what did she do here? 'I'd talked to him once about a case I was on. Didn't pan out. Could be he knew more than he was telling me. It's going to be hard to say now.' She took a deep breath, hating herself. 'I figure it was someone who wanted to take a swipe at me or Roarke. Most cops can keep their home addresses quiet. I can't.' She shrugged.

'Price you pay for falling for a public figure. You happy?' he said abruptly and turned to study her face.

'Sure.' She wondered if guilt was plastered on her forehead like a neon sign.

'Good. Good.' He paced again, jiggling the bag of nuts he habitually carried in his pocket and no longer seemed to have the appetite for. 'It's tough to be on the job and make a decent personal life. Frank did.'

'I know.'

'Alice's viewing is tonight. You going to make it?'

'I don't know, Feeney. I'll try.'

'It rips me, Dallas. It really rips me. My wife's with Brenda now. She's wrecked. Just wrecked. I couldn't handle it anymore so I came in. But I can't focus.'

'Why don't you go back home, Feeney?' She rose, reached out to touch his arm. 'Jus' go home. Maybe you and your wife could go away for a few days. You've got the time coming. Get away from this.'

'Maybe.' His eyes were bleak, heavy with bags. 'But where do you go to get away from what's always there?'

'Listen, Roarke's got this place in Mexico. It's great.' She was fumbling and knew it, desperate to give. 'It's got a monster view, and it's fully equipped. It would be.' She managed a smile. 'It's Roarke's. I'll square it with him. You can go there, take your family.'

'Take the family.' He repeated it slowly, finding the idea was almost soothing. 'Maybe I will. You never seem to make time to be with your family. I'll think about it,' he decided. 'Thanks.'

'It's nothing. It's Roarke. It's just there.' She turned blindly toward her desk. 'I'm sorry, Freeney, I've got to get it together for a media statement.'

'Sure.' He worked up a smile for her. 'I know how much you love that. I'll let you know about using the place.'

'Yeah, do that.' She stared hard at her screen until he went out. She'd followed orders, she reminded herself. She'd done the right thing.

So why did it make her feel like a traitor?

Chapter Eleven

She made the tail end of the viewing, grateful that Roarke had come with her. It was too familiar, the same memorial parlor, the same scents, many of the same people.

'I hate this,' she murmured. 'Sanitized death.'

'It comforts.'

Eve looked over to where Brenda was supported by her mother and her son while tears ran slowly down her cheeks. She had the glazed and delicate look of the heavily medicated.

'Does it?'

'It closes,' he corrected and took her cold hand in his. 'For some.'

'When it's my turn, don't do this. Recycle the parts, burn the rest. Get it done.'

He felt the fist clutch around his heart and gave her hand a hard squeeze. 'Don't.'

'Sorry. I tend to have morbid thoughts in places like this. Well.' Her room scan stopped when she spotted Isis. 'There's my witch.'

Roarke followed her gaze and studied the imposing woman with flame-colored hair and wearing a simple robe of pure white. She stood by the viewing box beside a man a full head shorter than she. He wore a plain, almost conservative suit, also in white. Their fingers were linked.

'The man with her?'

'I don't know him. Might be a member of her sect or whatever. Let's check it out.'

They moved across the room and by tacit agreement, flanked the couple. Eve looked down at Alice first, at the young face, composed now. Death had a way of relaxing the features. After the insult had passed.

'She's not here.' Isis spoke quietly. 'Her spirit still searches for peace. I'd hoped . . . I'd hoped to find her here. I'm sorry I missed you today, Dallas. We were closed in Alice's memory.'

'You weren't at home, either.'

'No, we gathered at another place, for our own ceremony. The man across the street told me you'd been looking for me.' A faint smile wisped around her mouth. 'He was concerned that I had a cop on my trail. He has a good heart, despite a certain imbalance.'

She stepped back to introduce the man beside her. 'This is Chas. My mate.'

Training kept Eve's eyes bland, but she was surprised. He was as ordinary as Isis was spectacular. His hair was a washed-out blond, thin in texture. His body was almost fragile, narrow in the shoulders, short in the leg. His square, unremarkable face was stopped just short of homely by a pair of surprisingly lovely deep gray eyes. When he smiled, it was with a sweetness that demanded a smile in return.

'I'm sorry to meet you under such sad circumstances. Isis told me you were a very strong and purposeful soul. I see she was right, as always.'

She nearly blinked at his voice. It was a deep, creamy baritone any opera singer would have wept for. She caught herself watching his mouth move and imagining a ventriloquist's dummy. It wasn't a voice that should have come out of that body and that face.

'I need to talk to you both as soon as possible.' She glanced around, wished for a discreet way to slip out and conduct an interview. It would have to wait. 'This is Roarke.'

'Yes, I know.' Isis offered a hand. 'We've met before.'

'Have we?' His smile was politely curious. 'I can't imagine forgetting meeting a beautiful woman.'

'Another time, another place.' Her eyes stayed on his. 'Another life. You saved mine once.'

'That was wise of me.'

'Yes, it was. And kind. Perhaps someday you'll revisit the county of Cork and see a small stone dance alone in a fallow field . . . and you'll remember.' She slipped the silver cross she wore off her neck, handed it to him. 'You gave me a talisman then. Similar to this Celtic cross. I suppose that's why I wore it tonight. To close a circle.'

The metal was warmer against his hand than it should have been, and it stirred something in cloudy memory he didn't care to explore. 'Thank you.' He slipped it into his pocket.

'One day I may return the favor you did me.' She turned to Eve then. 'I'll speak with you whenever you like. Chas?'

'Of course, whenever it's convenient for you, Lieutenant Dallas. Will you attend our ceremony? We'd very much like to share it with you. Night after next. We have a small place upstate. It's quiet and private and, when the weather cooperates, perfect for outdoor rites. I hope you—'

He broke off, his stunning eyes going dark. His thin body shifting to what Eve recognized immediately as a guard stance. 'He's not one of us,' he said.

She glanced around, spotted a man in a dark suit. His face was cell-block white and framed by a black wedge of hair. The suit was expensive, his skin wan, making him appear both sickly and successful.

He started toward the viewing box, saw the group already there. In one jerky move he turned on his heel and hurried out.

'I'll check it out.'

She was moving quickly when Roarke caught up with her. 'We'll check it out.'

'It would be better if you stayed inside with them.'

'I'm staying with you.'

She only shot him a frustrated look. 'Don't cramp my style.'

'Wouldn't dream of it.'

The retreating man was nearly at a run as he hit the door. Eve only had to touch his arm to have him jolt. 'What? What do you want?' He whirled, pressing the door for release, backing out of it into the rainy night. 'I haven't done anything.'

'No? He sure looks guilty for an innocent man, doesn't he?' She took a firmer grip on his arm to keep him from rabbiting away. 'Maybe you should show me some ID.'

'I don't have to show you anything.'

'It's not necessary,' Roarke said smoothly. He'd gotten a better look now. 'Thomas Wineburg, isn't it? Of Wineburg Financial. You've nabbed yourself a deadly type here, Lieutenant. A banker. Third generation. Or is it fourth?'

'It's fifth,' Wineburg said, struggling to look down his narrow nose at what his family would consider new and not quite decent money. 'And I've done nothing to warrant being accosted by a police officer and a financial rogue.'

'I'm the cop,' Eve decided glancing at Roarke. 'You must be the financial rogue.'

'He's just mad because I don't use his bank.' Roarke flashed a wolfish grin. 'Aren't you, Tommy?'

'I have nothing to say to you.'

'Well, then, you can talk to me. What's the rush?'

'I – I have an appointment I'd forgotten. I'm quite late.'

'Then a couple more minutes won't matter. Are you a friend of the deceased's family?'

'No.'

'Oh, I get it, you just like to while away a rainy evening at a viewing parlor. I've heard that's the coming thing for singles.'

'I – I'd mistook the address.'

'I don't think so. What did you come to see? Or who?'

'I—' His eyes widened when Isis and Chas stepped out. 'Stay away from me.'

'I'm sorry, Dallas. We were concerned when you didn't come back.' Isis turned her exotic eyes on Wineburg. 'Your aura is dark and muddy. You dabble without belief. Toy with power beyond your scope. If you don't change your path, you damn yourself.'

'Keep her away from me.' Straining against Eve's grip, Wineburg cringed back.

'She's not hurting you. What do you know about Alice's death, Wineburg?'

'I don't know anything.' His voice went shrill. 'I don't know anything about anything. I mistook the address. I have an appointment. You can't hold me.'

No, she couldn't, but she could scare the hell out of him. 'I could take you down to Central, play with you awhile before your representative managed to get there. Wouldn't that be fun?'

'I haven't done anything.' To Eve's surprise and mild disgust, he began to sob like a baby. 'You have to let me go. I'm not part of this.'

'Part of what?'

'It was just for sex. That's all. Just for sex. I didn't know anybody would die. Blood everywhere. Everywhere. Dear God. I didn't know.'

'Where? What have you seen?'

He continued to sob, and when she started to shift her grip, he rammed his bony elbow hard into her gut, sending her flying violently back into Roarke so that they both hit the pavement.

Later, she could curse herself for letting him catch her off guard with his sniveling. But for now, she scrambled up, struggling to suck in air and gave chase.

Son of a bitch. She could only think it. He'd knocked the

wind out of her and prevented her from swearing aloud or shouting out an order for him to freeze.

She reached for her weapon just as he dove into an underground garage and darted into the forest of vehicles.

'Shit.' She had enough air for that, then snarled at Roarke as he rushed in behind her. 'Get out. Damn it, he's probably not armed, but you're sure as hell not. Call it in if you want to do something.'

'The day I let a pissant banker knock me on my ass and walk away has not come.' He veered off to circle around and left her scowling at him.

The security lights were blinding, but the opportunity for cover was endless. Echoes of running footsteps bounced off the floor and walls and ceiling. Trusting instinct, she moved left.

'Wineburg, you aren't helping yourself. You've got assaulting an officer on you now. You come out without making me dig you out, I might cut you a break.'

Crouched, she swung toward the narrow opening between cars, scanned under, behind, moved on.

'Roarke, hold still a minute, goddamn it, so I can tag location.' The echoes softened a bit, allowing her to strain her ears and venture farther to the left at running speed. He was heading up, she decided, hoping to lose himself on the next level.

She darted up the first ramp, then whirled and braced, weapon aimed, when footsteps pounded behind her. 'I should have known,' was all she said as Roarke passed her. She dug in and continued pursuit. 'He's heading up,' she snapped out. 'He keeps going, he'll corner himself. All the idiot has to do is stop, lay low. It would take a fucking platoon to find him in here.'

'He's scared. When you're scared, you run away.' He glanced at Eve, and felt ridiculously exhilarated as they hit the next ramp. 'Or some do.'

Then the footsteps silenced. Eve threw out an arm to hold

Roarke in place, held her breath as she strained to hear. 'What is that?' she whispered. 'What the hell is that sound?'

'Chanting.'

Her heart jumped. 'Jesus Christ.' She broke into a fresh run just as one long, terrified scream ripped the air. It seemed to go on, endlessly, high and inhuman and horrible. Then it snapped off into silence. She dragged out her communicator without breaking stride. 'Officer needs assistance. Officer needs assistance, parking garage, Forty-ninth and Second. Dallas, Lieutenant Eve in pursuit of . . . Goddamn it.'

'Dispatch, Dallas, Lieutenant Eve, please say again.'

She didn't bother to stare at the body spread in a growing pool of blood on the concrete floor. One glance at the terrified, wide eyes and the carved hilt of a knife plunged into the heart had been enough to determine death.

Wineburg had run the wrong way.

'I need backup, immediately. I've got a homicide. Perpetrator or perpetrators possibly still on premises. Dispatch all available units to this address for blockade and search. I need a field kit and my aide.'

'Received. Units en route. Dispatch out.'

'I've got to look,' she said to Roarke.

'Understood.'

'I don't have my clutch piece or I'd give it to you. I need you to stay here, with the body.'

Roarke looked down at Wineburg and felt a stir of pity. 'He's not going anywhere.'

'I need you to stay here,' she repeated. 'In case they come back this way. Don't be a hero.'

He nodded. 'You, either.'

She took one last glance at the body. 'Fuck,' she said wearily. 'I should have had a better grip on him.'

She moved off slowly, scanning cars and corners, but without much hope.

He'd watched her work before, studied and admired the efficient, concentrated field she created around the dead. Roarke wondered if she fully understood why she did it, or how she could, while examining a lifeless, violently dispatched body with such clear-cut objectivity, see through the pity that haunted her eyes.

He'd never asked her. He doubted he ever would.

He watched her order Peabody to record the scene from a different angle, saw her jerk her thumb at a uniform – obviously a rookie who wasn't holding up well. Sending him off on an errand, Roarke imagined, so he could be sick in private.

Some of them never got used to the blood or the smell of bladder and bowels releasing with death.

The lights were viciously bright, merciless, really. The heart wound had bled profusely. She'd worn heels and a little black suit to the viewing. Of course, she would ruin both now. She was kneeling beside the body, tearing her stockings on the concrete and removing the murder weapon now that the scene had been duly recorded.

She sealed it, bagged it for evidence, but he'd gotten a good look at it. The handle was a deep brown, possibly horn of some sort. Yet there had been no mistaking its similarity to the one left at the last murder. An athame. The knife of ritual.

'Bad business.'

Roarke made a sound of assent as Feeney walked up to him. The man looked uncharacteristically fragile, Roarke observed. Eve was right to be concerned about him.

'You know anything about it? I'm not getting much buzz except that Dallas was talking to him outside, he ran, and ended up dead.'

'That's about it. He seemed nervous about something. Apparently he had reason to be.' It wasn't a place they could go together, Roarke decided and shifted away from it. 'I hope you'll take Eve up on the offer of the house in Mexico.'

'I'll talk it over with my wife. I appreciate it.' Then he moved his shoulders. 'I guess she doesn't need me here. I should get home.' But he studied the scene another minute. Behind the fatigue in his eyes lurked the cop. 'Screwy business. Some guy getting stuck in here. Fancy knife took out that stiff left at your place last night, too, right?'

'The other had a black handle. Some sort of metal, I think.'

'Yeah, well . . .' He rocked back on his heels a moment. 'I'd better head home.'

He crossed to Eve, careful to avoid getting too close in his untreated shoes. She looked up, distracted, wiping the blood off her sealed hands with a rag.

And she watched him walk away until he was out of sight.

She rose, raked her not quite clean hands through her hair. 'Bag him,' she ordered, and walked to Roarke. 'I'm going to go in, do the report while it's fresh in my mind.'

'All right.' He took her arm.

'No, you should go home. I'll catch a ride with one of the team.'

'I'll take you.'

'Peabody—'

'Peabody can catch a ride with one of the team.' She needed a few minutes, he knew, to decompress. He touched a button on his wrist unit to signal his driver.

'I feel stupid going into Central in a limo,' she muttered.

'Really? I don't.' He walked her out of the garage, then around to the front of the funeral parlor. The limo streamed up to the curb. 'You can catch your breath,' he suggested as he slid in behind her. 'And I can have a brandy.' He poured one from a crystal decanter, and knowing Eve, programmed her coffee.

'Well, since we're going it this way, you can tell me what you know about Wineburg.'

'One of the irritating rich and pampered.'

She took the hot, rich coffee served in a thin, classy cup of bone china, and gave Roarke – his plush limo, his pricey brandy – a long, cool look. 'You're rich.'

'Yes.' He smiled. 'But pampered? Certainly not.' He swirled his brandy, kept smiling. 'That's what stops me from being irritating.'

'You think so?' The coffee helped, got her circuits running. 'So he was a banker. He ran Wineburg Financial.'

'Hardly. His father's still hale and hearty. This little fish would have been more of a minion. The type given busy-work and a useless title and a big office. He'd gobble up his expense account, shuffle forms, and have his cosmetician in for weekly sessions.'

'Okay, you didn't like him.'

'I didn't know him, actually.' He gave the brandy a lazy swirl and sip. 'Just the type. I don't have any business dealings with Wineburg. In the dawn of my . . . career, I needed some backing for a couple of projects. Legal projects,' he added at Eve's speculative look. 'They wouldn't let me in the door. I wasn't up to their level of client. So I went elsewhere, got the backing, and made a killing. Figuratively speaking. The Wineburg organization took it poorly.'

'So they're a conservative, established, family-run institution.'

'Exactly.'

'It would be embarrassing to have the scion . . . Would he be like the scion?'

'If there's such a thing as a minor scion, I suppose.'

'Okay if he was into Satanism, it probably wouldn't go down well at the company picnic.'

'It would turn the board of directors white with shock – and, family or not, this little Wineburg would have been out on his ass.'

'He didn't look like the type to risk it, but you never know. Sex, he said. Just for the sex. He could have been one of the ones who had at Alice. Then he's guilty or curious and comes by the viewing. The one thing he was, was scared. He saw something, Roarke. He saw someone murdered. I know it. If I'd gotten him in, I'd have pulled it out of him. I could have broken him in ten minutes.'

'Apparently, someone else thought so, too.'

'Someone who was right there. On the spot. Watching him. Watching the viewing.'

'Or watching you,' Roarke finished. 'Which is more likely.'

'I hope they keep watching, because before long, I'm going to turn around and bite them on the throat.' She glanced up as the limo pulled up to the front of Cop Central. Vaguely embarrassed, she peered out, hoping no cops were loitering nearby. She'd be ragged on for days. 'I'll see you at home. Couple hours.'

'I'll wait.'

'Don't be ridiculous. Go home.'

He simply leaned back, ordered the screen to engage and list the latest stock information. 'I'll wait,' he repeated and poured another brandy.

'Hardhead,' she muttered as she got out, then winced when someone called her name.

'Woowee, Dallas, going to slum with us working poor for awhile?'

'Bite me, Carter,' she muttered, and rushed inside before the delighted laughter forced her to break someone's face.

An hour later, she was back, bone weary and sparking mad. 'Carter just had it announced over the main that my carriage awaited anon. What an idiot. I don't know whether to kick his ass or yours.'

'Kick his,' Roarke suggested and draped an arm around her. He'd switched from work to pleasure mode and had an old video on screen.

She caught the scent of expensive tobacco clinging to the

air and wished she could claim it irritated her. But it soothed, along with his arm and the ancient black-and-white video.

'What is this?'

'Bogart and Bacall. First film together. She was nineteen, I think. Here's the line.'

Eve stretched out her legs and listened to Bacall ask Bogie if he knew how to whistle. Her lips twitched. 'Clever.'

'It's a good film. We'll have to watch it all the way through sometime. You're tense, Lieutenant.'

'Maybe.'

'We'll have to fix that.' He shifted, poured a stemmed glass full of straw-colored liquid. 'Drink.'

'What is it?'

'Wine, just wine.'

She sniffed it suspiciously. He wasn't above doctoring it, she knew. 'I was going to work a little when we get home. I need my head clear.'

'You have to shut down sometime. Relax. Your head can be clear in the morning.'

He had a point. She had too much data in her head, and none of it was helping. Four deaths now, and she was no closer. Maybe if she backed off for a few hours, she'd see better.

'Whoever did Wineburg was quick and quiet. And smart, going for the heart. Hit the throat like Lobar, and you get blood all over you. Hit the heart, it's over fast and with minimal mess.'

'Umm-hmm.' He began to knead the back of her neck. It was always a magnet for her stress.

'What were we, thirty, forty seconds behind? Fast, really fast. If Wineburg cracked, there could be another. I've got to get the membership list. There has to be a way.' She sipped at the wine. 'What were you and Feeney talking about?'

'Mexico. Stop worrying.'

'Okay, okay.' She leaned her head back, closed her eyes for what seemed like three seconds. But when she opened them

164

again, they were through the gates and pulling up in front of the house. 'Did I fall asleep?'

'For about five minutes.'

'That was just wine, right?'

'Absolutely. The next part of our program is a hot bath.'

'A bath isn't . . .' She reconsidered as they stepped inside. 'Actually, that sounds pretty good.'

Ten minutes later, while water gushed into the tub and swirled in the power of jets, it began to sound better. But she arched a brow when she saw Roarke begin to undress. 'Who's the bath for, me or you?'

'Us.' He gave her a tap on the butt, nudging her forward.

'That's fine then. It'll give you a chance to tell me all about saving the life of a beautiful woman.'

'Hmm.' He slipped into the frothy water, facing her. 'Oh. I can't be held responsible for actions that took place in a former life.' He passed her another glass of wine he'd had the foresight to pour. 'Now, can I?'

'I don't know. Isn't the theory something like you repeat things, or learn from them, or don't?' She held the glass aloft and dunked herself down, resurfacing with a sigh. 'You figure you were lovers, or what?'

Considering, he trailed a fingertip up and down Eve's leg. 'If she looked then the way she looks now, I'd certainly hope so.'

She gave him a sour smile. 'Yeah, I'd guess you'd go for the big, beautiful, exotic type then and now.' With a shrug, she drank more wine, then toyed with the stem. 'Most people figure you stepped wide of the mark with me.'

'Most people?'

She downed the rest of the wine, set the glass aside. 'Sure. I get the drift when we've got to make time with some of those rich and high-toned business associates of yours. Can't blame them for wondering what came over you. I'm not big, beautiful, or exotic.'

'No, you're not. Slim, lovely, strong. It's a wonder I looked twice.'

She felt ridiculous and flustered. He could do that to her just by the way he looked at her. 'I'm not fishing,' she muttered.

'And it surprises me that you'd give a damn what any of my associates thought of either one of us.'

'I don't.' Damn it, she'd stepped right in it. 'I was just making an observation. The wine's got my tongue running away with me.'

'You annoy me, Eve.' His voice was dangerously cool. A warning she recognized. 'Criticizing my taste.'

'Forget it.' She dunked again, surfaced like a shot when his hands clamped over her waist. 'Hey, what are you doing? Trying to drown me?' She blinked water out of her eyes and saw that his were indeed annoyed. 'Listen—'

'No, you listen. Or better yet.' He crushed his mouth to hers, hot, hungry, hurried. It made the top of her lead lift off and spin. 'We'll just move to the third part of our program a little early,' he said when he let her suck in a gulp of air. 'And I'll show you why I'm precisely on the mark with you, Lieutenant. Precisely. I don't make mistakes.'

She scowled at him even as the blood hummed under her skin. 'That arrogant routine doesn't work for me. I said it was the wine.'

'You won't blame what I can do to you on the wine,' he promised. He tilted his hands so that his thumbs traced the vulnerable fold between thigh and crotch. 'You won't blame it on the wine when I make you scream.'

'I won't scream.' But her head fell back as a moan tore through her lips. 'I can't breathe when you do that.'

'Then don't. Don't breathe.' He lifted her up until her breasts were above water, and his hands busy below. He dipped, caught one dripping point between his teeth. 'I'm going to take you. You're going to let me.'

'I don't want to be taken, unless I take back.' But even as

her arms came around him, he ripped her to peak, made her body buck and her arms go limp.

'Not this time.' He was suddenly ravenous for her, just this way, limp and open and mindless.

'How do you do that?' Her voice was weak and slurred.

He nearly chuckled, though the need was growing painful. Saying nothing, he stood, lifted her. Her eyes fluttered open as he carried her out of the bath.

'I want you in bed,' he said. 'I want you wet, inside and out. I want to feel your body tremble when I touch you.' He laid her down, fastened his mouth on her throat. 'And taste you.'

She felt drunk, too loose for control, too pliant for shock, as his hands got busy again. She bucked, she reached for him, but he slipped away, sliding down her damp body, hands fast, mouth urgent. She couldn't keep up. Now her body was tight, a white-knuckled fist, ready to strike. She came abruptly, violently, and didn't hear her own scream.

He took what he wanted. Everything. His blood pounded harder and hotter every time he dragged her over the next edge. Their flesh was wet with sweat now as he drove them both ruthlessly.

When the need to be inside of her was unbearable, he pulled her up, parted her legs until they clamped around his waist. And when her arms were around him as well, clinging, her body trembling hard against his, he gripped her hips and filled her in one deep stroke.

His mouth found her breast, felt the wild, ragged beat of her heart beneath the damp flesh. And when she climaxed again, vising around him like silk-coated iron, he held himself back.

'Look at me.' He arched her back, watching as her body shuddered, her hips moved. Arousal built fresh as he took himself deeper into her. 'Look at me, Eve.' He stroked his hands over her, molding each curve again while he continued to thrust, slow, steady. His breath came in pants. His control vibrated on a thin, fraying wire.

She opened her eyes. They were glazed, heavy, but they watched him. 'You're the one,' he said, and braced himself over her. 'You're the only.'

His mouth swooped down to hers, found it eager and open as he emptied himself into her.

For once, he slept first. She lay in the dark, listening to him breathe, stealing a little of his warmth as her own body cooled. Since he was asleep, she stroked his hair.

'I love you,' she murmured. 'I love you so much, I'm stupid about it.'

With a sigh, she settled down, closed her eyes, and willed her mind to empty.

Beside her, Roarke smiled into the dark.

He never slept first.

Chapter Twelve

In his midtown office high above the city, Roarke dealt with his last meeting of the morning. As originally scheduled, he should be concluding this business in Rotterdam, but he had arranged to take the meeting holographically so as to remain close to home. Close to Eve.

He sat at the head of his gleaming conference table, aware that his image sat at a similar one an ocean away. His assistant sat on his left, feeding him the necessary hard copy for his approval and signature. His translator sat on his right, as backup, should there be any problem with the computer headset's language program.

The board of ScanAir filled the other seats. Or their images did. It had been a very good year for Roarke Enterprises and its subsidiaries. It had not been a good year nor a good several years for ScanAir. Roarke was doing them the favor of buying them out.

From the stony expressions on several holographic faces, they were not entirely grateful.

The company needed to be right-sized, which meant several of the cushier positions would be adjusted in salary and responsibility. Some would be eliminated altogether. He had already hand-picked several men and women who were willing to relocate to Rotterdam and whip the skyline back into shape.

As the computer-generated translation of the contract droned in his ears, he watched the faces, the body language.

Occasionally, he conferred with his translator for subtleties and syntax.

He already knew every phrase, every word of the buyout agreement. He wasn't paying what the board had hoped for. Then again, they had hoped his examination of the company wouldn't turn up some of the more delicate – and well-hidden – financial difficulties.

He couldn't blame them for that. He would have done the same. But his examinations were always thorough and turned up everything.

He signed his name on each copy, added the date, then passed the contracts to his assistant for her to witness and seal. She rose, fed the contacts into a laser fax. Seconds later, the copy was across the ocean and being signed by his counterpart.

'Congratulations on your retirement, Mr Vanderlay,' Roarke said pleasantly when the countersigned and witnessed copies were faxed back to him. 'I hope you'll enjoy it.'

This was acknowledged by a brief nod and a short formal statement. The holograms winked off.

Roarke eased back, amused. 'People aren't always grateful when you give them large quantities of money, are they, Caro?'

'No, sir.' She was tidy, with hair shockingly white and gloriously styled. She rose, taking both the hard copy and the record disc of the transaction for filing. Her trim, rust-colored suit showed off beautifully shaped legs. 'They'll be less grateful when you turn ScanAir into a financial success. Within a year, I'd say.'

'Ten months.' He turned to the translator. 'Thank you, Petrov, your services were invaluable, as always.'

'My pleasure, sir.' He was a droid, created by one of Roarke's science arms. His body was slim, garbed in a well-cut dark suit. His face was attractive, but not distractingly so, and formed to simulate trustworthy middle age. Several of his line were leased by the UN.

'Give me an hour, Caro, before the next. I have some personal business to tend to.'

'You have a one o'clock lunch with the department heads of Sky Ways to discuss the absorption of ScanAir, and the publicity strategies.'

'Here, or off site?'

'Here, sir, in the executive dining hall. You approved the menu last week.' She smiled. 'In anticipation.'

'Right. I remember. I'll be there.' He moved through the side door and into his office. Before going to the desk, he engaged locks. It wasn't strictly necessary. Caro would never come in unannounced, but it paid in certain areas to be cautious. The work he intended to do couldn't go on his log. He would have preferred to handle it at home, but he was squeezed for time. And so, he thought, was Eve.

At his desk unit, he engaged the jamming field that would block any scan by CompuGuard. The law frowned on unauthorized hacking, and the penalties were stiff.

'Computer, membership data, Church of Satan, New York City branch, under direction of Selina Cross.'

Working ... That data is protected under religious privacy act. Request denied.

Roarke only smiled. He'd always preferred a challenge. 'Oh well, I think we can change your mind about that.' Prepared to enjoy himself, he slipped off his suit jacket, rolled up his sleeves, and got to work.

Downtown, Eve paced Dr Mira's pretty, designed-to-soothe office. She was never completely relaxed there. She trusted Mira's judgment; she always had. More recently, she had come to trust the doctor on a personal level. As much as it was possible. But it didn't make her relax.

Mira knew more about her than anyone. More, Eve suspected

than she knew about herself. Facing someone with that kind of intimate knowledge wasn't relaxing.

But she hadn't come to talk about personal matters, Eve reminded herself. She was here to talk murder.

Mira opened the door and stepped in. Her smile was slow and warm and personal. She always looked so . . . perfect, Eve decided. Never too glossy, never undone, never less than competent. Today, instead of her customary suit, Mira wore a slim, pumpkin-colored dress with a single-button matching coat of the same above-the-knee length. Her shoes were of a slightly darker tone and boasted the skinny heels that Eve always marveled a woman would wear by choice.

Mira offered both hands, a gesture of affection that simultaneously baffled and pleased Eve.

'It's good to see you back in fighting shape, Eve. No problem with the knee?'

'Oh?' With a faint frown Eve glanced down, remembering the injury she'd suffered while closing a recent case. 'No. The MTs did a good job. I'd forgotten about it.'

'A side affect of *your* job.' Mira settled in one of her scoop chairs. 'I'd think it would be a bit like childbirth.'

'Excuse me?'

'The ability to forget the pain, the trauma to both body and mind, and go on to do the same thing again. I've always believed women make good cops and doctors because they're inherently resilient that way. Won't you sit, have some tea, tell me what I can do for you?'

'I appreciate you fitting me in.' Eve sat, shifted restlessly. She always felt inclined to bare her soul once she was settled in this room with this woman. 'It's about a case I'm working on. I can't give you many details. There's an internal block.'

'I see.' Mira programmed tea. 'Tell me what you can.'

'One subject is a young woman, eighteen, very bright, and apparently very impressionable.'

'It's an age for explorations.' Mira took out the tea steaming fragrantly in delicate china cups, offered one to Eve.

Eve would drink it, but she wouldn't particularly like it. 'I suppose. The subject has family. Close family. Though the father is out of the picture, there is extended family – grandparents, cousins, that kind of thing. She wasn't – isn't,' Eve corrected, 'alone.'

Mira nodded. *Eve had been alone*, she thought, *brutally alone.*

'The subject had an interest in ancient religions and cultures, was studying same. Over the past year, she developed a certain interest in the occult.'

'Hmm. That's also fairly typical. Youth often explores various creeds and beliefs in order to find and cement their own. The occult, with its mystique and its possibilities is very attractive.'

'She became involved in Satanism.'

'As a dabbler?'

Eve frowned. She'd expected Mira to show some surprise or disapproval. Instead, she was sipping tea with that slight attentive smile playing around her mouth. 'If that means was she toying with it, I'd say she went deeper.'

'Initiated?'

'I'm not sure what that involves.'

'Depending on the sect, there would be slight variations. Broadly, it would entail a waiting period, the taking of vows, a physical mark on the body, generally on or near the genitalia. The initiate would be accepted into the coven with a ceremony. There would be an altar, a human one, probably female, within a circle. The princes of hell would be called while the initiate or initiates knelt. Symbolism would include flame, smoke, the ringing of a bell, graveyard dirt, preferably from an infant. They would be given water or wine mixed with urine to drink, then the high priest or priestess would mark the initiate with a ceremonial knife.'

'An athame.'

'Yes.' Mira smiled, as though pleased with a bright student.

173

'And though it's illegal, if the coven is able, they will then sacrifice a young goat. With some, the blood of the goat is mixed with wine and consumed. Once done, the coven engages in sex. The altar may be used by all or many. It would be considered both a duty and a pleasure.'

'Sounds like you've been there.'

'No, but I was allowed to observe a sabbat ceremony once. It was quite fascinating.'

'You don't actually believe that stuff.' Stunned, Eve set the cup aside. 'Calling up the devil.'

Mira lifted a smoothly arched brow. 'I believe in good and evil, Eve, and I don't by any means discount the likelihood of an ultimate good, or an ultimate evil. In my profession, and yours, we see too much of both to deny it.'

Humans committed evil, Eve thought. *Evil was human.* 'But devil worship?'

'Those who choose to focus their lives – and shall we say souls – on this creed generally do so for its freedom, its structure, and its celebration of selfishness. Others are seduced by the promise of power. And many by the sex.'

'*It was just sex.*' *That's what Wineburg had said, had sobbed*, Eve remembered, *before he died.*

'Your young woman, Eve, was likely drawn in first by the intellect. Satanism is centuries old, and like most pagan religions, predates Christianity. Why does it survive, and in some eras even prosper? It's filled with secrets and sins and sex, its rites are mysterious and elaborate. She would have wondered, and coming from a close and likely sheltered homelife, was at an age ripe for rebellions against the status quo.'

'The ceremony you described was similar to one she described to me. But she had only begun to observe and she was sexually used. She was a virgin, and was, I suspect drugged.'

'I see. There are always sects that diverge from the established rules of law. Some can be dangerous.'

'She had blanks, time losses, and became almost slavishly

174

devoted to two of the members. She backed away from her family and her studies. Until she witnessed the ritual murder of a child.'

'Human sacrifice is an old practice, and a deplorable one.' Mira sipped delicately. 'If drugs were involved, it's highly possible she was made an addict, dependent upon these people. That would explain the blanks. I take it the murder she witnessed shocked her away from the cult and its rituals.'

'She was terrified. She didn't go to her family, didn't report the incident. She ran to a witch.'

'A white witch? A Wiccan?'

Eve compressed her lips. 'She did what I expect would be considered a religious one eighty. Started burning white candles instead of black. And she lived in terror, claimed that one of the membership could turn into a raven.'

'Shape-shifting.' Thoughtfully, Mira rose to program more tea. 'Interesting.'

'She believed they would kill her, had killed someone close to her, though that death is for now officially listed under natural causes. I have no doubt they tormented her, found a way to play on her delusions and fears. I'm thinking some of that came from her own sense of guilt and shame.'

'You could be right. Emotions influence the intellect.'

'Just how much?' Eve demanded. 'Enough for her to see things that weren't there? Enough for her to run from an illusion into the path of an oncoming car and kill herself?'

Mira sat again. 'She's dead then. I'm sorry. Are you quite sure she ran from an illusion?'

'A trained observer was on the scene. There was nothing there. Except,' Eve added with a twist of her lips, 'a black cat.'

'The traditional familiar. That alone might have been enough to push her over the edge. Even if the cat was planted in order to frighten her, you would have a difficult time terming it homicide.'

'They played on her mind, drugged her, possibly used

hypnosis. They tormented her with tricks and 'link transmissions. Then they pushed her over. Damned if that isn't murder. And I will make it stick.'

'Taking religion, particularly religions the masses don't wish to acknowledge, into court won't be easy.'

'I don't care about easy. The people behind this cult are dirty. And I believe they have killed four people in the last two weeks.'

'Four.' Mira paused, set the cup down. 'The body that was left near your home. The details in the media were sketchy. It's connected?'

'Yeah. He was an initiate, and he had his throat slit by an athame. It was left in him, stuck in his groin with a note that condemned Satanism. He was strapped to an inverted pentagram.'

'Mutilation and murder.' Mira pursed her lips. 'If it was Wiccans, it's very much out of character. Very much against their creed.'

'People do things out of character and against their creeds all the time,' Eve said impatiently. 'But at this time, I suspect a member or members of his own cult. Another man was killed last night with an athame. We held it from the morning reports, but it'll be all over the media within a couple of hours. I was on scene, chasing him down. I didn't run fast enough.'

'He was killed quickly, without ritual? With a police officer in pursuit?' Mira shook her head. 'A desperate or arrogant move. If this was committed by the same people, it shows a growing boldness.'

'And maybe a taste for it. Blood becomes addictive. I want to know where the weaknesses are in the kind of personality who runs a cult like this. I've got a female, long yellow sheet involving illegal sex and drug trafficking. Bisexual. She heads up the club, lives well. Her companion is a well-built male who caters to her. She likes to show off,' Eve added, remembering the fire trick. 'She claims to be clairvoyant. She's edgy, with a slippery temper.'

'Pride would likely be the first weakness. If she's in a position of power and authority, she would likely take disrespect badly. Is she clairvoyant?'

'Are you serious?'

'Eve.' Mira sighed lightly. 'Psychic abilities exist, and always have. Studies have established that.'

'Yeah, yeah.' Eve waved a hand in dismissal. 'The Kijinsky Institute, for one. I've got a detailed report on the white witch from there. They claim she's off the charts.'

'And you don't agree with the Kijinsky Institute?'

'Crystal balls and palm reading? You're a scientist.'

'Yes, I am, and as such, I accept that science is fluid. It changes as we learn more about the universe and what inhabits it. Many well-respected scientists believe that we're born with what we can term this sixth sense, or a heightened sense, if you will. Some develop it, some block it. Most of us retain at least some level. We'd call it instinct, hunches, intuition. You rely on that yourself.'

'I rely on evidence, on facts.'

'You have hunches, Eve. And your intuition is a finely crafted tool. And Roarke.' She smiled when Eve's brows drew together. 'A man doesn't rise so high so young without a strong instinct for making the right move at the right time. Magic, if you want to use a more romantic term, exists.'

'You're telling me you believe in mind reading and spell casting?'

'I can intuit what's going through your mind right now.' Mira chuckled, finished her tea. 'Mira, you're thinking, is full of shit.'

Eve's lips curved in a reluctant smile of her own. 'Close enough.'

'Let me say this, since I believe it's part of what you came here for. Witchcraft, black and white, has existed since the dawn of humanity. And where there is power, there is benefit, and there is abuse. That, too, is the nature of humanity. We can't, through all our scientific and technical skill, destroy one without damaging the other. Power requires tending, as do beliefs, so we have our ceremonies and our rituals. We need the structure, the comfort, and yes, the mystery of them.'

'I don't have any problem with ceremonies and rituals, Dr Mira. Unless they cross the line of the law.'

'I would agree. But the law can also be fluid. It changes, adapts.'

'Murder stays murder. Whether it's accomplished with a stone spear or a laser blast.' Her eyes were dark and fierce. 'Or whether it's done with smoke and mirrors. I'll find the perpetrator, and no magic in the world is going to stop me.'

'No.' A small, niggling fear – what might have been called a hunch – knotted in Mira's gut. 'I would agree with that as well. You're not without power, Eve, and you'll match yours against this.' She folded her hands. 'I can provide you with a more detailed analysis on both Satanism and Wicca, if it might help.'

'I like to know what I'm dealing with. I'd appreciate it. Can you give me a profile of a typical member of both cults?'

'There isn't a typical member, any more than there are typical members of the Catholic faith or of Buddhism, but I can generalize certain personality types who are often attracted to the occult. The Wiccan the young woman went to, is she a suspect?'

'She's not the prime, but she's a suspect. Revenge is a strong motive, and if Satanists keep ending up with a ritual knife in vital organs, I won't overlook revenge.' Unable to resist, Eve ran her tongue over her teeth. 'But I suppose she'd be more likely to put a curse on them.'

'Check the nails and hair of your victims, or of any subsequent ones. If a curse is involved, there should be signs of recent snippings.'

'Yeah? I'll do that.' Eve rose. 'I appreciate the help.'

'I'll get you a report by tomorrow.'

'Great.' She started out, paused. 'You seem to know a lot about all of this. Is it the kind of thing you study for psychiatry?'

'To some extent, but I have a more personal interest and studied fairly extensively.' Her lips curved. 'My daughter is Wiccan.'

Eve's jaw dropped. 'Oh.' What the hell did she say now? 'Well. I guess that explains it.' Uncomfortable, she dug her hands into her pockets. 'Around here?'

'No, she lives in New Orleans. She finds it less restrictive there. I may be a bit unobjective on the matter, Eve, under the circumstances, but I think you'll find it's a lovely faith, very earthy and generous.'

'Sure.' Eve edged for the door. 'I'm going to observe a meeting tomorrow night.'

'You'll have to let me know what you think. And if you have questions I'm unable to answer, I'm sure my daughter would be happy to speak with you.'

'I'll let you know.' She headed to the elevator, blowing out a long breath. *Mira's daughter was a witch, for Christ's sake*, she thought. *That was a hell of a capper.*

She headed back to Central with the intention of rounding up Peabody, then heading to Wineburg's townhouse. She wanted to get a look at his lifestyle, his logs, and his personal records. She had a feeling a drone like him would have kept some private list of names and places.

The sweepers had already been through, routinely, and had turned up nothing of particular interest. But she could get lucky.

She passed Peabody in the bullpen as she swung through. 'My vehicle, fifteen minutes. I want to check my messages, make a couple of calls.'

'Yes, sir. Lieutenant—'

'Later,' Eve said shortly, hurrying by and missing Peabody's wince.

The reason for it was waiting in her office.

'Feeney?' She tugged her jacket off, tossed it on a chair: 'You decide to head to Mexico? You're going to need to call Roarke for the details. He should be—'

She broke off when Feeney stood up, walked over, and shut her door. It had only taken one look at his face to know.

'You lied to me.' There was a quaver in his voice that came as much from hurt as anger. But his eyes were flat and cold. 'You fucking lied to me. I trusted you. You've been investigating Frank behind my back. Over his own dead body.'

There was no point in denying, less in asking how he'd found out. She'd known he would. 'There was going to be an internal investigation. Whitney wanted me to clear him, and that's what I've done.'

'Internal investigation my ass. Nobody was cleaner than Frank.'

'I know that, Feeney. I was—'

'But you investigated. You went through his records, and you did it around me.'

'That's the way it had to be.'

'Bullshit. I goddamn trained you. You'd still be in uniform if I hadn't put you here. And you back stab me.' He stepped closer, fists clenched at his sides.

She preferred him to use them.

'You've got Alice's file open, suspected homicide. She was my goddaughter, and you don't tell me you think some son of a bitch killed her? You block me out of the investigation, you lie to me. You looked right in my face and lied to me.'

Her stomach had gone to ice. 'Yes.'

'You think she'd been drugged and raped and murdered, and you don't take me in?'

He'd gotten into the records, the reports, she realized. They'd been sealed and coded, but that wouldn't have stopped him if he'd gotten a whiff. And, she decided, he'd gotten one the night before, over Wineburg's body.

'I couldn't,' she said in a flat voice. 'Even if I hadn't been under orders, I couldn't. You were too close. You can't objectively assist on an investigation involving family.'

'What the hell do you know about family?' he exploded and made her jerk.

Yes, she'd have preferred his fists.

'Orders?' he continued, bitterness spewing out and scalding her. 'Fucking orders? Is that your line, Dallas? Is that your reason for treating me like some lame rookie? "Take a vacation, Feeney. Use my rich husband's fancy house in Mexico."' His lips peeled back in a sneer. 'That would have been fine for you, wouldn't it? Get me out of your way, shuffle me off and out from underfoot because I'm useless to you on this one.'

'No. God, Feeney—'

'I've gone through doors with you.' His voice was abruptly quiet, and made her throat burn. 'I trusted you. I'd have put my back up against yours anytime, anyplace. But no more. You're good, Dallas, but you're cold. The hell with you.'

She said nothing when he walked out, leaving her door swinging open. Could say nothing. He'd nailed it, she decided. And he'd nailed her.

'Dallas.' Peabody rushed the door. 'I couldn't—'

Eve cut her off, simply lifting a finger, turning her back. Slowly, with slow even breaths, she pulled her guts back in. Even then, they ached. She could still smell him in the room. That stupid cologne his wife always bought him.

'We're going to do a follow-up sweep of Wineburg's townhouse. Get your gear.'

Peabody opened her mouth, closed it again. Even if she'd known what to say, she didn't imagine it would be welcome. 'Yes, sir.'

Eve turned back. Her eyes were blank, cool, composed. 'Then let's move.'

Chapter Thirteen

She was in a pisser of a mood by the time she got home. She'd turned Wineburg's townhouse inside out, reworking every step already taken by the sweepers. For three hours she and Peabody had searched closets and drawers, run logs, and traced 'link records.

She found two dozen all-but-identical dark suits, shoes so glossy she'd seen her own scowl reflected in the tips, an incredibly boring collection of music discs. Though he'd had a lock box, the contents hadn't been very illuminating. Two thousand in cash, another ten in credits, and an extensive collection of hard-core pornographic videos might have given some insight into the man, but no solid leads toward his killer.

He'd kept no personal diary, and his appointment book listed times and dates and very little about the content of any meeting, personal or professional. His financial records were ordered and precise, as one might expect from a man who dealt with money as an occupation. All expenses and income were carefully logged. Though the large and regular bimonthly withdrawals from credit into cash over the last two-year period of Wineburg's fussy life gave Eve a solid notion just how Selina managed to live so well, the withdrawals were all logged under personal expenses.

The consistency of late-night appointments over the last two years, again bimonthly and always on the same date as the personal cash withdrawal, wasn't enough to establish a solid connection with Selina Cross's cult.

The lady herself was never mentioned.

He'd been divorced, childless, and he'd lived alone.

So she knocked on doors, talked to neighbors. Eve learned Wineburg hadn't been the sociable sort. He'd rarely had visitors, and none of his neighbors had been curious enough or would admit to paying close enough attention to any of those rare visitors to give a description.

She came away with nothing but a raw feeling in the gut and a mounting sense of frustration. She knew, without a doubt, that Wineburg had been part of Cross's cult, that he'd paid heavily, first monetarily and then with his life, for the privilege. But she was no closer to proving it, and her mind wasn't as focused on the business at hand as it should have been.

When she headed home, alone, Feeney's angry face and bitter words played back in her head, and frustration slammed up hard against misery.

She'd more than let him down, she knew. She had betrayed him by doing precisely what he had helped train her to do. She'd followed orders, she'd been a cop. She'd done her job.

But she hadn't been a friend, she thought, as her temples throbbed with stress. She'd weighed her loyalties, and in the end had chosen the job over the heart.

Cold, he'd called her, she remembered and squeezed her eyes shut. And cold she had been.

The cat padded to her the moment Eve stepped in the door, winding around her legs as she stepped into the foyer. She kept walking, cursing lightly when he tripped her. Summerset slipped out of a doorway.

'Roarke has been trying to reach you.'

'Yeah? Well, I've been busy.' She nudged Galahad away impatiently with her foot. 'Is he here?'

'Not as yet. You might reach him at his office.'

'I'll talk to him when he gets home.' She wanted a drink, something strong and mind-misting. Recognizing the danger and the weakness of that crutch, she turned away from the parlor and walked in the opposite direction. 'I'm not here to anybody else. Get it?'

'Certainly,' Summerset said stiffly.

As she strode away, Summerset bent and picked up the cat to stroke – something he never would have done had anyone been around to observe. 'The lieutenant is very unhappy,' Summerset murmured. 'Perhaps we should make a call.'

Galahad purred, stretched his neck in appreciation of Summerset's long, bony fingers. Their mutual affection was their little secret.

It would have surprised Eve, though she wasn't thinking of either of them. She took the stairs, moved through the indoor pool and garden area, and into the gym. Physical exertion, she knew, blocked emotional distress.

Keeping her mind blank, she changed into a black skin suit and high tops. She programmed the full body unit, ordering the machine to take her through a brutal series of reps and resistance exercises, gritting her teeth as the clipped computer voice demanded that she squat, lift, stretch, hold, repeat.

She'd worked up a satisfactory sweat by the time she switched machines for aerobics. The combo-unit took her on a punishing run, up inclines, down them, a race up endless flights of stairs. She'd set it for variety, and found the change of texture on her running surface from simulated asphalt to sand to grass to dirt interesting, but it wasn't doing anything to ease the ache in her belly.

You could run, she thought with dull fury, *but you couldn't hide*.

Her heart was pumping hard, her skin suit soaked with sweat, but her emotions were still fragile as glass. What she needed, Eve decided as she tugged on soft, protective gloves, was to pound on something.

She'd never tried out the sparring droid. It was one of Roarke's newest toys. The unit was a middleweight: six feet,

184

one ninety, and firmly muscled. Good reach, Eve decided with her hands on her hips as she sized him up.

She punched in the code on his storage tube. There was a faint hum as circuits were engaged. The unit opened dark, polite brown eyes. 'You wish a match?'

'Yeah, pal, I wish a match.'

'Boxing, karate – Korean or Japanese – tae kwon do, kung fu, street style. Self-defense programs are also available. Contact is optional.'

'Straight hand-to-hand,' she said, backing up and gesturing. 'Full contact.'

'Timed rounds?'

'Hell, no. We go till one of us is down, pal. And out.' She curled her fingers in a come-ahead gesture.

'Acknowledged.' There was a faint humming from the unit as he self-programmed. 'I outweigh you by approximately seventy pounds. If you prefer, my program includes a handicap—'

She brought her fist up hard and fast, an uppercut to the jaw that snapped his head back. 'There's my handicap. Come on.'

'As you wish.' He crouched as she did and began to circle. 'You did not indicate if you desired vocal additions to the program. Taunting, insults—' He staggered back as her foot whipped up and plowed into his guts. 'Compliments or suitable exclamations of pain are available.'

'Come at me, will you, for Christ's sake?'

He did, with a swiftness and force that had her stumbling back, nearly losing her footing. This, she decided as she pivoted and caught him backhanded, was more like it.

He blocked her next blow, shifted weight, and wrapped his arm around her throat. Eve planted her feet, elbowed, and flipped him over her shoulder. He was up like lightning before she could attempt a pin.

His gloved fist made a solid connection with her solar plexus, pushing a whoosh of air out of her lungs and ringing bright pain straight into her head. Doubled over, she followed through with a head butt, stomped hard on his instep.

When Roarke walked in ten minutes later, he watched his wife fly through the air and go skidding across the mat. Lifting a brow, he leaned back against the door and settled down to watch.

She didn't have time to gain her feet before the droid was on her, so she grabbed one of his ankles, twisted, hauled, and thrusted. Her mind was a blank now, a black blank. Her breath was heaving, and she could taste the metallic flavor of blood inside her mouth.

She went at her opponent like a hail storm, cold and relentless. Each jab, each blow, each kick given or received sang through her body with icy, primitive rage. Her eyes were flat with violence now, her fists merciless as she concentrated on the head, working the droid back, back.

Frowning, Roarke straightened. Her breath was wheezing out now, all but sobbing, yet she didn't stop. When the droid staggered, went down on its knees, she crouched for the kill.

'End program,' Roarke ordered, and caught his wife's rigid arm before she could kick the droid's lolling head. 'You're going to damage the unit,' he said mildly. 'It isn't designed for to the death.'

She bent over, resting her hands on her knees, to catch her breath. Her mind was full of red now, red rage, and she needed to clear it. 'Sorry, I guess I got carried away.' She eyed the droid, who remained slumped on his knees, mouth slack, eyes blank as a doll's. 'I'll run a diagnostic on it.'

'Don't worry about it.' He started to turn her to face him, but she broke away, moved across the room for a towel. 'In the mood for a fight?'

'I guess I wanted to pound something.'

'Should I suit up?' He was smiling a little. Until she lowered the towel. The rage had drained from her face. All that was left in her eyes was misery. 'What is it, Eve? What happened?'

'Nothing. Just a rough day.' She tossed the towel aside,

moved to the cold box unit for a bottle of mineral water. 'So far, Wineburg's house is a bust. Nothing there to help us. Sweepers didn't find anything in the garage, either. Didn't expect them to. I jabbed some at Cross again, and at Alban the Magnificent. Had a consult with Mira. Her daughter's a Wiccan. Can you beat that?'

It wasn't work, he thought, *that put that painful unhappiness in her eyes*. 'What is it?'

'Isn't that enough? It's going to be tough to get an objective consult from Mira when her daughter's into spellcasting. Then there's Peabody. She's caught a damn cold, and her head's so full of snot I have to say everything twice before it gets through.'

She was talking too fast, Eve realized. Words were tumbling out of her mouth and she couldn't seem to stop them. 'A hell of a lot of good she's going to be to me hacking and sneezing all goddamn day. The media picked up on Wineburg, and the fact that you and I were on scene when it went down. My 'link's jammed with fucking reporters. Leaks everywhere. Fucking leaks everywhere. Feeney found out I've been holding back on him.'

Ah, Roarke thought, *there we are*. 'He was hard on you?'

'Why shouldn't he be?' Her voice rose as she whirled and searched for temper to cover the hurt. 'He should've been able to trust me. I lied to him, right to his face.'

'What choice did you have?'

'There's always a choice.' She bit the words off, heaved the half-empty bottle at the wall, where it bounced and spewed out bubbling water. 'There's always a choice,' she repeated. 'I made mine. I knew how he felt about Frank, about Alice, but I blocked him out. I followed orders. I walked the line.'

She could feel the pain rising, straining to spew as the water had spewed out of the bottle. She fought to block it back. 'He was right, everything he said to me. Everything. I could have gone to him on the side.'

'Is that what you were trained to do? Is that what he trained you to do?'

'He made me,' she said fiercely. 'I owe him. I should have told him how it was going down.'

'No.' He stepped to her, took her by the shoulders. 'No, you couldn't.'

'I could have.' She shouted it. 'I should have. I wish to God I had.' And broke. Covered her face with her hands and broke. 'Oh God, what am I going to do?'

Roarke gathered her close. She cried rarely, a last resort, and always when the tears finally came they were vicious. 'He needs time. He's a cop, Eve. Part of him already understands. The rest just needs to catch up.'

'No.' Her hands fisted in his shirt, held on. 'The way he looked at me . . . I've lost him, Roarke. I've lost him. I swear I'd rather lose my badge.'

He waited while the tears stormed out, while her body shook with them. There was such strong emotions in her, he thought, rocking as her hands clenched and unclenched against his back. Emotions she'd spent a lifetime bottling up, so they were only the more potent when they broke free.

'Damn it.' She let out a breath, long and shaky. Her head felt achy, muffled, her throat raw. 'I hate doing that. It doesn't help.'

'More than you think.' He stroked a hand over her hair, then tipped it under her chin to lift her face. 'You need food and a decent night's sleep, so you can do what you need to do.'

'What I need to do?'

'Close the case. Once you have, you can put all this behind you.'

'Yeah.' She pushed her hands over her hot, wet cheeks. 'Close the case. That's the bottom line.' She hissed out a breath. 'That's the goddamn job.'

'That's justice.' He brushed a thumb over the dent in her chin. 'Isn't it?'

She looked up at him, her eyes reddened, swollen, exhausted. 'I don't know anymore.'

She didn't eat, and he didn't press her. There had been grief in his life, and he knew food wasn't the answer. He'd considered browbeating her into taking a sedative. That, he knew, would have been an ugly business. So he was grateful when she went to bed early. He made some excuse about a conference call.

From his office, he watched on the monitor until her restless twists and turns stopped, and she slept. What he had to do would take no more than an hour or two. He doubted she'd surface before then and miss him.

He'd never been to Feeney's. The apartment building was comfortably shabby, well-secured, and unpretentious. Roarke thought it suited the man. Because he didn't want to risk being refused entrance, he bypassed the security buzzer and entrance locks.

That suited him.

He strolled through the tiny lobby, caught the faint scent of a recent insect extermination. Though he approved the intent, he disliked the lingering reminder of it, and made a note to have it dealt with.

After all, he owned the building.

He stepped into an elevator, requested the third floor. He noticed when he stepped out again that the corridor carpet could use replacing. But it was well lit, the tiny beam on the security cameras blinking efficiently. The walls were clean and thick enough to muffle all but a faint hum of life behind closed doors.

A low drift of music, a quick rumble of laughter, a fretful baby's nighttime wail. Life, Roarke thought, and a pleasant one. He rang the bell at Feeney's door and waited.

His eyes stared soberly at the peep screen, continued to stare when Feeney's irritated voice came through the intercom.

'What the hell do you want? You slumming?'

'I don't think this building qualifies as a slum.'

'Anything does, compared to that palace you live in.'

'Do you want to discuss the difference in our living arrangements through the door, or are you going to ask me in?'

'I asked what you want.'

'You know why I'm here.' He quirked a brow, making sure it was just insulting enough. 'You've got guts enough to face me, don't you, Feeney?'

It had, as Roarke had expected, the right effect. The door swung open. Feeney stood, blocking entrance with his compact body braced for war, his rumpled face bright with fury. 'It's none of your fucking business.'

'On the contrary.' Roarke stood where he was, kept his voice even. 'It's very much my fucking business. But I don't believe it's any of your neighbors'.'

Teeth clenched, Feeney stepped back. 'Come in and say what you have to say, then get the hell out.'

'Is your wife at home?' Roarke asked when Feeney slammed the door at his back.

'She's got a girl's thing tonight.' Feeney inclined his head, much like a bull, Roarke thought, preparing to charge. 'You want to take a shot at me, you go ahead. I wouldn't mind pounding that pretty face of yours.'

'Christ Jesus, she's just like you.' Shaking his head, Roarke wandered the living room. Homey, he decided. Not quite tidy. The viewing screen was set on the ball game, the sound muted. The batter swung, the ball flew in total silence. 'What's the score?'

'Yanks are up by one, bottom of the seventh.' He caught himself on the verge of offering Roarke a beer, then stiffened again. 'She told you, didn't she? Filled you in right from the get-go.'

'She wasn't under orders not to. And she thought I could help.'

190

He could help, Feeney thought and tasted bitterness. *Her rich, fancy husband could help, but not her former trainer, not her former partner. Not the man who had worked side by side with her with pride, and goddamn it, affection, for ten years.* 'Doesn't make you less of a civilian.' His tired eyes went broody. 'You didn't even know Frank.'

'No, I didn't. But Eve did. She cared.'

'We'd been partners, me and Frank. We were friends. Family. She had no business bumping me out of it. That's how I feel, that's what I told her.'

'I'm sure you did.' Roarke turned away from the view screen, looked Feeney dead in the eye. 'And however you told her, it broke her heart.'

'Dented her feelings some.' Feeney walked away, picked up a half-empty bottle of beer. Even through the murky haze of his fury, he'd seen the devastation in her eyes when he'd come down on her. And had willed himself not to give a damn. 'She'll get over it.' He drank deeply, knowing the taste wouldn't overpower the bitterness lodged in his throat. 'She'll do her job. She just won't do it with me anymore.'

'I said you broke her heart. I meant it. How long have you known her, Feeney?' Roarke's voice hardened, demanding attention. 'Ten years, eleven? How many times have you seen her fall apart? I imagine you could count them on the fingers of one hand. Well, I watched her fall apart tonight.' He took a careful breath. Temper wasn't the answer here, not for any of them. 'If you wanted to crush her, you succeeded.'

'I told her how things were, that's all.' Guilt was already seeping in. He slammed down the bottle, determined to chase it away. 'Cops back each other, they trust each other or they've got nothing. She was digging on Frank. She should have come to me.'

'Is that what you'd have told her to do?' Roarke countered. 'Is that the kind of cop you helped her become? It wasn't you in Whitney's office, taking the orders, doing the job,' he went on without giving Feeney time to answer. 'And suffering for it.'

'No.' A fresh wave of bitterness passed through him. 'It wasn't me.' He sat, deliberately turned up the sound, and stared at the ancient battle on the screen.

Stubborn, thick-headed Irish bastard, Roarke thought with twin tugs of sympathy and impatience. 'You did me a favor once,' Roarke began. 'When I was first involved with Eve and I hurt her because I misunderstood a situation. You straightened me out on that, so I'm going to do you a similar favor.'

'I don't want your favors.'

'You'll have it, anyway.' Roarke sat in a chair comfortably sprung. He helped himself to Feeney's nearly empty bottle. 'What do you know about her father?'

'What?' Baffled now, Feeney turned his head and stared. 'What the hell does that have to do with anything?'

'It has everything to do with her. Did you know he beat her, tortured her, raped her repeatedly until she was eight years old?'

A muscle worked in Feeney's jaw as he turned away again, muted the screen. He'd known that she'd been found in an alley at eight, beaten, broken, sexually abused. That was on record, and he never worked with anyone without knowing their official data. But he hadn't known it was her father who'd done it. He'd suspected as much, but he hadn't known. His stomach twisted, his hands clenched.

'I'm sorry for that. She never brought it up.'

'She didn't always remember. Or, more likely, she did and refused to remember. She still has nightmares, flashbacks.'

'You got no business telling me this.'

'She'd likely say the same, but I'm telling you, anyway. She made herself what she is, and you helped. She'd go to the wall for you; you know that.'

'Cops back up cops. That's the job.'

'I'm not talking about the job. She loves you, and she

doesn't love easily. It's difficult for her to feel it, and to show it. Part of her may always be braced for betrayal, for a blow. You've been her father for ten years, Feeney. She didn't deserve to be broken again.'

Roarke stood, and saying nothing more, walked out.

Alone, Feeney raked his hands up over his face, into his wiry red hair, then let them drop on his lap.

It was six fifteen when Eve rolled over, blinked at the light streaming through the windows. Roarke preferred waking to sun. Unless she snuck out of bed or climbed in well after him, she didn't get her shot at pulling the privacy screens.

She felt logy, decided it was too much sleep, and started to slip out of bed.

Roarke's arm swept out and pinned her. 'Not yet.' His voice was husky, his eyes still closed as he tugged her back over.

'I'm awake. I can get an early start.' She wiggled. 'I've been in bed nearly nine hours. I can't sleep anymore.'

He opened one eye – sufficient to note that she did indeed look rested. 'You're a detective,' he pointed out. 'I'll bet if you investigated, you'd uncover the startling fact that there are activities that can be done in bed other than sleep.'

His lips curved as he rolled on top of her. 'Allow me to give you the first clue.'

It shouldn't have surprised her that he was already hard, or that she would be so instantly ready for him. He slid inside her, smooth, slow, deep, and watched the lingering sleep clear from her eyes into awareness.

'I think I've figured it out already.' She lifted her hips, matched his lazy pace.

'You're such a quick study.' He lowered his lips to nuzzle just under her jawline. 'I like this spot,' he murmured. 'And this one.' His hand trailed up her rib cage, cupped her breast.

The arousal was sweet, simple, and made her sigh. 'Let me know when you get to something you don't like.'

She wrapped her arms around him, her legs. He was so solid, so warm, the steady beat of his heart against hers so comforting. Pleasure built in gauzy layers, floating over her mind, stroking through her body.

'Go over for me.' He nibbled her lips, then swept his tongue inside to tangle with hers. To nip, to suck. 'Go over,' he repeated. 'Slow.'

'Well . . .' Her breath was already hitching, catching in her throat. 'Since you ask so nice.'

The climax rolled through her, one long, lingering wave. She felt him follow, caught in the same current, and pressed her cheek to his.

'Was that like a cookie?' she wondered.

'Hmmm?'

'You know, have a cookie. You'll feel better.' She put her hands on either side of his face, lifting it as he laughed. 'Were you making me feel better?'

'I certainly hope so. It worked for me.' He dipped his head to kiss her lightly. 'I wanted you. I always do.'

'It's funny how men can wake up with their brains in their cocks.'

'It makes us what we are.' Still chuckling, he rolled her over him, patted her butt. 'Let's take a shower. I'll give you another cookie.'

Thirty minutes later, she stumbled out of the shower and into the drying tube. He was a quick change artist when it came to mood, she thought dizzily. From lazy to amused to hot, steamy, mind-numbing sex, all in one short morning.

Because her system was still frazzled, she braced a hand against the curve of the tube as warm air blew around her. When he stepped out of the shower, she jabbed out a finger.

'Stay away from me. You grab me again, I'll have to take you down. I mean it. I've got work.'

He hummed a tune and used a towel. 'I like making love to

you in the morning. You only wake up fast if you get a call from dispatch or if I seduce you.'

'I'm awake now.' She stepped out, pushed a hand through her hair. Giving herself safe distance, she reached for a robe. 'Go look at the stock reports or something.'

'I intend to. You'll want breakfast,' he added as he left the room. 'I'll order it up.'

She started to tell him she wasn't hungry. She wasn't. But she knew without fuel she wouldn't make it through the day.

When she joined him in the bedroom, he was slipping into a shirt, his gaze focused on the table monitor where he could view the headlines and financial reports. She walked past him to her closet, chose plain gray trousers.

'I'm sorry I lost it last night.'

He lifted his gaze, noted she kept her back to him as she pawed out a shirt. 'You were upset. You had a right to be.'

'Anyway, I appreciate you not making me feel like an idiot.'

'How do you feel now?'

She jerked a shoulder. 'I've got a job to do.' She'd come to that end while she'd tossed her way into sleep. 'I'm going to do it. Maybe . . . Well, maybe if I do it right, Feeney won't hate me so much when it's over.'

'He doesn't hate you, Eve.' When she didn't answer, he let it drop. He'd already programmed their meal in the recessed AutoChef. 'I thought ham and eggs would do the trick this morning.'

He got the coffee first, brought it to the table in the sitting area.

'It'll do the trick any morning.' She pasted on a determined smile, went over to get the food herself. He ordered the viewing screen on Channel 75 while she shoveled in creamy eggs.

She scowled as the on-air reporter, glossy as a china doll at seven thirty in the morning, recited the data on the Wineburg homicide.

'Though Lieutenant Eve Dallas, assigned to the homicide division of NYPSD, was on the scene, only yards away from the murder site, the police have no solid leads. The investigation continues. This is the second stabbing death connected with Lieutenant Dallas in as many days. When asked if the cases are linked, Dallas refused to comment.'

'A ten-year-old kid with a vision defect could see they're linked, for Christ's sake.' She had been eating on automatic, and now shoved the plate aside. 'That Cross bitch is sitting in her hell house, laughing.'

Springing up, she began to pace. Roarke took it as a good sign. If she was angry, she wasn't feeling sorry for herself. He chose some fresh strawberry jam for his croissant.

'I'm going to nail her, I swear to God, I'm going to nail her. For all of them. I need to connect Wineburg to her. If I can do that, I can harass her some more. May not be enough to get me a warrant to toss her place, but I can keep on her ass.'

'Well, then.' Roarke wiped his fingers with a pale blue linen cloth, set it aside. 'I should be able to help you with that.'

As she continued to pace and mutter, he rose, walked to a dresser, took a sealed disc from a drawer. 'Lieutenant?'

'What? I'm thinking.'

'Then I won't interrupt your train of thought with the list of membership from Cross's cult.' With a half smile on his face, he tapped the disk against his palm and waited for her eyes to clear and shoot to him.

'The list? You got the membership roster? How?'

He cocked his head. 'You don't really want to know how, do you?'

'No.' She said it immediately. 'No, I guess I don't. Just tell me he's on it.' She closed her eyes briefly. 'Just tell me Wineburg's on the list.'

'He certainly is.'

Her grin flashed quick and fever bright. 'I love you.'

Roarke handed her the disc. 'I know you do.'

Chapter Fourteen

Feeney wanted to see Whitney first. So he made it early, and he made it personal. They, too, went back together a long way, Feeney thought as he pulled up in front of the neat two-level home in the 'burbs. He'd been here socially over the years. The commander's wife loved to throw parties.

His mood wasn't sociable now as he strode up the pebbled walk toward the quiet house in the wakening neighborhood. A few yards down, a dog was barking in high, monotonous yips. The bark had none of the faintly metallic ring that said droid, but held a vibrancy of flesh and blood. The kind of dog that shit in the yard, Feeney thought with a shake of his head, and scratched at fleas.

Leaves skittered playfully along the street, most of them making beelines for lawns. Lawns that were, in a neighborhood like this, tended like a religion.

Feeney, himself, didn't get 'burb life, where you had to rake and mow and water or hire someone to rake and mow and water. He'd raised his family in the city, used the public parks. Hell, you had to pay for them, anyway. He moved his shoulders restlessly, not quite comfortable with the morning silence.

Anna Whitney answered his knock, and though she couldn't have been expecting company at that hour, she was already decked out in a trim jumpsuit. Her light hair waved stylishly, and her makeup was subtle and perfect. Her lips curved in welcome. Her eyes may have flickered with surprise and curiosity, but she was too much the cop's wife to ask questions.

'Feeney, how nice to see you. Come in, please, have some coffee. Jack's just having his second cup in the kitchen.'

'Sorry to disturb you at home, Anna. I need a few minutes of the commander's time.'

'Of course. And how's Sheila?' she asked as she led the way down the hall toward the kitchen.

'She's fine.'

'She looked just wonderful the last time I saw her. Her new stylist is terrific. Jack, you've got company for coffee.' She breezed into the kitchen, caught the surprise, then the speculation in her husband's eyes. She knew enough to make a quick exit. 'I'll let you two chat. I've got a million things to do this morning. Feeney, you give Sheila my best, now.'

'I will. Thanks.' He waited until the door swung closed, never taking his eyes off Whitney's. 'Goddamn it, Jack.'

'This should be discussed in my office, Feeney.'

'I'm talking to you.' Feeney jabbed a finger. 'To someone I've known twenty-five years. To someone who knew Frank. Why'd you cut me out of this? Why did you order Dallas to lie to me?'

'That was my decision, Feeney. The investigation had to be on a need-to-know basis.'

'And I didn't need to know.'

'No.' Whitney folded his big hands. 'You didn't need to know.'

'Frank and I raised some of our kids together. Alice was my godchild. Frank and I rode as partners for five fucking years. Our wives are like sisters. Who the hell are you to decide I don't need to know he's being investigated?'

'Your commander,' Whitney said shortly and pushed his still steaming coffee aside. 'And the reasons you just stated are the very reasons I made the decision.'

'You pushed me aside. You know damn well my division should have been involved. You needed records.'

'Records were part of the problem,' Whitney said evenly. 'There was no record of a heart defect in his medical files, no record of a connection, personal or professional, between him and a known chemi-dealer.'

'Frank had nothing to do with illegals.'

'No records,' Whitney continued. 'And his closest friend is the best E-detective in the city.'

Feeney's eyes went wide, and his color rose hot. 'You think I wiped records? You had Dallas looking at me?'

'No, I didn't think you wiped records, but it wasn't something I could ignore with IAD breathing down my neck. Who would you have picked to do the work, Feeney?' Whitney demanded with an impatient gesture. 'I knew that Lieutenant Dallas would be thorough and careful and that she'd bust her ass to clear both you and Frank. I knew she had – contacts – that could access those records.'

Deluged by emotion, Feeney turned to stare out of the gleaming window into the backyard with its tidily mowed grass and majestic fall flowers. 'You put her in a bad spot. You ordered her into a lousy position, Jack. Is that what happens when you command? You put your troops' backs to the wall?'

'Yeah, that's what happens.' Whitney ran a hand over his dark, grizzled hair. 'You do what needs to be done, and you live with it. I had IAD drooling. My priority was to clear Frank and shield his family from anymore hardship. Dallas was my best shot. You trained her, Feeney, you know she was my best shot.'

'I trained her,' Feeney agreed, sick inside.

'What would you have done?' Whitney demanded. 'Straight, Feeney. You've got a dead cop who's been tagged buying illegals from a suspected dealer who's under surveillance. There were drugs in his system when he died. Your gut tells you no way, no way he was dirty. And maybe your heart's telling you, too, because you remember when you were both rookies. But IAD's got no gut, and it's got no heart. What would you have done?'

And because he'd had a sleepless night to think on it, to worry the steps, Feeney shook his head. 'I don't know. But I know I don't want your job. Commander.'

'You've got to be crazy to want this job.' Whitney's wide face relaxed slightly. 'Dallas has gone a long way to clearing Frank, and she took you out of it within the first twenty-four hours. She'd hardly had more than a week on this, and she's already cleared a path. With her reports, I've been able to back IAD off. They're not happy about Frank setting up his own sting, but they've eased the pressure.'

'That's good.' Feeney dug his hands into his pockets as he turned back. 'She's good. Christ, Jack, I hit her hard.'

Whitney's brows knit. 'You should have come to me. Going after her was off, Feeney. I gave the orders.'

'I took it personal. I made it personal.' He remembered how she'd looked at him, her face pale, her eyes blank. He'd seen people with that look before – victims, he thought now, who were used to taking a fist in the face. 'I've got to fix it with her.'

'She called in a couple minutes before you showed up. She's doing a follow-through on a new lead. At home.'

Feeney jerked his head in a nod. 'I'd like a couple hours personal time.'

'You've got it.'

'And I want in on this.'

Whitney sat back, considered. 'That'll be up to Dallas. She's primary. If we're opening this up, she chooses her own team.'

'Answer the 'link, will you, Peabody?' Eve continued to scan the data on-screen as her 'link beeped insistently. It was a wonder to her how many names she recognized from the social, political, and professional registers. It was doubtful she'd have recognized quite so many a year before, but connecting with Roarke had broadened her horizons.

'Doctors, lawyers,' she muttered. 'Christ, this guy's been to dinner here. And I think Roarke used to sleep with this woman. This dancer. She's got a hit on Broadway and a mile of leg.'

'It's Nadine,' Peabody announced and wondered if Eve was talking to herself or really wanted to share that particular information. She hacked, sneezed, then added in her now raspy voice. 'Furst.'

'Perfect.' Eve cleared the screen, just in case, and turned to the 'link. 'So, Nadine, what's the story?'

'You're the story, Dallas. Two dead people. It's dangerous to know you.'

'You're still breathing.'

'So far, so good. I thought you might be interested in some data that's come my way. We can do a trade.'

'Show me yours, maybe I'll show you mine.'

'Exclusive one on one, in your home, with you discussing the investigation of both knifings, for the noon broadcast.'

Eve didn't bother to snort. 'One on one reporting the status of my investigation, in my office, for the evening broadcast.'

'The first body was found at your house. I want in.'

'It was found outside on the sidewalk, and you're not getting in.'

Nadine huffed out a breath. The pout was for her own benefit. She knew better than to think it would budge Eve. 'I want the noon.'

Eve checked her watch, calculated, considered. 'I'll clear you into my office. Arrival time eleven forty-five. If I can make it, I'll be there. If not . . .'

'Damn it, we need setup time. Fifteen minutes isn't—'

'It's enough, Nadine, for someone as good as you are. Be sure your data makes this worth my while.'

'Make sure you don't look like a rag picker,' Nadine shot back. 'Do something with your hair, for God's sake.'

Rather than respond, Eve ended transmission. 'What is this obsession people have with my hair and wardrobe?' She raked a bad-tempered hand through the hair in question.

'Mavis told me you're overdue for a style session. Leonardo's bummed about it.'

'You hanging with Mavis?'

'I've gone down to catch her act a couple times.' She blew her nose heartily. Over-the-counters were pure crap, she decided. 'I like watching her.'

'I haven't had time for a style session,' Eve muttered. 'I trimmed it myself a couple days ago.'

'Yeah, I could tell.' At Eve's narrow look, Peabody smiled blandly. 'It looks just lovely, sir.'

'Kiss ass.' Eve switched her screen back on. 'And if you're finished with your critique of my personal appearance, maybe you'd like to run a few of these names.'

'I recognize some of them.' Peabody bent over Eve's shoulder. 'Louis Trivane: big shot celebrity lawyer. Gets the stars out of legal jams. Marianna Bingsley: department store heiress and professional manhunter. Carlo Mancinni, cosmetic enhancement guru – medical doctor – you have to be way rich to have him even consider doing body sculpting on you.'

'I know the names, Peabody. I want background, personal data, financial data, medical data, and arrests. I want to know the names of their spouses and kids and pets. I want to know when and how they connected with Cross and why they decided Satan was a cool guy.'

'It'll take days.' Peabody said it mournfully and reminded Eve painfully of Feeney. 'Even shooting them into the IRCCA.'

Eve said nothing. The International Resource Center on Criminal Activity was one of Feeney's prides and joys.

'If I could tag someone in the E-Division for help, we could cut the time in half. Maybe less.' Peabody jerked a shoulder. 'So, where do you want me to start?'

'We've got a hop on Wineburg, so dig deeper there, and on Lobar – Robert Mathias. Then start at the top and work down. I'll start at the bottom and work up. Look for withdrawls of large amounts at regular intervals. We damn well better have what we need when we meet in the middle.'

She narrowed her eyes, thinking. The financial data on Selina's cult would be protected by the Privacy Act and its status as a registered religion. Still, there was a chance, a slim one, that she'd been cocky enough to make deposits in her personal account.

That was a simple matter to check on. For the other, she would have to decide if the data would hold solid if she was able to access it, and to access it, she needed Roarke.

She'd wait, she decided, a day or two. Once they ascertained how much money the membership list was suspected of feeding into Selina's pockets, she'd reassess.

It would be tough to sell the PA on religious contributions as extortion, but it might be a start.

'With Wineburg's name linked to Cross's cult, I can pull her into Interview. I think we'll make it, say, around eleven thirty.'

'You've got the spot with Nadine at eleven forty-five.'

'Yeah.' Eve's smile spread. 'That'll work.'

'Oh.'

'It's not my fault if some big-nosed reporter finds out I'm questioning Selina Cross, knows I'm primary on two recent homicides, then puts two and two together.'

'And goes on air with it.'

'Might shake up some of these fine, upstanding Satanists. Some people get real chatty when they're shook. Get me that data, and I can shake them harder.'

'I bow to you.'

'Save it until we see if it works. You use this unit. I can

use one of Roarke's to make the first pass. Computer, copy disc, print out hard copy.' She glanced up at the movement in the doorway, went very still. 'Abort,' she murmured and braced to take the next hit from Feeney.

'Peabody.' He sent her a quiet look out of sleep-starved eyes. 'I need a moment with your lieutenant.'

'Sir?' Though she rose, Peabody waited for Eve's signal.

'Take a break, Peabody. Get yourself some coffee.'

'Yes, sir.' She headed out, feeling the needles of edgy tension prickling the air.

Eve didn't speak, simply stood. Her body was set, he noted, not to defend, but to absorb the next blow. Her eyes were carefully empty. But her hand that she braced on the desk shook. He stared at it a moment, amazed and ashamed that he'd caused that.

'Your, ah, Summerset said I should just come up.' It was warm in the room, but he didn't remove his rumpled overcoat. Instead, he shoved his hands in the pockets. 'I was off yesterday. Coming down on you was off. You were doing your job.'

He saw her lip tremble, as if she would speak or make some sound. Then she firmed it again and said nothing. She looked, he realized, whipped.

'You broke her heart.'

'Her father beat her, tortured her, raped her.'

'You've been her father for ten years.'

How the hell was he supposed to deal with that? And how could he possibly ignore it?

'The things I said – I shouldn't have.' He pulled his hands free to scrub them hard over his face. 'Jesus, Dallas. I'm sorry.'

'Did you mean them?' It was out before she could stop it. She held up a hand, turned away, stared blindly out the window.

'I wanted to mean them. I was pissed.' He crossed to her,

his hands flapping uselessly. 'I got no excuse,' he began. He touched her, then snatched his fingers away from her shoulder when she cringed. 'I got no excuse,' he said again after a steadying breath. 'And you got a right to step back from me. I jumped hard where I shouldn't have jumped.'

'You don't trust me now.' She skimmed the back of her hand over her cheek, ashamed the single tear had gotten past her guard.

'That's bullshit, Dallas. There's nobody I trust more. Look, goddamn it, it takes a laser hit to get me to apologize to my own wife. I'm telling you I'm sorry.' Impatient now, he grabbed her arm, pulled her around. She froze. Her eyes were bright, tears sheening them but not, thank Christ, falling. 'Don't go female on me, Dallas. I can't kick myself in the ass much harder than I already am.'

He jerked up his chin, tapped a finger on it. 'Go ahead. Free shot. We won't say anything about you punching out a superior officer.'

'I don't want to hit you.'

'Goddamn it, I outrank you. I said take your shot.'

A ghost of a smile flitted around her mouth. He looked so fierce, she thought, those drooping camel eyes sparking with temper and frustration. 'Maybe after you shave. That stubble'd skin my knuckles.'

Relief flooded through him at the slight curve of her lips. 'You're going soft. Living the high life with that rich Irish son of a bitch.'

'I beat hell out of a sparring droid last night. One of Roarke's finest.'

'Yeah?' Pride swelled in him, ridiculously.

She tucked her tongue in her cheek. 'I pretended it was you.'

He grinned, took out the bag of candied almonds from his pocket, offered it. 'E-detectives don't have to use their fists. They use their brains.'

'You taught me to use both.'

'And to follow orders,' he added, his eyes resting on hers again. 'I'd have been ashamed of you if you'd forgotten that. You did right, Dallas, for Frank, for the department. For me,' he said and watched her eyes swim again. 'Don't do that.' His voice shook with the plea. 'Don't start that shit. That's an order.'

She swiped the back of her hand under her nose. 'I'm not doing anything.'

He waited a moment, just to be sure she wasn't going to lose it and embarrass them both. When her eyes cleared, he nodded in both relief and approval. 'Good.' He jiggled the bag in his hand. 'Now, are you going to let me in?'

She opened her mouth, shut it.

'I've seen Whitney,' he told her. Feeney found he wanted to smile. This was the cop he'd trained. Solid, sturdy, and straight. 'Chewed him out in his own kitchen.'

'Did you?' She lifted her brows. 'I'd like to have seen it.'

'Trouble was, once it was over, I had to agree with him. He'd picked the best cop for the job. I know you've been busting ass to push IAD out of the picture, clear Frank. Me,' he added. 'And I know you've been working on finding out who did him and Alice.' He had to take a breath because it hurt, still hurt. 'I want in, Dallas. I'm going to tell you straight, I need in to clear this out of my gut. Whitney said it was up to you.'

The tension seeped out of her. She could give him this, give both of them this. 'Let's get to work.'

Eve was so pleased to have Selina Cross in Interview, she'd missed anticipating the obvious bonus of having her represented by Louis Trivane. She flashed grins at both of them as she secured the door to Interview Room A.

'Ms Cross, I appreciate your cooperation. Mr Trivane.'

'Eve—'

'Lieutenant Dallas,' she corrected, snapping off the grin. 'We're not socializing here.'

'You know each other.' Selina's eyes went icy, pinned her lawyer.

'Your representative knows my husband on a social level. I'm acquainted with a number of attorneys in the city, Ms Cross. This doesn't affect my or their job performance. We'll go on record.'

Eve engaged the recorder, recited the pertinent data. After reading the revised Miranda, she sat. 'You've exercised your right to an attorney, Ms Cross.'

'I certainly have. I've already been harassed by you twice, Lieutenant Dallas. I prefer that this continued harassment go on record.'

'Me, too.' Eve smiled. 'You were acquainted with Robert Mathias, also known as Lobar.'

'He *was* Lobar,' Selina corrected. 'It was his chosen name.'

'*Was* is the operative word, seeing as he's in a refrigerated unit at the morgue. And so is Thomas Wineburg. Are you acquainted with him?'

'I don't believe I've had the pleasure.'

'Well, that's interesting. He was a member of your cult.'

Selina set her chin, waved away Trivane as he leaned forward to speak to her. 'I can't be expected to recognize the name of every member of my church, Dallas. We are . . .' She spread her hands on the small table. 'Legion.'

'Maybe this will refresh your memory.' Eve opened a file, took a still out, and slid it across the table. Death shots were always ugly.

Selina studied it with a small smile tugging at her mouth. A finger of the hand she wore webbed again today traced the spread of harsh red blood. 'I can't say for certain. We meet in the dark.' Her gaze lifted to Eve. 'It's our way.'

'I can say for certain. Both he and Lobar were yours, and both were murdered with a style of knife used in your rituals.'

207

'An athame, yes. We are not the only religion who uses such an instrument in ceremony. I feel, after this violence, this persecution of members of my church, the police should be concerned with protecting us rather than pointing fingers. Obviously, there is a person or persons determined to eliminate us.'

'I figured you had your own protection. Doesn't your master look out for his own?'

'Your mockery only shows your ignorance.'

'Having sex with an eighteen-year-old delinquent shows yours. Did you have sex with Wineburg, too?'

'I said I can't be sure I knew him. But if I did, I very likely had sex with him.'

'Selina.' Trivane cut her off, his voice firm. 'You're goading my client, Lieutenant. She's stated she can't positively identify this victim.'

'She knew him. Both of you did. He was a weasel. Do you know what a weasel is in cop-speak, Ms Cross? An informant.' Eve rose, leaned over, bending her body close to Selina's. 'Were you worried about how much he'd told me? Is that why you arranged for him to die? Were you having him followed?' She slanted her gaze toward Trivane briefly. 'Maybe you have all your . . . faithful followed.'

'I see whatever I need to see in the smoke.'

'Yeah, in the smoke. The psychic's version of the Peeping Tom. It was risky for Wineburg to come by the viewing room. Why do you suppose he wanted a look at Alice? Had he been there the night she was drugged, raped? Did you let him have her?'

'Alice was an initiate. A willing one.'

'She was a child, a confused one. You like luring the young, don't you? They're so much more interesting than stubby fools like Wineburg. With their firm bodies, their malleable minds. People like Wineburg and the distinguished counsel here, they're just for the money, and the cachet. But those like Alice, they're so tender. So tasty.'

Selina looked up smugly through her thick, dark lashes. 'She was. She enjoyed and was enjoyed. She didn't have to be lured, Dallas. She came to me.'

'Now she's dead. Three deaths. Your members must be getting nervous.' Eve smiled thinly at Trivane. 'I would be.'

'Martyrdom isn't new, Dallas. People have been killed because of their faith for centuries. And still, the faith survives. We'll survive. We'll triumph.'

Eve took out another still, slapped it on the table. 'He didn't.'

It was Lobar, his mutilated body caught it the garish lights of the crime scene. The wound on his throat gaped open like a scream.

It was Trivane who Eve watched. His eyes blinked rapidly, horror flickering through. His skin went pasty, and his chest rose and fell in jerks.

'He didn't survive,' Eve said softly, 'did he, Selina?'

'His death is a symbol. He will not be forgotten.'

'Do you own an athame?'

'I own several, naturally.'

'Like this?' She took out another photo, this one a close-up of the weapon left pinned into Lobar. Blood crusted the blade.

'I have several,' Selina repeated. 'Some similar to this, as one might expect. But I don't recognize this particular one.'

'Hallucinogens were found in Lobar's system. You use drugs during rituals.'

'Herbals, and some chemicals. All legal.'

'Not everything found in Lobar's system was on the legal list.'

'I can't be responsible for the choices other people make.'

'He was with you the night he died. Was he using?'

'He had taken the ritual wine. If he took something otherwise, it was without my knowledge.'

'You have priors as a chemi-dealer.'

'And paid my debt to so-called society. You have nothing on me, Lieutenant.'

'I have three bodies. And they're yours. I've got a dead cop, and he's on you, too. I'm closing in on you, Selina. Step by step.'

'Keep out of my face.'

'Or?'

'Do you know pain, Dallas?' Selina's voice went low and thick. 'Do you know the pain that eats at the stomach like drops of acid spreading? You beg for relief, but none comes. The pain becomes agony, and agony almost pleasure. The pain becomes so intense, so unspeakable that if a knife came to your hand, you would gladly slice through your own guts to cut out the source of it.'

'Would I,' Eve said coolly. 'Would I really?'

'I can offer you that. I can offer you pain.'

Eve smiled, and her smile was slow and humorless. 'That slips into the area of threatening a police officer. And that'll get you some time in a cage until your lawyer finesses you out again.'

'You bitch.' Furious that she'd been trapped so neatly and with so little effort, Selina sprang to her feet. 'You can't hold me for that.'

'Sure, I can. Selina Cross, you're under arrest for verbal threat to physically harm a police officer.'

She was fast, but Eve's reflexes were sharp. She blocked the first blow as Selina flew at her. But the second rapid swipe caught her along the throat with those lethal dark nails. She smelled her own blood and indulged herself by bringing her elbow up to ram Selina's chin.

The dark eyes rolled back, went glassy. 'Looks like we add resisting arrest. You're going to have your hands full for the next couple hours, counselor.'

He hadn't moved, not a muscle. Trivane continued to sit, staring at the photos of the dead. When Feeney opened the

210

door, a uniform behind him, Eve nodded. 'Book her,' she ordered. 'Verbal threat and resisting.'

Selina staggered as Eve passed her to the uniform. But her eyes cleared and fixed on Eve's face with bubbling malice. She began to speak softly, in a chant that rose and fell almost musically. She swiveled her head, looking over her shoulder as the uniform took her out.

Eve dabbed fingers on her throat, disgusted when they came away smeared with blood. 'Did you catch what she was saying there?'

Feeney took out a handkerchief, handed it to her. 'Sounded like Latin, bastardized some. My mother made me learn when I was a kid. Had delusions about me becoming a priest.'

'See if you can make any of it out from the record. We may be able to add to the charges. Shit, this burns. Interview is concluded,' she added and logged the time and date. 'Trivane, you want to talk to me?'

'What?' He looked over, swallowed, shook his head. 'I'll see my client, Lieutenant, as soon as she's booked. These charges won't hold.'

Eve held out her bloody fingers. 'Oh, I think they will. Take a good look, Louis.' She stepped closer, jammed her fingers under his nose. 'It could be yours next time.'

'I'll see my client,' he repeated, and his face was still white as death as he hurried from the room.

'That bitch is loony,' Feeney commented.

'Tell me something I don't know.'

'She hates your ever fucking guts,' he said pleasantly, happy to be in tandem again. 'But you knew that, too. Put the hoodoo on you.'

'Huh?'

'Cursed you.' He winked at her. 'Let me know if you start getting stomach cramps. You're starting to get to her.'

'Not enough,' Eve murmured. 'But my money's on the lawyer. Let's keep a man on him, Feeney. I don't want him ending up dead before he breaks. It was the way he looked at the shot of Lobar. Shock, then something like recognition.' She shook her head. 'Let's not lose him.' She glanced at her watch, hummed with satisfaction. 'Just in time to make my nooner with Nadine.'

'You want to have that neck looked after. Nasty.'

'Later.' She headed out, moving fast. Nadine wouldn't miss the injury. Nor, Eve thought, would the all-seeing eye of the camera.

'What the hell happened to you?' Nadine demanded. She stopped pacing, stopped looking at her watch.

'Little problem in Interview.'

'You cut it close, Dallas, we got two minutes before air. You don't have time to clean up.'

'Fine, we'll go like we are.'

'Get a voice and light level,' Nadine told her camera operator. She took out a mirrored compact, polishing up her face when she sat. 'Looks like female,' she added. 'Long, nasty nails, four separate grooves.'

'Yeah.' Eve patted the already stained handkerchief against the wound. 'Somebody was curious, they could check booking, get the data.'

Nadine's eyes went sharp. 'I imagine someone could,' she purred. 'You didn't do anything with your hair.'

'I cut it.'

'I meant anything constructive. Coming up in thirty. Set, Suzanna?'

The operator made a circle of forefinger and thumb. 'The fresh blood shows up real good. Nice touch.'

'Gee, thanks.' Eve settled back, hooked one booted foot over her knee. 'Let's keep this short, Nadine. I haven't seen yours yet.'

'Here's a preview then. What local white witch is the son of infamous mass murderer David Baines Conroy, who is

212

currently doing five separate life stretches, no parole options, in maximum lockup on Penal Station Omega?'

'Who—'

'In five,' Nadine said sweetly, delighted to have snagged Eve's full attention. 'Four, three . . .' She signaled the last of the countdown with her fingers, below camera level. On cue, she stared into the camera with sober eyes. 'Good afternoon, this is Nadine Furst, leading off the noon hour with an exclusive interview with homicide Lieutenant Eve Dallas in her office at Cop Central . . .'

Eve was prepared for the questions. She knew Nadine's style well, too well to allow herself to be rattled by the information that had been dumped on her seconds before air time. As, she imagined, Nadine had hoped. She answered briefly, carefully, and knew she was bumping up Channel 75's and Nadine's rating points with every on-the-air second.

'The department is proceeding with the belief that the cases are connected as evidence indicates. Though different weapons were left at the scene of each murder, they are of similar style.'

'Can you describe the weapons?'

'I can't comment on that.'

'But they were knives.'

'They were sharp instruments. I'm not at liberty to go into any more detail. Doing so would jeopardize our investigation at this point.'

'The second victim. You were pursuing him at the time of his death. Why?'

She was ready for this, had already decided to exploit the question for her own benefit. 'Thomas Wineburg had indicated he had information which would be useful to my investigation.'

'What information?'

Zip, Eve thought, but kept her eyes level. 'I'm not at liberty

213

to divulge that. I can only say we spoke, and he became agitated and ran. I pursued.'

'And he was killed.'

'That's correct. Running didn't help him.'

Annoyed that her director indicated her time was up through her earpiece, Nadine wound the interview to a close. 'And we're clear. Suzanna?' Nadine simply gestured to the door and sent her operator out. 'Off the record,' she began.

'Nope. Gimme.'

'All right then.' Nadine sat back, crossed her pretty legs. 'Charles Forte took his mother's maiden name legally twelve years ago after his father was convicted of the ritual slayings of five people. It's believed he killed countless others, but it's never been proved. The bodies have never been found.'

'I know the story behind Conroy. I didn't know he had a kid.'

'That was kept locked. Privacy Act. The family was already out of it. The mother had divorced and relocated a few years before Baines was caught. The kid was sixteen when she took him and left. Twenty-one when his father was tried and convicted. My sources claim the son attended court every day.'

Eve thought of the small, unassuming man she'd met at Alice's viewing. Son of a monster. How much of that came through the blood? She thought of her own father, nearly shuddered. 'I appreciate it. If it comes to anything, I'll owe you.'

'Yeah, you will. I've got lots of data on cults in the city. Nothing as dramatic as this, but it may lead somewhere. Meanwhile, if you were in Interview with someone pissed off enough to try to slice your jugular, should I assume you have a suspect?'

Eve studied her nails. She supposed some would have said she was overdue for a manicure. 'I can't comment on that. You know, Nadine, cameras aren't allowed down in Booking.'

'Damn shame. Thanks for the spot, Dallas. I'll be in touch.'

'Do that.' Eve watched her stroll out, had no doubt Nadine was making tracks to Booking. And that Selina Cross was going to have her name broadcast by the end of the noon report.

All in all, she decided, *not a bad morning*.

Wincing, she dragged through her drawers hoping for a first aid kit.

Chapter Fifteen

'I won't make it home.' Eve juggled the call to Roarke while her computer searched for all data on David Baines Conroy. 'Can you swing by here about six? We can drive upstate for the witch party.'

Roarke lifted an elegant brow. 'As long as it's not in your vehicle.' He frowned, gestured. 'Come a little closer to the screen. What now?' he asked.

'What do you mean, "What now"? I'm busy.'

'No, your neck.'

'Oh, that.' She touched her fingers to the still-raw scratches. She'd never found that first aid kit. 'A difference of opinion. I won.'

'Naturally. Put something on it, Lieutenant. I should be able to make it there by six thirty. We can eat on the way.'

'Fine.' *Eat on the way?* 'Wait a minute. Don't bring the limo.'

He only smiled. 'Six thirty.'

'I mean it, Roarke, don't—' She hissed when the screen blanked. 'Damn.' With a sigh, she swiveled back to the computer.

The IRCCA was a fount of data on this one, she thought. she skimmed through, pausing over pertinent facts on David Baines Conroy.

Divorced, one child, male, Charles, born January 22, 2025,

custody awarded to mother, Ellen Forte.

Big surprise, Eve thought. Mass murderers weren't generally given custody of minor children. 'Let's get down to it,' she murmured. 'Charges and convictions.'

Charged and convicted, Murder in the first, torture killing, posthumous rape, and dismemberment of Doreen Harden, mixed race female, age 23. Sentenced to life, maximum facility, no parole option.
Charged and convicted, Murder in the first, rape, torture killing, and dismemberment of Emma Tangent, black female, age 25. Sentenced to life, maximum facility, no parole option.
Charged and convicted, Murder in the first, sodomy, rape, torture killing, and dismemberment of Lowell McBride, white male, age 18. Sentenced to life, maximum facility, no parole option.
Charged and convicted, Murder in the first, rape, torture killing, and dismemberment of Darla Fitz, mixed race female, age 23. Sentenced to life, maximum facility, no parole options.
Charged and convicted, Murder in the first, sodomy, posthumous rape, torture killing, and dismemberment of Martin Savoy, mixed race male, age 20. Sentenced to life, maximum facility, no parole options.
Currently serving term on Penal Station Omega.
Suspected of twelve additional murders, cases open. Insufficient evidence to charge. Primary investigators available on request.

'List primaries,' Eve ordered and watched as names and data scrolled. 'Moved around, did you, Conroy?' she muttered, noting that the detectives in charge were scattered all over the country.

She'd still been a teenager when Conroy had dominated the news. She remembered snatches, weeping family members

217

begging Conroy to tell them where to find the remains of loved ones, grim-faced cops giving statements, and Conroy himself, a quiet face slashed with vicious, dark eyes.

They'd called him evil, she remembered. The Antichrist. That was the term used over and over again to describe him, to try, perhaps, to separate him from the human.

But he'd been human enough to conceive a child. A son. And that son was on her current list of suspects. Maybe, just maybe, she'd been focused too relentlessly on Selina Cross.

The son was drawn to power, she mused. Witchcraft was about power, wasn't it? He'd known at least one of the victims. And two had been killed with a knife. Conroy had been very handy with a knife.

He'd also claimed to have been the instrument of a god, she recalled, scanning data. Yes, there, there in one of his rambling statements. She highlighted. 'Give me audio on this.'

Working . . .

'I am a force beyond you,' Conroy's voice crooned out, beautiful diction, almost musical. The son's voice, Eve thought, was equally charismatic. 'I am the instrument of the god of vengeance and pain. What I do in his name is grand. Tremble before me for I will never be vanquished. I am legion.'

'You are garbage,' Eve corrected. *Legion.* Cross had used the same term. Interesting . . . *Had Conroy dabbled in Satanism,* she wondered, *in witchcraft? And had the son been attracted to the same areas?*

Just how much, she wondered, *did Charles Forte know about his father's work? And how did he feel about it?*

'Computer, run Charles Forte of this city, formerly Charles Conroy, son of David Baines Conroy, all data.

As the information beeped on, she tapped her fingers on the desk and considered. The mother had taken her son to New York, which meant, Eve mused, that the boy had traveled back to attend the trial. He'd made the effort, likely over his mother's objections. Dropped out of college, second term. Studied pharmaceuticals. Very-interesting. Licensed as a chemical drone, worked on drug cloning and manufacture. Moved around quite a bit, she noted. Like his dear old dad. Then settled back in New York, co-owner of Spirit Quest.

She leaned back, unconsciously rubbing her wounded throat. No marriages, no children, no arrests. She played a hunch.

'Medical data.'

Charles Forte, age six, broken hand. Age six, minor concussion, abdominal bruising. Age seven, second-degree burns, forearms. Age seven, concussion and fractured tibia.

The list went on through childhood in a pattern that made Eve's stomach clench. 'Hold. Probability of child abuse?'

Probability ninety-eight percent.

'Why the hell wasn't it picked up?'

Medical records indicate treatment was issued at varying hospitals in varying cities over course of ten years. No record of requested search through National Child Abuse Prevention Agency.

'Idiots. Idiots.' She rubbed her hands over her face, pressing hard on the headache now brewing in the center of her forehead. It was too close to home.

'List any psychiatric treatment or available psychological profiles.'

Subject entered Miller Clinic voluntarily as outpatient. Doctor of record, Ernest Renfrew from February 2045 to September 2047. Files sealed. No other data.

'Okay, that's enough to chew on. Save data, file Forte, Charles, case number 34299-H. Cross-reference, Conroy. Disengage when complete.'

She glanced up as Feeney stuck his head in her doorway. 'Cross just got sprung.'

'Well, it was too good to last.'

'You have anybody look at those cat scratches?'

'I will. Got a minute?'

'Sure.'

'David Baines Conroy.'

Feeney whistled, made himself comfortable on the corner of her desk. 'That's going back. Sick bastard. Cut his victims up when he was done with them. Kept the parts in a portable cold box. Had a trailer, traveled around. Preaching.'

'Preaching?'

'Well, that's not exactly the term. Set himself up as a sort of Antichrist. Lots of shit about anarchy, freedom to pursue carnal pleasures, opening the gates of Hell. That sort of thing. Figures he plucked most of his victims off the road. Itinerant LCs. At least three they pinned him on were licensed companions. Hookers have always been easy marks for psychos.'

'He was found competent to stand trial.'

'Passed the tests. Legally, he was sane. In reality, a real whacko.'

'He had a family.'

'Yeah, yeah, that's right.' Feeney closed his eyes to try to bring it back. 'I was still working Homicide then, and there wasn't a cop on planet who wasn't personally caught up by the case. Never did any of his work here, that we know of, but I remember he had a wife. Pale, jumpy little woman. Left him – before he got snagged seems to me. And there was a kid, a boy. Spooky.'

'Why?'

'He had his old man's eyes. Except they were dead, you know? I remember thinking we might be tracking him one day. In his father's footsteps. Then they ducked under the Privacy Act, and nobody ever heard of them again.'

'Until now.' Eve kept her eyes level. 'I'm seeing Conroy's son tonight. At a witch's coven.'

Roarke brought the limo. She'd been certain he would, just to annoy her. She'd have stayed annoyed if he hadn't seen that the AutoChef was stocked, Italian style.

Eve was wolfing down manicotti before they crossed the Jacqueline Onassis Bridge. But she shook her head at the burgundy he poured.

'I'm on duty,' she said with her mouth full.

'I'm not.' He sipped, studied her. 'Why haven't you taken care of that?' he asked, brushing gentle fingers over her throat.

'I got tied up.'

'Now, that's something we've yet to explore.' He smiled genially when she goggled at him. 'Just a thought. I caught the replay of your little tête-à-tête with Nadine on the way over to Central. I'm surprised you agreed to it.'

'It was a trade. I got my share.' She leaned forward, engaged the privacy shield between them and the driver. 'And I'd better fill you in before we join in tonight's festivities.'

She detailed the new line she was pursuing, then sampled one of the sweet, fat olives on the antipasto tray. 'It bumps him up a few notches on the list,' she concluded.

'The sins of the father?'

'Sometimes it works that way.'

He said nothing a moment. They both had reason to be uncomfortable with the theory. 'You know best, Lieutenant, but isn't it just as likely circumstances would push him to the opposite pole?'

'He knew Alice, he has knowledge of chemicals. Her grandfather had chemicals in his system, and she'd been hallucinating. The other two victims were ritual slayings. Forte belongs to a cult. I can't ignore the steps.'

'He looked remarkably unhomicidal to me.'

She poked through the antipasto, selected a marinated pepper. 'I once took down this little old lady, looked like everybody's favorite granny. She took in stray cats and baked cookies for the neighborhood kids. Grew geraniums on her windowsill.' Enjoying the bite, Eve chose another pepper. 'She'd lured a half a dozen kids into her apartment, and had fed their internal organs to the kitties before we nailed her.'

'Charming story.' Roarke slipped his plate into the holding slot. 'Point taken.' Reaching into his pocket, he took out the amulet Isis had given him the night before, slipped it over Eve's neck.

'What's this for?'

'It looks better on you than me.'

She narrowed her eyes at him. 'Bull. You're being superstitious.'

'No, I'm not,' he lied and set her plate in with his before he shifted and began to unbutton her shirt.

'Hey, what are you doing?'

'Passing the time.' His hands, clever and quick, swooped down to take her breasts. 'It'll take an hour to get there by car.'

'I'm not having sex in the back of a limo,' she told him. 'It's—'

'Delicious,' he finished and replaced his hands with his mouth.

She felt remarkably limber and relaxed by the time the limo turned onto a narrow country road. Here the trees were plentiful, the stars brilliant, and the dark complete. Half-denuded trees arched over the roadway, tunneling them in. She caught the glinting gold eyes of what might have been a fox as a shadow darted across the road and into the woods.

'Feeney and Peabody still behind us?'

'Hmm.' Roarke tucked his shirt back into his trousers. 'It would seem so. 'You're putting that on inside out,' he said mildly and grinned.

'Hell.' Eve struggled back out of the shirt, pulled the arms through, and tried again. 'Don't look so smug, I just pretended to enjoy that.'

'Darling Eve.' He took her hand, kissed it. 'You're too good to me.'

'You're telling me.' She slipped the amulet off, looped it over his head. 'You wear it.' Before he could object, she caught his face in her hands. 'Please.'

'You don't believe in it, anyway.'

'No.' She tucked it under his shirt, patted it. 'But I think you do. Your driver knows where he's going?'

'The directions from Isis are programmed in.' He checked his watch. 'By my calculations, we should be nearly there.'

'Looks like we're nowhere if you ask me.' She stared out the window. Nothing but dark, trees, and more dark. 'I'd rather be on my own turf. Hard to believe there's this much nothing less than two hours' drive from New York.'

'You're such an urbanite.'

'And you're not?'

He moved his shoulders. 'The country's an interesting place to visit for short periods of time. Quiet can be restful.'

'It makes me edgy.' They turned onto another winding road. 'And everything looks the same. There's no . . . action,' she decided. 'Now, you stroll into Central or Green-peace Park and you're bound to run into a mugger or chemi head at least. Maybe an unlicensed hooker, couple of perverts.'

She glanced back, saw he was grinning at her. 'Well?'

'Life with you has such . . . color.'

She snorted, strapped on her side arm. 'Yeah, like everything was gray in your little world before I came along. All that wine, women, and money. Must have been pretty tedious.'

'The ennui,' he said on a sigh, 'was unspeakable. I might have faded away from it if you hadn't tried to hang a murder or two on me.'

'Just your lucky day.' She caught the glimmer of lights through the trees as the car turned up a steep, rutted incline. 'Thank Christ. Looks like the party's already under way.'

'Try not to sneer.' Roarke patted her knee. 'It would offend our hosts.'

'I'm not going to sneer.' She already was. 'I want impressions. Not just of Forte, of everybody. And if you happen to recognize a face, let me know.' She took a small device out of her bag, slipped it into her pocket.

'Micro recorder?' Roarke clucked his tongue. 'I believe that's illegal. Not to mention rude.'

'I don't know what you're talking about.'

'And unnecessary,' he added. He turned his wrist, tapped a tiny button on the side of his watch. 'This one is much more efficient. I should know. I manufacture both brands.' He smiled as the car stopped at the edge of a small clearing. 'I believe we've arrived.'

Eve spotted Isis first. She was impossible to miss. The sheer, white robe she wore seemed to glow out of the dark like moonlight. Her hair was left long and loose, flowing over her shoulders. A gold band studded with colored stones circled her brow. Her long, narrow feet were bare.

224

'Blessed be,' she said and disconcerted Eve by kissing both her cheeks. She greeted Roarke the same way, then turned back to Eve. 'You're injured.' Before Eve could respond, she lay fingers against the scratches. 'Poison.'

'Poison?' Eve had visions of vicious nails dipped into a slow-acting brew that crept through the bloodstream.

'Not of the physical but of the spiritual kind. I feel Selina here.' Her eyes stayed on Eve's as she lowered her hand to Eve's shoulder. 'This won't do. Mirium, please welcome our other guests.' She spoke to a small, dark-skinned woman as Feeney's rattletrap of a car bumped up the road. 'Chas will see to your wound.'

'It's fine. I'll see an MT in the morning.'

'I don't think that will be necessary. Please come this way. It's unhealthy to have even this much of her here.'

She led the way around the clearing. Eve could see a wide circle formed by a ring of white candles. People stood outside it chatting, she mused, as they might at a midtown cocktail party. Dress varied. Robes, suits, long and short skirts.

Twenty in all, by her count, ranging in age from eighteen to eighty with a mixture of race and gender. There seemed no specific type. Coolers were stacked nearby, which, she supposed, explained why several members were sipping drinks. Conversation was muted, punctuated by the occasional laugh.

Chas turned from a folding table as they approached. He wore a simple blue unisuit and soft shoes in the same tone. He smiled, noting Eve's suspicious scan of the table.

'Witch's tools,' he told her.

Red cords, a white-handled knife. *An athame*, she thought. She saw more candles, a small brass gong, a whip, a gleaming silver sword, colored bottles, bowls, and cups.

'Interesting.'

'It's an old ritual, requiring old tools. But you're hurt.' He took a step toward her, his hand lifting, then pausing when she aimed a cool, warning look. 'I beg your pardon. It looks painful.'

'Chas is a healer.' Isis curved her lips in challenge. 'Consider this a demonstration. After all, you did come to observe, didn't you? And your mate wears protection.'

And so, Eve thought, feeling the comfortable weight of her weapon, did she.

'Okay, demonstrate.' She tilted her head, inviting Chas to examine the scratches.

His fingers were surprisingly cool, surprisingly soothing as they played over her abraded skin. She kept her eyes on his, watched them focus, then flicker. 'You're fortunate,' he murmured. 'The result didn't equal the intent. Will you relax your mind?'

His gaze lifted from his hand, met hers. 'The mind and body are one,' he said quietly in that lovely voice. 'One guides the other, one heals the other. Let me ease this.'

She thought she felt warmth move through her, from the point where his fingers lay, into her head, down through her body, until a drowsiness seeped through. She jerked herself alert, saw him smile quietly. 'I won't hurt you.'

He turned, picked up an amber bottle, uncorked the stopper and dabbed clear, floral-scented liquid on his hands.

'This is a balm, an old recipe with modern additions.' He spread it gently, his fingers following the path Selina's nails had raked. 'It will heal clean, and there will be no more discomfort.'

'You know your chemicals, don't you?'

'This is an herbal base.' He took a cloth from his pocket, wiped his fingers. 'But yes, I do.'

'I'd like to talk to you about that.' She waited a beat, her eyes keen. 'And about your father.'

She saw the demand hit home in the way his pupils dilated, then contracted. Then Isis was stepping between them, fury glorious on her face.

'You've been invited here; this place is sacred. You have no right—'

'Isis.' Chas touched her arm. 'She has a mission. We all do.' He looked at Eve, seemed to gather himself. 'Yes, I'll speak with you, when you wish. But this isn't the place to bring despair. The ceremony's about to begin.'

'We won't stop you.'

'Will tomorrow, nine o'clock, at Spirit Quest, be suitable?'

'That's fine.'

'Excuse me.'

'Do you always repay kindness with pain?' Isis demanded in a furious undertone as Chas stepped away. Then she shook her head, aimed her gaze deliberately at Roarke. 'You are welcome to observe, and we hope you and your companions will show the proper respect for our rite tonight. You aren't permitted within the magic circle.'

As she swept away, Eve slipped her hands into her pockets. 'Well, now I've got two witches pissed off at me.' She looked over as Peabody hurried to her side.

'It's an initiation,' Peabody whispered. 'I got it from the big gorgeous witch in the Italian suit.' She smiled across the clearing at a man with burnished bronze hair and a million-watt smile. 'Jesus, makes a woman consider converting.'

'Get a grip on yourself, Peabody.' Eve nodded at Feeney.

'My sainted mother would be saying half a dozen rosaries tonight if she knew where I was.' He pushed on a grin to cover nerves. 'Damn spooky place. Nothing out here but a lot of nothing.'

Roarke sighed, slipped an arm around Eve's waist. 'Cut from the same cloth,' he murmured and turned as the rite began.

The young woman Isis had called Mirium stood outside the circle of candles and was bound and blindfolded by two men. Everyone, but for the observers, was now naked. Skin glowed,

227

white and dark and gold in the streaming moonlight. Deeper in the woods night birds called liltingly.

Itchy, Eve slid a hand inside her jacket, felt the weight of her weapon.

The red cords were used for the binding of the initiate, leaving a kind of tether. As the ankle cord was attached, Chas spoke.

'Feet neither bound nor free.'

And there was unmistakable joy and reverence in his voice.

Curious, Eve watched the casting of the circle, the opening ritual. The mood was, she had to admit, happy. Overhead, the moon swam, sprinkling light, silvering the trees. Owls hooted – an odd sound that rippled through her blood. Nudity seemed to be ignored. There was none of the surreptitious groping or sly glances she knew she'd have seen at any city sex club.

Chas took up the athame, making Eve's hand close on her weapon as he held it to the postulant's heart. He spoke, his words rising and falling on the smoky breeze.

'I have two passwords,' Mirium answered. 'Perfect love and perfect trust.'

He smiled. 'All who have such are doubly welcome. I give you a third to pass you through this dread door.'

He handed the knife to the man beside him, then kissed Mirium. As a father might kiss a child, Eve thought, frowning. Chas walked around the postulant, embraced her, then gently nudged her forward into the circle. Behind them, the second man traced the tip of the athame over the empty space, as if to close them in.

There was chanting now as Chas led Mirium around the circle, as she was turned by hands after hands in a playful child's game of dizziness and disorientation. A bell rang three times.

It was Chas who knelt, speaking, then kissing the postulant's feet, her knees, her belly just above the pubis, her breasts, then her lips.

She'd thought it would be sexual, Eve mused. But it had been more . . . loving than that.

'Impressions?' She murmured to Roarke.

'Charming and powerful. Religious.' He slid his hand up and covered the one that still curled around her weapon, gently tugging it away. 'And harmless. Sexual, certainly, but in a very balanced and respectful sense. And yes, I see one or two people I recognize.'

'I'll want names.'

As the rite continued, she reached up absently to rub her throat. She found the skin smooth, unbroken, and free of pain.

As she dropped her hand, Chas looked at her, met her eyes. And smiled again.

Chapter Sixteen

Spirit Quest wasn't open for business when Eve arrived with Peabody. But Chas was there, waiting on the sidewalk, sipping something that steamed out of a recycle cup.

'Good morning.' The air was just chilled enough to have slapped color into his cheek. 'I wonder if we could talk upstairs, in our apartment, rather than in the shop.'

'Cops bad for business?' Eve asked.

'Well, we could say that the early customers might be disconcerted. And we do open in half an hour. I assume you don't need Isis.'

'Not at the moment.'

'I appreciate it. If you could, ah, give me just a moment.' He shot her a sheepish look. 'Isis prefers not to have caffeine in the house. I'm weak,' he said, taking another sip. 'She knows I sneak off every morning to feed my addiction and pretends not to. It's foolish, but it makes us happy.'

'Take your time. You get that across the street?'

'That would be a little too close to home. And to be honest, the coffee's filthy there. They make a decent cup down at the corner deli.' He sipped again with obvious pleasure. 'I gave up cigarettes years ago, even herbals, but I can't quite do without a cup of coffee. Did you enjoy the ceremony last night?'

'It was interesting.' Since the morning air was sharp, she tucked her ungloved hands in her pockets. Traffic, both street and air, was beginning to thin a little with the first commuter rush passing. 'Getting a little brisk to run around naked in the woods, isn't it?'

'Yes. We probably won't hold any more outdoor ceremonies this year. Certainly not skyclad. But Mirium had her heart set on being initiated to first-degree witch before Samhain.'

'Samhain.'

'Halloween,' he and Peabody said together. She shuffled her feet as he smiled at her. 'Free-Ager,' she muttered.

'Ah, there are some basic similarities.' He finished off his coffee, stepped over to a recycling bin, and neatly slipped the cup in the slot. 'You have a cold, Officer.'

'Yes, sir.' Peabody sniffled, determinedly blocked a sneeze.

'I have something that should ease that. One of our members recognized you, Lieutenant. She said she'd given you a reading lately. On the night, actually, that Alice died.'

'That's right.'

'Cassandra is very skilled and very sweet-natured,' Chas began as he started up the steps. 'She feels she should have been able to see more clearly, to tell you that Alice was in danger. She believes you are.' He paused, looked back. 'She hoped that you're still carrying the stone she gave you.'

'It's around somewhere.'

He let out a sound that might have been a sigh. 'How's your neck?'

'Good as new.'

'I see it's healed cleanly.'

'Yeah, and quickly. What was in that stuff you put on it?'

Humor flickered in his eyes, surprising her. 'Oh, just some tongue of bat, a little eye of newt.' He opened the door to a musical chime of bells. 'Please be comfortable. I'll get you some tea to warm you up since I kept you standing.'

'You don't have to bother.'

'It's no bother at all. Just be a moment.'

He slipped through a doorway, and Eve took the time to study his living quarters.

She wouldn't call them simple. Obviously, a lot of the stock from the shelves downstairs made its way up here. Large, many-speared hunks of crystals decorated an oval table and circled a copper urn filled with fall flowers. An intricate tapestry hung on the wall over a curved, blue sofa. Men and women, suns and moons, a castle with flame spewing from the arrow slits.

'The major arcana,' Peabody told her as Eve stepped up for a closer look. She sneezed once, violently, and dug out a tissue. 'The Tarot. It looks old, hand-worked.'

'Expensive,' Eve decided. Art such as this didn't come cheaply.

There were statues in pewter and carved from smooth stone. Wizards and dragons, two-headed dogs, sinuous women with delicate wings. Another wall was covered with odd, attractive symbols in splashes of color.

'From the Book of Kells.' Peabody lifted her shoulders at Eve's curious glance. 'My mother likes to embroider the symbols, like on pillows and samplers. They look nice. It's a nice place.' And it didn't give her the willies like the Cross apartment. 'Eccentric, but nice.'

'Business must be good for them to be able to afford the antiques, the metalwork, the art.'

'The business does well enough,' Chas said as he came back with a tray laden with a flower patterned ceramic pot and cups. 'And I had some resources of my own before we opened.'

'Inheritance?'

'No.' He set the tray down on a circular coffee table. 'Savings, investments. Chemical engineers are well paid.'

'But you gave it all up to work retail.'

'I gave it up,' he said simply. 'I was unhappy in my work. I was unhappy in my life.'

'Therapy didn't help.'

He met her eyes again, though it seemed to cost him. 'It didn't hurt. Please sit down. I'll answer your questions.'

'She can't make you go through this, Chas.' Isis slipped into the room like smoke. Her gown was gray today, the color of storm clouds, and swirled around her ankles as she moved to him. 'You're entitled to your privacy, under any law.'

'I can insist that he answer my questions,' Eve corrected. 'I'm investigating murder here. He is, of course, entitled to counsel.'

'It isn't a lawyer he needs, but peace.' Isis whirled, her eyes alive with emotion, and Chas took her hands, lifted them to his lips, pressed his face to them.

'I have peace,' he said quietly. 'I have you. Don't worry so. You have to go down and open, and I have to do this.'

'Let me stay.'

He shook his head, and the look they exchanged had Eve staring in surprise. It was baffling enough to speculate on their physical relationship, but what she saw pass between them wasn't sex. It was love. It was devotion.

It should have been laughable, the way Isis had to lean down, bend that goddess body to reach his lips with hers. Instead, it was poignant.

'You have only to call,' she told him. 'Only to wish for me.'

'I know.' He gave her hand a quick, intimate pat to send her off. She shot Eve one last look of barely controlled rage and swept out.

'I doubt I would have survived without her,' Chas said as he stared at the door. 'You're a strong woman, Lieutenant. It would be difficult for you to understand that kind of need, that kind of dependence.'

Once she would have agreed. Now she wasn't so sure. 'I'd like to record this conversation, Mr Forte.'

'Yes, of course.' He sat, and as Peabody engaged her recorder, mechanically poured the tea. He listened without glancing up as Eve recited the traditional caution.

'Do you understand your rights and obligations?'

'Yes. Would you care for sweetener?'

She looked down at her tea with some impatience. It smelled suspiciously like what Mira insisted on serving her. 'No.'

'I've added a bit of honey to yours, Officer.' He sent Peabody a sweet smile. 'And a bit of . . . something else. I think you'll find it soothing.'

'Smells pretty good.' Cautious, Peabody sipped, tasted home, and smiled back. 'Thanks.'

'When's the last time you saw your father?'

Caught off guard by the abruptness of Eve's question, Chas looked up quickly. The hand holding his cup shook once, violently. 'The day he was sentenced. I went to the hearing and I watched them take him away. They kept him in full restraints and they closed and locked the door on his life.'

'And how did you feel about that?'

'Ashamed. Relieved. Desperately unhappy. Or perhaps just desperate. He was my father.' Chas took a deep gulp of tea, as some men might take a gulp of whiskey. 'I hated him with all of my heart, all of my soul.'

'Because he killed?'

'Because he was my father. I hurt my mother deeply by insisting on attending his trial. But she was too battered emotionally to stop me from doing as I chose. She could never stop him, either. Though she did leave him eventually. She took me and left him, which was, I think, a surprise to all of us.'

He stared down into his cup, as if contemplating the pattern of the leaves skimming the bottom. 'I hated her, too, for a very, very long time. Hate can define a person, can't it, Lieutenant? It can twist them into an ugly shape.'

'Is that what happened to you?'

'Nearly. Ours was not a happy home. You wouldn't expect that it could be with a man like my father dominating it. You suspect I could be like him.' Chas's sensual voice remained calm. But his eyes were swirling with emotions.

It was the eyes you watched during interview, Eve thought. The words often meant nothing. 'Are you?'

'"Blood will tell." Is that Shakespeare?' He shook his head a little. 'I'm not quite sure. But isn't that what all children live with, and fear no matter what their parents, that blood will tell?'

She lived with it, she feared it, but she couldn't allow herself to be swayed by it. 'How strong an influence was he on your life?'

'There couldn't have been a stronger one. You're an efficient investigator, Lieutenant. I'm sure you've studied the records by now, run the discs, watched them. You would have seen a charismatic man, terrifyingly so. A man who considered himself above the law – any and all laws. That kind of steely arrogance is in itself compelling.'

'Evil can be compelling to some.'

'Yes.' His lips curved without humor. 'You'd know that, in your line of work. He wasn't a man you could . . . fight, on a physical or emotional level. He's strong. Very strong.'

Chas closed his eyes a moment, reliving what he was constantly struggling to put to death. 'I was afraid I could be like him, considered giving back the most precious gift I'd been given. Life.'

'You attempted self-termination?'

'I never got as far as the attempt, just the plan. The first time, I was ten.' He sipped tea again, determined to soothe himself. 'Can you imagine a child of ten pondering suicide?'

Yes, she could, all too well. She'd been younger yet when she had pondered it. 'He abused you?'

'Abuse is such a weak term, don't you think? He beat me. He never seemed to be in a rage when he did. He just struck out at unexpected moments, snapping a bone, raising a fist, with the absent calm another man might display while flicking away a fly.'

His fist was clenched on his knee. Deliberately, Chas opened

235

his hand, spread his fingers. 'He struck like a shark, fast and in utter silence. There was never a warning, never a gauge. My life, my pain, was totally dependent on his whim. I've had my time in Hell,' he said softly, almost as a prayer.

'No one helped you?' Eve asked. 'Attempted to intervene?'

'We never stayed in one place very long, and were allowed to form no attachments or friendships. He claimed he needed to spread the word. And he would snap a bone, raise a fist, then take me into a treatment center himself. A concerned father.'

'You told no one?'

'He was my father, it was my life.' Chas lifted his hands, let them fall. 'Who was I to tell?'

Neither had she told anyone, Eve thought. Neither had she had anyone to tell.

'And for quite a while, I believed him when he said it was just.' Chas's eyes flickered. 'And I certainly believed him when he told me there would be terrible pain and terrible punishment if I said anything. I was thirteen when he sodomized me for the first time. It was a ritual, he told me, when he bound my hands and I wept. A rite of passage. Sex was life. It was necessary to take it. He would take me on the journey as was his duty and his right.'

He picked up the tea pot, poured, set it neatly aside. 'I don't know if it was rape. I didn't struggle. I didn't beg him to stop. I simply cried without sound and submitted.'

'It was rape,' Peabody said, and her voice was very quiet.

'Well . . .' He found he couldn't drink the tea he'd just poured but lifted the cup, held it. 'I told no one. Even years later when they had him in a cage, I didn't tell the police. I didn't believe they would hold him. I simply didn't believe they could. He was too strong, too powerful, and all the blood on his hands seemed to add to it. Oddly enough, it was the sex that pushed my mother to run, and take me. Not the violence, not the little boy with broken bones or even the deaths I think she knew he'd caused. It was the sight of him kneeling over me on his altar, with the black candles lit. He didn't see her, but I did. I saw her face when she stepped into the room. She left me there, let him finish with me, and that night when he went out, we ran.'

'And still she didn't go to the police.'

'No.' He looked at Eve. 'I know you believe if she had, lives might have been saved. But fear is a very personal emotion. Survival was her only goal. When they arrested him, I went to the trial, every day. I was sure he would stop it somehow. Even when they said they would lock him away, I still didn't believe. I erased his name, and I tried to slip into normality. I took a job that interested me, that I had some talent for. And I allowed myself to get close to no one. There was a rage in me. I would look at a face and hate it because it was happy. Or it was sad. I hated them all for their unshadowed existence. And like my father, I didn't stay in one place very long. And when I found myself considering suicide again with great calm and great seriousness, I was frightened enough to seek help.'

He was able to smile again. 'It was, though I didn't realize it at the time, the beginning for me, taking that step, allowing myself to speak the unspeakable. I learned to accept my own innocence, and to forgive my mother. But the rage was still there, this hard, secret knot inside me. Then I met Isis.'

'Through your interest in the occult,' Eve prompted.

'Through my study of it, as part of my therapy.' He drank his tea now, and his lips were curved. 'I was angry and rude. Religion of any kind was an abomination to me, and I detested what she stood for. She was so beautiful, so full of light. I hated her for that. She challenged me to come to a ceremony, to observe much as you did last night. I preferred to think of myself as a scientist. I would go, I thought, to prove there was nothing in her faith but old words repeated by fools. Just as there had been nothing in my father's creed but an excuse to hurt and dominate.

'I stood back, separate, cynical, and secretly enraged. I hated them for their simplicity and their devotion. Hadn't I seen that same captured look on the faces of those who'd gathered to hear my father speak? I wanted nothing to do with it, with them, but I was drawn back. Three times I went back and watched, and though I didn't know it, I had begun to heal. And one night, on Alban Eilir, the Spring Equinox, Isis asked me into her home. When we were alone, she told me that she had recognized me. I panicked. I'd tried so hard to bury all of that, all of him. She said she hadn't meant from this life, though I could see in her eyes that she knew. She knew who I was, what I'd come from. She told me I had a great capacity for healing, and I would discover it once I had healed myself. Then she seduced me.'

He gave a short laugh, and in it was great warmth. 'Imagine my surprise when this beautiful woman led me to her bed. I went along like a puppy, half eager, half terrified. She was the first woman I'd had, and the only one I've been with. And on the night of the Spring Equinox, that hard, secret knot inside me began to dissolve.

'She loves me. And the miracle of that made me believe in other miracles. I became Wiccan, I embraced and was embraced by the craft. I learned to heal myself and others. The only person I've ever harmed in my life has been myself. But I understand better than Isis with all her insights, the lure of violence, of selfishness, of bowing to another master.'

She believed him, yet too much of his past mirrored her own for her to trust her instincts. 'You've gone to a great deal of effort to hide your connection with your father.'

'Wouldn't you?'

'Did Alice know?'

'Alice was innocence. She was youth. There were no David Baines Conroys in her life. Until Selina Cross.'

'And Cross is an intelligent and vindictive woman. If she'd discovered your secret, she might have used Alice, and others, to blackmail you. Would the members of your cult trust you if they knew your history?'

'Since that's never been tested, I don't have the answer. I'd prefer, certainly, to keep my privacy.'

'And on the night Alice was killed, you were here. Alone with Isis.'

'Yes, and we were here, alone, on the night Lobar was killed. You know I was on hand at the last murder, again with Isis. And yes.' He smiled slightly. 'I have no doubt she would lie for me. But while she would live with a murderer's son, she would never live with a murderer. It's against everything she is.'

'She loves you.'

'Yes.'

'And you love her.'

'Yes.' He blinked, and horror filled his eyes. 'You can't believe she'd have a part in any of this, beyond the fact that she loved Alice, cared for her as a mother would a sick child. She's incapable of hurting anyone.'

'Mr. Forte, everyone is capable.'

'You don't think he's involved,' Peabody said as they started down the outside stairs.

'There's history of aberrant behavior in his family. He has an expert knowledge of chemicals, including hallucinogens and herbals. He has no alibi for any of the incidents. He was associated with Alice, closely enough that she may have stumbled across the secret he's been hiding for years, and that exposed, could destroy his cult.'

She paused, tapping her fingers against the rail as she ticked off her mental list. 'He has good reason to hate Selina Cross and her membership, to want to punish them as he couldn't punish his father. He was on hand when Wineburg started to break, and could have easily circled around and killed him. That gives him motive and opportunity, and with his background, the potential for violent behavior.'

'He's made himself a decent life after a nightmare child-hood,' Peabody protested. 'You can't condemn him for what his father did.'

Eve stared out at the street and fought her own demons. 'I'm not condemning him, Peabody, I'm investigating every possibility. Consider this.' She turned. 'If Alice knew, and told Frank, his reaction might very well have been to demand she break off the connection. It's likely, following this line of speculation, that he confronted Forte himself, even threatened him with exposure if he didn't break off his influence. He was in Homicide when Conroy was taken in, and he'd have known and remembered every filthy detail.'

'Yes, but—'

'And Alice moved into her own place. She continued to work part time for Isis, but she no longer lived here. Why did she move out, away from here, when she was afraid?'

'I don't know,' Peabody admitted.

'And we can't ask her.' Eve turned back, started down the stairs again, then swore when she saw the boy leaning on her vehicle. 'Well, hell.'

She strode down, straight over to Jamie. 'Get your butt off my hood. This is an official vehicle.'

'An official piece of shit,' he corrected with a quick, sassy grin. 'The city puts you cops into recycled garbage heaps. A high-profile detective like you ought to have better.'

'I'll tell the chief you said so next time I'm in the Tower. What are you doing here?'

'Just hanging.' His grin flashed again. 'And I ditched the shadow you put on me. He's good.' Jamie tucked his thumbs in his pockets. 'I'm better.'

'Why aren't you in school?'

'Don't bother to call the Truant Brigade, Lieutenant, it's Saturday.'

How the hell was she supposed to keep track? 'Then why

aren't you terrorizing one of the sky malls like a normal delinquent?'

His grin spread. 'I hate sky malls. They're so yesterday. Caught you on Channel 75.'

'Did you drop by for my autograph?'

'You scrawl it on a credit slip, I could outfit this heap of yours and make it rock.' He looked past her toward the shop. 'I got a load of the witch through the glass. She's doing some heavy retail today.'

Eve glanced back, noted the customers browsing inside. 'You've seen her before.'

'Yeah, couple times when I tailed Alice.'

'Ever see anything interesting?'

'Nope. Everybody's always wearing clothes in there.' He wiggled his brows. 'A guy has to hope. I studied up on Wicca. They liked to be naked a lot. Did see the head witch kick a guy out of the shop once.'

'Really.' It was Eve's turn to lean on the hood. 'Why?'

'Couldn't say, but she was maximum pissed. I could see they were having words, and I thought she was going to belt him. Especially when he shoved her.'

'He shoved her.'

'Yeah. I thought about going in then, though she was a hell of a lot bigger than he was. Still, guys got no business pushing women around. But whatever she said had him backing off. Backing way off until he was backing right out of the door. And he went off in a big hurry.'

'What did he look like?'

'Skinny dude, five ten, maybe a hundred and twenty-five. Couple years older than me. Long black hair, red tips. Long face, with his incisors fanged. Red eyes. Light complexion. Turned out in tight black leather, no shirt, couple of tattoos, but I was too far away to make them out.'

He shot her a smile, grim around the edges. 'Sounds familiar, doesn't it? Last time I saw him, he wasn't looking so jazzy.'

241

Lobar, Eve thought, exchanging a glance with Peabody. The kid had given a solid and nearly professional description. 'And when was this? When did you see the incident?'

'The day—' His voice cracked a little, so he cleared his throat. 'The day before Alice died.'

'And what did Isis do after Lobar?'

'She made a call. Couple minutes later the dude she lives with came on the run. They talked for a couple minutes, real intense, then she put up the Closed sign and they went into the back room. Ticked me off,' he added. 'I could have followed the leather guy.'

'You want to stop tailing people, Jamie. They make you, they tend to get annoyed.'

'People I tail don't make me. I'm too good.'

'You thought you were good at B and E too,' she reminded him dryly and watched as his color rose.

'That was different. Look, the guy that was stabbed, he was right there, at Alice's viewing. It has to be connected, to her, to that Lobar creep, and I got a right to know.'

She straightened. 'Are you requesting the status of my investigation?'

'Yeah, yeah, right.' He rolled his eyes skyward. 'What's the status of your investigation?'

'Ongoing,' she said shortly, then jerked a thumb. 'Now, scram.'

'I got a right to know,' he insisted. 'Survivors of victims, and all that.'

'You're the grandson of a cop,' she reminded him. 'You know I'm not going to tell you anything. And you're a minor. I don't have to tell you anything. Now, go play somewhere else, kid, before I have Peabody here roust you for loitering.'

The muscles of his jaw tightened and jumped. 'I'm not a kid. And if you don't deal with Alice's killer, I will.'

Eve snagged his arm by the jacket before he could storm away. 'Don't cross the line,' she said very quietly. She kept her face close to his, forcing him to look directly into her eyes. 'You want justice, you'll get it. I'll by God get it for you. You want revenge, I'll slap you in a cage. You remember what Frank stood for, and what your sister was, and then you think it all through again. Now, get out of here.'

'I loved them.' He jerked his arm free, but not before she saw tears rush into his eyes. 'Fuck your justice. And fuck you.'

She let him walk because, though the language had been an adult's, the tears had been a child's.

'The kid's hurting,' Peabody murmured.

'I know.' So was she now. 'Tail him, will you, just to be sure he doesn't get in any trouble. Give it thirty minutes, until he calms down, then beep your location. I'll pick you up.'

'You going to talk to Isis?'

'Yeah, let's see what she and Lobar had to say to each other. Oh, and Peabody, watch your step. Jamie's a clever kid. If he made one of Roarke's men, he's likely to make you.'

Peabody flashed a smile. 'I think I can manage to tail a kid for a few blocks.'

Trusting her aide to keep Jamie out of trouble, Eve walked into Spirit Quest. The air swam with incense and the scented melted wax from dozens of candles. The October sun was strong and gleamed in shooting colors through hanging prisms.

The look Isis sent her held none of that exotic welcome.

'You've finished with Chas, Lieutenant?'

'For now. I'd like a few minutes.'

Isis turned to answer a question from a customer on a blend of herbs to enhance memory. 'Steep it for five minutes,' Isis told her. 'Then strain it. You'll need to drink it daily for at least a week. If it doesn't help, let me know.' She turned her head back to Eve. 'As you can see, this is a bad time.'

'I'll be quick. I'm just curious about the visit you had from Lobar here, a few days before he ended up with his throat slashed.'

She'd kept her voice down, but left her intention clear.

They would talk, in private, or in public. The location was up to Isis.

'I don't think I misjudged you,' Isis said quietly, 'but you make me doubt myself.' She signaled to a young woman Eve recognized from the initiation rite. 'Jane will handle the customers,' Isis said as she started toward the back room. 'But I don't want to leave her long. She's very new at shop work.'

'Alice's replacement.'

Isis's eyes burned. 'No one could replace Alice.'

She entered what appeared to be a combination of office and storeroom. On the reinforced plastic shelves were gargoyles, candles, sealed bins of dried herbs, clear stoppered bottles filled with liquids of varying hues.

On the small desk was a very modern and efficient computer and communication system. 'Jazzy equipment,' Eve commented. 'Very now.'

'We don't eschew technology, Lieutenant. We adapt, and we use what is available to us. It's always been so.' She gestured to a chair with a high, carved back, took another for herself, one with armrests shaped like wings. 'You said you would be quick. But first I need to know if you intend to leave Chas in peace.'

'My priority is closing a case, not the peace of mind of a suspect.'

'How could you suspect him?' Her hands curled around the armrests as she leaned forward. 'You, of all people, know what he's overcome.'

'If his past is relevant—'

'Is yours?' Isis demanded. 'Is the fact that you survived a nightmare to your credit or to your detriment?'

'My past is my business,' Eve said evenly, 'and you know nothing about it.'

'What comes to me, comes in flashes and impressions. Stronger in some cases than others. I know you suffered and were innocent. Just as Chas is. I know you carry scars and harbor doubts. As he does. I know you struggle to make your own peace. And I see a room.'

Her voice changed, deepened, just as her eyes did. 'A small, cold room washed with dirty red light. And a child, battered and bleeding, huddled in a corner. The pain is unspeakable, beyond endurance. And I see a man. He's covered with blood. His face is—'

'Stop it.' Eve's heart was hammering, choking off her air. For a moment, she'd been back there, back in that child who'd crawled whimpering like an animal into the corner with blood staining her hands. 'Damn you.'

'I'm sorry.' Isis lifted a hand to press it to her own heart, and it trembled. 'I'm so very sorry. That's not my way. I let anger take over.' She shut her eyes tight. 'I'm so very sorry.'

Chapter Seventeen

Eve lurched out of the chair. There was no room to pace, to prowl, to steam off the dregs of memory. 'I'm aware,' she began coldly, 'that you have what is commonly called heightened psychic skill. HPS is still being studied. I have a report on my desk right now. So you've got a talent, Isis. Congratulations. Now, stay the hell out of my head.'

'I will.' Pity swam in her eyes and couldn't be blinked away. She'd seen much more than she'd expected or intended. 'I can only apologize again. Part of me wanted to hurt you. I didn't control it.'

'It must be hard to control it when you're angry. When you're threatened. When you see a weakness and can exploit it.'

Isis took a careful breath. Her system was still rocked, not only by what she'd seen, but what she'd done. 'It isn't my way. It's against the foundation of my faith. I will cause no harm.' She lifted her hands, rubbing her fingertips under her eyes to dry them. 'I'll answer your questions. You wanted to know about Lobar.'

'You were seen arguing with him here in the store, the day before Alice died.'

'Was I?' She drew her composure back, cloaked it over her. 'It's always a mistake to believe yourself alone. Yes, he was here. Yes, we had words.'

'About?'

'Alice, most specifically. He was a misguided young man, filled with a dangerous self-importance. He thought himself powerful. He was not.'

'Alice wasn't here, she wasn't working that day?'

'No. I'd hoped she'd spend time with her family, connect with them again through her grandfather's death. That was the primary reason I'd encouraged her to move out of here and into a place of her own. I'd asked her not to come in for a few days. Lobar expected her to be here. I don't believe he was sent, but came on his own. Maybe to prove himself.'

'And you argued.'

'Yes. He said that I couldn't hide her, that she'd never get away. She'd broken the law – the law that Cross and those who belong to her subscribe to. He said her punishment would be torture and pain and death.'

'He threatened her life, and you didn't tell me. I was here before, and I questioned you.'

'No, I didn't tell you. I considered it no more than a clash of wills, his against mine. He was no more than a pawn. I didn't require HPS to intuit that. He only wanted to upset me, to prove his superiority. His way of doing so was to describe, graphically, what he had done to Alice sexually.' She drew another breath. 'And he told me that I had been promised to him. That when I was taken in, when my power was crushed, he would be the first to lay hands on me. Then he told me what he intended to do and how much I would enjoy it. He invited me to sample some of his many talents then and there, so that I would see how much more of a man he was than Chas. I laughed at him.'

'Did he assault you?'

'He pushed me. He was angry. I'd deliberately baited him into it. Then I used it. An old spell,' she said with a flick of her hand. 'What you might call a mirror or boomerang spell, so that what he was sending toward me – all the darkness, the violence, the hate – was reflected back at him, and when

247

reflected, enlarged.' She smiled a little. 'He left quickly, and very frightened. He didn't come back.'

'And you were frightened?'

'Yes, on a physical level, I was.'

'You called Forte.'

'He's my mate.' Isis lifted her chin. 'I have no secrets from him, and I depend on him.'

'He'd have been angry.'

'No.' Eyes level, she shook her head. 'Concerned, yes. We cast a circle, performed a rite for protection and for purification. We were content. I should have seen,' she continued, with regret shimmering in her voice. 'I should have seen that Alice was their goal. Pride made me believe they would turn on me, that they wouldn't dare touch her while she was under my protection. Maybe I wasn't as honest with you as I might have been, Dallas, because without my pride blinding me, I know Alice might still be alive.'

Guilt was there, Eve decided as she drove off to pick up Peabody. And guilt could lead to retribution. Frank and Alice had been killed by a different method than Lobar and Wineburg. The deaths were connected, she was certain, but the connection didn't mean they'd all been committed by the same hand.

She wanted to get back to Central, run a probability scan. There was enough data for it now. And if the numbers warranted it, she could go to Whitney and request the manpower for a twenty-four-seven watch on both groups of suspects.

Damn the budget, she thought as she fought traffic. She'd need a high probability ratio to wangle the expense of time, money, and manpower. But Peabody and Feeney weren't enough to keep round-the-clock tabs on everyone involved.

Including Jamie, she thought. The kid was looking for trouble. She believed he was smart enough to find it.

Peabody hopped in when Eve swung to the curb at Seventh

and Forty-seventh. Across the sidewalk, the rowdy noise and computerized warfare of a VR den spilled out of the open doorway. It nicked the ordinance on noise pollution, but Eve figured the proprietors were willing to risk a fine or two in order to lure in tourists and the bored.

'He in there?'

'Yes, sir.' Peabody looked hopefully at the rising steam from a glida grill. She could smell fresh soy burgers and oil fries. It was near enough to lunch to make her stomach yearn and her heart sink at the thought of facing the slop served at the Eatery back at Central. 'Do you mind if I grab something from this cart?'

Eve shot an impatient look out the window. 'Aren't you supposed to starve a cold or something?'

'I never could keep that straight. Anyway,' Peabody took a long deep breath through her nose, 'I feel great. That tea did the trick.'

'Yeah, yeah. Make it quick, and eat it on the way.'

'Do you want anything?' Peabody asked over her shoulder as she pushed out of the car.

'No. Snap it up and let's roll.'

Drugs, sex, Satan, and power, Eve mused. *A religious war? Hadn't humans fought and died for beliefs since the dawn of time? Animals fought for territory; people fought for territory as well. And for gain, for passion, for beliefs. For the hell of it.*

They killed, she thought, *very much for the same reasons.*

'Got two of everything,' Peabody announced and set the thin cardboard filled with food on the seat between them. 'Just in case. If you don't want it, I can probably choke it down. It's the first time I've had an appetite in two days.'

She bit into the loaded burger while Eve waited for a break in traffic. 'The kid led me on quite a route. Walked off his mad for ten blocks, caught an uptown tram, got off, headed west. And talk about appetite. He hit a cart on Sixth and downed two real pig dogs, and a mega scoop of fries. Hit another a block down for an orange Freezie, which happens to be a personal favorite of mine. Before he went into the VR den, he tagged this guy for three candy bars.'

'Growing boy,' Eve commented, and shot out like a bullet when she saw a slim gap in traffic. Horns bellowed in protest. 'As long as he's eating junk and playing VR, he should stay out of trouble.'

Inside the whoops and whistles of the arcade, Jamie sneered at the holograms battling on his personal screen. He listened to the exchange in Eve's car, courtesy of his earpiece, and the micro recorder and location device he'd planted.

Yeah, it had been worth the risk, he decided, diddling with the VR controls with his mind wandering. Of course, it hadn't been that much of a challenge. Not only was the cop car a rolling heap of refuse, but its security system was rinky. At least when it came up against the skills of the master of electronics.

Dallas wouldn't tell him what was going on, he thought grimly and destroyed the holo image of an urban tough. He'd just keep tabs on things his own way. And he'd deal with things his own way.

Whoever had killed his sister had better prepare to die.

Eve ran the probability program with mixed results. The computer agreed, by a ninety-six percentile, that the four cases were connected. The numbers dropped ten points when it came to tagging different perpetrators.

Charles Forte scored high on the index, as did Selina Cross. For Alban, she continued to run up against insufficient data.

Frustrated, she buzzed Feeney. 'I've got some data I want to download on you. For a probability scan. Can you see what you can do with the numbers?'

He wiggled his brows. 'You want them higher or lower?'

She laughed, shook her head. 'I want them higher, but I want it solid. Could be I'm missing something.'

'Shoot it over, I'll take a look.'

'Appreciate it. And there's something else. I'm running into blanks every time I try to access data on this Alban character. The guys in his thirties. There has to be more on him. I'm not getting education, medical, family history. There's no criminal record, not even an illegal zone stop. My take is he had it wiped.'

'Takes a lot of talent and a lot of money to wipe it clean. Something's always somewhere.'

She thought of Roarke, and the suspiciously limited data on record. Well, he had a lot of talent, she reminded herself. And a lot of money. 'I figured if anybody could find anything . . .'

'Yeah, flatter me, kid.' He winked. 'I'll get back to you.'

'Thanks, Feeney.'

'Was that Feeney?' Mavis bounced in, literally, on new air pump, stack-heeled, neon yellow sneakers. 'Shoot, you zipped off. I wanted to talk to him.'

Eve ran her tongue around her teeth. Mavis was decked out in classic Mavis style. Her hair matched her sneakers and made the eyes burn. She wore it in a spiral mass of curls that exploded up as much as down. Her slacks were glossy simulated rubber, dipped well below the glinting red stone in her navel, and hugged every curve. Her blouse, if it could be called that, was a snug band of material that matched the slacks and almost covered her breasts.

Over it all she wore a transparent duster.

'Anybody try to arrest you on the way in?'

'No, but I think the desk sergeant had an orgasm.' Mavis fluttered emerald green lashes and dropped into a chair. 'Great outfit, huh? Just off Leonardo's drawing board. So, are you ready?'

'Ready? For what?'

'We've got a salon date. Trina shuffled you in. I left the

message on your unit. Twice.' She narrowed her eyes at Eve. 'Don't tell me you didn't get it, because I know you did. You logged it out.'

Logged it out, Eve remembered. And ignored it. 'Mavis, I don't have time to play hair.'

'You haven't taken lunch today. I checked with the desk sarge,' Mavis said smugly. 'Before his orgasm. You can eat while Trina whips you into shape.'

'I don't want to be whipped into shape.'

'It wouldn't be so bad if you hadn't hacked at it again yourself.' Mavis rose, picked up Eve's jacket. 'You might as well come quietly. I'm just going to keep hounding you. Log out for lunch, take an hour. You'll be back and making our city safe by one thirty.'

Because it was easier than arguing. Eve snatched the jacket, shrugged it on. 'Just the hair. I'm not having her put all the gunk on my face.'

'Dallas, relax.' Mavis began to tug her out. 'Enjoy being a girl.'

Eve snapped out her log book to mark time, scanning Mavis's rubber clad butt bouncing along. 'I don't think that means the same thing to you as it does to me.'

Maybe it was the fumes – the potions and lotions, the oils and dyes and lacquers so typical in salons – but Eve found inspiration striking as she tipped back in her treatment chair.

She wasn't sure how they'd gotten her to take off her clothes, submit to the indignity of the body smoother, the facial, the poking and prodding. She had managed to put her foot down – her bare, now toenail-painted foot down – when the discussion had veered toward temporary tattoos and body piercing.

Othewise, she was a hostage, coated with goop, her hair covered with the spermlike cream Trina swore by. Privately, she could admit she was deeply terrified of Trina with her snapping scissors and green glop. That's why she kept her

eyes shut during the procedure, so as not to imagine herself
emerging looking like a Trina clone with frizzed fuchsia hair
and torpedo breasts.

'Been too long,' Trina lectured. 'I told you, you need regular
treatments. You got the basics, but you don't enhance, you lose
the edge. If you came in regular, it wouldn't take so long to
bring you back.'

She didn't want to be brought back, Eve thought. She wanted
to be left alone. She suppressed a shudder as she felt something
buzzing around her eyes. Brow shaping, she reminded herself
and struggled to calm. Trina was not tattooing a smiley face
on her forehead.

'I've got to get back. I've got work.'

'Don't rush me. Magic takes time.'

Magic, Eve thought and rolled her eyes, causing Trina to
hiss at her. *Everybody was obsessed with magic, it seemed.*

She frowned, listening to Mavis chirp happily about a new
body polish that gave the skin a gold glow. 'This is mag, Trina.
I've got to try it full body. Leonardo would lap it up.'

'You can get it temp, and edible. Six flavors on the market
now. Apricot's real popular.'

Potions and lotions, Eve thought. *Smoke and mirrors. Rites
and rituals.* She opened her eyes to slits, saw Mavis and Trina
huddled over a vial of gold liquid. *Mavis with her neon hair*,
she thought with odd affection, *Trina with her pink frizz.*

Weird sisters.

Weird sisters, she thought again and sat up. Trina let out
another hiss.

'Back down, Dallas. You got two minutes left.'

'Mavis, you said you used to run a psychic con.'

'Sure.' Mavis fluttered her newly painted neon nails.
'Madam Electra sees all, knows all. Or Ariel, the sad-
eyed sprite.' She dipped her head, managed to look delicate and forlorn. 'I guess I had about six grifts on that
theme.'

'You could spot somebody pulling the same grift?'

'Shit, are you kidding? From three blocks with sunshades on.'

'You were good,' Eve considered. 'I never saw you in that gig, but you were good in the others.'

'You busted me.'

'I'm better.' Eve flashed a smile and felt the glop on her face ooze. 'Listen; there's this place you could check out for me,' she began as Trina marched over and shoved her back into the horizontal. 'Both of you,' she added, eyeing Trina.

'Hey, is this a cop deal?'

'Maybe.'

'Frigid,' Trina said and pushed Eve back toward the rinsing bowl.

'You could scope it out.' Eve squeezed her eyes shut as water flooded. 'See if you can get the clerk – her name's Jane – to talk. Give me a rundown. They don't come clean with cops.'

'Who does?' Trina wanted to know.

'I want impressions,' Eve continued. 'You're interested in herbs, in mind expansion, love potions, sex enhancers. Soothers.

'Illegals?' It didn't take Mavis long to catch on. 'You think they might be dealing?'

'It's a possibility I need to confirm or eliminate. You could spot it every bit as quick as an undercover. And you could spot a grift. If they're hosing customers. If they're playing any cons. The money's coming from somewhere.'

'This could rock, Mavis.' Trina grinned. 'You and me, a couple of detectives. Like Sherlock and Dr Jekyll.'

'Decent. I thought it was Dr Holmes, though.'

Eve closed her eyes again.

Must be the fumes, she decided.

When she arrived home, Mavis and Trina were there, entertaining Roarke with their exploits. Eve scooped up the cat and followed the laughter.

'I bought this lotion to rub on,' Trina was saying. 'It's supposed to bring out the animal in men. Like pheromones.' She stuck her long arm under Roarke's nose. 'What's it do for you?'

'If I wasn't married to a woman who carries a weapon, I'd . . .' He trailed off, grinned. 'Hello, darling.'

'You could finish the thought,' Eve told him and dumped Galahad in his lap.

'I'll wait until you're unarmed.'

'Dallas, it was so, so decent.' Mavis popped up, waving her glass of wine so that the straw-colored liquid sloshed to the rim. 'I can't wait to get home and tell Leonardo. But Trina and I, we wanted to grab some nutrition, you know, and come right over and report. You should see all the stuff I bought.'

She started to dive into one of several shopping bags with the Spirit Quest logo. Eve resisted groaning and tugged Mavis's arm. 'Talk now, show later. I must have lost my mind, sending the two of you in there. I tell you,' she said whirling to Roarke. 'It's the fumes in those places. That's what makes people sit there and let themselves be shaved and painted and pierced.'

His eyes clouded briefly. 'Pierced? Where, exactly?'

'Oh, she wouldn't go for the nipple job.' Trina waved a hand. 'Said she'd zap me if I came near her with the jabber.'

'Good girl,' Roarke murmured. 'I'm proud of your restraint.'

Because her head was starting to ache, Eve poured herself a glass of wine. 'Did the two of you do anything in there but spend your credits?'

'We had readings,' Mavis told her. 'Genuinely iced. I've got an adventurous soul, and my narcissism is balanced by a generous heart.'

Eve couldn't help it; she laughed. 'You don't have to be

psychic to read that one, Mavis. You just have to have eyes. You did go in dressed like that, right?'

Mavis dangled her neon sneaker. 'Sure. Jane, the clerk, was real helpful, seemed to know her herbs. We judged her sincere, right Trina?'

'Jane was sincere,' Trina agreed, soberly. 'Kinda dull. I could fix her up with a couple sessions. A little high-lighter, some body work. Now, the goddess, hard to improve on that one.'

'Isis.' Eve sat up. 'She was there?'

'She came out of the back while we were doing the herb thing,' Mavis put in. 'I was saying how I wanted something to improve my performance level, boost my stage energy. See, when you're working a grift, you hang better if you believe the con. So if you can do true, it's mag.'

'I was looking for sex stuff.' Trina smiled sinuously. 'Stuff to attract men, lift sexual performance. And I said how I had this stressful job. Kept me tense and edgy. Over-the-counters just weren't cutting it for me. So I thought they might have something more potent, and I didn't mind the cost.'

'They had lots of blends.' Mavis took up the story. 'I didn't see anything off. Fact is, she said how drugs weren't the answer. What we wanted was the natural way. Like holistic.'

'Holistic,' Trina agreed. 'We nudged her, flashed credits and stuff, but she wasn't buying. Or I guess that would be selling.'

'The Amazon Queen went into the back.' Mavis picked up the story. 'Came back with this mix.' Hair flying, Mavis dug into her shopping bag, tossed the smaller, clear bag to Eve. 'Said I should sample it, and wouldn't charge me. She wants me to let her know if it worked for me. You can test it out, but I'd say it's clean.'

'Who gave you the reading?'

'Isis. She didn't look too keen when she came in.' Mavis tipped back her glass. 'We were playing it up, you know. I

256

went with the wide-eyed giggle act. Oohed and aahed a lot over the stock.'

Eve shifted her gaze to the shopping bags. 'I see you carried the act through.'

'I liked the stuff.' Mavis grinned, unrepentant. 'Then AQ, you know, Amazon Queen, she started to get into it. I had my sights on this A-one crystal ball, a green one. What did she call it, Trina?'

'Tourma-something.'

'Tourmaline,' Roarke provided.

'Yeah, right. Tourmaline. She steered me away, said it was for relaxing, for soothing, and if I wanted energy, I should go for the orange one. For, like, vitality.'

'More expensive?' Eve assumed.

'No, cheaper. Way cheaper. She said how the green one wasn't for me. She thought I had a friend who could use it, someone close to me who carried too much stress. But she should choose it for herself, when she was ready.'

Eve grunted, frowned.

'Then she gave us a reading. Mega. She said how she was glad we'd come in. She'd needed the positive energy. She wouldn't charge us for the readings. I liked her, Dallas. She hasn't got the eyes of a grifter.'

'Okay, thanks. I'll check out the package.' One way to make money, Eve mused, was to round up repeat customers. And a sure way to insure repeaters was to addict them.

'We got to make it.' Mavis was up again, gathering her bags. 'I bought this candle for romance. I want to see if it works. See you Tuesday night.'

'Tuesday?'

Mavis tapped her platform sneaker. 'Our Halloween party, Dallas. You said you'd come.'

'I must have been drunk.'

'No, you weren't. Nine o'clock, our place. Everybody's coming. I even tagged Feeney. See you.'

'Loosen up,' Trina advised as she strolled out. 'Wear a costume.'

'Not in this lifetime,' Eve muttered. 'Well.' She bounced the small bag of leaves and seeds in her hand. 'That was probably a monumental waste of time.'

'They enjoyed themselves. And you'll feel better once you analyze that mix.'

'I suppose. I'm not getting anywhere.' Eve set the bag on the table. 'I keep taking wrong turns. I can feel it.'

'Enough wrong turns, and you usually end up in the right place after all.' He leaned forward, set his hands on her shoulders, and began to rub. 'Mavis has a close friend who carries around too much stress.' He worked on the knots. 'I wonder who that could be?'

'Shut up.'

He chuckled, kissed the nape of her neck. 'You smell wonderful.'

'It's that goop Trina poured all over me.'

'She mentioned it. She said I'd enjoy it.' He sniffed her neck again, made her chuckle. 'And I am. She also said she managed to hold you down for a full body treatment. I'm to pay particular attention to your butt.'

'*She* certainly did. She tried to talk me into a temp tattoo of a rosebud on my right cheek.' She started to sigh, then bolted up, grabbing her ass. 'Jesus Christ, she had me on the table for ten minutes. You don't think she snuck one on.'

Roarke lifted a brow, then smiled slowly as he rose. 'I'll have to make it my job to find out.'

Chapter Eighteen

She had a rosebud on her ass, and wasn't happy about it. Standing naked in the bathroom, Eve adjusted the trifold mirror until she could get a good look.

'I think I could bust her for this,' she muttered.

'Decorating a cop's posterior without a license?' Roarke suggested as he strolled in. 'Felonious reproduction of floral imagery?'

'You're getting a big charge out of this, aren't you?' Miffed, Eve snagged a robe off the hook.

'Darling Eve, I thought I made it perfectly clear last night I was on your side of the issue. Didn't I do my best to chew it off?'

She would not laugh, she ordered herself as she bit down hard on her tongue. There was nothing funny about it. 'I've got to get some solution or something. Whatever they make to get it off.'

'What's your hurry? It's rather . . . sweet.'

'What if I have to go in for a disinfect? Or need to shower or change at the station? Do you know what kind of grief a butt tattoo's going to get me?'

He slid his arms around her, clever enough to get them under rather than over the robe. 'You're not working today.'

'I'm going in. I've got to check my unit, see if Feeney shot back some data.'

'And it won't make any difference if you do it Monday morning. We've got the day off.'

'To do what?'

He merely smiled, slid his hands lower to stroke her rosebud.

'Didn't we just do that?'

'It bears repeating,' he mused, 'but it could wait a bit. Why don't we spend the day lazing around the pool?'

Lazing around the pool? It had a certain appeal. 'Well, maybe . . .'

'In Martinique. Don't bother to pack,' he told her, planting a quick kiss on her mouth. 'You won't need anything but what you're wearing.'

She spent the day in Martinique, wearing nothing but a smile and a rosebud. That might have been why she was dragging a bit more than usual on Monday morning.

'You look tired, Lieutenant.' Peabody dug a bag out from her field kit, set two fresh cream donuts on the desk. She was still beaming over the fact that she'd gotten them through the bullpen without the hounds sniffing them out. 'And sort of tanned.' She peered closer. 'You get a flash?'

'No. Just got some sun yesterday, that's all.'

'It rained all day.'

'Not where I was,' Eve muttered and filled her mouth with pastry. 'I've got a probability ratio to run by the commander. Feeney worked some numbers, we're still pretty light, but I'm going to shoot for round-the-clocks on the top suspects.'

'I don't suppose you want my probability ratio on your chances of getting it. New interoffice came down this morning about excess overtime.'

'Fuck it. It's not excess if it's necessary. Whitney could play it to the chief – and the chief could play it to the mayor. We've got two high-profile homicides, generating a lot of media. We need the manpower to close them and turn off the heat.'

Peabody risked a smile. 'You rehearsing your pitch.'

'Maybe.' She blew out a breath. 'If the numbers were a few

points higher, I wouldn't have to pitch so hard. There are too many people involved; that's the problem.' Lifting her hands, she pressed her fingers to her eyes. 'We've got to run the name of every member of both cults. Over two hundred people. Say we eliminate half on data and profile, then we've still got a hundred to tag, check alibis.'

'Days of work,' Peabody agreed. 'The commander would probably spring for a couple of uniforms to knock on doors, sweep out the obvious noninvolved.'

'I'm not sure there are any obvious noninvolved.' Eve pushed away from her desk. 'It took more than one person to transport Lobar's body, strap him onto that form. And it took a vehicle.'

'None of the primes owns a vehicle large enough to have carried and concealed the body and the pentagram.'

'Maybe one of the membership does. We run names through vehicle licensing. Failing that, we start checking on rentals, vehicles reported stolen on the night of the murder.' She pushed at her hair. 'And it's just as likely whoever dumped him jumped a vehicle from one of the long-term lots, and nobody ever noticed.'

'Do we check, anyway?'

'Yeah, we check, anyway. Maybe Feeney can spare some-body in EDD to do some of the grunt work. Meanwhile, you get started, and I'll go begging to the commander.' She punched her 'link when it beeped. 'Dallas, Homicide.'

'I need to talk to you.'

'Louis?'

Eve cocked a brow. 'You want to talk about the charges against your client regarding resisting, you talk to the PA.'

'I need to talk to you,' he repeated, and she watched as he lifted his hand to his mouth and began to gnaw away his perfect manicure. 'Alone. Privately. As soon as possible.'

She lowered a hand, signaling Peabody to keep back and out of view. 'What about?'

'I can't talk about it on the 'link. I'm on my pocket unit, but even that's risky. I need you to meet me.'

'Come here.'

'No, no, they may be following me. I don't know. I can't be sure. I'm being careful.'

Had he made the shadow Feeney'd put on him, Eve wondered, or was he just being paranoid? 'Who might be following you?'

'You've got to meet me,' he insisted. 'At my club. The Luxury on Park. Level Five. I'll leave your name at the desk.'

'Give me some incentive, Louis. I've got a full plate here.'

'I think – I think I saw a murder. Just you, Eve. I won't talk to anyone else. Make sure you're not followed. Hurry.'

Eve pursed her lips at the blank screen. 'Well, that's incentive. I think we've caught a break, Peabody. See if you can sweet-talk Feeney into giving you an extra pair of hands from EDD.'

'You're not going to meet him alone,' Peabody protested as Eve grabbed her bag.

'I can handle one scared lawyer.' Eve bent down, checked the clinch piece strapped to her ankle. 'We've got a man outside the club in any case. And I'm leaving my communicator on. Monitor.'

'Yes, sir. Watch your back.'

The fifth floor of the Luxury Club held twenty private suites for the members' use. Meetings of a professional or private nature could be held there. Each suite was individually decorated to depict its own era, and each contained a complete communication and entertainment center.

Parties could be held there, of the large or the intimate nature. The catering department was unsurpassed in a city often preoccupied with food and drink. Licensed companions were available through the concierge for a small additional service charge.

Louis always booked Suite 5-C. He enjoyed the opulence of the eighteenth-century French style with its emphasis on the decorative. The rich fabrics of the upholstery on curved-backed chairs and velvet settees appealed to his love of texture. He enjoyed the thick, dark draperies, the gold tassels, the gleam of gilt on pier glass mirrors. He had entertained his wife, as well as an assortment of lovers, in the wide, high, canopy bed.

He considered this period to have embodied hedonism, self-indulgence, and a devotion to earthly pleasures.

Royalty had ruled and had done as it pleased. And hadn't art flourished? If peasants had starved outside the privileged walls, that was simply a societal mirror of nature's natural selection. The chosen few had lived life to the hilt.

And here, in midtown Manhattan, three hundred years later, he could enjoy the fruits of their indulgence.

But he wasn't enjoying them now. He paced, drinking unblended scotch in quick, jerky gulps. Terror was a dew on his brow that refused to be wiped away. His stomach roiled, his heart rabbitted in his chest.

He'd seen murder. He was nearly sure of it. It was all so hazy, all so surreal, like a virtual reality program with elements missing.

The secret room, the smoke, voices – his own among them – lifted in chant. The taste, lingering on the tongue, of warm, tainted wine.

Those were all so familiar, a part of his life now for three years. He'd joined the cult because he believed in its basic principles of pleasure, and he'd enjoyed the rituals: the robes, the masks, the words repeated and repeated while candles guttered into pools of black wax.

And the sex had been incredible.

But something was happening. He found himself obsessing

263

about meetings, desperately craving that first deep gulp of ceremonial wine. And then there were the blackouts, holes in his memory. He'd be logy and slow to focus the morning after a rite.

Recently, he'd found blood dried under his nails and couldn't remember how it had gotten there.

But he was starting to. The crime scene photos Eve had shown him had clicked something open in his mind. And had filled that opening with shock and horror. Images swirled behind his eyes. Smoke swirling, voices chanting. Flesh gleaming from sex, the moans and grunts of vicious mating. Dank black hair swaying, bony hips pumping.

Then the spray of blood, the gush of it, spurting out like that final cry of sexual release.

Selina with her feral, feline smile, the knife dripping in her hand. Lobar – God it had been Lobar – sliding from the altar, his throat gaping wide like a screaming mouth.

Murder. Nervously, he twitched the heavy drapes open a fraction, let his frightened eyes search the street below. He'd seen a blood sacrifice, and not of a goat. Of a man.

Had he dipped his fingers into that open throat? Had he slipped them between his lips to taste the fresh blood? Had he done something so abhorrent?

My God, dear God, had there been others? Other nights, other sacrifices? Could he have witnessed and blanked it from his mind?

He was a civilized man, Louis told himself as he jerked the draperies back into place. He was a husband and a father. He was a respected attorney. He wasn't an accessory to murder. He couldn't be.

With his breath coming fast and short, he poured more scotch, stared at himself in one of the ornately framed mirrors. He saw a man who hadn't slept, hadn't eaten, hadn't seen his family in days.

He was afraid to sleep. The images might come more clearly

in sleep. He was afraid to eat, sure the food would clog in his throat and kill him.

And he was mortally afraid for his family.

Wineburg had been at the ceremony. Wineburg had stood beside him and had seen what he had seen.

And Wineburg was dead.

Wineburg had had no wife, no children. But Louis did. If he was in danger and went home, would they come for him there? He had begun to understand during those long, sleepless nights, when liquor was his only company, that he was ashamed at the thought of his children discovering what he had participated in.

He had to protect them and himself. He was safe here, he assured himself. No one could get inside the suite unless he opened the door.

Possibly, he was overreacting. He mopped his sweating forehead with an already sodden handkerchief. Stress, overwork, too many late nights. Perhaps he was having a small breakdown. He should see a doctor.

He would. He would see a doctor. He would take his family and go away for a few weeks. A vacation, a time to relax, to reevaluate. He would break off from the cult. Obviously, it wasn't good for him. God knew it was costing him a small fortune in the bimonthly contributions. He'd gotten in too deeply somehow, forgotten he'd entered into the cult out of curiosity and a thirst for selfish sex.

He'd swallowed too deeply of wine and smoke, and it was making him imagine things.

But he'd had blood under his nails.

Louis covered his face, tried to catch his breath. It didn't matter, he thought. None of it mattered. He shouldn't have called Eve. He shouldn't have panicked. She would think him mad; or worse, an accessory.

Selina was his client. He owed his client his loyalty as well as his professional skill.

But he could see her, a knife gripped in her hand as she sliced it across exposed flesh.

Louis stumbled across the suite, into the master bath and, collapsing, vomited up scotch and terror. When the cramps passed, he pulled himself up. He leaned over the sink, croaked out a request for water, at forty degrees. It poured out of the curved gold faucet, splashed into the blindingly white sink and cooled his fevered skin.

He wept a moment, shoulders trembling, sobs echoing off the shining tiles. Then he lifted his head, forced himself to look in the mirror once more.

He had seen what he had seen. It was time to face it. He would tell Eve everything and shift his burden into her hands.

He felt a moment of relief, sweet in its intensity. He wanted to call his wife, hear his children's voices, see their faces.

A movement reflected in the glass had him whirling, had his heart bounding into his throat. 'How did you get in here?'

'Housekeeping, sir.' The dark woman in the trim black-and-white maid's uniform held a stack of fluffy towels. She smiled.

'I don't want housekeeping.' He passed a shaking hand over his face. 'I'm expecting someone shortly. Just leave the towels and . . .' His hand slid slowly to his side. 'I know you. I know you.'

Through the smoke, he thought through the cracked ice of fresh terror. *One of the faces in the smoke.*

'Of course you do, Louis.' Her smile never wavered as she dropped the towels and revealed the athame she held. 'We fucked just last week.'

He had time to draw breath for a scream before she plunged the knife into his throat.

Eve strode out of the elevator, bristling with annoyance. The reception droid had kept her waiting five full minutes while

266

he checked her ID. He'd given her a hassle over taking her weapon into the club. She'd been considering just using it on him to shut him up when the day manager had bustled out full of apologies.

The fact that they'd both been aware he'd been apologizing to Roarke's wife rather than Eve Dallas had only irritated her.

She'd deal with him later, she promised herself. See how the Luxury Club would like a full-scale inspection by the Department of Health, maybe a visit from Vice to check out their LCs. She had strings she could pull to insure the management a couple of days of minor hell.

She turned toward 5-C, started to punch the buzzer under the peep screen. Her gaze flickered over the security light. It beeped green for disengaged.

She drew her weapon. 'Peabody?'

'Here, sir.' Though her voice was muffled against Eve's shirt pocket.

'The door's unlocked here. I'm going in.'

'Do you want backup, Lieutenant?'

'Not yet. Stay on me.'

She slipped inside, soundlessly, shut the door at her back. She kept to her defensive crouch, sweeping her weapon and her gaze through the room.

Fancy furniture, ugly and overdone in her mind, a rumpled suit jacket, a half-empty bottle. Drapes drawn. Quiet.

She stepped farther into the room, but kept near the wall, guarding her own back as she circled. No one hid behind the furniture, behind the drapes. The small kitchen was empty and apparently unused.

She stepped to the doorway of the bedroom, again crouched, again sweeping her weapon. The bed was made, heaped with decorative pillows and apparently hadn't been slept in. Her gaze moved to the closet, the firmly shut carved doors.

She sidestepped toward it, then heard the sounds from the

267

bathroom. Quick, heavy breathing, grunts of effort, a distinctly female chuckle. It passed through her mind that Louis might be having a quick roll with the LC of his choice, and she gritted her teeth in annoyance.

But she didn't relax her guard.

She stepped left, shifted her weight, and swung to the doorway.

The smell hit her an instant before she saw it.

'Jesus. Jesus Christ.'

'Lieutenant?' Peabody's voice, ringing with concern, piped out of her pocket.

'Back off.' Eve leveled her weapon at the woman. 'Drop the knife and back off.'

'Sending backup now. Give me your situation, Lieutenant.'

'I've got a homicide. Really fresh. I said back the hell off.'

The woman only smiled. She straddled Louis, or what was left of him. Blood pooled on the floor, splattered the white tiles, coated her hands and face. The stench of it, and the gore, was thick as smoke.

Louis, Eve noted, was well beyond hope. He'd been gutted and disemboweled. And he was busily being eviscerated.

'He's already dead,' the woman said pleasantly.

'I can see that. Put down the knife.' Eve took a step closer, gesturing with the weapon. 'Put it down and move away from him. Slow. Face down on the floor, hand behind your back.'

'It had to be done.' She slid her leg over the body until she was kneeling beside it, like a mourner over a grave. 'Don't you recognize me?'

'Yeah.' Even through the mask of blood, Eve had made the face. And she'd remembered the voice, the sweetness of it. 'Mirium, right? First-degree witch. Now, drop the fucking knife and kiss the floor. Hands behind you.'

'All right.' Obligingly, Mirium set the knife aside, barely glancing at it when Eve trapped it under her heel, sent it skidding across the room well out of reach. 'He told me to be quick. In and out. I lost track of time.'

Eve tugged her restraints from her rear pocket, snapped them in place over Mirium's wrists. 'He?'

'Chas. He said I could do this one all by myself, but to be fast.' She let out a sigh. 'I guess I wasn't fast enough.'

With her mouth thin, Eve looked down at Louis Trivane. No, she thought *I* wasn't fast enough. 'You copy that, Peabody?'

'Yes, sir.'

'Pick up Charles Forte for questioning. Do it personally, and take two uniforms for backup. Don't approach him alone.'

'Affirmative. Do you have the situation under control there, Lieutenant?'

Eve stepped back from the blood running in a rivulet toward her boots. 'Yeah,' she said. 'I've got it.'

She showered and changed before the interviews. The ten minutes it took was necessary. She'd all but bathed in Louis Trivane's blood before she'd released his body to the ME. If anyone in the lockers noticed the elegant little flower on her ass, there was no comment.

The buzz on the state of this particular crime scene had already swarmed through the station.

'I'm taking Mirium first,' Eve told Feeney as she studied the dainty woman through the one-way glass.

'You could take a break, Dallas. Word is, it was pretty rough over there this morning.'

'You always think you've seen it all,' she murmured. 'But you never do. There's always something else.' She blew out a breath. 'I want to do it now. I want to close this.'

'Okay. Duet or solo?'

'Solo. She's going to talk. She's on something . . .' Eve shook her head. 'Maybe she's just plain crazy, but I think she's using. I'm going to get her to sign for a chemi-scan. The PA doesn't like confessions given under the influence.'

'I'll order one up.'

'Thanks.' She moved past him, walked into the room. Mirium's face had been washed clean of blood. She wore a baggy disposable shift in police station beige. And still managed to look like a young, eager fairy.

Eve set the recorder, entered standard, then sat. 'You know I've got you tagged, Mirium, so we don't have to take that dance. You murdered Louis Trivane.'

'Yes.'

'What are you on?'

'On?'

'Doesn't look like straight Zeus, you're too mellow. Will you agree to a drug scan?'

'I don't want to.' Her pretty mouth pouted; her dark eyes sulked. 'Maybe later I'll change my mind.' She pursed her lips and plucked at the thin skirt of the shift. 'Can I get some of my own clothes? This thing's itchy, and it offends the eye.'

'Yeah, we're real worried about that right now. Why did you kill Louis Trivane?'

'He was evil. Chas said so.'

'By Chas you're referring to Charles Forte.'

'Yes, but no one calls him Charles. It's just Chas.'

'And Chas told you Louis was evil. Did he ask you to kill Louis?'

'He said I could. Other times I just got to watch. But this time I got to do it myself. There was a lot of blood.' She lifted a hand, studied it carefully. 'Gone now.'

'What other times, Mirium?'

'Oh, other times.' She moved her shoulders. 'Blood purifies.'

'Did you assist or witness other murders?'

'Sure. Death is a transition. I got to do this one. It was a very powerful act. I cut the demon out of him. Demons exist, and we fight them.'

'By killing the people they inhabit.'

'Yes. He said you were smart.' Mirium beamed at her out

of slanted black eyes. 'But you'll never touch him. He's too far removed from your law.'

'Let's go back to Louis. Tell me about it.'

'Well, I have a friend on staff at the Luxury. All I had to do was screw him, and that was okay. I like to screw. Then I slipped one of the master codes in my pocket. You can get in most anywhere with a master. I put on one of the maids' dresses, so no one would bother me, and I went right on in Louis's suite. I took him towels. He was in the bathroom. He'd been sick, I could smell it. Then I stabbed him. I went for the throat, just like I was supposed to. Then I guess I got into it.'

She moved her shoulders again, sent Eve a mischievous smile. 'It's kind of like punching a knife through a pillow, you know. And it makes this sucky noise. Then I cut the demon out of him, and you came. I guess I'd finished, anyway.'

'Yeah, I guess you had. How long have you known Chas?'

'Oh, a couple of years. We like to make it in the park, in the daytime, because you never know if somebody's going to come along and see.'

'How does Isis feel about that?'

'Oh, she doesn't know.' Mirium rolled her eyes. 'She wouldn't like it.'

'How does she feel about the murders?'

Mirium's brows knit and her eyes unfocused for a moment. 'The murders? She doesn't know. Does she? No, we wouldn't tell her about that.'

'So it's just between you and Chas.'

'Between me and Chas.' Her eyes fluttered, stayed blank. 'I guess. Sure.'

'Have you told anyone else in the coven?'

'The coven?' She laid her fingers on her lips, tapped them. 'No, no, it's our secret. Our little secret.'

'What about Wineburg?'

'Who?'

'In the parking garage. The banker. Do you remember?'

'I didn't get to do that.' She bit her bottom lip now, shook her head. 'No, he did that. He was supposed to bring me the heart, but he didn't. He said there wasn't time.'

'And Lobar?'

'Lobar, Lobar.' Her fingers kept tapping. 'No, that was different. Wasn't it? I can't remember. I'm getting a headache.' Her voice turned petulant. 'I don't want to talk anymore now. I'm tired.' She laid her hands down on her folded arms and closed her eyes.

Eve watched her for a moment. There wasn't any point in pushing now, she decided. She had enough.

Eve signaled a uniform. Mirium murmured sulkily as Eve slipped the restraints back into place. 'Take her down to Psych. Get Mira to do the evaluation, if possible; make a note to request permission for a drug scan.'

'Yes, sir.' Eve stepped to the door behind them, pushed a call button. 'Have Forte brought to Interview Room C.'

It occurred to her that she would like to lay her head on pillowed arms herself. Instead, she turned down the corridor into the observation area. Peabody stood beside Feeney.

'I want you in on this, Peabody. What did you think of her, Feeney?'

'She's whacked.' He held out his bag of nuts. 'Whether it's psych or induced, I dunno. Looks like a mix of both to me.'

'That was my take. How come she seemed so damn normal the other night?' Then she pulled her hands through her hair and laughed. 'I can't believe I'm saying that. She was standing naked in the woods letting Forte kiss her crotch.'

She lowered her hands, pressed them to her eyes, then dropped them. 'His father never used a partner. That was never hinted at. He worked alone.'

'So, he's got a different style,' Feeney said. 'Whacked or not, the girl pinned Forte.'

'It doesn't feel right to me,' Peabody murmured, and Eve turned to her with a mildly interested glance.

'What doesn't feel right, Officer?'

Detecting the light trace of sarcasm, Peabody lifted her jaw. 'Wiccans don't kill.'

'People kill,' Eve reminded her. 'And not everybody takes their religion seriously. Had any red meat lately?'

The flush worked up from under Peabody's starched uniform collar. Free-Agers were strict vegan and used no animal by-products. 'That's different.'

'I walked in on a murder,' Eve said shortly. 'The woman with the knife in her hand identified Charles Forte as her accomplice. That's fact. I don't want you to take anything but fact into that interview room. Understood?'

'Yes, sir.' Peabody stiffened her shoulders. 'Perfectly.' But she stood in place a moment longer when Eve strode off.

'She's had a rough morning,' Feeney said sympathetically. 'I got a quick scan of the first crime scene shots. It doesn't get any rougher.'

'I know.' But she shook her head, watching as Charles Forte was led into the room behind the glass. 'But it just doesn't feel right.'

She turned away, headed around the corner, and stepped into the interview room just as Eve was reading Forte his rights.

'I don't understand.'

'You don't understand your rights and obligations?'

'No, no, I understand them. I don't understand why I'm here.' There was puzzlement and a vague sense of disappointment as he turned his gaze toward Peabody. 'If you'd wanted to speak with me again, you had only to ask. I would have met you, or come in voluntarily. It wasn't necessary to send three uniformed officers to my home.'

'I thought it was necessary,' Eve answered shortly. 'Do you want counsel or representation at this time, Mr Forte?'

'No.' He shifted in agitation, tried to ignore the fact that he

273

was inside a police facility. Like his father. 'Just tell me what you want to know. I'll try to help you.'

'Tell me about Louis Trivane.'

'I'm sorry.' He shook his head. 'I don't know anyone by that name.'

'Do you usually send your handmaids out to murder strangers?'

'What?' His face went white as he pushed himself to his feet. 'What are you talking about?'

'Sit down.' Eve snapped the order out. 'Louis Trivane was murdered two hours ago by Mirium Hopkins.'

'Mirium? That's ridiculous. That's impossible.'

'It's very possible. I walked in while she was cutting out his liver.'

Chas swayed, then sank onto his chair. 'There's a mistake. It couldn't be.'

'I think the mistake was yours.' Eve rose, wandered over, then leaned over his shoulder. 'You should pick your weapons more carefully. When you use defective ones, they can turn on you.'

'I don't know what you mean. May I have some water? I don't understand this.'

Eve jerked a thumb to Peabody, signaling her to pour a glass. 'Mirium told me everything, Chas. She told me that you were lovers, that you neglected to bring her Wineburg's heart as promised, and that you'd allowed her to execute Trivane herself. Blood purifies.'

'No.' He lifted the glass in both hands and still slopped water over the edge as he tried to drink. 'No.'

'Your father liked to slice people up. Did he show you how it was done? How many other defective tools have you used? Did you dispose of them after you'd finished with them? Keep any souvenirs?'

She continued to hammer at him while he sat, just sat, shaking his head slowly from side to side.

'Was this your version of a religious war, Chas? Eliminate the enemy? Cut out the demons? Your father was a self-styled Satanist, and he'd made your life a misery. You couldn't kill him, you can't get to him now. But there are others. Are they substitutes? When you kill them, are you killing him, hacking him to pieces because of what he did to you?'

He squeezed his eyes tight, began to rock. 'God. My God. Oh God.'

'You can help yourself here. Tell me why, tell me how. Explain it to me, Chas. I may be able to cut you a break. Tell me about Alice. About Lobar.'

'No. No.' When he lifted his head, his eyes were streaming. 'I'm not my father.'

Eve didn't flinch, didn't look away from the desperate plea in his eyes. 'Aren't you?' Then she stepped back and let him sob.

Chapter Nineteen

She worked him for an hour, relentlessly pushing, then backtracking, then shifting directions. She kept the death photos on the table, dealt out like grisly playing cards.

How many more, she demanded. How many more images of the dead should there be?

Through it all, he wept and denied, wept and was silent.

When she turned him over to holding, his eyes stayed on hers until he was led around the corner and away. But it was the look in Peabody's eyes that caught her and had her waiting until they were alone.

'Problem, Officer?'

Observing the interrogation had been like watching a wolf toy and tear at a wounded deer. Peabody drew a breath, braced. 'Yes, sir. I didn't like your interview technique.'

'Didn't you?'

'It seemed overly harsh. Cruel. Using his father, over and over again, directing him to look at the stills.'

Eve's stomach was raw, her nerves scraped clean, but her voice was cool, her hands steady, as she gathered up the stills. 'Maybe I should have asked him politely to please confess so we could all go home and get back to our comfy lives. Don't know why I didn't think of it. I'll make a note to try it the next time I have a murder suspect in interview.'

Peabody wanted to wince, managed not to. 'It just seemed

to me, Lieutenant, particularly since the suspect had no representation—'

'Did I read him his rights, Officer?'

'Yes, sir, but—'

'Did he verify that he understood those rights?'

Peabody pulled back, nodded slowly. 'Yes, sir.'

'Can you estimate, Officer Peabody, how many interviews you've conducted on homicide cases?'

'Sir, I—'

'I can't,' Eve snapped, and her eyes went from cool to hot. 'I can't, because there's been too fucking many of them. You want to take a look at the stills again? You want to see this guy with his guts spilled out all over the tiles? Maybe it'll toughen you up a little, because if my interview techniques upset you, Peabody, you're in the wrong career.'

Eve strode to the door, then whirled back while Peabody stood where she was at rigid attention. 'And I expect my aide to back me up, not question me because she happens to have a soft spot for witches. If you can't handle that, Officer Peabody, I'll approve your request for transfer. Understood?'

'Yes, sir.' Peabody let out a shaky breath as Eve's boots clicked down the corridor. 'Understood,' she said to herself and shut her eyes.

'A little rough on her,' Feeney commented when he caught up.

'Don't you start on me.'

He only held up a hand. 'Isis came in voluntarily. I put her in Room B.'

With a jerk of the head, Eve changed directions and pulled open the door of Room B.

Isis stopped her restless pacing and spun around. 'How could you do this to him? How could you bring him here? He's terrified of places like this.'

'Charles Forte is being held for questioning in the stabbing death of Louis Trivane, among others.' In contrast to Isis's raised and furious voice, Eve's was cold and flat. 'He has not yet been charged.'

'Charged?' Her golden skin paled. 'You can't believe Chas had anything to do with a murder. Trivane? We don't know any Louis Trivane.'

'And you know everyone Forte knows, Isis?' Eve set the file on the table, kept her hand on it as if to remind herself what was inside. 'You know everything he does and thinks and plans?'

'We are as close as it's possible for human bodies and minds and souls to be. There is no harm in him.' The temper drained out of her. Now her voice trembled. 'Let me take him home. Please.'

Eve met the pleading eyes straight on, forced herself not to feel. 'Did you know, being as close as it's possible, that he'd decided to get equally close, bodily speaking, with Mirium?'

'Mirium?' Isis blinked once, then nearly laughed. 'That's ridiculous.'

'She told me herself. She smiled when she told me.' Remembering that, bringing that image back, dried up any sympathy. 'She smiled as she straddled what was left of Louis Trivane, while his blood was smeared all over her hands and her face and the knife she held.'

As her legs went weak, Isis reached out blindly to brace a hand on the back of a chair. 'Mirium killed someone? That's impossible.'

'I thought all things were possible in your sphere. I walked in on her little ceremony myself.' Eve's fingers curled on the file, but she didn't open it. There was still pity, after all, for the woman who loved and believed. 'She was very cooperative, happily told me that Forte had allowed her to kill Trivane herself. Unlike the others, where she only observed.'

Using her hand to keep her balance, Isis stepped unsteadily around the chair, eased herself into it. 'She's lying.' There was a lance in her heart, quivering there. 'Chas has nothing to do with this. How could I have missed this part of her?' Closing her eyes, Isis rocked herself gently. 'How could I not have seen? We initiated her, we took her in. We made her one of us.'

'Can't see everything, can you?' Eve angled her head. 'I think you should be more worried about your vision as it applies to Charles Forte.'

'No.' She opened her eyes again. There was misery in them, but behind it was a steel Eve recognized. 'There's no one I see more clearly than Chas. She's lying.'

'She'll be tested. In the meantime, you may want to rethink allowing yourself to be used as his alibi. He's betrayed your trust,' Eve said, stepping closer. 'It could have been you, Isis, at any time. Mirium's younger, probably more biddable. I wonder how much longer he'd have pretended to let you run the show.'

'How can you not understand what there is between us when you have it yourself? Do you think the word of some disturbed young woman would make me doubt the man I love? Would it make you doubt Roarke?'

'It's not my personal life that's in dire straits here,' Eve said evenly. 'It's yours. If you care for him so much, then cooperate with me. It's the only way to stop him, and to get him help.'

'Help?' Isis's mouth twisted. 'You don't want to help him. You want him to be guilty, you want him to be punished, because of where he came from. Because of his father.'

Eve looked down at the folder in her hands, the plain tan cover that hid the terrible images of terrible death. 'You're wrong.' She spoke quietly now, almost to herself. 'I wanted him to be innocent. Because of his father.'

Then she lifted her gaze, met Isis's. 'The warrant will have come through by now. We'll search your shop and your apartment. Whatever we find can be used against you as well.'

'It won't matter.' Isis forced herself to stand. 'You won't find anything to help you.'

279

'You're entitled to be present during the search.'

'No. I'll stay here. I want to see Chas.'

'You're not related or legally married—'

'Dallas.' Isis interrupted quietly. 'You have a heart. Please listen to it and let me see him.'

Yes, she had a heart. And it ached to see the plea in the eyes of a strong woman. 'I can give you five minutes through security glass.' As she wrenched the door open, she set her teeth. 'Tell him to get a lawyer, for God's sake.'

In the storeroom of Spirit Quest and in a workroom in the apartment above, were dozens of bottles and containers and boxes. They were filled with liquid and powder and leaves and seeds. She found organized records detailing the contents and their uses.

Eve ordered everything sent to the lab for analysis.

She found knives, carved handles and plain, long-bladed and short. She tagged a sweeper, ordered him to scan for traces of blood. Ceremonial robes and street clothes were scanned as well.

She blocked out the voices – sweepers never worked quietly – and went about her job with focused efficiency.

And there, under a neatly folded stack of robes kept fresh in a chest smelling of rosemary and cedar, she found the balled-up and bloody black robe.

'Here.' She signaled to a sweeper. 'Scan it.'

'Nice sample.' The sweeper snapped her gum, ran the nozzle of her shoulder unit over the cloth. 'Mostly on the sleeves.' Behind her protective goggles, the sweeper's eyes were mildly bored. 'Human,' she confirmed. 'A neg. Can't tell you much more with a portable.'

'That's enough.' Eve slid the robe into a bag, sealed and labeled it for evidence. 'Wineburg was A negative.' She looked at Peabody as she handed the bag to her. 'Careless of him, wasn't it?'

'Yes, sir.' Dutifully, Peabody stored the bag in her evidence kit. 'It would seem so.'

'Lobar was O positive.' She moved to another chest, hauled back the domed lid. 'Keep looking.'

Twilight had settled with its dim light and fitful breezes when she climbed back in her car. Since the tension was still simmering between her and Peabody, she didn't bother to speak but engaged her car 'link instead.

'Lieutenant Dallas for Dr Mira.'

'Dr Mira is in session,' the receptionist said politely. 'I'll be happy to log your message.'

'Has she tested Mirium Hopkins?'

'One moment while I check the logs.' The receptionist slid her gaze to the side, then back. 'That session has been rescheduled for eight thirty tomorrow morning.'

'Rescheduled, why?'

'The log notes indicate that the subject complained of severe head pain, and on examination by the physician on duty, was medicated.'

'Who was the physician on duty?' Eve asked through clenched teeth.

'Dr Arthur Simon.'

'Simon Says; figures.' Disgusted, Eve whipped her car around a slow-moving maxibus packed with commuters. 'He'll give you a double tranq for a hangnail.'

The receptionist grimaced in sympathy. 'I'm sorry, Lieutenant, but the subject was already medicated before her scheduled testing. Dr Mira is unable to proceed until morning.'

'Fine. Terrific. Ask her to let me know as soon as she's done.' Eve broke transmission. 'Son of a bitch. I'm going in to take a look at her, myself. Deliver the bags to the lab, Peabody, with a request for rush – for what good that does. Then you're off duty.'

'You'll interview Forte again tonight.'

'That's right.'

'Sir, I request to be present during interview.'

'Request denied,' Eve said shortly as she pulled into the garage at Central. 'I said you're off duty.' She shoved out of the car and walked away.

It was midnight and her own head was aching viciously. The house was quiet when she slipped in, dragged herself up the stairs. It didn't surprise her to see Roarke, awake and on the bedroom 'link. She glanced at the monitor as she passed through and recognized the young, eager face of one of the engineers assigned to the Olympus Resort.

It made her think of the last few days of her honeymoon. There had been death there, as well. Big surprise, she thought as she leaned over the sink and splashed her face with cold water. There was never any escaping it.

She toweled off, then walked to the bed to sit and remove her boots. When they hit the floor, the effort of undressing further seemed beyond her. She crawled onto the bed and lay across it, facedown.

Roarke listened to his engineer with half an ear while he watched her. He knew the signs, the shadowed eyes, the pale skin, the slow, deliberate movements. She'd worked herself to the breaking point again – a habit that both fascinated and frustrated him.

'I'll get back to you on that tomorrow,' he said and abruptly ended transmission. 'You've had a bad one, Lieutenant.'

She didn't stir when he straddled her and began to knead her neck and shoulders. 'I know there's been worse,' she murmured. 'I just can't think of when right now.'

'Louis Trivane's murder has been all over the news.'

'Goddamn vultures.'

He unhooked her weapon harness, wiggled it off her, and set it aside. 'A prominent attorney gets himself hacked up in an exclusive private club, it's news.' Competently, he worked his thumbs up her spine. 'Nadine's called here several times.'

'Yeah, she's buzzed Central, too. I don't have time for her.'

'Mmm.' He tugged her shirt free of her slacks, and used the heels of his hands. 'Did you walk in on it, or was that added for entertainment value?'

'No, I walked in on it. Maybe if that idiot droid at the desk hadn't—' She broke off, shook her head. 'I was too late. She'd already opened him up. She was still working on him, like a kid with a science project. She implicated Charles Forte.'

'That's out, too.'

'Of course it is,' she said with a sigh. 'You can't plug all the leaks.'

'You have him in custody?'

'We're questioning him. I'm questioning him. He denies everything. I found physical evidence in his apartment, but he still denies everything.'

Denies, she thought, *while looking shocked, dislocated, terrified.*

'Oh shit.' She turned her head, pressed her face into the spread. 'Oh shit.'

'Come on.' He kissed the top of her head lightly. 'Let's get you undressed and into bed.'

'Don't baby me.'

'Try to stop me.'

She started to shift, then moved quickly before she'd realized her intent or the need. She had her arms around him, her face buried against his shoulder, her eyes squeezed tight as if to block out visions.

'You're always here. Even when you're not.'

'We're not alone, anymore. Either of us.' Because he thought she needed it, he lifted her onto his lap. 'Talk to me. You've got more than murder and evidence on your mind.'

'I'm not a good person.' She blurted it out before she could stop herself. 'I'm a good cop, but I'm not a good person. I can't afford to be.'

'That's nonsense, Eve.'

'It's not. It's true. You just don't want to see it, that's all.' She pulled back so she could look at him. 'When you love somebody, you can handle the little faults, but you don't want to see the big ones. You don't want to admit what the person you've attached yourself to is capable of, so you pretend it's not there.'

'What are you capable of that I'm blind to?'

'I beat Forte into pulp. Not physically,' she continued, dragging her hair away from her face. 'That's too easy, that's too clean. I ripped him to pieces emotionally. I wanted to. I wanted him to tell me what he'd done so I could finish it, close it away. And when Peabody had the balls to tell me she disapproved of my interview techniques, I trounced her. I sent her off duty so I could go back in and hammer at him again.'

He was silent a moment, then rose to turn the covers down. 'So let me recap. You walked in on a mutilation in progress, took the killer into custody, a killer who implicated Charles Forte in this and in other murders. This is a matter of days after you discover a mutilated body on your doorstep.'

'It can't be personal.'

'I beg your pardon, Lieutenant, but that's bullshit. To continue,' he said, coming around to unbutton her shirt, 'you then take Charles Forte in for interview, a man you suspect with good cause is responsible for several violent deaths. You play hardball, something which your aide whom you're training, and who, though highly competent, has considerably less experience than yourself in these matters, disapproves of. A police officer who did not walk into a room and find a woman gleefully carving a man into pieces. The news reports were quite specific,' he told her.

'And,' he added before Eve could speak, 'you then reprimanded your aide when she questioned your judgment,

284

subsequently sending her off duty so that you could resume your interrogation. Does that about sum it up?'

Frowning, she studied the top of his head as he bent to pull off her slacks. 'You're making it black and white. It's not.'

'It never is.' He swung her legs into bed, pushed her down gently. 'I'll tell you what it makes you, Eve. It makes you a good cop, a dedicated one. And a human one.' He undressed, slipped into bed beside her. 'And that being the case, it's probably best if I divorce you and get on with my life.' He pulled her close until her head cozied into the curve of his shoulder. 'Obviously, up till now, I've been blind to your hideous character flaws.'

'You make me sound like an idiot.'

'Good, I intended to.' He kissed her temple, ordered the lights to dim. 'Now, go to sleep.'

She turned her head so that she could smell his skin on her way to sleep. 'I don't think I can let you have that divorce,' she said on a sigh.

'No?'

'Uh-uh. No way I'm giving up the coffee.'

Eve arrived at her office at eight A.M. She had already been by the lab to harass them, which had, in part, cheered her. Her 'link was beeping with an incoming when she opened the door.

And Peabody stood at attention beside her desk.

'You're early, Peabody.' Eve moved to the 'link, coded in, and waited for the messages to dispense. 'You're not on for thirty minutes.'

'I wanted to speak to you, Lieutenant, before I came on duty.'

'All right.' Eve put the messages on hold, turned to give Peabody her full attention. 'You look like hell,' she commented.

Peabody kept her gaze steady. She knew how she looked. She hadn't eaten or slept. Symptoms, she knew that were embarrassingly similar to those she displayed when a love affair ended badly. And this, she'd realized during the long night, was worse than any breakup with a man.

'I would like to formally apologize, Lieutenant, for statements made after the Forte interview. It was insubordinate and incorrect to question your methods. I hope that my lack of judgment in this matter will not influence you to dismiss me from this case, or from this division.'

Eve sat, leaned back in a chair that creakily begged for lubricant. 'Is that all, Officer Peabody?'

'Yes, sir. Except to say—'

'If you've got more to say, pull the stick out of your butt first. You're off duty and off the record.'

Peabody's shoulders slumped slightly, but in defeat rather than relaxation. 'I'm sorry. Watching him fall to pieces that way got to me. I wasn't able to divorce myself from the situation and view it objectively. I don't believe – don't want to believe,' she corrected, 'that he's responsible. It tainted my viewpoint.'

'Objectivity's essential. And, more often than any of us want to admit, impossible. I wasn't completely objective either, which is why I overreacted to your comments. I apologize for that.'

Surprise and relief spread through her. Peabody found them both easier to swallow than crow and fear. 'Will you keep me on?'

'I've got an investment in you.' Leaving it at that, Eve turned back to her 'link.

Behind Eve's back, Peabody closed her eyes tightly, dug for composure. She took a breath, swallowed hard, and found it. 'So, does this mean we've made up?'

Eve slanted a look at Peabody's hopeful grin. 'Why don't I have any coffee?' She engaged the 'link, let her messages run. The first had barely begun when Peabody set a steaming cup at her elbow.

'Come on, Dallas, come on. Give me a break. I can go on with an update any time, day or night. Get back to me damn it. Just a couple details.'

'Not going to happen, Nadine,' Eve murmured and zipped through the next three messages from the reporter, all increasingly desperate.

There was a communication from the ME, with the autopsy report. Eve downloaded and ordered a hard copy print. Finally, a relay from the lab which verified the blood on the robe was Wineburg's.

'I can't see it,' Peabody said quietly. 'Why can't I see it? It's all there.' She lifted her shoulders, let them fall. 'It's all right there.'

'We charge him and book him.' Eve rubbed a finger up and down the center of her forehead. 'Murder one on Wineburg. We'll hold off on the conspiracy to murder on Trivane until Mira's done the testing. Have him brought up for interview again, Peabody. We'll see how many more we can pin to him.'

'Why Alice?' Peabody asked. 'Why Frank?'

'He didn't do them. They're not his.'

'Separate cases? You still think Selina's responsible for them?'

'I know she is. But we're a long way from proving it.'

She spent the day going over reports, filing her own. By noon, when she faced Chas in interview again, she was ready to try a different tack.

She studied his chosen representative, a young, sad-eyed woman who, by Eve's estimate, could barely be old enough to have passed the bar. She didn't bother to sigh as she recognized the woman from the initiation ceremony.

A lawyer witch, she mused. And wondered if that would be considered a redundancy.

'This is your chosen counsel, Mr Forte?'

'Yes.' His face was a sickly gray, his eyes shades darker. 'Leila has agreed to help me.'

'Very well. You've been charged with murder, Mr Forte.'

'I've requested a bail hearing,' Leila began and passed Eve some paperwork. 'It's scheduled for two P.M. today.'

'You won't get bail.' Eve handed the papers to Peabody. 'And it won't delay this very long.'

'I didn't even know the man who was killed,' Chas began. 'I'd never seen him before that night. I was with you.'

'Which puts you on the scene at the time, giving you opportunity. Motive?' She leaned back. 'You were there, you knew he was about to break, to talk. His blood wasn't the first to spill, was it, Mr Forte?'

'I don't know anything about it.' His voice quavered. He took a breath, laid his hand over Leila's as if for support. Their fingers linked and his voice came stronger. 'I've never harmed anyone in my life. It's against everything I believe, everything I've made myself. I've told you. I held nothing back from you, trusting you to understand.'

'Do you own a black robe? Natural silk, wrap style, floor length?'

'I own many robes. But I don't care for black.'

Eve held a hand out, waited until Peabody put the sealed garment into it. 'Then you don't recognize this?'

'It's not mine.' He seemed to relax a little. 'That doesn't belong to me.'

'No? Yet it was found in a chest in the bedroom of the apartment you share with Isis. Carelessly, perhaps quickly hidden under a stack of other robes. There's blood on it, Mr Forte. Wineburg's blood.'

'No.' He cringed back. 'That's not possible.'

'It's a fact. Your representative is free to study the lab report. I wonder if Isis will recognize it. It might . . . jog her memory.'

'She has nothing to do with this. Nothing to do with any

288

of this.' Panic had him lurching up. 'You can't suspect her of—'

'Of what?' Eve cocked her head. 'Of being an accessory? She lives with you, works with you, she sleeps with you. Even if she's just been protecting you, it puts her in it.'

'She can't be drawn into this. She can't be put through this. Leave her alone.' He leaned forward, resting trembling hands on the table. 'Leave her alone, Promise me that, and I'll tell you whatever you want to hear.'

'Chas.' Leila stood, put a firm hand on his shoulder. 'Sit down. Don't say anything else. My client has nothing further to say at this time, Lieutenant. I need to confer with him and request privacy to do so.'

Eve took her measure. The woman no longer looked young and sad-eyed, but cool and determined. 'There won't be a deal, counselor, not on this one.' She rose, signaled Peabody. 'But a full confession might get him a psych facility rather than a maximum lockup. Think about it.'

She swore under her breath once she was outside the room. 'She'll put a lid on him. He'll do what she tells him because he's too scared not to.'

Eve paced a yard down the corridor then back. 'I've got to get to Mira. She's bound to be done by now with testing. You contact the PA's office. We need somebody down here. Maybe if we have a prosecutor talk to his rep lawyer to lawyer, we can open it up.'

'Isis cracked him.' Peabody glanced back toward the door as they headed away. 'He really loves her.'

'There's all kinds of love, isn't there?'

'I don't get why he had sex with Mirium.'

'There's all kinds of sex, too. Some is straight manipulation.' She turned into her office to call Mira.

Chapter Twenty

Delusional, sociopathic, an addictive and easily influenced personality. Eve tossed Mira's report aside. She hadn't needed a psychiatrist to tell her Mirium was a lunatic with no conscience. She'd seen that for herself.

Or that she had obsessive leanings toward the occult, a low intelligence quotient, and a capacity for violence.

Mira's recommendation for further testing, and for treatment as a mentally defective might have been sound, but it didn't change the facts.

Mirium had butchered a man in cold blood, and would more than likely do her time in the quiet rooms of a mental health facility.

The truth testing hadn't been much more helpful. It indicated the subject was telling the truth – as the subject saw the truth. There were gaps and hitches and confusion.

Likely due, Eve noted, glancing at the drug scan results, from having a half dozen illegal substances bouncing around in her system.

'Lieutenant?' Peabody stepped in, waited for Eve to look up. 'Schultz from the PA's office just tagged me.'

'What's the status?'

'The lawyer won't budge. She's pushing for a truth test, but Forte keeps refusing. Schultz thinks she's stalling, says she wants forty-eight to study all the reports and evidence. It'll keep Forte in since bail was denied, but she's insisting.

Schultz thinks Forte's ready to roll over, but she's keeping him on a short leash.'

'Schultz give you all that?'

'Yeah, well, I think he was looking to make time. Fresh divorce.'

'Oh.' Eve lifted a brow. 'And he likes a woman in uniform.'

'I'd say it's more like he likes a human with breasts at this point. Bottom line, he doesn't think we're getting any more tonight. The lawyer exercised her client's right for minimum break. Schultz agreed to talk more in the morning. He's headed out.'

'All right. Maybe it's best to give them both time to stew. We'll swing by Isis's place. May be able to shake her.'

'You've got it pretty well wrapped.' Peabody fell into step beside her. 'You'll be able to relax some tonight at the party.'

'Party?' Eve stopped dead. 'Mavis's party? That's tonight? Hell.'

'So speaks the party animal,' Peabody said dryly. 'Personally, I'm looking forward to it. It's been a shitty week.'

'Halloween's supposed to be for kids, so they can blackmail adults into forking over junk food. Grown men and women running around in dopey costumes. It's embarrassing.'

'Actually it's an old, revered tradition with its roots in earth religions.'

'Don't get started,' Eve warned as they rode down to the garage. She eyed Peabody suspiciously. 'You're not actually wearing a costume.'

'How else can I guarantee getting my share of candy?' Peabody brushed some lint from the front of her uniform.

The store was dark, and so was the apartment. No one answered the knock on any door. Eve considered, checked her watch. 'I'm going to stake it out for a couple of hours. I'd rather hit her tonight.'

'She's probably at the sabbat ceremony.'

'I don't figure she's in the mood for naked dancing under the circumstances. I'll stick. You can catch transpo from here.'

'I can stay.'

'It's not necessary. If she doesn't show in a couple hours, I'll head to Mavis's.'

'Like that?' Peabody scanned Eve's faded jeans, worn boots, and battered jacket. 'Don't you want to wear something more . . . festive?'

'No. I'll see you there.' Eve climbed back in the car, lowered the window. 'So, what are you wearing?'

'It's a secret,' Peabody said with a grin and walked off to catch a tram home.

'Embarrassing,' Eve decided, and settling back, engaged her 'link. The system put her through to Roarke at his mid-town office.

'Just caught me,' he told her, and noted the edge of the steering wheel on the monitor. 'Obviously, you're not at home getting yourself ready for tonight's festivities.'

'Obviously not. I've got a couple more hours here, so I'll meet you at Mavis's. We can duck out early.'

'I can see you're already looking forward to an exciting evening.'

'Halloween.' She glanced over as a ghoul, a six-foot pink rabbit, and a mutant transexual crossed the street in front of her car. 'I just don't get it.'

'Darling Eve, for some it's simply an excuse to be foolish. For others it's a serious holy day. Samhain, the beginning of Celtic winter. The beginning of the year, the turn of it with the old dying and the new yet unborn. On this night the veil between is very thin.'

'Boy.' She gave a mock shudder. 'Now I'm spooked.'

'Tonight we'll concentrate on using it as an excuse to be foolish. Want to get drunk and have wild sex?'

'Yeah.' Her lips twitched. 'That sounds pretty good.'

'We could get started now. A little 'link sex.'

'That would be illegal over an official line. Besides, you never know when Dispatch is going to get nosey.'

'Then I won't mention how much I want to get my hands on you. My mouth on you. How exciting it is to feel you under me, when I'm inside you and you arch back, struggling to breathe and fist your hands in my hair.'

'No, don't mention it,' she told him as the muscles in her thighs tingled and went lax. 'I'll see you in a couple hours. We'll, ah, go home early. Then you could mention it.'

'Eve?'

'Yeah?'

'I adore you.' With a silky, satisfied smile on his face, he disengaged.

She blew out a long, slow breath. 'When am I going to get used to this?' she muttered.

The sex was mind-scrambling enough. She'd never thought of the act as any more than a necessary and mildly pleasurable physical release. Until Roarke. He could turn her dry-mouthed and needy with a look. But more was the hold he had on her heart in that firm, possessive grip that was alternately comforting and terrifying.

She'd never understood the demanding power of love.

Frowning, she looked back at the apartment across the street. Hadn't that been what she'd seen there? Power and love? Isis was a strong, powerful woman. Could love have blinded her so completely?

It wasn't impossible, Eve mused. But it was . . . disappointing, she admitted. For herself, she knew Roarke had spent much of his life skirting the law. Hell, she thought, he'd stomped on it.

She knew he'd stolen, cheated, finagled. She knew he'd killed. The abused child from the mean streets of Dublin had done what he'd needed to do to survive. Then had done as he'd liked to profit. She couldn't entirely blame him for either.

Yet, if he used his power and his position today to kill, what would she do? Would she stop loving him? She wasn't sure, but she was sure that she would know. And the code that she lived by wouldn't allow her to turn a blind eye to murder.

Maybe the code Isis lived by wasn't as strong.

And yet, as she sat in the dark with the sharp little teeth of the wind biting at her windows, she found she couldn't balance it.

Forte had all but confessed now, she reminded herself. Once she'd confronted him with the robe, with the evidence, he'd started toward surrender.

That wasn't entirely true, she thought. It was when she'd brought Isis into it that he'd changed directions.

Protecting her. Shielding her. Sacrificing for her.

With a new theme playing in her mind, she got out of the car, crossed the street.

A number of people wandered the street, many of them in costumes. Even as she stepped over the curb, a gaggle of teenagers rushed by, making enough noise to wake the dead. No one paid any attention to a lone woman in a leather jacket climbing the stairs to a dark apartment.

She stood on the landing a moment, scanning the street, the surrounding buildings. It was an area where people minded their own business, she decided. And wouldn't the neighbors be accustomed to seeing people – perhaps the-less-than-usual type of person – going up and into the apartment.

To test her theory farther, Eve tried the door. Finding it locked, she simply fished a master code out of her pocket. She had the door open in seconds and waited just outside it for the sound of a security alarm.

There was only silence inside.

No security, she decided, and resisted the temptation to go in. The average civilian wouldn't have access to a master, but there were other ways of popping unsecured locks.

Hadn't the apartment been empty the day before? With both Forte and Isis at Central, how easy would it have been for someone to slip in, to plant a bloodstained robe in an obvious place?

Eve shut the door again and stood arguing with herself. Mirium had implicated him. She'd said his name as she sat on the floor, blood still running from her hands.

Delusional, sociopathic, easily influenced.

Damn it. Eve trooped down the steps, back to her car. The evidence was there, wasn't it? Motive, opportunity. It was a fucking textbook checklist. She even had a confessed accomplice in custody.

An accomplice he'd been sleeping with on the side. Having sex in Central Park, using his influence to bring her into the coven right under his lover's nose.

It fit, she told herself. And that was the trouble. It slid so well into place it was as if someone had oiled the slot. All you had to do was leave out love – selfless, devoted, unquestioning love. Add that, and it scraped along the sides of that slot, screaming in protest.

If there was a chance it was a setup, and that she was being used to make it click, she was damn well going to find out. She considered calling Peabody, started to reach for her 'link, when she heard the scream. She was out of the car, her hand on her weapon, when she spotted the black-robed figure dragging a woman into the shadows.

'Police.' She rushed forward, drawing. 'Back off.'

He did more than that. He ran. When Eve reached the woman, she was lying facedown, moaning. Holstering her weapon, she crouched down.

'How bad did he hurt you?' As she rolled the woman over, she saw the glint of a blade. It was pressed, keenedged, against her stomach before she saw Selina's face.

'All I have to do is push, just a little.' Selina smiled. 'I'd enjoy that. But for now . . .' Her hand tapped against Eve's throat. She felt the pressure and the sting an instant before her vision blurred.

'Now you're going to help me to the car. Or it's going to look that way if anyone notices.' Smiling, Selina put her arms around Eve, keeping close so it appeared she was being lifted to her feet. 'And if you don't do exactly what I say, your guts will hit the sidewalk and I'll be gone before you realize you're dead.'

Eve's head was swimming, her legs like rubber as Selina led her down the sidewalk. 'Get in,' Selina ordered, 'slide over.'

She found herself obeying dully, while a part of her mind screamed in protest. 'Not so smart now, are you, Lieutenant Dallas? Not so cool. We led you right where we wanted you. Stupid bitch. How do you set this thing to auto?'

'I—' She couldn't think. Fear couldn't get through the haze, nor could anger or training. She stared blankly at the controls. 'Auto?'

Her voice was enough. The vehicle shuddered, then hummed discordantly.

'I don't believe you're in any shape to drive.' Selina threw back her head and laughed. 'Give it the address. My apartment. We have a very special ceremony in mind for you.'

Mechanically, Eve repeated the address and stared straight ahead as the vehicle slowly slid from the curb. 'Not Forte,' she managed, struggling to snap back. 'It was never him.'

'That pathetic excuse for a man? He couldn't kill a fly if it landed on his dick. If he's got one. But he and that half-breed Wiccan are going to pay. You've seen to that, haven't you? They thought they could save poor little Alice. Well, so did her stupid grandfather. See where it got them. No one challenges me and lives. You'll find out just how much power I have very soon now. And you'll beg me to kill you and end it.'

'You killed them all.'

'Every one of them.' Selina leaned closer. 'And more. Many more. I enjoy the children most. They're so . . . fresh. I walked right in on the grandfather, used his weakness for females. Sobbed, told him I was afraid for my life. Alban would kill me. Then I slipped the drugs into his drink and I killed him. I wanted blood but, well, it was nearly as satisfying to watch his eyes as he realized he was dying. You've seen how the eyes die first, haven't you, Dallas? They die first.'

'Yes.' The mists were moving back to the corners of her mind. She could feel her legs and arms tingle as the nerves pumped back to life. 'Yes, they do.'

'And Alice. I was almost sorry when we had to end that. Tormenting her day after day was so arousing. They way she would jump at a cat or a bird. Droids. Easily programmed. We used the cat that night, had it speak to her with my voice. We were waiting for her, we had plans for her, but she ran into the street and killed herself instead.

'So we'll do to you what we'd planned for her. Here we are now.'

As the car veered toward the curb, Eve tested her hand, forced it into a fist. She struck out, backhanded, felt the satisfying connection with flesh and bone. Then the door was wrenched open behind her, hands clenched around her throat.

And the world went black.

'She should be here by now.' Though her apartment was filled with people and noise and wildly spinning lights, Mavis pouted. 'She promised.'

'She'll be right along.' Roarke managed to avoid being butted by a red-robed bull, lifted a brow at the manic call of 'Toro!' An angel spun by, desperately dancing with a headless corpse.

'I really wanted her to see what Leonardo and I have done with the place.' Proud, Mavis turned a quick circle. 'She'd never recognize her old digs, would she?'

Roarke scanned the magenta walls with their uninhibited splashes and streaks of cerise and periwinkle. The furniture consisted of heaps of glossy pillows and glass tubes. In keeping with the event, streamers of orange and black swayed everywhere. Skeletons danced, witches flew, and black cats arched.

'No.' He could agree with complete honesty. 'She'd never recognize her old apartment. You've done . . . wonders.'

'We just love it. And we've got the best landlord on planet.' She kissed him enthusiastically.

While he hoped her purple lipstick hadn't transferred to his face, he smiled. 'My favorite tenant.'

'Could you call her, Roarke?' With fingers tipped the same shade, she plucked at his sleeve. 'Just give her a little goose.'

'Of course. Go play hostess, and don't worry. I'll get her here.'

'Thanks.' She rolled off on glittery, red-wheeled shoes.

Roarke turned with the idea of hunting up somewhere quiet to make his call, then blinked at the apparition. 'Peabody?'

Her elaborately painted face fell. 'You recognized me.'

'Barely.' With a faint smile, he stepped back to take a full measure.

Long blonde hair swirled over her shoulders, down her back, over the tiny scallop-shaped bra that covered her breasts. From the waist down, she was encased in shimmering green.

'You make a lovely mermaid.'

'Thanks.' She perked up again. 'It took me forever to rig myself out.'

'How the hell do you walk?'

'I've got a cutout for my feet, the skirt of the tail covers it.' She wiggled back. 'Pretty restrictive to movement though. Where's Dallas?' She twisted her head to search. 'I want her to get a load of it.'

'She isn't here yet.'

'No?' Because she hadn't worn her watch, she peered down at his. 'It's almost ten. She was only going to stake out Isis's place for a couple hours then come straight here.'

'I was about to call her.'

'Good idea.' Peabody tried to ignore the prickle of nerves. 'She's probably stalling. She hates stuff like this.'

'Yes, you're right.' But she'd have been there for Mavis, he thought as he slipped into the corner. And for him.

When her 'link went unanswered, he bypassed security and called through her communicator. There was a humming buzz that indicated it was on standby, but it went unanswered.

'Something's wrong,' he said when he stepped back up to Peabody. 'She isn't picking up.'

'Let me get my bag, try her communicator.'

'I already tried it,' he said shortly. 'She isn't picking up. She was staking out Spirit Quest?'

'Yeah, she wanted to talk to Isis . . . let me get out of this costume. We'll go check it out.'

'I can't wait for you.' He pushed his way through the crowd as Peabody shuffled and looked for Feeney.

She thought it was a dream at first when she woke, groggy and hot. Her head spun, and when she tried to lift a hand to it, she found she couldn't move.

Panic rushed in first. Her hands were bound. He'd often tied her hands when she was a child. Tied her to the bed, clamped a hand over her mouth to hold in her screams when he raped her.

She pulled at them, felt the vague, faraway pain of the straps cutting into her wrists. Her breath sobbed out as she struggled. Her legs were secured as well, tied down at the ankles so that her thighs were spread.

She whipsawed her head, trying to see. Shadows shifted through the room, chased by the flickering lights of dozens of candles. She could see herself in a mirror, a wall of black glass that reflected images and light.

She wasn't a child, and it wasn't her father who had tied her.

She forced down the panic. It wouldn't help. It never did. She'd been drugged, she told herself. She'd been brought here, stripped naked, and tied to a marble slab like a piece of meat.

Selina Cross meant to kill her, and maybe worse, unless she could keep her mind clear and fight back. She continued to work at her wrist straps, twisting, tugging, while she forced her mind to focus.

Where was she? In the apartment, most likely, though she couldn't quite remember. The club would have been too dangerous, full of people. It was more private here, in this room. This room where Alice had seen a child sacrificed.

What time was it? God, how long had she been out? Roarke was going to be pissed. She bit her lip hard enough to draw blood to hold back the bubble of hysteria.

They would miss her, wonder about her. Peabody knew her last location, and they would check it out.

And what good would that do her?

Eve closed her eyes to wait for calm. She was on her own, she told herself. And she meant to survive.

The mirrored wall slid open and Selina, draped in an open black robe, slipped through. 'Ah, you're awake. I wanted you awake and aware before we started.'

Alban stepped in behind her. He wore a similar robe and the fierce, toothed mask of a boar. Saying nothing, he picked up a thick candle, set it between Eve's thighs. He stepped back, lifted an ivory-handled athame from a black pillow, then held it aloft.

'Now, we begin.'

Roarke opened the door of his car when his pocket 'link beeped. He whipped it out. 'Eve?'

'It's Jamie. I know where she is. They've got her. You have to hurry.'

'Where is she?' As he spoke, Roarke climbed behind the wheel.

'That Cross bitch. They've got her inside the apartment. Or

300

I think they do. I lost transmission when they got her out of the car.'

Roarke didn't wait, but pushed the accelerator and flew through traffic. 'What transmission?'

'I bugged her car. I wanted to know what was going on. I planted a transmitter. I heard stuff tonight. Cross told her to put the car on auto, go to the apartment. Dallas must've been drugged or something, because she sounded weird. And Cross said how she'd killed my grandfather and Alice.' His voice flooded with tears. 'She killed them both. And kids. And Christ . . .'

'Where are you?'

'I'm right outside their place. I'm going in.'

'Stay out. Goddamn it, you listen to me. Stay out. I'll be there in two minutes. Call the cops. Report a break-in, a fire, anything, but get them there. Understand me?'

'She killed my sister.' Jamie's voice was suddenly calm and cold. 'And I'm going to kill her.'

'Stay out,' Roarke repeated, swearing as the transmission ended. Digging for control, he called Mavis's, snapped out a demand for Peabody when the call was answered with wild laughter.

He was already pulling up at Selina's building when Peabody answered. 'Roarke. Feeney and I are heading to Spirit Quest right—'

'She's not there. Cross has her, most likely in the apartment building. I'm there now, and I'm going in.'

'Jesus, don't do anything crazy. I'll call for a cruiser. Feeney and I are on our way.'

'There's a young boy in there, too. You'd better hurry.'

With no weapon but his wits and his will, he rushed the door.

They were chanting over her. Alban had lighted a fire in a black cauldron and the smoke was thick and overly sweet.

301

Selina had discarded her robe and was now slowly rubbing glistening oil over her body.

'Ever been raped by a woman? I'm going to hurt you when I do it. So will he. And we won't kill you quickly, the way we did Lobar, the way we told Mirium to kill Trivane. It's going to be slow and unspeakably painful.'

Eve's head was clear now, brutally clear. Her wrists burned, slicked with her own blood as she continued to strain against the straps. 'Is this how you call up your demons? Your religion's a sham. You just like to rape and kill. It makes you a degenerate, just like any creep crawling in the gutter.'

Selina brought her hand back, whipped it down hard over Eve's face. 'I want to kill her now.'

'Soon, my love.' Alban crooned it. 'You don't want to rush the moment.'

He reached into a box, pulled a black cockerel out. It clucked and squawked, wings flapping as Alban held it over Eve's body. He spoke in Latin now, his voice musical, as he took the knife and sliced off the head. Blood gushed out, steaming over Eve's torso. Beside her, Selina moaned in ecstasy.

'Blood, for the master.'

'Yes, my love.' He turned to her. 'The master must have blood.' And very calmly, very quickly, he raked the knife over Selina's throat. 'You have been so . . . tedious,' he murmured when she stumbled back, breath gurgling as she grabbed at her throat. 'Useful, but tedious.'

When she collapsed, he stepped over her, removed the mask, set it aside. 'Enough of the pageantry. She enjoyed it. I find it stifling.' He smiled, charmingly. 'I don't intend to make you suffer. There's no purpose in it.'

The stench of blood was nauseating. Using all her will, Eve concentrated on his face. 'Why did you kill her?'

'She'd ceased to be useful. She's quite insane, you know. Too many chemicals, I suspect, in addition to a defective personality. She liked me to beat her before sex.' He shook his head. 'There were times I actually enjoyed it. The beating part, anyway. She was very clever with chemicals.' Absently, he ran a hand up and down Eve's calf. 'And I discovered with the right direction, the proper incentive, she was a clever businesswoman. We've made an enormous amount of money over the last couple of years. And, of course, there's the membership contributions. People will pay ridiculous amounts of money for sex and the possibility of immortality.'

'So it was just a con.'

'Come on, Dallas. Calling up demons, selling the soul.' He chuckled, delighted. 'It's the best grift I've ever run, but it's hit its peak. Now Selina . . .' He glanced down, idly rubbed a thumb over his chin. 'She became quite serious about it. She actually believed she had power.' He studied the sprawled body with something like amused pity. 'That she could see in the smoke, call up the devil.' He smiled again, made the ageless sign for lunacy by circling his finger at his temple.

A sham, Eve thought, *from the beginning, nothing but a long con for profit.* 'Most grifters don't add human sacrifice to the theme.'

'I'm not most grifters, and a few realistic ceremonies kept Selina in line. She developed a taste for blood. So did I,' he admitted. 'That I did find addicting. Taking a life is a powerful thing, an arousing thing.'

He let his gaze roam over her, appreciating the slim, subtle lines. Selina had been all lush curves, just on the point of overabundance. 'I may have you first, after all. It seems a waste not to.'

Everything in her revolted at the thought. 'You were the one who had sex with Mirium, you were the one who told her to kill Trivane, to infiltrate the Wiccans.'

'She is the most malleable of women. And under a little

303

chemical inducement, some posthypnotic suggestion, selectively forgetful.'

'It was never Selina. That's where I was off. You weren't her lap dog. She was yours.'

'That's very accurate. She was losing control. I've known that for some time. She did the cop on her own.' His mouth thinned in annoyance. 'That was the beginning of the end for this, and for her. He'd never have pinned us, and should have been left to fumble around until he gave up.'

'You're wrong. Frank wouldn't have given up.'

'Hardly matters now, does it?' He turned away, taking up a small vial and a pressure injector. 'I'll give you just a bit, to take the edge off. You're really quite attractive. I can make you enjoy it when I rape you.'

'There aren't enough drugs in the world for that.'

'You're wrong,' he murmured and walked toward her.

Roarke had to force himself not to enter the apartment at a run. If she was inside and in trouble, his rushing in could do her more harm than good. He closed the door quietly at his back. Since the security had already been bypassed, he knew Jamie had gone in.

Still, the movement at his side had him lashing out, grabbing at the throat.

'It's me. It's Jamie. I can't get into the room. They've installed something new. I can't bypass.'

'Where is it?'

'There, that wall. I haven't heard anything, but they're in there. They have to be.'

'Go outside.'

'I won't. And you're wasting time.'

'Then stay back,' Roarke ordered, refusing to waste more.

He approached the wall, running his fingers over it, ordering himself to be thorough, methodical, while every instinct in him screamed to hurry.

If there was a device, it was well concealed. Reaching into his pocket, he took out his daily log, tapped in a program. He thought he caught the distant wail of a siren.

'What is that?' Jamie demanded in a whisper. 'Jesus, is that a jammer? I've never seen one worked into a pocket diary.'

'You're not the only one who knows the tricks.' He began to play it over the wall, cursing it for being too slow, too inefficient. Abruptly, it emitted a low hum, beeped twice. 'There's the little bastard.'

As the door slid open, he crouched and, baring his teeth, prepared to spring.

She strained away from the injector, but it pressed against her upper arm, then just as quickly, was removed.

'No.' With a quick laugh, Alban, set it aside. 'Not for sex. That would be unfair to you and a blow to my pride. Afterward, I'll put you under deeply so you won't feel the knife. It's the least I can do.'

'Just kill me, you son of a bitch.' With a final vicious pull, she popped the strap, dragged one arm free, and shot her fist into his face. But when she reached for the knife lying beside her, it clattered to the floor.

Then, for just a moment, she thought the demons of hell had been loosed after all.

He came in like a wolf, with a snarl and a lunge. The force of Roarke's attack sent Alban flying back, sent candles flying to gutter out in pools of blood.

Rearing up, Eve struggled to free her other hand, and panic left no room for shock as she spotted Jamie. 'Hurry up, for Christ's sake. Get the knife, cut me loose. Hurry!'

His stomach was heaving, but he stepped over Selina's body, grabbed the knife. Keeping his eyes locked on her wrist, he hacked at the strap.

'Give it to me. I can get the rest.' Her gaze was locked on Roarke, the desperate struggle over the bloody floor. Fire was

305

beginning to live in the corner, growing from upended candle to hungry flame. 'There's the cops,' she said when she heard the siren. 'Go let them in.'

'The door's unlocked.' He said it calmly, flatly, as he moved to her feet to cut her ankles free.

'Do something about that fire in the corner,' she ordered as she scrambled down.

'No, let it burn. Let the whole damn place burn to the ground.'

'Put it out,' she snapped again, then leapt like a madwoman onto Alban's back. 'You bastard, you son of a bitch.' Even as she dragged his head back, Roarke's fist flew up and cracked against his face.

'Get the hell back,' Roarke demanded. 'He's mine.'

They rolled over in a violent tangle of limbs to discover only two of them were still conscious.

'Did he hurt you?' Roarke's eyes were still wild when he grabbed her arms. 'Did he put his hands on you?'

'No.' She had to be calm now, she realized, for he wasn't. She wasn't entirely sure what Roarke was capable of when he was in this state. 'He never touched me. You took care of that. I'm all right.'

'You were taking care of yourself, as usual, when I got here.' He lifted her hand, stared at the blood seeping from the abrasions on her wrist, and lifted it to his lips. 'I could kill him for that. Just for that alone.'

'Stop. It's part of the job.'

He was struggling to accept that. His jacket was ruined, a bloody mess, but he took it off and wrapped it around her. 'You're naked.'

'Yeah, I noticed. I don't know what they did with my clothes, but I'd just as soon be wearing something other than skin when the troops get here.'

She rose, discovered she wasn't entirely steady on her feet. 'They drugged me,' she explained, shaking her head to clear it as Roarke moved her away, eased her down to sit on a clear spot on the floor.

'Just get your breath back. I have to put out that fire.'

'Good thinking.' She drew a couple of cleansing breaths as he used one of the robes to smother the flames flicking along the floor. Then she shot to her feet, cried out. 'No. Jamie, don't.' She took the first running steps forward, but it was already too late.

Face white, Jamie got to his feet. The knife still wet with Alban's blood was in his hand. 'They killed my family.' His eyes were huge, the pupils pinpricks as he offered the knife to Eve. 'I don't care what you do to me. He won't ever kill anyone else's sister.'

She heard the footsteps rushing through the outside door, and following instinct, gripped the athame by the handle so that her own fingerprints were on it. 'Shut up. Just shut the hell up. Peabody.' Eve turned as her aide rushed in, weapon drawn. 'Get me something to wear, will you?'

Peabody's breath came out in three unsteady puffs as she scanned the carnage. 'Yes, sir. Are you all right?'

'I'm fine. Cross and Alban ambushed me, drugged me up, and got me here. They've both confessed to the murders of Frank Wojinski and Alice Lingstrom, Lobar, Wineburg, and conspiracy to murder Trivane. Alban killed Selina, for reasons I will detail in my report. Alban was killed during the struggle to contain him. It was confusing, I'm not sure exactly how it happened. I don't think it matters.'

'No.' Feeney stood beside Peabody, scanned Jamie's face, then Eve's. And he knew. 'I don't think it matters now. Come on, Jamie, you shouldn't be in here now.'

'Lieutenant, with respect. I think it would be best if you and Roarke went home and cleaned up. You're a little too in tune with the season, so to speak.'

Eve glanced at Roarke, grimaced. Blood and smoke coated his face. 'You look disgusting.'

'You should see yourself, Lieutenant.' He slipped an arm around her. 'I think Peabody has a point. We'll find a blanket. That should be sufficient to get you home without you freezing or getting arrested.'

She wanted a bath so desperately she could have wept. 'Okay. I'll be back in an hour.'

'Dallas, it isn't necessary for you to come back tonight.'

'An hour,' she repeated. 'Secure the scene, call the ME. Get that boy an MT. He's shocky. Contact Whitney. He'll want to know what happened here, and I want Charles Forte released as soon as possible.'

Eve tugged Roarke's jacket more securely around her. 'You were right about him, Peabody. Your instincts were on target. They're good instincts.'

'Thank you, Lieutenant.'

'Use them again. If that boy says anything that doesn't jibe with my brief statement of the events, ignore him. He's emotionally wrecked and in shock. I don't want him questioned tonight by anyone.'

Peabody nodded, kept her eyes carefully blank. 'Yes, sir. I'll see that he's taken home. I'll remain on scene until you return.'

'Do that.' Eve turned, started to button the jacket.

'By the way, Dallas?'

'What, Peabody?'

'That's a lovely tattoo. New?'

Eve clamped her teeth together, strode toward the door with as much dignity as she could manage. 'See?' She jabbed a finger into Roarke's chest as they walked down the corridor. 'I told you I'd be humiliated by that stupid rosebud.'

'You've been drugged, slapped, tied up naked, and nearly killed, but a rose on your butt humiliates you?'

'All that other stuff's the job. The rosebud's personal.'

Laughing, he swung his arm around her shoulders, hugging her close. 'Christ, Lieutenant, I love you.'

If you enjoyed *Ceremony in Death*,
you won't want to miss J. D. Robb's
next exciting novel . . .

VENGEANCE

IN

DEATH

The business of murder took time, patience, skill, and a tolerance for the monotonous. Lieutenant Eve Dallas had them all.

She knew the act of murder required none of these. All too often, a life was taken on impulse, in rage, for amusement, or simply out of stupidity. It was the last of these, in Eve's mind, that had led one John Henry Bonning to throw one Charles Michael Renekee out a twelve-story window on Avenue D.

She had Bonning in interview and calculated that it would take another twenty minutes tops to shake a confession out of him, another fifteen to book him and file her report. She might just make it home on time.

'Come on, Boner.' It was her veteran cop talking to veteran bad guy. Level ground, her turf. 'Do yourself a favor. A confession, and you can go for self-defense and diminished capacity. We can tie this up by dinnertime. I hear they're serving pasta surprise in lockup tonight.'

'Never touched him.' Bonning folded his oversized lips, tapped his long, fat fingers. 'Fucker jumped.'

With a sigh, Eve sat down at the little metal table in Interview A. She didn't want Bonning to lawyer himself and gum up the works. All she had to do was keep him from saying those words, steer him in the direction she was already heading, and she had a wrap.

Second-rate chemi-dealers like Bonning were invariably slow-witted, but sooner or later he'd whine for a representative. It was an old shuffle and dodge, as timeless as murder itself. As the year 2058 stumbled to an end, the business of murder remained basically unchanged.

'He jumped – a quick gainer out the window. Now, why'd he do that, Boner?'

Bonning furrowed his ape-sized forehead into deep thought. 'Because he was a crazy bastard?'

'That's a good guess, Boner, but it's not going to qualify you for round two of our stump-the-cops sweepstakes.'

It took him about thirty pondering seconds, then his lips stretched out into a grin. 'Funny. Pretty funny, Dallas.'

'Yeah, I'm thinking of moonlighting as a stand-up. But, going back to my day job, the two of you were cooking up some Erotica in your porta lab on Avenue D, and Renekee – being a crazy bastard – just got some hair up his ass and jumped out a window – right through the glass – and dived twelve stories, bounced off the roof of a Rapid Cab, scared the living shit out of a couple of tourists from Topeka in the backseat, then rolled off to leak his brains onto the street.'

'Sure did bounce,' Bonning said with what passed for a wondering smile. 'Who'da thought?'

She didn't intend to go for murder one, and figured if she went for murder two, the court-appointed rep would bargain Bonning down to manslaughter. Chemi-dealers greasing chemi-dealers didn't make Justice flip up her blindfold and grin in anticipation. He'd do more time for the illegals paraphernalia than he would for the homicide. And even combining the two, it was doubtful he'd do more than a three-year stretch in lockup.

She folded her arms on the table, leaned forward. 'Boner, do I look stupid?'

Taking the question at face value, Bonning narrowed his eyes to take a careful study. She had big brown eyes, but they weren't soft. She had a pretty, wide mouth, but it didn't smile. 'Look like a cop,' he decided.

'Good answer. Don't try to hose me here, Boner. You and your business partner had a falling-out, you got pissed off, and terminated your professional and personal relationship by heaving his dumb ass out the window.' She held up a hand before Bonning could deny again. 'This is the way I see it. You got into, maybe dissing each other over the profits, the methods, a woman. You both got hot. So maybe he comes at you. You've got to defend yourself, right?'

'Man's got a right,' Bonning agreed, nodding rapidly as the story sang to him. 'But we didn't get into nothing. He just tried to fly.'

'Where'd you get the bloody lip, the black eye? How come your knuckles are ripped up?'

Bonning stretched his lips into a toothy grin. 'Bar fight.'

'When? Where?'

'Who remembers?'

'You'd better. And you know, Boner, after we run the tests on the blood we scraped from your knuckles, and we find blood mixed with yours. We get his DNA off your fat fingers, I'm going for premeditated: maximum lockup, life, no parole.'

His eyes blinked rapidly, as if his brain was processing new and baffling data. 'Come on, Dallas, that's just bullshit. You ain't gonna convince nobody I walked in there thinking to kill old Chuckaroo. We were buds.'

Her eyes steady on his, Eve pulled out her communicator. 'Last chance to help yourself. I call my aide, have her get the test results, I'm booking you on murder one.'

'Wasn't no murder.' He wanted to believe she was bluffing. *You couldn't read those eyes*, he thought, wetting his lips. *Couldn't read those cop's eyes*. 'It was an accident,' he claimed, inspired. Eve only shook her head. 'Yeah, we were busting a little and he . . . tripped and went headlong out the window.'

'Now you're insulting me. A grown man doesn't trip out a window that's three feet off the floor.' Eve flicked on her communicator. 'Officer Peabody.'

Within seconds, Peabody's round and sober faced filled the communicator screen. 'Yes, sir.'

'I need the blood test results on Bonning. Have them sent directly to Interview A – and alert the PA that I have a murder in the first.'

'Now, hold on, back up, don't be going there.' Bonning ran the back of his hand over his mouth. He struggled a moment, telling himself she'd never get him on the big one. But Dallas had a rep for pinning fatter moths than him to the wall.

'You had your chance Boner. Peabody—'

'He came at me, like you said. He came at me. He went crazy. I'll tell you how it went down, straight shit. I want to make a statement.'

'Peabody, delay those orders. Inform the PA that Mr Bonning is making a statement of straight shit.'

Peabody's lips never twitched. 'Yes, sir.'

Eve slipped the communicator back in her pocket, then folded her hands on the edge of the table and smiled pleasantly. 'Okay, Boner, tell me how it went down.'

Fifty minutes later, Eve strolled into her tiny office in New York's Cop Central. She did look like a cop – not just the weapon harness slung over her shoulder, the worn boots and faded jeans. Cop was in her eyes – eyes that missed little. They were a dark whiskey color, and they rarely flinched. Her face was angular, sharp at the cheekbones, and set off by a surprisingly generous mouth and a shallow dent in the chin.

She walked in a long-limbed, loose-gaited style – she was in no hurry. Pleased with herself, she raked her fingers through her short, casually cropped brown hair as she sat behind her desk.

She would file her report, zing off copies to all necessary parties, then log out for the day. Outside the streaked and narrow window behind her, the commuter air traffic was already in a snarl. The blat of airbus horns and the endless snicking of traffic copter blades didn't bother her. It was, after all, one of the theme songs of New York.

'Engage,' she ordered, then hissed when her computer remained stubbornly blank. 'Damn it, don't start this. Engage. Turn on, you bastard.'

'You've got to feed it your personal pass number,' Peabody said as she stepped inside.

'I thought these were back on voice ID.'

'Were. Snafued. Supposed on be back up to speed by the end of the week.'

'Pain in the butt,' Eve complained. 'How many numbers are we supposed to remember? Two, five, zero, nine.' She blew out a breath as her unit coughed to life. 'They'd better come up with the new system they promised the department.' She slipped a disc into the unit. 'Save to Bonning, John Henry, case number 4572077-H. Copy report to Whitney, Commander.'

'Nice, quick work on Bonning, Dallas.'

'The man's got a brain the size of a pistachio. Tossed his partner out the window because they got into a fight over who owed who a stinking twenty credits. And he's trying to tell me he was defending himself, in fear for his life. The guy he tossed was a hundred pounds lighter and six inches shorter. Asshole,' she said with a resigned sigh. 'You'd have thought Boner would have cooked up the guy had a knife or swung a bat at him.'

She sat back, circled her neck, surprised and pleased that there was barely any tension to be willed away. 'They should all be this easy.'

She listened with half an ear to the hum and rumble of the early air traffic outside her window. One of the commuter trams was blasting out its spiel on economical rates and convenience.

'Weekly, monthly, yearly terms available! Sign onto EZ TRAM, your friendly and reliable air transport service. Begin and end your workday in style.'

If you liked the packed in like sweaty sardines style, Eve thought. With the chilly November rain that had been falling all

315

day, she imagined both air and street snarls would be hideous. The perfect end to the day.

'That wraps it,' she said and grabbed her battered leather jacket. 'I'm clocking out – on time for a change. Any hot plans for the weekend, Peabody?'

'My usual, flicking off men like flies, breaking hearts, crushing souls.'

Eve shot a quick grin at her aide's sober face. The sturdy Peabody, she thought – a cop from the crown of her dark bowl-cut hair to her shiny regulation shoes. 'You're such a wild woman, Peabody. I don't know how you keep up the pace.'

'Yeah, that's me, queen of the party girls.' With a dry smile, Peabody reached for the door just as Eve's tele-link beeped. Both of them scowled at the unit. 'Thirty seconds and we'd have been on the skywalk down.'

'Probably just Roarke calling to remind me we've got this dinner party deal tonight.' Eve flicked the unit on. 'Homicide, Dallas.'

The screen swam with colors – dark, ugly, clashing colors. Music, low octave, slow paced, crept out of the speaker. Automatically, Eve tapped the command for trace, watched the Unable to Comply message scroll across the bottom of the screen.

Peabody whipped out her porta-link, stepping aside to contact central control as the caller spoke.

'You're supposed to be the best the city has to offer, Lieutenant Dallas. Just how good are you?'

'Unidentified contact and/or jammed transmissions to police officers are illegal. I'm obliged to caution you that this transmission is being traced through CompuGuard, and it's being recorded.'

'I'm aware of that. Since I've just committed what worldly society would consider first-degree murder, I'm not overly concerned about minor nuisances like electronic violations. I've been blessed by the Lord.'

'Oh yeah?' Terrific, she thought, just what she needed.

'I have been called on to do His work, and have washed myself in the blood of His enemy.'

'Does he have a lot of them? I mean, you'd think He would just, what, smite them down Himself instead of enlisting you to do the dirty work.'

There was a pause, a long one, where only the dirge played through. 'I have to expect you to be flippant.' The voice was harder now, and edgier. Temper barely suppressed. 'As one of the godless, how could you understand divine retribution? I'll put this on your level. A riddle. Do you enjoy riddles, Lieutenant Dallas?'

'No.' She slid her gaze toward Peabody, got a quick, frustrated head shake. 'But I bet you do.'

'They relax the mind and soothe the spirit. The name of this little riddle is Revenge. You'll find the first son of the old sod in the lap of luxury, atop his silver tower where the river runs dark below and water falls from a great height. He begged for his life, and then for his death. Never repenting his great sin, he is already damned.'

'Why did you kill him?'

'Because this is the task I was born for.'

'God told you that you were born to kill?' Eve pushed for trace again, fought with frustration. 'How'd He let you know? Did he call you up on your 'link, send a fax? Maybe He met you in a bar?'

'You won't doubt me.' The sound of breathing grew louder, strained, shaky. 'You think because you're a woman in a position of authority that I'm less? You won't doubt me for much longer. I contacted you, Lieutenant. Remember this is in my charge. Woman may guide and comfort man, but man was created to protect, defend, to avenge.'

'God tell you that, too? I guess that proves He's a man, after all. Mostly ego.'

'You'll tremble before Him, before me.'

'Yeah, right.' Hoping his video was clear, Eve examined her nails. 'I'm already shaking.'

'My work is holy. It is terrible and divine. From Proverbs, Lieutenant, 28:17. "If a man is burdened with the blood of another, let him be a fugitive until death; let no one help him." This one's days as a fugitive are done – and no one helped him.'

'If you killed him, what does that make you?'

'The wrath of God. You have twenty-four hours to prove you're worthy. Don't disappoint me.'

'I won't disappoint you, asshole,' Eve muttered as the transmission ended. 'Anything, Peabody?'

'Nothing. He jammed the tracers good and proper. They can't give us so much as on or off planet.'

'He's on planet,' she muttered and sat. 'He wants to be close enough to watch.'

'Could be a crank.'

'I don't think so. A fanatic, but not a crank. Computer, run buildings, residential and commercial, with the word *luxury*, in New York City, with view of the East River or the Hudson.' She tapped her fingers. 'I hate puzzle games.'

'I kind of like them.' Brows knit, Peabody leaned over Eve's shoulder as the computer went to work.

Luxury Arms
Sterling Luxury
Luxury Place
Luxury Towers

Eve pounced. 'Access visual of Luxury Towers, onscreen.'

Working . . .

The image popped, a towering spear of silver with sunlight glinting off the steel and shimmering on the Hudson at its

318

base. On the far west side, a stylish waterfall tumbled down a complex arrangement of tubes and channels.

'Gotcha.'

'Can't be that easy,' Peabody objected.

'He wanted it easy.' Because, Eve thought, someone was already dead. 'He wants to play and he wants to preen. Can't do either until we're in it. Computer, access name of residents on the top floor of the Luxury Towers.'

Working ... Penthouse is owned by The Brennen Group and is New York base for Thomas X. Brennen of Dublin, Ireland, age forty-two, married, three children, president and CEO of The Brennen Group, an entertainment and communications agency.

'Let's check it out, Peabody. We'll notify Dispatch on the way.'

'Request backup?'

'We'll get the lay of the land first.' Eve adjusted the strap on her weapon harness and shrugged into her jacket.

The traffic was just as bad as she'd suspected, bumping and grinding over wet streets, buzzing overhead like disoriented bees. Glide-carts huddled under wide umbrellas and did no business she could see. Steam rolled up out of their grills, obscuring vision and stinking up the air.

'Get the operator to access Brennen's home number, Peabody. If it's a hoax and he's alive, it'd be nice to keep it that way.'

'On it,' Peabody said and pulled out her 'link.

Annoyed with the traffic delays, Eve sounded her siren. She'd have had the same response if she'd leaned out the window and shouted. Cars remained packed together like lovers, giving not an inch.

'No answer,' Peabody told her. 'Voice mail announcement

319

says he's away for two weeks beginning today.'

'Let's hope he's bellied up to a bar in Dublin.' She scanned the traffic again, gauged her options. 'I have to do it.'

'Ah, Lieutenant, not in this vehicle.'

Then Peabody, the stalwart cop, gritted her teeth and squeezed her eyes shut in terror as Eve stabbed the vertical lift. The car shuddered, creaked, and lifted six inches off the ground. Hit it again with a bone shuddering thud.

'Goddamn piece of dog shit.' Eve used her fist this time, punching the control hard enough to bruise her knuckles. They did a shaky lift, wobbled, then streamed forward as Eve jabbed the accelerator. She nipped the edge of an umbrella, causing the glide-cart hawker to squeal in fury and hotfoot in pursuit for a half block.

'The damn hawker nearly caught the bumper.' More amazed than angry now, Eve shook her head. 'A guy in air boots nearly outran a cop ride. What's the world coming to, Peabody?'

Eyes stubbornly shut, Peabody didn't move a muscle. 'I'm sorry, sir, you're interrupting my praying.'

Eve kept the sirens on, delivering them to the front entrance of the Luxury Towers. The descent was rough enough to click her teeth together, but she missed the glossy fender of an XRII airstream convertible by at least an inch.

The doorman was across the sidewalk like a silver bullet, his face a combination of insult and horror as he wrenched open the door of her industrial beige city clunker.

'Madam, you cannot park this . . . thing here.'

Eve flicked off the siren, flipped out her badge. 'Oh yeah, I can.'

His mouth only stiffened further as he scanned her ID. 'If you would please pull into the garage.'

Maybe it was because he reminded her of Summerset, the butler who had Roarke's affection and loyalty and her disdain, but she pushed her face into his, eyes glittering. 'It stays where

I put it, pal. And unless you want me to tell my aide to write you up for obstructing an officer, you'll buzz me inside and up to Thomas Brennen's penthouse.'

He sucked air through his nose. 'That is quite impossible. Mr Brennen is away.'

'Peabody, get this . . . citizen's name and ID number and arrange to have him transported to Cop Central for booking.'

'Yes, sir.'

'You can't arrest me.' His shiny black boots did a quick dance on the sidewalk. 'I'm doing my job.'

'You're interfering with mine, and guess whose job the judge is going to think is more important?'

Eve watched the way his mouth worked before it settled in a thin, disapproving line. Oh yeah, she thought, he was Summerset to a tee, even though he was twenty pounds heavier and three inches shorter than the bane of her existence.

'Very well, but you can be sure I will contact the chief of police and security about your conduct.' He studied her badge again. 'Lieutenant.'

'Feel free.' With a signal to Peabody, she followed the doorman's stiff back to the entrance, where he activated his droid backup to man the post.

Inside the shining silver doors, the lobby of the Luxury Towers was a tropical garden with towering palms, flowing hibiscus, and twittering birds. A large pool surrounded a splashing fountain in the shape of a generously curved woman, naked to the waist and holding a golden fish.

The doorman keyed in a code at a glass tube, silently gestured Eve and Peabody inside. Unhappy with the transport, Eve stayed rooted to the center while Peabody all but pressed her nose against the glass on the ascent.

Sixty-two floors later, the tube opened into a smaller garden lobby, no less abundant. The doorman paused by a security screen outside double-arched doors of highly polished steel.

'Doorman Strobie, escorting Lieutenant Dallas of the NYPSD and aide.'

'Mr Brennen is not in residence at this time,' came the response in a soothing voice with a musical Irish lilt.

Eve merely elbowed Strobie aside. 'This is a police emergency.' She lifted her badge to the electronic eye for verification. 'Entrance is imperative.'

'One moment, Lieutenant.' There was a quiet hum as her face and ID were scanned, then a discreet click of locks. 'Entrance permitted, please be aware that this residence is protected by Scan-Eye.'

'Recorder on, Peabody. Back off, Strobie.' Eve put one hand on the door, the other on her weapon, and shouldered it open.

The smell struck her first, and made her swear. She'd smelled violent death too many times to mistake it.

Blood painted the blue silk walls of the living area, a grisly, incomprehensible graffiti. She saw the first piece of Thomas X. Brennen on the cloud-soft carpet. His hand lay palm up, fingers curled toward her as if to beckon or to plead. It had been severed at the wrist.

She heard Strobie gag behind her, heard him stumble back into the lobby and the fresh, floral air. She stepped into the stench. She drew her weapon now, sweeping with it as she covered the room. Her instincts told her what had been done there was over, and whoever had done it was safely away, but she stuck close to procedure, making her way slowly over the carpet, avoiding the gore when she could.

'If Strobie's finished vomiting, ask him the way to the master bedroom.'

'Down the hall to the left,' Peabody said a moment later. 'But he's still heaving out here.'

'Find him a bucket, then secure the elevator and this door.'

Eve started down the hall. The smell grew riper, thicker.

She began to breathe through her teeth. The door to the bedroom wasn't secure. Through the crack came a slash of bright, artificial light and the majestic sounds of Mozart.

What was left of Brennen was stretched out on a lakesized bed with a stylish mirrored canopy. One arm had been chained with silver links to the bedpost. Eve imagined they would find his feet somewhere in the spacious apartment.

Undoubtedly, the walls were well soundproofed, but surely the man had screamed long and loud before he died. How long had it taken, she wondered, as she studied the body. How much pain could a man stand before the brain turned off and the body gave out?

Thomas Brennen would know the answer, to the second.

He'd been stripped naked, his hand and both his feet amputated. The one eye he had left stared in blind horror at the mirrored reflection of his own mutilated form. He'd been disemboweled.

'Sweet Jesus Christ,' Peabody whispered from the doorway. 'Holy Mother of God.'

'I need the field kit. We'll seal up, call this in. Find out where his family is. Call this in through EDD, Feeney if he's on, and have him put a media jammer on before you give any details. Let's keep the details quiet as long as possible.'

Peabody had to swallow hard twice before she was sure her lunch would stay down. 'Yes, sir.'

'Get Strobie and secure him before he can babble about this.'

When Eve turned, Peabody saw a shadow of pity in her eyes, then it was gone and they were flat and cool again. 'Let's get moving. I want to fry this son of a bitch.'

It was nearly midnight before Eve dragged herself up the stairs to her own front door. Her stomach was raw, her eyes burning, her head roaring. The stench of vicious death clung to her, though she'd scrubbed off a layer of skin in the locker room showers before heading home.

What she wanted most was oblivion, and she said one desperate and sincere prayer that she wouldn't see the wreckage of Thomas Brennen when she closed her eyes to sleep.

The door opened before she could reach it. Summerset stood with the glittery light of the foyer chandelier behind him, his tall, bony body all but quivering with dislike.

'You are unpardonably late, Lieutenant. Your guests are preparing to leave.'

Guests? Her overtaxed mind struggled with the word before she remembered. *A dinner party. She was supposed to care about a dinner party after the night she'd put in?*

'Kiss my ass,' she invited and started past him.

His thin fingers caught at her arm. 'As Roarke's wife, you're expected to perform certain social duties, such as assisting him in hosting an important affair such as this evening's dinner.'

Fury outdistanced fatigue in a heartbeat. Her hand curled into a fist at her side. 'Step back before I—'

'Eve darling.'

Roarke's voice, managing to convey welcome, amusement, and caution in two words, stopped her curled fist from lifting and following through. Scowling, she turned, saw him just outside the parlor doorway. It wasn't the formal black that made him breathtaking. Eve knew he had a lean, muscled body that could stop a woman's heart no matter what he wore – or didn't wear. His hair flowed, dark as night and nearly to his shoulders, to frame a face she often thought belonged on a Renaissance painting. Sharp bones, eyes bluer than prized cobalt, a mouth fashioned to spout poetry, issue orders, and drive a woman to madness.

In less than a year, he had broken through her defenses, unlocked her heart, and most surprising of all, had gained not only her love but her trust.

And he could still annoy her.

She considered him the first and only miracle in her life.

'I'm late. Sorry.' It was more of a challenge than an apology, delivered like a bullet. He acknowledged it with an easy smile and a lifted eyebrow.

'I'm sure it was unavoidable.' He held out a hand. When she crossed the foyer and took it, he found hers stiff and cold. In her aged-whiskey eyes he saw both fury and fatigue. He'd grown used to seeing both there. She was pale, which worried him. He recognized the smears on her jeans as dried blood, and hoped it wasn't her own.

He gave her hand a quick, intimate squeeze before bringing it to his lips, his eyes steady on hers. 'You're tired, Lieutenant,' he murmured, the wisp of Ireland magical in his voice. 'I'm just moving them along. Only a few minutes more, all right?'

'Sure, yeah. Fine.' Her temper began to cool. 'I'm sorry I screwed this up. I know it was important.' Beyond him in the beautifully furnished parlor, she saw more than a dozen elegant men and women, formally dressed, gems winking, silks rustling. Something of her reluctance must have shown on her face before she smoothed it away, because he laughed.

'Five minutes, Eve. I doubt this can be as bad as whatever you faced tonight.'

He ushered her in, a man as comfortable with wealth and privilege as with the stench of alleys and violence. Seamlessly, he introduced his wife to those she'd yet to meet, cued her on the names of those she'd socialized with at at another time, all the while nudging the dinner party guests toward the door.

Eve smelled rich perfumes and wine, the fragrant smoke from the applewood logs simmering discreetly in the fireplace. But under it all, the sensory memory stink of blood and gore remained.

He wondered if she knew how staggering she was, standing there amid the glitter in her scarred jacket and smeared denim, her short, untidy hair haloing a pale face, accenting dark, tired eyes, her long, rangy body held straight through what he knew was an act of sheer will.

She was, he thought, courage in human form.

But when they closed the door on the last guest, she shook her head. 'Summerset's right. I'm just not equipped for this Roarke's wife stuff.'

'You are my wife.'

'Doesn't mean I'm any good at it. I let you down. I should've—' She stopped talking because his mouth was on hers. It was warm, possessive, and it untied the knots in the back of her neck. Without realizing she'd moved, Eve wrapped her arms around his waist and just held on.

'There,' he murmured. 'That's better. This is my business.' He lifted her chin, skimming a finger in the slight dent centered in it. 'My job. You have yours.'

'It was a big deal, though. Some whatzit merger.'

'Scottoline merger – more of a buyout, really, and it should be finalized by the middle of next week, even without your delightful presence at the dinner table. Still, you might have called. I worried.'

'I forgot. I can't always remember. I'm not used to this.' She jammed her hands in her pockets and paced down the wide hall and back. 'I'm not used to this. Every time I think I am, I'm not. Then I come walking in here with all the mega-rich, looking like a street junkie.'

'On the contrary, you look like a cop. I believe several of our guests were quite impressed with the glimpse of your weapon under your jacket, and the trace of blood on your jeans. It's not yours, I take it.'

'No.' Suddenly, she just couldn't stand up any longer. She turned to the steps, climbed two, and sat. Because it was Roarke, she allowed herself to cover her face with her hands.

He sat beside her, draped an arm over her shoulders. 'It was bad.'

'Almost always you can say you've seen as bad, even worse. It's most always true. I can't say that this time.' Her stomach still clenched and rolled. 'I've never seen worse.'

He knew what she lived with, had seen a great deal of it himself. 'Do you want to tell me?'

'No, Christ no, I don't want to think about it for a few hours. I don't want to think about anything.'

'I can help you there.'

For the first time in hours, she smiled. 'I bet you can.'

'Let's start this way.' He rose and plucked her off the step, up into his arms.

'You don't have to carry me. I'm okay.'

He flashed a grin at her as he started up. 'Maybe it makes me feel manly.'

'In that case . . .' She wound her arms around his neck, rested her head on his shoulder. It felt good. Very good. 'The least I can do after standing you up tonight is make you feel manly.'

'The very least,' he agreed.

Witness in Death
Opening night at New York's New Globe Theatre turns from stage scene to crime scene when the leading man is stabbed to death right on centre stage. And Eve Dallas is not just the primary – she's a witness.

Judgement in Death
In an uptown strip joint a cop is found bludgeoned to death. The weapon's a baseball bat. The motive is a mystery. It's a case of serious overkill that pushes Eve Dallas straight into overdrive

Betrayal in Death
At the luxurious Roarke Palace Hotel, a maid is brutally murdered. And Eve must face a terrifying possibility that the real target may, in fact, be her husband, Roarke...

Seduction in Death
Lieutenant Eve Dallas is searching for a Casanova killer with a deadly appetite for seduction...

Reunion in Death
A surprise party turns into a murder scene and Eve Dallas is called to investigate. The killer is Julie Dockport. No one at the party knows who she is. But Detective Eve Dallas remembers her all too well. Eve was personally responsible for her incarceration nearly ten years ago.

Divided in Death
Roarke's security specialist Reva Ewing is the prime suspect in a double homicide – accused of killing her adulterous husband and his lover. But despite having every reason for wanting both of them dead, Reva protests her innocence…

Visions in Death
Eve Dallas' latest case involves the murder of a young mother. Psychic Celina Sanchez claims to be having visions of the killer and though Eve remains sceptical of Celina's abilities, she will use all the resources she can to track down the killer before he strikes again....

A SELECTION OF NOVELS AVAILABLE FROM PIATKUS BOOKS

0 7499 3406 9	**Naked in Death**	*Nora Roberts/J.D.Robb*	£6.99
0 7499 3407 7	**Glory in Death**	*Nora Roberts/J.D.Robb*	£6.99
0 7499 3408 5	**Immortal in Death**	*Nora Roberts/J.D.Robb*	£6.99
0 7499 3411 5	**Rapture in Death**	*Nora Roberts/J.D.Robb*	£6.99
0 7499 3412 3	**Ceremony in Death**	*Nora Roberts/J.D.Robb*	£6.99
0 7499 3413 6	**Vengeance in Death**	*Nora Roberts/J.D.Robb*	£6.99
0 7499 3416 6	**Holiday in Death**	*Nora Roberts/J.D.Robb*	£5.99
0 7499 3417 4	**Conspiracy in Death**	*Nora Roberts/J.D.Robb*	£6.99
0 7499 3418 2	**Loyalty in Death**	*Nora Roberts/J.D.Robb*	£6.99
0 7499 3436 0	**Witness in Death**	*Nora Roberts/J.D.Robb*	£6.99
0 7499 3437 9	**Judgement in Death**	*Nora Roberts/J.D.Robb*	£6.99
0 7499 3438 7	**Betrayal in Death**	*Nora Roberts/J.D.Robb*	£6.99
0 7499 3439 5	**Seduction in Death**	*Nora Roberts/J.D.Robb*	£6.99
0 7499 3440 9	**Reunion in Death**	*Nora Roberts/J.D.Robb*	£6.99
0 7499 3444 1	**Divided in Death**	*Nora Roberts/J.D.Robb*	£6.99
0 7499 3499 9	**Vision in Death**	*Nora Roberts/J.D.Robb*	£6.99